T0188318

"From the very first line, I knew *Four Weekends and a Funeral* was going to be one of my favorite books. Ellie Palmer has such a compelling voice—razor-sharp wit wrapped up in beautiful warmth—that every word she writes leaps off the page. The fresh take on fake dating hooked me from the start, and the perfectly balanced mix of serious topics and electric banter made it unputdownable. I'll devour anything Ellie Palmer writes."

—Jessica Joyce, author of *You, with a View*

"A charming rom-com dripping with witty banter and heartfelt moments. Despite their rocky start, Alison and Adam's chemistry leapt off the page with the sweetest tension as their relationship progressed. But what was special about this book for me was the realistic exploration of survivor guilt and grief as Alison learned to accept herself and her new body as a carrier of the BRCA1 genetic mutation. As a carrier myself, I loved how this difficult diagnosis was handled with care and nuance by the author. A stunning debut!"

—Farah Heron, author of *Accidentally Engaged*

"With her debut novel, Ellie Palmer has managed to accomplish what most authors never do and that is create the perfect romantic comedy. *Four Weekends and a Funeral* is a masterfully penned, pitch-perfect romance full of humor, so much heart, and swoon-worthy moments as well as brilliant puns, poignant observations about life, important representation, and believable character development. Adam, Alison, and all their friends, even the dead ones, come alive on the page and make you care so hard and pine for their happily ever after." —Meredith Schorr, author of *As Seen on TV*

Four Weekends and a Funeral

A NOVEL

Ellie Palmer

G. P. PUTNAM'S SONS
New York

PUTNAM
— EST. 1838 —

G. P. PUTNAM'S SONS
Publishers Since 1838
An imprint of Penguin Random House LLC
penguinrandomhouse.com

Library of Congress Cataloging-in-Publication Data

Names: Palmer, Ellie, 1989– author.
Title: Four weekends and a funeral: a novel / Ellie Palmer.
Description: New York: G. P. Putnam's Sons, 2024.
Identifiers: LCCN 2024011301 (print) | LCCN 2024011302 (ebook) |
ISBN 9780593714300 (trade paperback) | ISBN 9780593714317 (epub)
Subjects: LCGFT: Romance fiction. | Novels.
Classification: LCC PS3616.A33887 F68 2024 (print) |
LCC PS3616.A33887 (ebook) | DDC 813/.6—dc23/eng/20240329
LC record available at https://lccn.loc.gov/2024011301
LC ebook record available at https://lccn.loc.gov/2024011302

Printed in the United States of America
1st Printing

Book design by Tiffany Estreicher

For Chris:
You always believed this was possible,
and that's only one of the millions
of things I love about you.

Four
Weekends
and a
Funeral

1

We Start with the Funeral

WHEN I LEARN I'm still dating Sam Lewis, I'm at his funeral.

Mara and I drift into St. Ignatius Catholic Church twenty minutes early.

"You're sloshing," she tells me out of the side of her mouth.

"Puddle in the parking lot." The wet squish of my foot into damp insole punctuates my words.

I grip her elbow when we reach the threshold, as if I'm guiding her toward the vaguely familiar faces of my ex-boyfriend's friends and loved ones. Really, she's the one who's keeping me upright. Such is her duty as my best friend, though her striking, angular features and statuesque frame make her an only slightly more discreet companion than an emotional-support corgi.

Today, we're a study in contrasts. Where Mara is tall and steady in her stacked heels, I'm short and unwieldy in my waterlogged, machine-washable flats. Her auburn hair is spun up neatly in a French twist while my long brown curls fall messily around my face, because I'm thirty years old and still can't follow a YouTube hair tutorial.

She shakes herself from my death grip to unbutton her coat, revealing a pristinely black, Woolite-commercial-ready sweater topping a pair of effortlessly chic wide-leg trousers. I—as a chronically reckless washer of dark woolens—had nothing so perfectly Burial Black to don for the funeral of a man who'd gently dumped me in a rowboat. I settled for a faded charcoal dress and a cardigan that exists somewhere between pea green and the color of the dead late-autumn grass. I hope it snows soon. I'm already so sick of fall. I'm already so sick of today.

The wooden doors thud behind us, announcing our arrival. I suppose it's not ordinary to bring a plus-one to these sorts of things, but the funeral of my most recent ex is no ordinary occasion.

My eyes search the front hall for someone I know. More accurately, I'm hoping to see *no one* I know and confirmation that I'm in the wrong place.

No, no. Not your *Sam Lewis,* a stranger might say. *A different Sam Lewis.* Though he hasn't been *my* Sam Lewis for six weeks—if he ever really was.

But I recognize his friend Russell immediately, and relief and disappointment flood my chest like an inflowing tide. Today is real. This is no mistake.

We sidle up to his group, and Russell introduces himself to Mara with an overly familiar hug. I watch her struggle against her natural urge to recoil. Russell Rossi is an adventure seeker, a shameless flirt, and a level of attractive that loops all the way back around to unattractive. He's uncanny valley–level hot and a self-proclaimed "hugger."

Since Mara once described a high five from her accountant as "inappropriately chummy," I swoop in to hug Russell myself. He presses his whole body against me and holds it approximately three seconds too long. Releasing me from his grip, he presents me to the group as "Alison Mullally, Sam's girlfriend."

"Former girlfriend," I correct Russell.

"Well, obviously, babe," Russell says dismissively before returning to his conversation.

His words snap against my skin like a rubber band. I stand there dumbly while the group continues speaking about people I don't know and sharing memories I don't have. The words *He broke up with me six weeks ago* sit on my tongue.

My mouth opens and shuts once, twice, and then a third time. With each second that passes, my correction morphs into an uncomfortable non sequitur in a conversation that's moved on. All of my explanations dissolve in my mouth like sour cotton candy.

Sam's mom joins our circle, greeting each of us with a cool, stiff embrace. I can hardly look at her when she pulls me close, murmuring into my putrid-colored sweater—so quietly I almost can't make it out—"I'm just grateful he found you before . . ."

My role in this tragic drama finally clicks into place.

At funerals, we're all present tense in relation to the dead. Judy Lewis *is* his mom. Rachel *is* his sister. I'm introduced over and over as his girlfriend. *This is Alison, Sam's girlfriend.* Only Sam is past tense.

To this group, I *am* Sam's girlfriend. No one interrogates the seriousness of our relationship to determine how much grief I'm allowed. We could have been together two weeks or ten years—though any of his Instagram followers could see I surfaced around June. I never made it to his TikTok. *A relationship wouldn't fit the "nomad" aesthetic,* he said.

Dread pools in my belly while I hover between lukewarm coffee carafes, overhearing alternate versions of my love life making their way through the sympathy floral arrangements. Most timelines diverge at the annual Lewis family Labor Day party.

In my version of events, Sam dumped me three days prior. Mrs. Lewis, on the other hand, was sad to hear of my bout with food poisoning. Russell's still bummed I was out of town and missed his epic bonfire—the tallest one yet! A few people are sure they saw me there.

In every story but mine, I was still with Sam on Labor Day, and I was still dating him when he crashed his rental car last Tuesday in Sedona on a spur-of-the-moment climbing trip. Therefore, at his funeral, I'm Sam Lewis's girlfriend—possibly in perpetuity.

Part of me wonders if Sam's lie means that he felt more for me than he ever let on, but I immediately dismiss the thought. It's more likely that the breakup didn't warrant a special announcement. My departure would have been self-explanatory when he showed up with a new girlfriend at the next big event. It just so happens that event is today, and he can't be here for it.

As the crowd filters into the church, I yank Mara through a set of heavy double doors into a parochial school hallway, decorated with brightly colored drawings of Jesus on the cross demonstrating varying levels of artistic competency.

Mara stumbles over her feet. "Alison, what the—"

"Why would they all think . . . ?" I can't seem to find the words as nausea clenches my throat.

"Why didn't you correct anyone?" Mara asks. Her tall

frame settles against the beige cubbies lining the school hallway.

"I tried!" She challenges my excuse with a barely perceptible eye roll. "What did you want me to do? Say 'No, Mrs. Lewis, I'm sure you don't have enough on your plate today, so let me be the one to tell you that we broke up six weeks ago'?"

She dismisses her pulsing phone with a frown. "At least *he* dumped *you*. Less culpability."

My teeth worry at my bottom lip. "I think that makes it worse somehow."

Mara's phone pulses again, more violently this time, and she soundtracks her question with furious thumb taps. "Why'd you want us to come then?"

My feet squelch as I pace the small opening of Ms. Dubicki's classroom door. "His mom wanted me here . . . which suddenly makes a bit more sense. But we're trying to stay friends. *Were*, I mean," I correct myself, an apostrophe the difference between life and death. "Who're you texting during my crisis?"

"The Guy," she grumbles. Mara manages the campaign of a potential mayoral candidate whom she refers to only as "the Guy." Her texting demeanor—all stiff shoulders and flared nostrils—broadcasts her frustration with her newest candidate. "And since we're clearly doing this"—she gestures in a circle between us—"I'm briefing Chelsea to get us all on the same page. She has *thoughts*."

"*This*? What is . . ." I rip my silent phone out of my coat pocket and groan at my missed notifications from Chelsea Olsen, the other member of our trio. "You can't text 'Al is dating Sam' in the group chat with no further context. Chelsea's asking if it's a 'Devon Sawa *Casper* scenario.'"

While Mara is a classic old soul—with the confidence and jaded perspective that comes from having done it all and seen it all—Chelsea's soul is fresh and new. The possibilities for her are always endless, so when Mara texts a coded message about my waking nightmare, Chelsea's first thought is that I've fallen into a paranormal romance with a ghost.

"Don't answer that. Never admit to anything in writing. Keep all your statements on message. Right now, the story is you're still dating Sam."

"I don't need a story. I need to set this straight." I take a deep, restorative breath before losing steam and slumping next to Mara against the cubbies. "How do I do that?"

"The Notes-app apology on Instagram is always a classic. But I think you can just tell his mom there's been a misunderstanding."

"Yeah. Yes, of course." Anxiety twists my stomach. "I think I need a second."

My eyes drift to the glowing fire exit and the sign below it that reads CAUTION. ALARM WILL SOUND.

Before I can properly consider escape routes, a gorgeous blond woman barges through the hallway doors. "Is one of you Alison?" the stranger asks. "Russell said Sam's girlfriend went this way." She stops short, somehow perfectly positioned in the single ray of sunshine pouring into the dark, nearly windowless hallway so that she's bathed in light like an angel of death. But then her wild eyes slam into me with recognition. Damn it, Russell. "Alison? I'm Rachel, Sam's sister."

As soon as she says her name, I see it. Rachel Lewis looks so much like her brother, the same ocean-blue eyes and beachy blond waves. Without a stitch of makeup, she glows in her simple black cotton dress. I suppress the inappropriate urge to ask for her skin-care routine.

The words *Sam's girlfriend* ring in my head like an alarm. This is the confrontation I've been hurtling toward—to rehash my dumping by the man we're all here to mourn. My body braces for impact. "There's been a misunderstanding," I explain in the passive voice like a true politician. Mara should be proud. "I'm Sam's *ex*-girlfriend. I'm not sure how, but—"

She cuts me off with a dismissive hand wave. "I know all of that. Who have *you* told?"

I stop analyzing each of her eerily Sam-like features and finally take in Rachel's demeanor. She's shifting her weight from foot to foot and peering over her shoulder like an intrepid reporter handling an increasingly volatile source, the kindergartners' coat hooks a stand-in for a darkened parking garage.

I squint at Rachel. "Told?"

"That you're broken up. Tell me you didn't tell anyone." Her eyes are pleading with me.

I look at Mara before answering. "I tried to correct Russell, but it went over his head."

"Wait, I'm sorry. You *know*?" Mara asks, transforming into "Work Mara" like a corporate Animorph.

"He had me take Alison's name off the plane ticket to Chile. Of course I know," Rachel explains, leaning toward us. "But I'm the only one who does."

Back when I was dating Sam and feigning wild impulsivity, Sam promised he'd "figure out" my flight and accommodations if I'd join him in Chile. *Just say yes. The rest will work itself out,* he assured me. I'd thought it was some sort of "the universe will provide" mantra, but apparently, "the universe" was his flight attendant sister.

Mara snaps her head in my direction. "Plane ticket?"

"Sam invited me on his January Patagonia trip," I answer, my shoulders stiffening under my friend's narrowed gaze.

"And you agreed?" Mara asks. "Of your own free will?"

Rachel's waving arms cut into our aside of meaningful looks and shrugs. "We don't have much time," she instructs, her voice vibrating with a panicked energy. "I'm giving the eulogy in a few minutes, and I need to know that you'll go along with this."

"What do you mean, 'go along'?" Mara folds her arms.

Rachel pulls me closer by my forearm, gripping so desperately pain shoots to my fingertips. "Sam didn't want my mom to know he broke up with you. She'd been on him about 'getting serious' and 'settling down,' and she likes you. You're stable." She means *dull*. "Despite all his achievements, the only thing that matters to my parents right now is that he was finally settling down with a nice girl." Her voice puts *nice girl* in scare quotes. Whether she's objecting to nice girls in general or attributing the term to *me*, no one's asking follow-up questions.

I tilt my head to the side, trying to process this bizarre turn of events. "You want me to . . . pretend?"

She nods her head as if still convincing herself. "It's one day. You guys only dated for a minute, and when the grief fog lifts, they'll forget all about you. I—we just need you to be 'the girlfriend' today. Please." She swallows the last word, but I hear it all the same. Tears pool at the corners of her eyes, and she blinks them away. The sight of her tortured expression pulls at a painful rock in my chest, and I bite on the insides of my cheeks to keep from crying too.

The thought of Sam worrying that his bold, undaunted life wasn't enough cuts me in a way I can't explain. I want to tell him I admired his unsettled life, but I can't. I can't tell him anything ever again, and neither can this despairing woman in front of me.

But pretending is something I *can* do.

I peel Rachel's hand from my arm and offer her a smile I hope is encouraging. "Of course. Whoever you need me to be."

As far as funerals go, this one's vibrating with energy. The church is packed in the way it only is for Easter Sunday, Christmas Eve, and the funerals of young people. Mara and I are directed to a pew near the front, and I realize too late the usher has provided us prime mourner real estate.

We're in the second row, directly behind the immediate family, mixed in with cousins and lifelong family friends. As a discarded summer fling, I brought reinforcement and dressed for the back pew to hide beside former coworkers and high school acquaintances. Instead, I'm up front on full display as Sam Lewis's Current Girlfriend (capital C, capital G).

Rachel delivers the eulogy. She starts with childhood stories of tree climbing and broken arms. Sam's early wanderlust and his adrenaline-junkie thirst for adventure. His penchant for taking spur-of-the-moment vacations and wilderness hikes without a word to anyone. A frustrating attribute in life sounds so charming in death. I recognize the man she describes as Sam, but he's flattened—a flawless sum total of sweet stories and wacky anecdotes.

I always thought Sam was living precisely the *right* life. He was effervescent and spontaneous, always wanting to try a new spot, always leaving for an exciting trip. He was zero to one hundred in every facet of life. He was impulsive and did things that scared him "for the story." If anyone was really living, it was Sam.

He introduced me to his parents and invited me on a two-week backpacking trip through the Patagonian Andes after only a few dates, as if that were a completely ordinary way to approach a new relationship.

I thought being with him would make me adventurous in a hurry, but it just made me tired. I hoped I'd eventually acclimate to his lifestyle, like a climber adjusting to changing altitude, but it only got more exhausting and difficult to breathe. Finally, he cut me loose.

Sometimes I don't think you even like hiking or parasailing or rock climbing, he said when he ended it. *I want to know* you, *but it's like you're pretending to be someone else.*

I feel the weight of everyone's eyes on my back as the grief swims beneath my breastbone, but my sorrow isn't what it looks like. I miss Sam as my friend, as the guy who burned hot and bright like the sun, everyone helpless against his gravitational pull.

After "On Eagle's Wings," I perk up at the introduction of the next reader, biting back an inappropriate smirk when the priest directs "Adam Berg, Sam's best friend" to the pulpit. Sam's oldest friend and college roommate, the mythical Adam Berg, is known to me—and now *only* me—as the North Shore Grump.

A character in many of Sam's stories, Adam lives two hours

away in Duluth, and though I've been on countless group chats with the man for last-minute invitations to events and spontaneous weekend trips, we've never met. Adam was always quick to respond with a curt "Can't" or "Nope." (My responses were often rejections as well, but far more regretful and long-winded.) As with Bigfoot or the Loch Ness Monster, it seemed doubtful I'd ever catch a glimpse of Sam's supposed "closest friend."

When he finally approaches the lectern, I'm surprised. He looks nothing like the aspiring wilderness influencers Sam surrounded himself with. It's not that Adam's not good-looking—he is—but he's a different brand of "unkempt handsome white guy." Where Sam had the easy, windswept attractiveness of a man dismounting a Jet Ski, Adam manages to look like he hasn't slept in days but also just woke up. His rumpled dark brown hair and beard are a bit overgrown, like he's missed a haircut or three. Partway through Philippians 4:8, he fights with the starchy shirt collar under his charcoal suit, which I'm certain is either borrowed or has been sitting at the bottom of his closet since a wedding years ago.

At the final sentence, he peers into the packed church, and his eyes pierce mine like a tranquilizer dart, sending pins and needles down my spine. Before it can render me boneless, his look transforms into a puzzling combination of recognition and embarrassment, like the expression of someone who stole a stranger's parking spot only to share an elevator with them five minutes later.

My insides clench, but before I can make sense of his expression, the phone I'm certain I silenced chirps in my coat pocket. In the millisecond it takes to lift my eyes back to the front, his gaze has drifted away. He steps down from the pulpit without a second glance.

I turn toward Mara to exchange telepathic looks of *Did you see that?* and *Seriously, what is his deal?* But she's flipping through her hymnal, unaffected by the stare of the elusive Adam Berg.

I take advantage of the uncomfortable lull in the proceedings and wake up my phone. The alert that broke through the quiet settings stares back at me:

> **Message from the Future: Get in a hike this weekend with Sam!! Chile is everything you imagined, but only because you put in the training back in October!**
>
>

A guttural sound wrenches itself from my throat, reverberating throughout the church. I feel the weight of every set of eyes on me.

"That's the girlfriend," someone explains among the echoey chorus of sympathetic murmurs.

Because now I *am* "the girlfriend." Sam Lewis is stuck with me—even in death.

2

The Luncheon

SAM USED TO leave reminders in my calendar when we were dating. He called them "Messages from the Future." It was part of the life philosophy he promoted on his motivational Instagram platform—the inspirational messages captioning photos of his sharp jawline admiring sunsets on Kilimanjaro.

If I casually mentioned wanting something, it became a message. They were written from the point of view of my future self, saying things like, "You started training for the marathon today, and now you're killing it!" or "I'm so grateful you bought a ticket to Croatia today, because you're there right now and it's breathtaking."

You could never daydream with Sam. Everything was achievable. Everything was within reach. Money, time, and prior commitments were never an excuse for not living your best life. He never understood why I didn't like the messages. To him, each message from the future was a statement of potential. To me, they were a reminder of how I was falling short.

He must've loaded a bunch of countdowns for the Patagonia trip when I agreed to go. After the breakup, I got a "100 days" reminder, but it wasn't nearly as alarming when they were just notes from a man who'd friend-zoned me, as opposed to this eerily timed post-death dispatch.

"Sorry about your seat belt pillow," Mara says from the driver's seat of her Jeep. She points her chin at my unadorned belt strap. "They threw it away when I got the car detailed."

I stare out the window into the boat club parking lot with my forehead pressed to the glass. "It's fine." And it is. I only really needed a pillow strapped to my seat belt during my mastectomy and reconstruction. Since then, it's just been too cozy to chuck.

Six years ago, when my mom was diagnosed with Stage 2 breast cancer, the rest of my family got tested for the BRCA1 genetic mutation. My sister, Emma, was negative. I drew the short pink straw.

With my genetics, I have an 85 percent chance of having breast cancer during my lifetime. It's a noncommittal, *likely, eventually,* diagnosis. That 15 percent is like glimpsing an oasis in a desert—there's some reason to hope, but you're probably going to be drinking sand. My doctor couldn't say anything for sure other than I'm *likely, eventually* doomed. Or I was.

About a year and a half ago, I bit the bullet and got a preventative double mastectomy, removing my breast tissue, nipples, sensation—the whole deal. Six months later, I underwent breast reconstruction and am now less likely to develop breast cancer than women without the mutation.

After a slew of awkward one-night stands and failed first dates, I started dating Sam. Sam always felt less like a boyfriend and more like a higher plane to aspire to, someone who could transform me through proximity—and the occasional motivational calendar notification—into someone worthy of having escaped a *likely, eventually* death sentence. A person worthy of the cheat code I'd used.

Mara taps my arm from the driver's seat. "It's one afternoon, Al. And it's almost over. We just need to get through the luncheon and then you can deal with all of these feelings in the privacy of your therapist's office," she tells me, assuming I'm lost in thought over the current deception.

I brush off her suggestion with a weak wave, because I stopped seeing Denise months ago. "Thanks for driving me today."

"It's less for your benefit and more for the safety of the greater Twin Cities metropolitan area. I can't remember the last time you drove yourself somewhere." She peers over her sleek sunglasses, which are either pricey designer frames or only look expensive because that is the power of Mara Montgomery-Kline. "I'm not certain you still know how."

This is a lie. Not the part about my masterminding my life around walkability, public transit, and any other measures to avoid driving my beat-up Subaru across town, but the part about her presence being for anyone's benefit other than mine. But since Mara feels deep discomfort acknowledging that she possesses the capacity for feelings beyond "ruthlessly ambitious" and "hungry," I let it slide.

I flip the visor and rub smeared mascara from my under eyes with my ring finger. "Okay. Play something fun before we go in. Give us a lift."

"I think belting it out in the parking lot of your boyfriend's wake is going to send the wrong message." She turns toward me, clasping my hands in hers like she would a jittery candidate's before a debate. "You can handle this. We can handle this. Let's roll!"

But we can't handle this, and things quickly fall apart at the luncheon.

From the moment we enter the hall—all wood paneling and nautical stripes as far as the eye can see—the event is already in minor crisis. Since the caterer failed to mark the gluten-free brunch options, I volunteer to identify and label them for Mrs. Lewis, in hopes of both hiding in the kitchen and busying myself.

Unfortunately, this gesture only serves to amplify my position as "grieving partner" rather than achieve my primary goal of evaporating into thin air. In the industrial kitchen, the waiters swap pitying looks in my direction. The bartender leads me in a quick healing meditation for grief, which involves placing both hands between my breasts. I participate, hoping it will end the interaction faster, but this is a miscalculation.

Sam's family and friends find me, offering their condolences in a mini receiving line between stainless steel prep tables. Most of these mourners fall into one of two categories: strangers I'm confident I've never met but who claim to remember me specifically, or vaguely familiar people I'll never place, no matter how intensely I stare at them.

"This is . . . uncomfortable," Mara murmurs when we're finally alone. Her curly penmanship on the "gluten-free" labels is impeccable, and it only fuels my fury.

"I know," I snap. I press my pen too hard, and the *f* in *free* bleeds across the index card. "But if I stand out there with all of Sam's loved ones for one more second, my skin will walk off without me and serve appetizers."

She scrunches her nose. "That's an *unsettling* image."

We both look up as the scrape of the metal door announces another entrance into the kitchen.

A young server juggling three coffee carafes tilts her navy-polo-clad torso into the kitchen. "We need a tray of GF French toast. The celiacs are getting restless." She tips her head in the direction of the crowded room filled with a shockingly high number of gluten-intolerant mourners. Something about the way she treats us—not like characters in a tragic romance but as two women standing between her and a fat tip—recenters me. She bounces the open door on her hip impatiently.

Mara fills her arms with a metal pan of sugar-dusted slices. "I'll take care of this. You continue hiding behind the chafing dishes."

"I prefer the term *strategic avoidance*," I call out after her. Using her body as a doorstop, our server friend lets Mara through the doorway, but before she too can make her way into the dining room, I watch her eyes clock an intruder into my sanctuary of stainless steel and bulk bins of mini French vanilla creamers.

"Alison!" Mrs. Lewis's voice precedes her, sparkling and sweet, and for a moment, I expect to see the woman I met on the Fourth of July. Vibrant and fizzy, she was wearing a hot pink and teal kaftan and pushing a signature cocktail she had created for the event.

Today, she's unrecognizable. Her eyes are the same blue as Sam's, but flat and red rimmed with dried tears. There's no color in her cheeks, and she looks beyond exhausted, like her bones are too heavy to carry with her. She drags a man through the kitchen door behind her.

"There you are. I've been looking everywhere. Have you met Sam's best friend, Adam? Adam, this is Sam's girlfriend, Alison." She gestures to the man behind her, whose gaze is glued to the floor.

Adam's strange expression during the service flashes in my brain, and I seriously consider whether I can run away before his eyes rise to meet mine. But I'm too late.

When he looks up, I'm surprised by his appearance. I figured the North Shore Grump would have a tall, broad frame fit for a northern cryptid, but on that body, I'd imagined a face to match his bland, curt personality: a man as off-putting as his text persona.

What I did *not* imagine? That Adam Berg would be that particular brand of approachably handsome that compels you to lean in closer with his every blink and half smile. Or he would be if his ruggedly handsome features weren't frozen in a scowl.

Still, there's something undeniably gentle about his dark brown eyes, even now, when they're as unfocused as Mrs. Lewis's.

For a moment, I feel safe, until something in his face flickers and those seemingly harmless eyes skewer me with a look that sets me so off-balance, I nearly announce, *I'm Sam's current girlfriend,* like the world's worst undercover cop.

"No," I finally respond. "We haven't met. I'm Alison." Grateful my brain's produced the right words in the correct order, I extend my hand toward Adam.

He moves with a slight start, as if he nearly forgot what a

handshake is. He takes my hand in his, and I finally understand why people compare hands to paws. His hands aren't especially hairy, but they're rough and big, at least twice the size of mine. When he gives me that same look of unease he did in the church, I brace myself.

"I've seen pictures of you with Sam," he says simply, and I let out an inward sigh of relief. His tone reveals nothing aside from moderate embarrassment to have recognized me off of Instagram alone. Though a discomfort with social media would be in stark contrast to Sam—who once referred to making dinner together as a "collab"—I grab hold of this explanation like it's a buoy in choppy waters.

Still, I can't release the tight knot that formed at the base of my shoulders the moment he gave me that look in the church. That *look*. It told me that if anyone was going to see through this whole farce, it was Adam Berg.

"He told me so much about you when he was planning his visit for Oktoberfest," I say, filling the pause when he doesn't. I'm incapable of letting anyone twist in silent discomfort. I inherited my mother's compulsion to make others feel at ease.

"I thought he *did* visit for Oktoberfest," Mrs. Lewis interjects. Adam grips my palm tighter, examining me with a keen gaze.

I extract my hand. "Yes. Of course."

Adam's hard jaw ticks as they both wait for my explanation. Less than one hour after agreeing to play "the girlfriend," I've already stepped into a conversational minefield.

Mara bursts through the door. "We need two more trays, and I'm covering for Taylor while she takes her fifteen." She sees us and stops short.

"Got it." A young server with floppy hair and ear gauges

dutifully loops around her and grabs another tray of French toast.

"The service has been really great," Adam tells Mara, handing her the second dish from the prep table.

Oh god. He thinks she works here, which isn't an absurd presumption considering we're hiding with the kitchen staff.

Mara pauses, no doubt deciding how to play this. "Thanks," she replies. Her eyes question me, but at my subtle head shake, she traitorously escapes through the screeching door.

Adam's and Mrs. Lewis's eyes dart back to me. I clear my throat.

Why did I let Mara leave? I should've tied our ankles together with kitchen twine, ensuring her supportive cooperation with walking, talking, and other basic behaviors expected of a grief-stricken girlfriend until we could mount an escape.

Relief rattles up my ribs at another scrape of the metal door, but it's only Sam's father trudging purposefully across the tile floor, not Benedict Mara or even a well-timed rodent to clear the room.

"Walter says if we sell before January, we can avoid further tax complications," Dr. Richard Lewis tells his wife, holding his lit phone in the palm of his hand.

"You were on the phone with Walter *now*? During our . . ." Mrs. Lewis abandons the sentence, the thought too painful to complete. Her voice is a lid on a boiling pot.

Undeterred, his left forefinger presses against the silvery hair at his temple as he continues, "One of Sam's friends is a Realtor, and he was saying if we list it by December first, we might have everything settled before the Cookie Party."

"The Cookie Party?" she repeats, sounding as if she's never heard of either cookies or parties.

Her hands smooth her black dress. It looks expensive but not perfectly tailored. She probably bought it for this occasion. The image of her wandering the Ridgedale Center Nordstrom with a slow gait and vacant blue eyes slices my abdomen like a shard of glass.

She recovers and trills, "Richard, we're not discussing this," through a pasted-on smile.

"Judy, we have to discuss this. You won't go in his apartment, and I can schedule the movers, but if we want to arrange for them to pack Sam's belongings—"

"*Strangers* are not touching our son's things." Her voice is sharp. It seems to catch her husband off guard; he jumps the tiniest bit before pulling his round tortoiseshell glasses off his nose and wiping them with the bottom of his suit jacket.

His foggy eyes stare at his lenses. "I'm sorry, JuJu," he says, and suddenly I'm back on their deck holding Sam's hand while Dr. Lewis calls out to his wife from behind the grill. From the sad, sweet look in her eyes, I suspect Mrs. Lewis is there too. "I know you don't want to, but . . . it's something we need to deal with," he says, but the word *we* sounds startlingly similar to *I*.

Adam stuffs his hands in his pockets as the image in front of us comes into sharp focus, kitchen noise clattering all around us. Neither parent can bear their son's sudden death. While Mrs. Lewis is collapsing beneath its crushing weight, Dr. Lewis is hoping to outrun it, as if checking off lists and calling accountants from now until eternity will be enough to evade the grief chasing him down.

My gut twists imagining what it would feel like to suffer an unfathomable loss, only to be left with nothing besides the business of death—burials, estate sales, and everything else required to ease your son from the world.

I look into their weary blue eyes. Sam's eyes. What must it be like to look into the mirror and see your son's eyes, knowing you'll never see his again? It isn't natural to grieve for your child. The unfairness of it presses into my lungs so hard I need a gulp of air.

Only, when I open my mouth to breathe—before I've even had a second to consider what a colossally bad idea this is—I hear myself volunteer, "I can do it."

"You'll go through Sam's things for us?" The smallest glimmer of light shines through Mrs. Lewis's expression. "You'll pack his things and get his condo ready to sell?" Her hopeful expression presses on the pleasure center in my brain that lights up when I'm doing something right even when it hurts a little.

"Of course." I stretch the words into so many syllables, desperate for a bystander to jump in and stop this. "Whatever you need me to do, I can do it."

Mrs. Lewis claps her hands together. "That would be wonderful, Alison. I'm so grateful. I've always admired how dependable you are. I'm always telling Sam how perfect you are for him." She slips into the present tense again. I can't correct her. Rather than comment, I stare at the mysterious stain on the wall behind her head.

Adam clears his throat. "She doesn't need to . . . I can handle it, Judy. It's fine."

I glance at him sidelong. "Don't you live two hours away?"

"There are weekends." He manages not to sound like an

irredeemable asshole when he explains the concept of calendars to me, which is an absolute feat. "And I'm sure there's some small house projects to do if they need it sold by the end of the year. You won't want to do that." His words are technically directed at me, but his attention has barely left the Lewises.

Every so often I've caught him chancing glances at me like I'm a piece of food in someone's teeth. He's nice enough not to stare but can't help but anxiously track my movements. His subtle awareness makes my skin tight.

I don't *like* the idea of packing up my ex-boyfriend's apartment, but I like the idea of ceding the task to the North Shore Grump even less.

"I love small house projects." I narrow my eyes. I'm obviously lying but that's beside the point. "Small house projects are my favorite."

"Adam, I thought you were too busy to take on side work," Dr. Lewis says.

Adam bristles. "This isn't *side work*. I'll make time for Sam."

I don't like how we're talking about Sam, as if he's only in the next room and not permanently displaced to our memories.

Mrs. Lewis spins her silver pendant necklace with her fingers. "It should really be Alison, Adam. She'll know what's special for us."

She looks to me to reinforce this assumption, which only makes my insides fold in on themselves.

"We can both do it," I manage.

Mrs. Lewis beams, her husband nods—crossing an item off of his mental to-do list—and Adam pinches the bridge of his nose like I've sentenced him to one weekend trapped inside a freight elevator.

Why am I like this?

Because Sam's gone and all this family wants is for their son to have had a girlfriend willing to shoulder one small piece of the burden bearing down on them.

Being the woman they need right now is the least I can do. It won't make up for the loss of their son, but it might make this moment more tolerable. I can't disappoint this family, today of all days.

And whether Adam wants to believe it or not, I can help him too.

"Adam and I will handle everything."

3

A Steadier Ford

2:17 PM
Alison:
Hi Adam! It's Alison! Is there a time I should come by
on Saturday? Anything I can bring?

WINTER COMES QUICKLY in Minnesota. One day,
you're enjoying a beautiful fall morning in a light
denim jacket. The next, you're hunting through
the bottom of your closet for a parka so you can dig your car
out of the snow. Sometimes we get our first good snowfall in
the middle of October.

Not this year. The day after Sam's funeral, it's in the high
forties and warm enough to force my two best friends on the
hike my dead ex-boyfriend proposed between his eulogy and
communion.

Driving to a suburban man-made nature trail feels inade-
quate, but it's the best I can do on my haunted iCal's short
notice. The path is too groomed and well maintained, and
I can still hear the highway in the distance. It's hardly a

communion with nature. Sam wouldn't even count it as a hike—more of an unproductive stroll to nowhere.

"I left you alone for ten minutes." A twig snaps beneath Mara's bright white sneakers, which have never seen the outside of a Life Time Fitness. She's always a bit twitchy this far away from cell reception, because, in her words, "You never know where you'll be when the Guy—I don't know—accidentally posts a Reel of his dick set to 'Unholy.'"

The specificity of that "hypothetical" haunts me to this day.

"You abandoned me in my time of need."

The reflective strip on her Lululemon running jacket catches in the sun as her hand swipes at something in the air. "I assumed you could handle yourself well enough to *not* volunteer to pack up your dead ex-boyfriend's home for his family. You hear how insane that sounds, right?"

"No way, Al. I love how committed you are to fake-dating their son. It's sweet." Coconut-scented blond strands whip into my mouth as Chelsea spins in the direction of whatever creature is pounding on a neighboring tree. "Ooh, a red-bellied woodpecker!"

Chelsea's always been an animal lover, but years of teaching fourth-grade science have turned her passing interest in Minnesota fauna into a mild obsession. The only barrier to her hoarding formerly stray cats is her landlord Joel, whose strict no-pet policy forced her to rehome Colonel Corduroy, the one-eyed calico she found wandering around the state fairgrounds.

"I'm not 'fake-dating' . . . ," I start to argue before accepting defeat, swatting at the mosquito dive-bombing my face. Most summer bugs have died or gone indoors, and only the most stubborn tiny vampires remain. They can feel the cool breeze of winter closing in on them, and the beasts are reckless with nothing to lose.

"'Fake-dating' assumes a level of participation on Sam's part that Al can't rely on." Mara high-steps over a swarm of ground hornets crawling along the grass. When I close my eyes, I swear I can feel them creeping up my hiking boots and push down the shudder rising up my back.

Chelsea yanks her eyes away from the majesty of nature. "This won't interfere with my kids' holiday concert, right? Half of the parents will be away for travel hockey, and we need bodies. If you bail, send someone else in your place. It's a one-in, one-out situation."

"Don't worry," I say to ease her mind. "I'll be there with bells on."

"I'm ninety percent sure you're kidding, but please don't. It'll really mess with the handbell choir's Rihanna cover, and Kaylee and Hunter are already holding on to that bridge by a thread."

I pull a water bottle out of my belt bag. "You gave the children bells?"

"Don't pretend you're not intrigued by a ringing rendition of 'Umbrella.'" Chelsea stuffs her hands in the pocket of her highlighter-pink hoodie, popping a brow.

"We said we're coming. Please stop telling us about it," Mara begs.

Chelsea rolls her eyes at us. "I should have rescheduled rehearsal yesterday. If I'd known it was going to get all cloak-and-dagger at Sam's service, I would've been your 'plus-two.' Oh, I could've done an accent! I've been bingeing *Bachelor in Paradise Australia,* and my Aussie accent is getting good."

Chelsea says "getting good" in an accent not authentic to any region of the Commonwealth.

Mara holds her phone above her head as if cell service will strike her arm like a lightning rod in a storm. "You're staying on top of *Real Housewives* too, right? There is always *Housewives* trivia." Her question is a thinly veiled directive.

Along with Chelsea's coworker Patrick, Chelsea and I are part of a bar trivia team that Mara takes far too seriously. Every year, we participate in a league championship on New Year's Day, and every year, we never make it past the quarter-finals. Our poor showing only fuels Mara's competitive nature for the year ahead.

"Don't worry, Mar. I'm just as devoted to the cause as ever." Chelsea turns back to me. "Why didn't Sam tell anyone you broke up?" The million-dollar question.

"Rachel said his parents wanted to see him settled, and he couldn't face them until he was in another relationship. They're a bit intense about that stuff. His mom, especially." I grimace, remembering how Mrs. Lewis—after a couple of Bud Light Limes at her Fourth of July party—more than once inquired after the state of my womb. I knew she was trying to parlay her unsubtle questions into an open discussion of babies, family, and the general state of my reproductive health, but I wasn't in the mood to discuss how my BRCA diagnosis complicated all of these decisions while on a pontoon boat with my brand-new boyfriend's mom as "Party in the USA" thrummed in the background. "Being 'the girlfriend' is the absolute least I can do. It's just packing stuff up. And his friend Adam will be helping me. It'll take—what—one day? Maybe two? Then it's done."

"There's a friend? What's this friend's deal? Is he hot?" Chelsea prods, kicking up dirt along the trail.

I stumble on the uneven terrain. "What? No!" I shriek too quickly as Mara shouts, "Yes! It's a disaster."

"Oooh. Twist." Chelsea rubs her hands together, greedy for any crumbs of salaciousness.

"He's completely Al's type," Mara says, trying her phone toward the ground now, getting increasingly desperate.

"I don't have a type," I argue, but my voice is shrill and defensive.

"So, like . . . a beardy Indiana Jones?" Chelsea inquires. Mara nods without looking up from her device.

"I think I would have noticed if he looked like a young Harrison Ford." I trip over a rock, trying, and failing, to make the messy maneuver look like a natural human movement.

Sure, Adam is handsome, but all of Sam's friends are. Collected in one room, they look like a casting call for a North Face catalog. If anything about him was uniquely attractive to me, I didn't register it. Everything about the day felt wrong, like we were all victims of a horrifying practical joke gone too far.

Mara rolls her eyes. "Oh, *you* noticed. And it was reciprocated."

I fidget with my sleeve. "You saw us talking for one second."

She levels me with a look that says one second was all she needed.

Did I? Did he? I inwardly shudder at the possibility I was subconsciously ogling guests at my boyfriend's funeral. Well, ex-boyfriend, but no one else knew that!

Chelsea's eyes are bright with mischief. "It's more of an energy than a look you go for, like a grumpy intellectual who just emerged disheveled from a cave and has no time for your funny business."

Mara piles on. "Like a scruffy guy who'll argue with you while mounting your TV."

"That's not my type. Sam wasn't like that."

Chelsea tilts her head in serious deliberation. "No, he was Greg Kinnear in *Sabrina,* even though it was obvious to anyone with eyes she was going to end up with Harrison Ford. But Sam was definitely in the Harrison Ford extended universe. I, for one, want to see you with a steadier Ford. Like in *Witness* or *Working Girl.*"

"He's such a jerk in *Working Girl*," I say, but no one's listening.

Chelsea picks a bundle of pine needles from the forest floor and smells it, pleasure crinkling the corners of her eyes. Jealousy blooms in my chest. Ever since my mastectomy, I've made myself go on a hike every week, hoping I'd grow to love these regular meditations with nature and my body. I have not. Give me a choice between a mountain, a beach, and a meadow, and I'll choose "D: None of the Above" every time. Humans have mastered climate control. Why move backward?

With every weekend hike, every personal-growth memoir I devour, every trip down the river in a canoe, I'm hoping to become the kind of person who feels compelled to sniff at a twig just for the simple joy of it.

But I'm still me, and I'd rather smell a cookie.

It's like you're pretending to be someone else.

"Yes! Sweet baby Jesus, I have a bar." Mara teeters on a boulder, hovering her phone in the air and engaging every core muscle for balance.

The branches open up behind my friend's precarious yoga

pose, and I can just make out crystal-blue water in the distance. Lush pine trees surround the small lake, their reflections dancing in the glittering light of the surface. The last dregs of fall foliage cling to the branches of the neighboring deciduous trees, dotting the scene with sparse bits of oranges and reds like it's an unfinished landscape watercolor.

Even I have to admit, there's something hopeful about witnessing seasons, the way even the air is capable of radical change. The guilt in my chest unfurls—the smallest bit—and I reward my attitude shift with a rest on a neighboring rock.

Mara and Chelsea are already typing on their screens, so I pull out my phone too. I started a text conversation with the North Shore Grump on the drive, feeling buzzy first-day-of-school nerves for some unknown reason.

When he didn't immediately respond, I hid my phone under my water bottle in the backseat of Mara's Jeep and reopened my text messages with Sam. I've been picking at that scab since I learned of his death.

I should've been relieved that all of our post-breakup communications were dreadfully civil, friendly even. There was no acrimony. No cruel jabs. No unfortunate drunk voicemails on either end. The exchanges were absolutely devoid of substance. It was almost as if we didn't mean anything to each other at all.

SEPTEMBER 9:

2:30 PM
Sam
Is my green jacket at your place?

3:12 PM

Alison:

It is. You can grab it after 5.

4:36 PM

Sam:

I'll swing over around 6 then. 😊

SEPTEMBER 30:

8:42 AM

Sam:

Happy Birthday!!

9:03 AM

Alison:

Thanks!

OCTOBER 9:

10:19 AM

Alison:

I'm glad we ran into you at trivia last night. Thanks
for your help with the sports questions!

12:37 PM

Sam:

I could tell it thrilled Mara to finally win.

12:39 PM
Sam:
We should do it again. I'll bring a ringer.

OCTOBER 16:

8:47 PM
Alison:
Tell me this is a joke.

After that, there's nothing.

I shift my butt on the damp rock and tap on my missed text from Adam.

3:04 PM
Adam:
No.

No? No to what? To whether I can bring something on Saturday? Or is this his way of saying there's "no" good time for me to come over? Ever? There isn't even punctuation or an emoji to offer clues. What am I supposed to do with a one-syllable answer to a multipart question?

I stuff my phone in the pocket of my fleece. Minutes pass before Mara clasps her hands together and announces, "I think we can count this as a moderate success and quit while we're ahead. It's getting very *True Detective*-y out here, and I don't have time to solve a murder today."

Chelsea pulls her foot into a standing quad stretch. "Yeah,

I need to head out soon. Ritter wants me to stay over to-night."

She at least has the decency to look guilty for cutting our afternoon short, but her excuse being her new boyfriend Ritter—a crypto entrepreneur—is adding insult to injury. I like him even less than Mara's most recent ex-girlfriend, who shoplifted "for political reasons" and once brought a whole rotisserie chicken into a movie theater.

My head flops backward in defeat. "Fine. You're both dismissed. Thank you for accompanying me to this future crime scene."

I didn't tell them about the iCal alert from Sam or why my need to be on a trail, any trail, couldn't wait. I wasn't sure they'd understand. I'm not sure *I* do.

I fall in step behind Chelsea, who leads us downhill at double speed. "I've decided to view this whole 'fake girl-friend' business as a good thing," Chelsea says. I hear Mara snort behind us. "Physically sorting through his belongings will help you mentally sort your feelings. Put it all in literal and metaphorical boxes."

"It's a bit on the nose, Chels." One of my feet slides out from under me on a rotting crab apple, but Mara grabs my arm from behind so I don't slip to the ground.

"Maybe Chelsea's right." Mara's tone is kind, if not entirely convincing. "It might help you process your grief. It's a bit of an emotional minefield, and this has already been such a hard year for you."

She distills it all down to two words—*hard year*.

I was sure I'd processed the BRCA diagnosis six years ago, when I first tested positive. My mom was still sick, and maybe I was fooling myself, but I thought I had it under control. I had a plan. I had a binder. I had a gratitude journal, for chrissake! But when I finally had the mastectomy, something changed.

The physical pain of a surgeon carving out my breast tissue, removing my nipples, and inserting expanders was more than I anticipated, but physical pain was still something everyone around me could understand. As a cancer survivor, my mom could relate to my grief over losing parts of my body so closely tied to my femininity and sexuality. She too felt the alienness of adapting to the new numb bits that had replaced them.

But knowing no one else who'd had a preventative mastectomy, no one else who'd cheated cancer, I felt utterly alone with the knot of guilt that took root beneath my silicone implants. The guilt that—after a second chance had been plopped in my lap—I was going to go back to being just plain me.

I made it a point to be *more*. I started hiking, mountain climbing, water skiing, and anything else that looked adventurous. But then Sam—wild and worthy Sam—died, and it felt like someone grabbed each end of the knot in my chest and pulled it apart.

The parking lot appears ahead, and I dig deep for a smile. "Yeah, maybe the packing will be good for me."

With two bars of service, I shoot off a text to the North Shore Grump.

3:59 PM
Alison:
See you at 10 AM.

Then I send a slew of cheery emojis. Just to really piss him off.

4

Half-Used Bottle of Men's Dove

I ALWAYS LIKED THAT Sam lived off the Green Line. There are only two light railways in the Twin Cities, and the Green Line starts in front of my apartment in Saint Paul and crosses in front of Sam's in Minneapolis.

I've always loved public transportation, particularly trains. My earliest memory is of setting up a model train under the Christmas tree to weave through our gifts. Sometime in high school, my rail enthusiasm went into hibernation—the popular kids weren't as fascinated by engines—but every Christmas, my dad unpacked the model set and I let my inner train geek run wild.

The train lurches to a stop on Saturday morning, one week after the funeral and my single-syllable exchange with Adam. I'm plopped into the heart of Sam's neighborhood, made up of assertively hip converted warehouses along the river, but Sam's condo is not in one of those unattainably chic buildings. His is in a new complex stacked on top of a pricey organic grocery store, a "green" dry cleaner, and a florist—a redundant beacon of gentrification.

I'm at the door when a rush of grief and embarrassment

rolls over my skin like a hot flash. My fingers are poised to text Sam to let me up. My stomach flips, and my mouth tastes of acid and Cheerios.

On my exhale, the feeling recedes like a tide, leaving only my embarrassment as evidence it was ever there in the first place. A patch of wet sand buried in my chest. I'm debating whether I can scale the building's exterior in a heeled leather boot when a young woman with a tiny white dog dressed as a sushi roll for Halloween exits. I'm in.

"Hello?" I announce myself, slowly opening the unlocked door to Sam's apartment. I unbutton my wool coat and hang it on the teak coatrack next to a thick, denim men's jacket with rough tan lining.

I haven't been to this apartment for two months, but everything that made it essentially Sam's is the same, down to the basket of dirty clothes on the washer.

"I'm starting in the bathroom." Adam's voice echoes through the open door into the hallway.

The first time Sam invited me over to his apartment, which boasts so much natural light it borders on oppressive, I saw the home of a new boyfriend with all the intoxicating potential that came with it. During those early days, I pictured us taking trips to the places where he'd bought the woven tapestries on his walls. The brown leather couch and vintage trunk in his living room were where we might relax and kick our feet up after a long return flight. The dark countertop was the surface on which he'd make us coffee after we woke up slowly in each other's arms.

When he dumped me, the rooms were sapped of their magic possibilities. Because—self-conscious of my new breasts—I always found excuses not to sleep over. We never ended up traveling together, and now I know that most of his art is from West Elm.

Now that he's gone, I try to look at the space as nothing but real estate. Cluttered real estate.

I assault Adam with a cheery "Happy Halloween!" upon my intrusion into the bathroom.

"There's a spare set of keys on the counter. I didn't see any of your stuff around, so I figured you didn't have one."

Sidestepping my lack of keys, I respond, "Starting with the bathroom. Very brave."

The side of his face doesn't register my attempt at levity.

I push the bathroom door wide, and the scratch of the metal trash can against the floor bounces off every white ceramic surface in the modern space. My entrance is so loud and so inelegant that his failure to acknowledge it has to be deliberate.

He's sitting on the edge of the spa bathtub, so I'm left to make do with the lidded toilet. The back of Adam's neck radiates irritation, but somehow, I still notice that he smells good—notes of firewood, hot coffee, and soap, but that last one might be the eleven or so mostly empty bottles of shampoo and body wash lying next to him on the white hexagonal tile. A few are economy sized, but most are hotel filched.

Adam grimaces at a dark gray bottle of body wash, the dried bits of creamy light blue soap crusted down the side in a hardened drip. "I'm tossing anything perishable or mildewy first. I emptied the fridge, so that's dealt with."

"You work fast." I hold my hand out for the soap.

"Did you want anything in the fridge?" Judgment rings through his tone.

"No. It's fine. Fast is good. Better than good," I prattle,

flailing my arms. Mercifully, the shower curtain has ob-scured his face, so he can't see me.

"I would've been faster, but Judy asked me to wait for you."

It's faint, but if I listen, I can hear how put out he is by having to consider me at all.

"In case I want to keep his half-used bottle of men's Dove?" I hold the bottle up like a slimy trophy before setting it next to the other soaps on the floor.

He grunts, turning away from me.

I promised Sam's sister I'd play along, I remind myself. *For Sam and his family. Sam. Sam. Sam.*

"I'm sorry. It was nice of you to make sure." I hesitate, briefly wondering whether Sam's Current Girlfriend would be able to part with his things so easily. "I've never been much for remembering people through their stuff, but I'm glad to help sort through it all, especially for his family," I say, to remind him why we're both here.

Adam points at the trash can, his face expressionless. I uncap a tube of hair pomade and inhale the scent one last time before tossing it in with a low clunk. I don't know why I do it—or why I do it with the other hair products—before discarding it forever. It doesn't conjure a feeling or a particular memory, just Sam's smell. One small, static part of him I can hardly remember.

I wipe dried toothpaste off the inside of the medicine cabi-net with a sponge while Adam rubs Goo Gone on a mysteri-ous, tacky stain Sam hid behind a painting. Every so often, I attempt friendly conversation. Adam always seems to thwart it.

"Adam."

He doesn't respond.

Adam lost his best friend, I remind myself.

"Adam," I repeat, touching my hand to his forearm. His eyes dart to my fingers and then up to my eyes. I'm intending a reassuring, supportive pat of camaraderie—a *You and me, buddy, we're in this together* gesture. What I'm delivering is more of a tentative middle-school-dance hold.

My self-preservation instincts are screaming at me to remove the offending hand and run out the door in humiliation, but I can't.

It's my first proper look at Adam since the luncheon, and he looks completely different outside the context of a funeral. His eyes are just as striking as before, but today, there's a warmth to them, like hot chocolate so decadent and rich, coffee shops would have to call it "drinking chocolate."

His dark brown hair is oddly swoopy, like he's been nervously tugging at it. Under the lights of the bathroom vanity, I see the way his beard is dusted with gray hairs and wonder if I might be into this silvery detail if I allowed myself to examine my reaction to it. Which I will not.

The whole "unkempt man of the woods" thing is a more appealing picture in his comfortable posture and regular clothes—jeans, off-white Henley, and Red Wing leather boots showing signs of serious wear. His shirtsleeves are pushed up to his elbows, doing that sexy-magic thing Henleys do to male bodies by pulling tight through the chest and arms to make shoulders look their brawniest and forearms look their forearmiest.

He's not sculpted in the way Sam was—a body that required hours of targeted work to maintain. Adam's body is muscled in the way men are when they develop strength through chopping wood in the forest.

And now I'm imagining Adam chopping wood in the forest. But it's not as if he's passively accepting my appraisal. He's looking back, his gaze heavy on my skin like fingertips padding along the blush blooming on my neck, my cheeks, the tips of my ears. I shudder to think what he's cataloging about *me*.

It's at this moment the realization crashes into me. Mara was right, and if I wasn't noticing him at the funeral, I am now, while I'm perched on the toilet lid in my dead ex-boyfriend's bathroom. Neither the location of this revelation nor the flush creeping up my body in this current moment is ideal.

His mouth turns down at the corners as we run out the clock on what would be a normal amount of time to look at another person. I can either acknowledge it and make a joke or tear my arm away and cower in shame and denial.

I choose the latter, dropping his arm to ask, "You didn't empty the freezer, did you?" I'm out of the bathroom and crossing the living room toward the kitchen before his mouth can form a response.

He yells from his seat on the bathtub. "Some of it, but I left behind—"

"Yahtzee!" I smile into the glowing freezer, letting the cold air cool my cheeks.

"The Thin Mints or the sugar-free JonnyPops?" His gruff voice carries down the hall.

I pluck out the green box. "The Thin Mints, obviously."

"I don't know how he has those. He never ate sugar, and I can't remember the last time I saw a Girl Scout."

"It was April." But it sounds like "Erroll," because my mouth is already full of cookies. "And he has them because I left them here." I considered texting after our breakup to arrange a drop-off, but that seemed like Thin Mint–junkie behavior, and keeping a stash in my freezer from April to January is my hard line. "They're best frozen. You want one?"

"I try to hold off on cookies until at least noon." He sounds only vaguely disgusted by my sugar addiction.

"Your loss. They're perfect with coffee. Speaking of coffee . . ." I stretch out the word, searching the crowded countertop.

"In the fridge." His voice still echoes from the bathroom.

I grab a tall, slim can of cold coffee from the fridge, but when Adam speaks again, I don't dare leave the kitchen island. Shouting across the house has facilitated my longest conversation with him yet. Plus, this position prevents me from noticing more of his physical attributes—an added bonus.

"I got a six-pack of some cold coffee from the market on the ground floor. There are beans in the cabinet, but Sam doesn't have a coffeemaker."

"He's a member of the Cult of Pour-Over." I crack open my can of cold brew and admire Sam's shelf of mismatched mugs—souvenirs from vacations past and time abroad.

"We're talking about him like he's still here. He *drinks* pour-over coffee. He *has* cookies in the freezer. I keep doing that," he says, his voice sounding sad and a little frustrated.

I walk back toward the bathroom and see Adam sitting on the side of the tub peeling at a shampoo label. He throws it in the trash before tying off the bag and removing it from the can in one movement.

"This needs to go out."

He doesn't say anything else before walking out the door.

It takes the rest of the day to empty the kitchen cabinets and wipe their interiors. Sam wasn't much for deep cleaning, so I spend a fair amount of time scraping at mysterious, hard chunks.

I can best describe the rest of my interactions with Adam as *stiff*.

He doesn't talk to me again other than the occasional inquiry into the location of tape measures, pens, and additional utility items. I'm not as familiar with Sam's place as Adam thinks I am, and there are multiple drawers in contention for the One True Junk Drawer. I have to stall with anecdotes until I stumble upon his requests, which only further agitates him.

"You talk a lot," he observes. His tone doesn't impart judgment, but there is literally no way to take the words *you talk a lot* as anything other than a moderately less confrontational version of *please don't talk so much,* as if I'm a precocious child or a particularly chatty parrot.

I don't take the bait. Instead, we work in complete silence for about an hour, and I notice every second of it.

I open yet another drawer of bric-a-brac and find boxes of little cocktail umbrellas. Sam bought them for a party here in June, right when we started seeing each other.

I'd been envious of how effortless he was socially. He introduced me to a small group chatting about their indoor soccer league, and before I realized it, he had floated off to enamor a new group of people over a game of beer pong. I tried to find my groove in a group of strangers but had nothing to add to his friend's complaints about her infrared sauna installation. Before long, I found myself leaning against the kitchen island, fiddling with the paper umbrellas and pretending to text.

I wander into the living room, twirling a paper umbrella between my fingers. "Did we meet at the Summer Kickoff?" I ask Adam.

He's around the corner now, removing art from the walls and wrapping it in bubble wrap. Just out of sight, I can only imagine the perplexed look on his face when he asks, "Is that a parade?"

"No. It was what Sam called the party he threw this past June. I didn't know anyone there, so I was wondering if we met without realizing it." Though now that I've said it, I find it hard to believe. Adam would've stuck out like a sore thumb at that party. He probably would've been hiding near the food with me.

"I didn't make it down this year," he says, with no sign of forthcoming embellishment. I can hear my attempt at conversation flopping to the ground like a dead, wet fish.

Black marks on the living room wall catch my eye. I noisily pull back the end table by the couch to reveal three years of beer pong scores written on the wall in Sharpie and curse. "I forgot about the scoreboard."

I remember seeing people keeping score on the wall at the party and thinking, *I wish I could be like that*—be the kind of person who doesn't worry about his walls until he has to move out. Now he never has to.

"I didn't know he was still doing that." Adam's voice breaks through my thoughts. Without warning, he's in the living room only a few feet away from me. He stares at the scrawl with a pinched forehead. "I don't think his family knows what rough shape this place is in. He was barely around to take care of it, and when he was, he treated it like a frat house. If I'm only coming down on weekends, this'll take me the rest of the month."

I offer him a bright smile. "I'm here to help." My voice sounds desperate for approval.

He grunts and walks back to the hallway, returning to his task.

"Do you need anything before I go?"

"Nope. I don't need anything from you," he says quietly, and though his tone doesn't precisely convey an insult, I simply can't rule it out.

"Okay. When will you be here next?"

"All day tomorrow. I'm staying at my sister's tonight."

"That makes sense. I wouldn't expect you to drive back to Duluth tonight."

He finally turns to face me. With a sheet of bubble wrap still in his hands, he folds his arms across his chest in challenge. His eyes look me up and down—clinically, impersonally, like an MRI machine scanning for anomalies—until he returns his gaze to the mass-produced modern art print on the wall. "I'm glad you approve."

This conversation feels like a game I'm losing, but I double down on friendliness. I can't help it. "See you tomorrow?" I despise the cheery eagerness in my voice.

He releases a long exhale, drained by one day with me. "I'll be here."

Then so will I. Unfortunately.

———

HALLOWEEN REVELERS ARE meandering along the sidewalk, already several hours into their debauchery. It's warmer than the weather forecast predicted, so every painted face and sexy cat eye is a bit drippy. When I board the light rail back to Saint Paul, a steampunk zombie argues with Frank N. Furter in that loud, lazy way only drunk people do.

"It's like, it's like, you don't even care! You don't even care!" the zombie yells over Frank, who's slurring back, "You didn't even ask! You never ask!"

More costumed twenty-somethings hop on, and I get off early. Despite the weather apps predicting the first snow-storm of the year tonight, the breeze is warm on my skin, and I'd rather walk five extra minutes if it means escaping an in-toxicated Addams Family.

When I turned thirty, a switch flipped, and holidays that once felt shiny and limitless started to look sweaty and claus-trophobic. I fight the throngs of face paint and latex masks—which will undoubtedly end up in the street at one a.m., when their owners realize just how little those things breathe—all the way to my apartment, where I change into my low-effort costume before heading back into the mess.

"Tell me we have a table!" I beg the blond milkmaid braids I hope belong to Chelsea when I step into the crowded pizza place that hosts Halloween-themed trivia.

Chelsea spins on her stool away from the bar and gives me a delighted, if slightly demented, grin. "Ahh! You're here!" She pulls me into a suffocating hug and knocks me into the red laminate bar counter. My forehead bumps her cat ears askew as she rocks us back and forth, alternating between screaming across the room and loudly whispering in my ear over the blaring alt-rock, "MarsBars! Al is HERE! Al is here. I was so worried."

When she releases me, I spot Patrick Finley—our reliable

fourth in trivia—hovering next to her in a navy sweater vest emblazoned with a giant gold *R*.

"Archie for Halloween? Again?" I point at his red hair and overall lack of creativity.

Chelsea sways into his chest. "I told him he should upgrade to *Riverdale* Archie next year. The youths don't know about the comic book. Ooh! Does Mara have cheese bread?" Chelsea gallops off to the table Mara's guarding.

I plop into her abandoned stool next to Patrick's, the splitting vinyl scraping my pants. "So . . . Chelsea's drunk."

He grimaces. "It happened slowly and then all at once. Two hours of food, water, and Mara should do the trick." Patrick's eyes examine Chelsea across the room as she struggles momentarily with her straw. "I'm grabbing another pitcher of water, just in case. Can you watch her?" I give him a nod before weaving through the bodies.

Mara, in a blue striped button-up with a tie and suspenders, looks me up and down as I slide into the booth. "What's this? We all have to be in costume for the extra point."

I gesture to my hiking boots and olive cargo pants. "I'm Cheryl Strayed. She wrote *Wild*. Reese Witherspoon was in the movie."

"I know who Cheryl Strayed is. What I don't know is in what world you think a reference to a memoir from the early 2010s is an appropriate Halloween costume."

"She's from Minnesota."

"Don't insult me by pretending you put effort into this." Mara poises her pen over our team's trivia sheet. "I'm writing down Laura Dern from *Jurassic Park*. Any objections?"

"I would never object to being Laura Dern. Who are you supposed to be?"

"Gordon Gekko." She tsks, disappointed I even had to ask.

I bob my head in agreement. Her outfit and red-brown slicked-back lob definitely resemble a vamped-up version of the famous Michael Douglas look.

"See how you immediately got it, and I didn't need to summarize a nonfiction book from ten years ago?"

"Yes, I understand. Now, hand me the image page. Laura Dern needs to make her guesses before the live questions start." I take the sheet from Mara and analyze the iconic horror villains for clues.

"I'm buying him out!" A splotchy-faced, sexy minion runs to our table. I assume she's lost until she presents her phone to Chelsea. "I wrote the email and everything."

Chelsea takes the stranger by the hand. "Sadie, you're doing the right thing. If he didn't respect you as a girlfriend, he won't respect you as a partner in your hemp water business. But maybe leave that email in the 'drafts' tonight?" she advises with a one-eyed squint.

Chelsea's the kind of drunk who has profound conversations in women's bathrooms. Even when she's sober, lost souls tend to find Chelsea wherever she goes.

With the interloper gone, Mara rubs Chelsea's shoulders like a cornerman with his champion boxer. "Okay, Chels. Eat some pizza and look alive. We'll need you sharp out there."

Chelsea's responsible for earth science, math, and reality television; I cover general pop culture, TV, movies, and geography; Patrick is our resident academic; and Mara is in charge of politics, music, and basically everything else. Sports is our team's Achilles' heel.

We tend to stick to official Twin Cities Trivia League events. At participating bars throughout the Cities, league hosts provide each team a blank front sheet at the start, with the back covered in a series of images based on a theme. The night always ends with a music round. No phones are allowed, and host rulings are always final.

Top-ranked teams qualify for a yearly tournament on New Year's Day. Besides happiness for her friends and success in her career, winning that tournament is the thing Mara wants most in this world.

By the time we get to the halfway point, Chelsea is mostly herself but without volume control. Every answer she gives is followed by Mara's and Patrick's loud shushes. When she yells out "*Scream 2!*" during the third round, Patrick covers her mouth and tells her with an easy laugh, "Chels, you're giving away the farm!"

Mara knows most of the songs in the final music round but hums one to herself, hoping the last elusive ditty will come to her before the host grabs our sheets for scoring. Patrick asks over Mara's musical mutterings, "How's the railroad business, Al?"

Patrick always asks me about work in what I suspect is a fishing expedition to figure out what I do. If pressed, he'd probably admit that he thinks I'm a Gilded Age railroad tycoon who wears a monocle to the office. In reality, I'm a transportation consultant, specializing in public transit systems, but I'm too pleased with his vision of me as a Monopoly character to ever fully explain it to him.

"Booming." I pantomime twirling my mustache. "But we're all very concerned with the rise of zeppelins."

His face crinkles into a smile before turning uncomfortably serious. "I was sorry to hear about Sam. I can't imagine what you're going through."

I tilt my head side to side as if the movement will arrange my thoughts. "Yeah, it's still hard to believe he's gone."

"He was a good guy. Chelsea said you were at his house today?"

"His friend and I are getting the condo ready to sell," I tell him between bites of room-temperature pizza.

"Why?"

"She's Sam's girlfriend again!" Chelsea announces at top volume.

"Like a Patrick Swayze *Ghost* situation?" he asks.

Chelsea claps like an excited toddler. "That's what I said! But Devon Sawa."

He turns toward Chelsea with a wide grin. "Classic film. Or Bruce Willis in *The Sixth Sense*."

"Or *Casper Meets Wendy*."

"Now you're just naming Casper movies."

"You took the other ghost movie I know." Chelsea grabs his arm playfully, her face stuck in a beatific smile.

He tears his eyes from hers when his phone buzzes. "Shit. Mara, can you turn in the answer sheet? I need to use my phone. Josie left like ten messages."

Chelsea's face goes slack. Mara grumbles but catches the host on his way to the front. Patrick is dialing before he's shaken off Chelsea's hand.

Mara gestures at an exiting Patrick. "This mind-meld thing you two do is adorable, but it isn't helping the situation with Josie."

"We're just friends. He's been dating Josie forever, and *I* have several Petfinder profiles bookmarked on my web browser. There's an elderly Russian blue that's really ticking all my boxes." Chelsea sniffs a pepperoni and sets it back down, her face green around the gills.

I grab her hand across the booth. "What happened to Ritter?"

"We broke up." Chelsea waves off my supportive friend assault, and the movement loosens a lock of hair from her braid crown. "It's for the best. I told him my love languages were gifts and acts of service, so he bought me an NFT of a meme he had to explain to me."

Mara grimaces. "Yikes."

"Onward and upward! I'm either going on a total man hiatus or applying for *The Bachelor*."

"*Bachelor*," I vote.

"Neither," Mara argues.

"I'm too old for *The Bachelor* anyway. Once you hit thirty, you get the 'crazy and desperate' edit." Chelsea fights a losing battle with her loose hair strand before finally retreating to the bathroom with a huff.

Mara raises her brows. "That's a disaster waiting to happen."

"Speaking of disasters," I say. "Sam's best friend might hate me. Probably."

Her eyes crinkle to slits. "What did you do?"

"Nothing! I'm perfect!"

"Does he know Sam dumped you?"

I shoo her negativity away with my free hand. "Okay—it was very nearly amicable—but no, he never mentioned anything, and I wasn't about to tell him. He spoke like seven words the whole day. Is that enough of a reason to flake on Sam's family and avoid them for eternity?"

"For me? Yes. But you're the one who has to live with telling a grieving family you can't be bothered to box up some dishes."

I slope my head into my palm.

"Are you still into 'the friend'? Adam, is it?" Mara asks.

"I was never *into* 'the friend'!"

Chelsea slides back into her side of the booth with her refreshed, perfectly imperfect hairstyle. "Oh, thank god! I was worried you were talking about me. So Al's in love with Sam's friend. Go."

I pale at the accusation and turn to find Patrick, who's placing the scored answer sheet into Mara's greedy hands. "That's so messed up. That would be like if Demi Moore left Patrick Swayze for Whoopi Goldberg."

Chelsea's teeth tear into discarded pizza crust. "That would be such a good movie!"

Irritation scrunches my features. "No, we're not . . . He won't even talk to me. We're two people stuck together until we finish the job, never to speak again. Then I'll no longer be Demi Moore. Or Whoopi Goldberg. I lost track of Patrick's analogy."

Chelsea gives me a playful wink. "Oh, Al. You're a total Demi."

My groan is cut short by the announcement of our narrow victory. While Mara whoops in unhinged euphoria, Chelsea redirects our prize pizza to a group of crying Harley Quinns, who appear to need it more than we do.

The streets are still bursting when I trudge home, bracing myself for another day in Adam's company.

5

But It Didn't Snow

THE NEXT MORNING, the early November chill bites at my face the moment I step off the light rail into the Minneapolis air. The season is well past its peak, and most of the trees are naked sticks with only the last bits of fall foliage clinging to them.

Fall's the season I like the least because it's the most fleeting one. It's always orange and vibrant in my memories, with a pumpkin coffee in my hand to warm me just a bit. In reality, that fantasy season lasts about ten days, tops. The rest of the season is cold, dead, and gray.

The only saving grace is that today is November 1—the official start to the Christmas season, per the reigning queen of Christmas, Mariah Carey. People all over the city will be decorating their trees, wrapping their rooflines with twinkle lights, and decking their halls.

Tonight, I'll break out a spruce-tree-scented three-wick candle (the more wicks, the better), plug in my tabletop artificial tree, and queue up a Christmas movie. Until then, I'll be stacking plates and mugs with the North Shore Grump.

The apartment door is unlocked when I arrive. I announce my presence by telling Adam I'm making coffee and take his silence as drowsy assent. My mindless chatter fills the quiet as I open a bag of the coffee and the toasty aroma of the beans fills my nostrils.

I shoot three feet into the air when Adam—a man who I was *certain* was puttering around the bedroom—strolls through the front door like a goddamned teleporter. Coffee beans scatter across the counter and onto the wood floor with little clinks. I gasp and grab the kitchen island to settle myself—beans crunching under my feet—as Adam surveys the mess.

I recover my breath over the sound of the last beans clattering off the counter. "You scared the crap out of me. I was talking to you in the other room this whole time."

"Did I answer?" His lips press together in amusement, and I'm certain he's never met anyone he finds more ridiculous.

I scoop the smashed beans off the floor and into the trash. "What were you doing outside?"

"Looking for Sam's car. Did you move it last night?" His question sounds suspiciously like an accusation.

"I don't have the keys. It should be in his spot in the underground lot."

"I moved it to the street so you'd have a place to park." He seems annoyed that solving this mystery requires so much conversing with me.

"I take the train."

"What train? Do you mean that streetcar thing? Do people use that? It stops like every block," he says, apparently more baffled by this development than by the missing car.

"It's more of a tram. Did you move the car back last night?"

I ask, already pulling out my phone to check my alerts. "Yep. There was a snow emergency."

He stares at me blankly.

"You can't park on the street during a snow emergency. The city tows your car, and it's like a three-hundred-dollar ticket."

"I know what a snow emergency is. It's just . . . but it didn't snow," he argues, either with me or the City of Minneapolis or possibly weather in general.

"It was supposed to snow, so they called a snow emergency. It probably got towed." I show him my text alerts.

"But it didn't snow." His brow furrows and frustration stiffens his shoulders.

"I'll look up which impound lot it went to."

"But it didn't snow!" he growls.

His hand grazes mine on its way to Sam's key fob on the kitchen island. The tiny flutter in my stomach at this skin-to-skin contact catches me by surprise.

"Welcome to the ruthless world of overnight street parking in Minneapolis," I say, stuffing my phone in my pocket.

We're not the only ones burned by the fickle Minnesota weather. Adam commiserates with at least a dozen other unlucky souls. "But it didn't even snow!" they exchange over and over in the cold echo chamber of the temporary impound lot.

The Cities are so vigilant about keeping streets cleared on plow routes that getting towed is practically a rite of passage. If Adam had a sense of humor, I'd offer to buy him a cupcake to commemorate the event.

All signs point to Adam *not* having a sense of humor, least of all about our current predicament.

Unlike impound facilities serviced by permanent structures with floors, walls, and a working HVAC system, Sam's car was brought to an overflow lot created for the winter towing season, which means we're standing in an open field where the city hosts community carnivals in the summer. The moment the temperature drops below freezing, it transforms into the seventh circle of hell, if hell were miserably cold.

Last night's icy rain has turned the patch of dirt in front of the canopy-covered counter into slippery, squishy mud. We shuffle forward in silence with the slow-moving, disgruntled clump, our only sign of progress our increasing proximity to the propane heater pushing dry, tepid gusts our way.

"Are your feet okay?" Adam asks.

His question catches me off guard. "What?"

"Are your shoes holding up in the mud? You're not cold?" His eyes scan my boots for deficiencies.

Adam's thick work boots were made for these conditions. My ankle boots—already caked in mud—are barely managing to keep my toes dry.

"I'm fine. Thanks."

"Good." He offers me a curt nod. If his words were an attempt at compassion, no one told his face.

When we finally make our way to the front of the line, Adam places himself directly in front of the attendant. It's a power move. *I'll handle this,* his stance commands. "I'm here to pick up a car. An SUV."

"Oh, yeah?" The large man shifts on his stool. His face is the kind that looks permanently tired, as though he's too far in sleep debt from the daily grind to ever dig himself out. Those sleepy eyes are fixed to the clipboard he's scrawling on.

"It's an SUV." Adam lifts the key fob as Exhibit A, but the

attendant doesn't so much as blink. "It's . . . uh . . . black or dark blue, maybe."

I push him aside with my hip. "It's a navy blue Acura. License plate number six seven two YKX. And it's one of those specialty state park plates." I hold up the picture of the plate displayed on my phone, but the attendant doesn't budge. "If that helps you find it."

Adam removes a money clip from his coat pocket and slaps Samuel Lewis's driver's license on the counter. "If that helps."

Finally, the attendant flips through the pages of the clipboard and walks away.

"You have a picture of his license plate on your phone?" Adam says. His posture suggests he's accusing me of something, but of what? I'm not sure.

"I emailed it to my landlady so she wouldn't have Sam towed. Why do you have his ID?" I accuse him right back.

"It was in his personal effects."

The cold formality of *personal effects* stops me in my tracks. "You mean from the morgue?" My voice is the angry whisper of an unwitting accomplice.

"Of course not! What is wrong with you? His wallet was in his luggage in the rental car. His parents had it all sent to the apartment."

"Then just say it was in the apartment. *Personal effects* sounds so creepy."

The attendant returns with a yellow receipt. "That will be three hundred twenty-two dollars and fifty-six cents. We take cash or checks. As soon as you pay, I can release the car to the registered owner . . ." He glances down at the receipt. "Samuel Lewis."

Adam pulls out a worn leather checkbook like an elderly

person paying for groceries, writes it out in barely legible scrawl, and hands it over. The attendant studies Adam's check. Then the two of us. Finally, the driver's license. "Neither of you are Samuel Lewis."

"That's the ID for Samuel Lewis." Adam points to the card in the attendant's hand.

"But it's not your ID. You're not Samuel Lewis. Based on the check, I'm guessing you're Adam Berg. I can only release the car to Samuel Lewis."

Adam rubs a hand over the back of his neck until he makes a decisive move for his pocket. "You have the money. We have the right ID. What if you show us to the car and look the other way on the names?" Adam slyly pushes a bill toward the attendant. He's expertly smooth, until he removes his large hand, revealing a ten-dollar bill.

The attendant snorts. Pointing to a sign under the canopy, he tells us, "Each day Samuel Lewis leaves his car here earns him a fifty-dollar fee."

"This is ridiculous," Adam argues, raking a hand through his hair. "It didn't even snow!"

The attendant's brows form a sharp V. "Kid, I don't handle the weather. I just tow the cars."

A truly idiotic idea pops into my brain, and I blurt, "Can I pick it up if I'm Samuel's wife?"

I can feel Adam's eyeballs burning a hole in the side of my face.

The attendant tilts his head. "Are you Samuel's wife?"

"Yes." My frozen feet stumble closer to the counter. "But I kept my last name," I add, in case he checks my ID.

"Do you have a marriage license with you?"

I reach into my leather crossbody, as if a marriage license

for me and my ex-boyfriend will appear inside like a divine miracle from the towing gods. "Do married people carry around their marriage licenses?"

"Married people don't ask that question." His eyes flit up, victorious, and then back to the clipboard.

He pushes back the check, driver's license, and paltry bribe and shoos us from his counter.

"Can you give us a second?" I pull Adam by the arm out of the attendant's earshot.

Adam angles his mouth down and murmurs directly into my ear, his hot breath moving strands of my hair. "So you're a widow now? My condolences."

I ignore him, pitching my voice low. "We should tell him he's dead."

He actually harrumphs—a sound I assumed existed exclusively in *Winnie the Pooh*. "They can't release a dead person's SUV to two random people."

"Maybe he'll feel sorry for us," I say. We pivot toward the stickler attendant, who is cracking sunflower seeds in his mouth while a red-haired woman weeps before him in frustration. He's unmoved by her hysterics as she sulks back into the ornery collective.

I rub my hands together for warmth as I brainstorm. "What about Sam's parents?"

"They winter in Florida. They've only been coming up for . . ." Adam's sentence falls away, and he adjusts his jacket anxiously.

"Right. Sorry."

The reality of Sam's death seems to wash over Adam anew.

Suddenly, brilliance strikes me. "Sir?" I recapture the attendant's attention. "One of my friends had her car towed, and another person was able to pick it up with a note. Is that an option for Sam?"

The attendant puffs a sigh out his nostrils. "It needs to be signed and notarized."

"Thank you!" I smack my hand on the counter triumphantly before making a heel turn toward the parking lot, assuming Adam is following. When we reach his beige truck, I yank at the door handle, but it doesn't budge. I pull two more times until Adam bleeps the locks, and his smug smirk smacks me in the face.

"I don't know why you're so confident. Dead men can't write notes, Alison." His flat, arrogant affect and eye crinkle remind me so much of Harrison Ford in *Working Girl,* I want to scream at Chelsea and Mara for putting the image in my head.

"We don't need Sam," I say when we're safely in his truck. "We just need a notary."

———

RUSSELL ROSSI IS the only notary I know socially. He does something in real estate that sounds a lot like being a Realtor, but, per him, it's decidedly not. He's been a fixture in Sam's social circle ever since they met camping near the Boundary Waters a few years ago, but I haven't seen him since the funeral. Had my correction about my role in Sam's life not gone completely over his head, I might have avoided this nightmare entirely.

Russell answers the door of his Lyndale duplex apartment shirtless—despite knowing we were on our way to his house.

"Alison, babe! Come in." He wraps me in a hug, and I awkwardly pat his bare, sweaty back. The two men exchange dude-bro nods. "Adam. Long time, no see. Well, before . . ."

Russell looks momentarily off-balance before leaning back and slapping his pecs in recovery. "I was lifting, but I always have time for you." Russell winks at me.

Even though he does nothing for me chemically, I giggle and inwardly groan at myself so loud I almost hear it.

Actually, I do hear it. I look behind me and find its source in Adam's disturbed expression. Russell winks a second time for good measure and disappears into an office.

"Something wrong?" I hiss at Adam, irritation ringing through my words.

"It's like I'm not even here. Should I find someone else to drive your boyfriend's car home? You guys seem to have—"

"Quiet. He's doing us a favor."

"What do you need stamped, babe?" Russell returns with a pouch. "You know, I don't normally work weekends. You'll have to make it up to me." Russell's voice is thick with interest, but I know better than to take it seriously. This is not my first encounter with Russell Rossi. Like a goldfish, he'll forget any apparent fascination with me about three seconds after I leave.

I lean against the kitchen counter, where he's setting up. "Sam's car got towed this morning, and they want something notarized that'll authorize me to pick it up."

Confusion cascades over Russell's face, dropping the Casanova curtain. "*From* Sam? I can't knowingly notarize a forged document. I took an oath."

"An oath?" Adam scoffs.

"Yeah, man. An oath. The whole point is to verify the

signers' identities to prevent whatever shit this is. Why didn't you move the car for the snow emergency?" Russell asks.

"It didn't . . ." Adam flutters his eyes shut rather than repeat himself. "We should get going."

Russell bobs his shoulders and rubs his left pec.

"Wait," I call out, because after enduring a wet, bare-chested embrace from this man, I refuse to leave empty-handed. "You only verify the identity of the signer, right? Not the enforceability of the letter?" I have the beginning of a bad idea forming, but it's the best we've got. I scribble on the notebook paper in front of me.

Alison Mullally is authorized to pick up Acura MDX #672 YKX registered to Samuel Lewis.

I hand Russell my ID and gesture to Adam to do the same. "We'll sign it as ourselves."

"Does Adam have the authority to—"

"We'll worry about its enforceability, but as you can see, no one's pretending to be anyone they're not." I press on.

Russell frowns, and I briefly switch tactics, offering my sweetest smile. "Can you verify our signatures? I can't tell you how much it would help us out." I pout my lips slightly. I've seen Chelsea pull off this move with great success, but I haven't practiced it enough to know whether I look sexy or constipated—high risk, high reward.

Russell reveals all of his perfect white capped teeth, and I know I've got him. He removes his stamp and ink pad from a pouch. I write in a loopy, purposefully illegible script. Adam seems to follow suit, or he just always signs like a toddler.

"Good luck." Russell scoff-laughs as he verifies our signatures with his stamp.

"Thanks." Adam's gratitude pains him.

Russell repacks his notary pouch. "Alison, you're sorting out who's getting Sam's stuff, right?"

"Not really. I'm helping Adam pack everything to get the condo ready for sale. We're not distributing anything." I look questioningly at Adam, but his eyes are narrowed on Russell.

"Sam promised me some mountaineering gear for the Patagonia trip. I mentioned it to Sam's mom at the funeral. She said I should talk to you about picking it up."

Adam slants him a seething look. "Our thirty-two-year-old friend promised you 'gear' in the event of his accidental death? And you asked his mom about it at her son's funeral?"

"He was giving it to me for the trip. What's your problem?" Russell flexes and crosses his arms defensively over his chest.

"That's fine, Russ." I collect the letter from the table, stepping between the two men before this display of testosterone gets out of hand. "Text me what to look for, and we'll figure something out."

Russell faces me with a cocky grin, but his eyes are fixed on Adam, watching for sudden movements. "Good. We can meet for drinks after. You're still coming to Patagonia in January, right? Sam wouldn't have wanted you to miss it." Russell doesn't wait for my response. "It'll be therapeutic. I always find returning to nature to be the perfect clean slate. A rebirth."

I remember when Sam invited me on this trip. We had only been on a few dates. It all sounded incredible—hiking in the mountains, camping under the stars every night, nothing but the pack on your back. He invited me along like it was nothing—like such an experience was even a possibility for a recovering homebody like me.

I said yes, and it was the most intoxicating feeling. I loved being the type of girl who agreed to spend two weeks in Patagonia with a handsome stranger. I could tell Sam liked *that* girl more than the real me. But the more time we spent together, the more obvious it was that, to me, the adventurous girl was still a goal. To him, she was a lie.

Adam grimaces, which only makes Russell's grin look toothier. Russell is as slick and uncontroversially handsome as a reality dating show contestant, while even Adam's sourest expression is undeniably trustworthy. It's the eyes, I think. They're solid and seemingly honest.

"You two can pick through Sam's stuff another time."

I look daggers at Adam before presenting my forced smile to Russell. "We better get going. Thanks for your help, Russell." I push Adam out the door before me.

"I'll text you," Russell calls out as I'm stepping into the truck.

Like him, Adam's truck is beige on beige on beige. Still, it's impressively tidy—not a speck of dust or McDonald's wrapper in sight.

Adam adjusts his mirrors from the driver's side of his bench seat. "If you want to stay here with him, I can figure out how to get the car back on my own."

"Why would I stay here?"

"Alison, baby, let's get a drink, just the two of us," he mocks.

My eyelashes flutter with faux sweetness. "Someone's cranky. I'm sure he would have invited you too if you hadn't been scowling at our only hope for getting the car."

"I wasn't scowling."

"So that deep ridge forming between your brows is just your face then. My mistake. Either way, you can't get rid of me yet. It's my name on the note."

"Don't let that stop you from shooting your shot with Russ. His shirt's already off, and he doesn't strike me as a generous lover. I can wait." He cranks up the heat and unbuttons the top two buttons of his khaki-colored coat.

My eye snags on the denim lining I recognize as the outside of yesterday's jacket. Does Adam only own one jacket? "Don't be gross. He's your friend."

"Uh, no. He was Sam's friend. And apparently *your* friend." Adam fastens his seat belt, the click of the buckle emphasizing the word. "Although I don't usually drape my sweaty body against my friends."

"Friends hug each other."

"That was not a hug," he says with a snort. "That was a full-body press. That was foreplay."

"He was being nice."

"The nicest. Tell me, do nice people claim their dead friend's stuff at his funeral? I'm trying to get a sense of how we're defining *nice* here." Adam gestures between us on the bench seat, tipping his mouth into that infuriating smirk that crinkles his eyes.

"He wants the gear for his trip. That's all." I pull my seat belt too aggressively, and it locks. I jerk at it uselessly three more times—trapped in a Three Stooges physical comedy bit against my will—before I've released it enough to get my belt to click. I let out an exhausted breath and gather the courage to face Adam.

He shakes his head, his mouth pushed up in what—on anyone else—would be an effortlessly handsome smile. "That was . . . wow."

"Please drive to the lot so this can be over," I say with the simmering rage achievable only by someone who's been moderately inconvenienced. "We have to deliver this note before the lot closes."

He twists toward me and extends his arm across the backrest to reverse out of Russell's drive. His finger grazes a strand of my hair, and he recoils like he's been burned. I'm suddenly very aware of how small this truck is. If I leaned back an inch, his hand would be cradling my neck. The thought makes my skin hot because my defective nervous system can't decipher the nuances of this dynamic.

He seems to notice this near-touch too and bends his elbow, resting his clenched fist behind the bench. "That note's a crime," he says, like a spark of electricity didn't just flicker between us.

"Are you a lawyer?"

"No. I'm a carpenter."

"Like Jesus?"

An irritated breath passes through his teeth. "No, like custom Nordic furniture."

"You're joking."

Adam's eyes flash to mine before returning to the road. "Why would I be joking?"

I round on him gleefully. "I didn't think Nordic furniture makers existed outside of Hallmark Christmas movies. Are you responsible for teaching a workaholic woman the true meaning of Christmas or is that a different grumpy carpenter? Do you guys work in shifts?"

"I've never been so happy to have no idea what someone is talking about."

"It's a compliment, really. Few jobs lend themselves to romantic proclamations of love in the form of matching rocking chairs."

"It's an ordinary vocation. There are many furniture makers in the world."

"I'm sure there are hot toy store owners too, but I've never met one." I blush, mortified that I called Adam hot while trying to insult him. Wasn't Harrison Ford a carpenter when he was discovered by George Lucas? The thought forces a shiver down my spine.

"This conversation is ridiculous." His eyes shoot death glares at a VW Golf that passes us without signaling. "And technically, I work for a building contractor. Furniture's a hobby until I get my business off the ground."

"What do you need to get it off the ground?"

He ignores the question and continues driving. He seems to deploy silence whenever he's finished speaking to me. This rankles me, for some reason.

I lean my head against the window, the glass cool against my temple. "I wish I had a Hallmark Christmas movie profession. I'd love to own a candy cane store."

"There's no market for that." He drums his thumb against the steering wheel. Adam is always in motion, I'm noticing, like an impatient child. I prattle on with my movie musings until I'm interrupted by my phone's vibrations.

"What?" he asks. His frown is a true upside-down smile, and if I didn't know better, I'd think he was disappointed I've stopped listing impractically twee Christmas movie occupations. It's an impressive look too. I thought only two-dimensional emojis could contort their lips with such severity. The stark contrast of hard lines formed by his chiseled jaw and the soft, cartoonish expression paints a surprisingly adorable picture.

"It's Russell." I read off my screen. "Following up about

something called a 'canyoneering harness.' Sounds uncomfortable."

"Is that why you're doing all this?" His voice bends, not quite angry. Hurt. "So you and Russell can pick through Sam's life for scraps?"

The whiplash from his words practically tosses me through the windshield. "Scraps? What are you—"

He jerks his hand through his messy hair, his jaw tightening like he's trying to barricade the words inside his mouth. "You don't need to stick around to get whatever you're hoping for. I'm sure Judy will let you have whatever you want."

"Why are you being such a jerk?" I spit the words out, fueled by my righteous indignation. "I'm helping Sam's family. Mrs. Lewis wanted *me* to do this."

"Because Judy thinks he was serious about you!" A wave of regret instantly washes over his face. He drags his eyes from the road to see the wreckage of his direct hit. "I didn't mean it like that. Well, I did, but I didn't mean to say it."

A bitter laugh shakes out of my throat. "Should I appreciate your honesty?"

"I only meant he didn't talk about you much, and when he did it always sounded so casual."

"Oh my god." My words fall out on a drained exhalation. From his defeated look, I can see he's not saying any of this to hurt me. And he's right—Sam broke up with me, after all—but it's humiliating to have your ex-boyfriend's indifference toward you detailed by a third party.

He adjusts and readjusts his grip on the wheel. "This isn't . . . I'm not saying this right."

"No, you've been very clear. You don't want me here, and Sam never cared about me. Or talked about me. Ever."

"That's not what I said. I said he didn't talk about you *much*." His eyes flit upward like he's thumbing through the dusty filing cabinet of his brain. "I remember him asking if I'd go skydiving in your place, because you refused to go." Based on the way his mouth practically trips over itself to soften its blow, my face must be doing something bad. "But he made you sound kind of funny when he told me about it."

"Skydiving is ridiculous. Why would I voluntarily participate in a flight's worst-case scenario? If you're not exiting a plane on the ground, something's gone horribly wrong."

"Yeah, that!" I get a glimpse of an animated Adam before it disappears behind his mask of detachment. "I liked that. I told him I couldn't agree more."

I can't tell if he realizes he's making this worse every time he opens his mouth. He's hitting on my every insecurity without even trying.

"Alison." Concern passes over his face. "I—"

"Don't worry about it," I cut him off. We sit in an unbearable silence the rest of the way back to the impound lot, and the fact that I bet he's loving my loss for words only fuels my quiet rage.

"There's no way this scheme works," he says when he throws the truck into park.

"Have a little faith in me, Berg." I slam the truck door shut. Icy moisture pricks my nose, and I hold out my hand to marvel at the perfect cotton candy flakes floating down onto my glove. Finally, it's started to snow, and I can't even enjoy it.

We wait in line for the second time today and present our deliberately worded note to an even more apathetic attendant who's openly watching hockey on his phone. With a disinterested glance at the notebook paper I hand him, he accepts

Adam's check, and we trudge into deeper mud toward the navy SUV in the distance.

I step into a puddle of sludge, but when I pull my left foot forward, it refuses to follow. Tragically, my momentum doesn't stop. My stomach flips as my right foot slides out from under me, my left still mired in the muck.

It happens slowly enough for the thought to crystalize in my mind—*I'm about to faceplant into ice-cold mud*—but fast enough that I can only manage to yell, "SSSuuuuuhh-hhh!," which I assume is a portmanteau of many curse words.

I've extended my hands in acceptance of my filthy fate when Adam turns from beside me, his large frame meeting mine. "Whoa," he says, like I'm livestock. I lean into the wall of his body to catch my breath. It feels too good to rest here—even if only for a second—and when he's not pressing on my fears like they're a bruise, he's steady and warm, if a bit stiff.

"Are you okay?" His hands grip my arms and stand me back up with minimal effort. He ducks down, his eyes surveying my face for signs of damage. We're close—so close that I can make out the shape of snowflakes catching on his long eyelashes. His nearness overwhelms me.

The air bites at my cheeks, and I finally remember to breathe. It creates some much-needed space between us. "I'm fine. See?" I manage to pry my foot from the sludge as an unnecessary visual aid. He nods, his intense brown eyes splicing me in two.

We both register that he's still holding me by my arms and break apart. He walks ahead, and I quicken my unsteady pace to follow. The navy blue SUV appears in front of us. He wordlessly passes me the keys.

I open the car door, about to climb in, when I feel Adam's

hand brush against my arm. "Will I, uh . . . Are you coming back next weekend?" he asks.

I want to be angry with him, to write him off as an asshole unworthy of my time and effort, but his guilty face is so achingly genuine. It pulls at my heart like a loose thread. It's those infuriating eyes. They're so gentle and guileless that I have to look away when I tell him, "I'll see you Saturday."

"See you Saturday." His voice is low and sure, like he never told me he didn't want me here. Like it was never up for debate.

He turns away and walks back in the direction of his truck. He looks over his shoulder twice, and I scold myself because both times, I'm looking back, frozen in the spot where he left me, the warmth of his hands still skittering across my arms.

But I can't help but stare. Adam Berg has a phenomenal walk.

6

My Phantom Nipples

WHEN I STEP out into the Tuesday evening chill, I feel it. It's a split second of panic, followed by a rush of embarrassment—like losing your glasses only to find them on your face. It's the shock of the cold air hitting my sensationless breasts—the moment I feel my nipples showing through my thin shirt, then remembering all over again I don't have them.

When I was a teenager, I would sneak my mother's romance novels off her bookshelves, carefully replacing them before she noticed. Heroines had an awareness of their nipples I didn't understand at the time. I inhaled passages of women taking note of the specific states of nipple arousal—purpled, pinched, plumped, pebbled, and perky. These nipples all seemed to have a life of their own. I never really noticed the pair of nipples on my chest.

Now that I don't have nipples, though, I always notice them. I feel their absence pucker under my blouse like a phantom limb when I walk into a cool breeze. When Adam caught me in the car lot two days ago, I swear they pinched in a way that would make any Regency-era maiden blush.

But since I no longer have physical sensation on my breasts (no hot, no cold, no pain, no pleasure), what I do feel is a trick of the brain.

I constantly wonder what they'd be doing, like my old nipples still exist somewhere in the ether. They're a vacation fling I've lost track of and am now left dreaming about. What are they doing now? What would we be doing together? Is there a world where we could've made it work?

I hike up the box of Sam's flatware over my phantom nipples as I heave it into the back of my car in front of his apartment. Dr. Lewis asked Adam to leave the boxes we packed in their garage while he and his wife are in Florida, but after getting derailed by the no-snow emergency, the delivery duties fell on me.

Mara Tetrises the final box and clicks the trunk shut. "Just the one trip, right? I have a call with the Guy in an hour. He's mid-meltdown." She slides into the passenger seat.

My Subaru hums to life when I push the starter. "Someone caught wind of the secret baby?"

She checks her face in the mirror before flipping up the visor. "Ugh. I wish. My kingdom for a secret baby. That's a scandal I would rock. Is that all of the boxes?"

"Just from the kitchen. We've hardly made a dent in packing. Can you check if Adam texted the Lewises' garage code yet?" I pass her my unlocked phone before pulling out of Sam's parking lot.

Categorizing a screenshot of a text from my ex-boyfriend's dad as a "text from Adam" feels like a stretch. Adam's gone from monosyllabic responses to zero.

"Al, this text conversation is completely lopsided." Mara does nothing to conceal her cringe as she scrolls up to the beginning of the thread. "You're quadruple texting him for almost nothing in return."

"That's how he is with everyone."

"I kind of respect that level of misanthropy."

"He's dipped into some special reserves of hostility for me. Did I mention that he can't stand me?"

"You mentioned that in the apartment. And on the stairs. And when the box broke in the lobby."

I click on my blinker and squint into the late autumn sun. "I'm not used to being disliked. It rattles me."

"How are you not done with this apartment thing yet?" she asks, her tone steeped in judgment.

"It turns out Sam was pretty bad at home ownership. When he broke off part of the faucet handle, he just duct-taped it." I flit my eyes toward Mara, who's pursing her lips. "There's more stuff like that all over the place. We're not even close to done."

"Can't they hire someone?"

"I don't think they know how bad it is, and I feel wrong tattling to his parents." When Rachel told me he was lying to his parents about our relationship to appear more serious and settled, she introduced me to a part of Sam I had so much more in common with: a people pleaser performing a version of himself. I can't betray that guy, even if he broke up with me in the middle of a lake. "Adam seems determined to do it all himself, and I promised Sam's mom I'd help Adam."

"If he wants to do it all himself, let him," she says with a flick of her wrist.

I tilt my head, considering this. After all, Adam made it clear he didn't want me around, and though I agreed to pretend that Sam never dumped me, I can't imagine his family honestly cares which of his friends packs up his socks and paints the living room. If Adam wants the job so badly, why can't I give it to him?

"It'll free you up for weekend trivia before the tournament, and we desperately need the practice. I assigned Chelsea a couple of sports to study, but she's deep in a Formula 1 hole. Can you learn everything there is to know about baseball by January first?" Mara shines her intensity on me as I check my blind spot to exit the highway.

"Everything there is to know about America's oldest pastime? Sure," I respond dryly.

"Start with Minnesota baseball and work your way out in concentric circles." Mara says this like she's asking me to grab takeout on the way over—a wholly ordinary and simple request.

"You're insane."

"I'm a winner. We have to beat our nemesis once and for all."

Mara has a one-sided rivalry with another trivia team, Risky Quizness. They massacre us every time and have no idea who we are or that Mara hates them. It drives her batty. Consequently, she tends to overestimate Chelsea's and my desire to memorize sports stats. But as with most things involving Mara, resistance is futile.

"We have the other major areas covered. We need someone who knows sports if we want to win."

Sam knew sports. A few weeks after we broke up, Mara dragged us to a different bar every week, trying to qualify for the upcoming trivia tournament. One Tuesday, we wound up somewhere near Sam's job. He was perched on a stool near the back enjoying happy hour with coworkers.

I did what any normal woman would do in this situation: pretended not to see him, sparing us the obligatory awkward ex chitchat and endless "good"-ing. *You're doing good? I'm good too. Work's good. Good for you too? So good!* But Sam yelled across the bar, "Seriously, Mullally? You're gonna walk right past like that? Can we at least be civil, for the kids?" He gestured to Mara, Chelsea, and Patrick, and I busted out laughing.

We invited him over to our table, and it was . . . fun. It was like we were old friends who had never dated. Sam regaled us with stories of the strange people he'd run into at a campground near Badlands National Park and his new venture into getting his pilot's license. Patrick listened rapt, and Mara and Chelsea revealed their slightly mean nickname for him when we were together: Manic Pixie Dream Boy. He laughed good-naturedly in the way the unflinchingly self-assured can.

With Sam's encyclopedic knowledge of ESPN, we were able to win the night and qualify for the tournament. My favorite competitive sociopath, Mara, jumped into Sam's arms and screamed, "Suck it, Risky Bitchness!" who were not even there to receive the devastating blow. Chelsea thanked him for freeing her from Mara's crippling qualifying schedule. Patrick was just grateful for a buffer from Mara's intensity.

He wanted to join us for the tournament on New Year's Day, and I had smiled, realizing we were finally exactly what we were always supposed to be. It was like discovering the shirt you could never get over your head no matter how hard you tried had always been a pair of pants.

On autopilot, I pass several obscenely large lakefront houses. The Lewises' cheery floral mailbox snaps me back to reality, and I turn onto their drive, pea gravel crackling under my tires like Rice Krispies. Their cozy rambler's exterior doesn't look as grand as the neighboring McMansions built during the Clinton administration, but what it lacks in flimsy austere façade it makes up for in airy warmth. We park in front of the oversized garage, which I know holds two luxury SUVs, a couple Jet Skis, and a pontoon boat.

Mara punches in the code while I heave the boxes out of the trunk, yanking at my ill-fitting sports bra. With firm silicone implants and no nipples to speak of, I generally don't wear bras, but lifting stacked ceramic plates and other athletic endeavors require proper support. A too-tight bra leaves deep grooves and skin irritation I can't feel. Too loose and the jostling causes pins and needles throughout my chest— my brain filling in the gaps of assumed pain.

Preparing to lift the final box, I'm bent over, adjusting the band of my bra, when I hear the snap-crackle-pops of a car pulling up behind me. A white Lexus enters my field of vision, and Mrs. Lewis steps out of the passenger seat. She's dressed like a Nancy Meyers movie heroine in head-to-toe linen neutrals. The outfit's all wrong for Minnesota in November, but then again, she's supposed to be in Florida right now.

"We came home early," she says, because I must've said that last part out loud. She's slower than when I saw her last, like her grief is a weighted vest. "I'm glad I caught you. I was thinking about you the whole time we were gone. Is this all of it?"

Mrs. Lewis gestures between the open garage door and the box at my feet. Mara waves demurely and beelines out of sight. No chance she's rescuing me from my matinee performance as Sam's Current Girlfriend.

I shake my head. "I'm sorry. There's a lot more to do."

Apprehension pulls her face taut. Tears pool in her eyes, but she presses into the corners of them with her thumb and forefinger before they can fall.

Panic seeps into my chest. "It'll get done. Adam will be here every weekend. He's determined to do this for you," I say.

"I'm sorry, Alison, honey. The idea of having to pack up his . . . It's just . . ." She pulls me into her arms and says into my shoulder, "I can't tell you how grateful I am that we've had you to count on through all of this. Knowing someone who loved Sam is guiding the process, you can't imagine—" She stops herself. Her chest rises and falls in my arms until she takes a step back.

"I've always been so worried for him. I imagine every parent worries—about the big things especially, but about the little things too. And Sam always gave me so much to worry about." Her mouth curls up at the corners, like even now, she can't help but smile at her son. "When he was learning to walk, he would grab on to table legs and bookshelves to help him stand. But then he kept trying to pull himself higher up the bookcase, as if climbing was the real goal and we were all thinking too small. Gosh, I should've gotten a punch card from the ER for how many times I had to get that kid stitched up."

Her wistful expression deteriorates into a sad, broken thing. "They don't tell you . . . the worry doesn't go anywhere when they're gone, you know. I don't think it's supposed to. Your children hand it to you when they're born and you carry it with you until the end. But knowing he had you in his life . . . it helps a little. Like you're holding some of it for me."

She rubs my shoulder in the way my mom does. Maybe all

moms have this comforting gesture in their arsenal. What do they do with it when they lose the person it was made for?

"Adam and I will take care of it all," I promise, pressing my hand against the emotions cracking beneath my collarbone. "Don't worry about a thing."

Mrs. Lewis bends to touch the box next to me. Her hand falters, like there's a monster inside, poised to attack. Maybe for her, there is. She snaps her hand back. "Can you put that in the garage for me?" she asks, pointing to the cardboard box of her distilled grief.

With a wobbly smile, I move the last one into the garage, spying Mara hidden in the passenger seat in my peripheral vision. She's no doubt overheard this dreary exchange.

We don't say another word until we're back on the highway. "I'll let Chelsea and Patrick know you'll be busy every weekend this month," Mara states. It's not a question anymore. I'm in this with Adam until the end. "You're doing a good thing, Mullally." She rubs sympathetic circles on my right shoulder blade. "I just wish it wasn't at the expense of our trivia domination."

A single-syllable laugh breaks free from my throat, and I shrug her hand off. "Yes, this must be a very challenging time for *you*."

"Hey, let's not compare our problems." She turns up the volume on Mariah Carey and lets the queen of Christmas serenade us home.

7

My Schrödinger's Breasts

THE UPCOMING WEEKEND hangs over my week like a dark cloud, and by Friday, I've sat through six meetings—that should've been emails—as Sam's Current Girlfriend. But since the bereavement policy for the niche transportation consulting firm I work for doesn't extend beyond immediate family members anyway, it's a distinction without a difference.

My work is a four-block walk from my apartment and connected via skyway, a series of climate-controlled footbridges allowing Saint Paulites to walk most of downtown without ever going outside. It's a miracle in a cold snap, or in the rain, or on a day like today, which is both cold and rainy.

Josh Rosen looks at me and our other officemate Patty Tanaka over the Newton's cradle on his desk. "Kyle wants a word. Do you guys mind?"

He attempts to make direct eye contact with both of us while clacking away on his keyboard, but only I—the middle desk in our U-shaped configuration—look up. Josh is a fantastic, if loud, touch typist, while Patty methodically hunts and pecks.

The sharp clink of the metal paper clip Josh flicks onto Patty's desk breaks through her noise-canceling headphones. She finally looks up to ask, "Is Josh kicking us out?"

Josh is the HR rep for our regional office. He used to have a private room for personnel matters, but as we outgrew our cramped space, our boss, Daniella, pushed Josh into a shared office with Patty and me.

It's an open secret within the office that we're in desperate need of a newer, larger workspace that doesn't have an ill-tempered bird nesting in the front entry light fixture. Nevertheless, no one's in any real hurry to relocate.

We're on the fourth floor of a 1920s hotel that was repurposed into mixed-use office space, retail, and high-end condominiums sometime in the nineties. Aside from the occasional use of industrial gray carpeting—no doubt covering devastatingly gorgeous hardwood—the developers mostly stayed true to the art deco design, due to its historic significance as a place where F. Scott Fitzgerald may or may not have passed out drunk a few times and possibly wrote a bit of *The Beautiful and Damned*.

Nearly all old buildings in Saint Paul make similar claims.

Still, there's something inspiring about working to improve access to a city in a space that's rich in its history. I wouldn't want to be doing this work in a soulless office park, even if it meant Josh never again had to kick me out into the hallway when a coworker was overcome with the burning need to discuss break room food injustices.

I grab my phone and a notebook to look busy in the windowed conference room. Patty and I are team leaders who perform efficiency assessments, conduct feasibility studies, and present recommendations for improving services while cutting operational costs to our clients. Patty works primarily for our private developers on parking, traffic planning, and driveway locations, whereas I typically work on prospective government projects that rarely ever find funding.

Nothing we do can be done without our computers, but I flip a page in my Moleskine and pretend I'm doing something terribly important for the benefit of any supervisors passing our windowed room. When I was toiling away in Intro to Civil Engineering and Econ 101, no one told me how much excelling in a professional setting came down to looking the busiest.

Patty pulls out a spiral notebook and turns to a blank page. "Are you flying home for Thanksgiving?" she asks.

"Not until Christmas. I'll probably work on Thanksgiving again."

Patty shakes her head like this simply won't do. "You better take an incredible vacation this year, Alison. I'm serious. You're only young once."

In another life, Patty might have been an inaccessible art curator with her eco-friendly dresses, cat-eye glasses, and gray-streaked dark hair. In this one, she's the mom of our office—reminding Josh to pass around cards for birthdays and lecturing me about work-life balance.

"Sam was planning a big trip to Chile after the holidays. I was supposed to go too . . ." *Before he realized I didn't belong,* I almost add.

Patty's eyes go soft. She waits, giving me the space to say more about Sam, but I don't.

"Speaking of trips," I deflect, "how was Phoenix? You were visiting your sister, yeah? Or was it your cousin?"

Patty looks over her shoulder before leaning forward in her seat. I lean forward too, anticipating something juicy.

"I didn't visit my family last Friday," she starts, and I try not to let my face fall at how unscandalous this scandal is.

I'm fake-dating a dead man, Tanaka. The bar for tantalizing tidbits is set pretty high.

I stare at her in hopes she'll rise to the occasion.

"I was interviewing for a job with the hotel chain I consulted for this summer," she explains. "And yesterday, they made an offer."

A luxury hotel chain hired us when they started to expand into the northern Midwest. Patty led the project and provided parking plans and layout recommendations. Clearly, the company loved her ability to make parking solutions sound somewhat interesting.

"That's amazing, Patty!"

"Yeah?" A smile breaks free from her lips. "I thought you might be excited about one fewer desk in your office."

"No. I'm sad about that part. I'll have to kill time in conference rooms all on my own."

"I'm recommending you for my job," Patty confides. "Goodbye, government and public transit assignments."

"But I was hired for my public works background." I'm partially overstating it. I was hired because I revealed myself as a train geek in my urban planning freshman seminar and my professor—a transportation systems engineer and fellow rail enthusiast—volunteered himself as my advisor and connected me to an internship with this consulting firm.

I'm not a train conductor, as my six-year-old self dreamed of, but I'm providing research and insight into how expanding public transportation can serve communities who need it. Public transportation can connect people in a way that facilitates equity and community. I'm not sure I'd find the same fulfillment planning airport parking lots.

Patty sighs. "You do all of this work for these large-scale projects that never get funded. How many years did you put into that express train red-tape nightmare? With developers, you'll get to travel outside of Minnesota. You'll make corporate contacts. It's a way bigger playing field."

I can't articulate why the positives of Patty's job don't sound like positives to me. After all, opportunities, travel, and connections are what most ambitious people look for in a career.

"I'll think about it."

"No pressure," she assures me. "But I have to say, I thought you'd be more excited."

Josh's knock against the glass interrupts our conversation. "He's gone." Josh looks left and right before he mimes strangling himself.

He can hardly wait until our office door is closed to spill. "I hate that you guys aren't HR."

"Does Kyle still have a bee in his bonnet about 'reply all' emails?" Patty prods.

Josh types so furiously, smoke should be pouring from his keyboard. "I can neither confirm nor deny," he says.

Underneath his buttoned-up corporate drone appearance, Josh is a massive gossip. I suspect it's why he went into HR. A healthy penchant for gossip is my favorite trait in officemates, but since Josh is cursed with a confidentiality requirement, our meeting postmortems require a bit of inference.

My inbox dings with a new email from HR detailing the

grievances of an "anonymous" concerned team member on email reply etiquette.

I snort. "Josh! Let Kyle get back to his desk before you unmask him as the email hall monitor." I'm 87 percent sure Kyle steals my Sharpie rollerball pens when I leave for the day, but he's still a person.

"If someone wants to waste my precious time detailing their every minor issue to HR, they should be named and shamed. I don't want anyone thinking I'm personally upset about email etiquette or deviating from the fridge cleaning schedule."

Patty's index fingers are poised above her keyboard for her tiny game of whack-a-mole. "Joshy, no one suspects you care about the chore wheel. We see how little effort you put in when it's your turn."

"And everyone knows if it weren't for Kyle, you'd be on Reddit all day," I pile on.

Josh never ceases typing as he raises his eyebrow in challenge. "Oh yeah, Mullally? As opposed to all the time you spend logging self-help books on Goodreads? The dry-erase board behind you is reflective."

"Leave her alone. She's had a tough week." Patty steps in as mother hen.

I change the subject. "Josh, do I have enough vacation stored up to go to South America in January?"

"You? Probably. You never go anywhere."

"You're going on the trip? Is it for Sam?" Patty's heart is in her eyes, as if this might be a display of doomed romance and not whatever indescribable part of me needs to do something like this even if the idea of backpacking through mountain ranges without access to plumbing makes me shudder.

"Maybe."

On my way out the door for the day, I pop into my boss Daniella's office to let her know I'll be leaving early for an appointment.

"Put yourself on my cal next week to talk about Patty's position," she says, because Daniella Torres is the kind of corporate American who chops one syllable off of words for efficiency and uses *synergy* unironically.

The coffee in my stomach turns at the thought of meeting with Daniella to discuss a promotion I'm not sure I want, but that's a problem for Next Week Alison. Between packing my ex's apartment, playing the bereaved lover in front of the actually grieving best friend, and the ovarian ultrasound I nearly forgot about, This Week Alison's dance card is full.

For lunch, I eat a sad, wet turkey sub—it's been sitting in the office fridge for so long, I don't dare calculate its age—and pass the jealous faces of my coworkers who incorrectly assume I'm leaving early to enjoy a long weekend in the crisp afternoon air. Instead, I drive to the imaging center, fantasizing about alternate Friday afternoons for alternate Alisons with unremarkable breast tissue and ovaries.

Dragging my feet into my semiannual ovarian ultrasound, I flop onto a gray couch with uninviting wipe-clean fabric. I try to occupy myself with my phone but am immediately foiled by a text notification from my mom. It's a link to an article, showing only the title: "Facing Hereditary Risk: Why Are These Empowered Women Preventatively Removing Their Fallopian Tubes?"

Irritation swells in my belly at my mom's obvious ovarian agenda. She stopped ramping up to BRCA chitchat long ago, preferring to open with some variation of "Remember your ovaries? They aren't safe either."

I stuff an AirPod in my right ear; press play on my latest audiobook, featuring a man who shakes himself awake from his unfulfilling life by quitting his job to bike from Oregon to Patagonia; and hide my mom's message in my pocket—out of sight, out of mind—until a nurse in scrubs calls my name. A giant diagram of a woman's reproductive organs greets me on the other side of the double doors.

As someone who's had mammograms, breast ultrasounds, and chest MRIs multiple times per year for the past six years, I'm no stranger to an unpleasant examination. Still, the ovarian ultrasound takes the cake.

The problem with this exam is that ovaries are hard to image, making ovarian cancer difficult to detect. But since my BRCA mutation is linked to an estimated 46 percent risk of developing ovarian cancer in my lifetime, frequent ovarian ultrasounds are a necessary evil until I remove the spiteful little sacks.

After I change into a gown, the ultrasound tech gestures for me to lie back on the exam table, which looks like an unholy marriage of gynecological stirrups and a La-Z-Boy, and starts in with the transabdominal ultrasound. The warm gel on my belly does nothing to offset the overall chill of the cold, dark room. We stay there for a couple of images before it's time for the main event: the transvaginal ultrasound. A transvaginal ultrasound involves inserting a long, thin wand—covered with a plastic sheath and conducting gel—into my vagina. Fun, right?

What makes this experience so uncomfortable is not the

length of the procedure (no more than ten minutes) or even the size of the ultrasound wand (though it's *not* small). It's how the ultrasound technician roots around my body in search of each ovary.

"Excited for the weekend?" Marie, today's ultrasound technician, asks.

Am I excited to pack my dead ex-boyfriend's belongings with his friend who obviously doesn't want me around? No.

But since I've never met an ultrasound tech who wanted an honest answer during transvaginal chitchat, I say, "Oh, sure!"

Marie starts slow and optimistic, but her movements become more desperate as the time drags on. The wand moves inside me like it's an oversized couch and I am a doorway, the ultrasound tech the determined moving crew. *To the right. No, left. What if we try it at an angle like . . . ? No, push it up from the bottom. Use your back. Pivot!*

"Alison, dear. I can't find your right ovary. Can you lower your leg to the floor so I can try from another angle?" Her eyes crease with a pitying smile.

In this position, I'm poised to make direct eye contact with Marie, something neither of us wants. My pulse quickens as she roots around with greater gusto, and I stare down the painting behind her head—a lake motif so bland it's as if the room's designer was worried hotel art would be too provocative.

The procedure eventually ends, and Marie hands me a towel to mop up the leftover gel before leaving me to put my underwear back on.

"Your doctor will review the findings with you over the phone sometime next week," Marie tells me as she closes the exam room door behind her.

. . .

Since my mom artfully pried my appointment time out of me when we last spoke, I should've expected she wouldn't wait for my call. Still, bitterness coils in my chest when I see her name light up the screen before I've even unlocked my front door.

"Alison!" she shouts into the receiver. "I don't have long. I'm on episode two of the Kentucky cult documentary."

"*You* called *me*," I answer, fiddling with my key in my dead bolt.

I live in a historic brick building in Saint Paul originally renovated to house artists. Now it's mostly occupied by government workers, young professionals, and the occasional minor league baseball player.

My front door bounces off my tiny entry table when I open it too far. The large windows, high ceilings, and exposed brickwork once made the studio feel spacious and airy when it was empty. It wasn't until I tried to fit a table into the kitchenette that I discovered a studio was too small a space for an average-sized human to spend most of their waking hours.

Every piece of furniture is nearly touching another piece of furniture, as if I arranged the whole room for the world's most straightforward game of The Floor Is Lava. I shimmy myself between a kitchen chair and the vintage table I rescued from a rummage sale to hang my coat on a wall hook.

"Right, right," my mom responds. "It's just as well. This episode has been about a bunch of people doing yoga in a strip mall. I'm not missing much."

I toss my keys into a little ceramic bowl. "Next episode, they take over a school board. Then it gets *really* nuts."

"Oh, I know them!" I have to pull the phone back from

my ear because of the volume of her shriek. "A few years before Emma was born, I went to a meeting. Everyone wore wool scarves *inside*. It was so odd. I never went back."

I find this completely unsurprising. My mom was the Forrest Gump of 1980s cults. If a cult was recruiting, my mother had a brief encounter with them. My sister and I have a few theories on this, ranging from benign to conspiratorial—what if Mom is the actual cult leader?

The most likely answer is that my mom is both the perfect and most disastrous recruit. She's outgoing, she's trusting, and she wants to please people, but unlike the ideal recruit, she loves herself precisely as she is and has no desire to reach nirvana at your expensive weekend retreat. Also, she detests a sign-up sheet.

When she exhales, I can hear her mentally ramping up to the real purpose of her call. "What were the results of the ultrasound?" Enough small talk.

I kick off my boots one at a time. "And here I thought you'd called to talk about true crime." I hoped we could have one conversation about something other than my cancer risk, but who was I kidding?

She tuts. "Alison."

"My doctor hasn't reviewed the results yet."

"My doctor always called right away."

"I'd hope so. You had cancer. I just don't have boobs."

I swear I can hear her roll her eyes. When she pauses, I pounce before she can fill the quiet herself. Neither of us has ever been able to hold a silence. It slips between our hands like a wet bar of soap.

"I went on a beautiful prairie hike yesterday after work," I say to fill space.

"You told Emma you were lost in 'Murder Field.'"

I did tell her that. The thing about the prairie in the early winter: it's just dead, hard ground. The waterlogged soil turns to solid dirt with the steep drop in temperature. The trees are naked. The sky is gray. It's the perfect setting to find a body in the cold open of a prestige crime drama, so, naturally, I shared my location with my sister so my family would have closure in the event of my disappearance from the barren wasteland abutting a rural highway.

"I didn't realize you discussed anything about me aside from the present state of my tubes and ovaries."

I want to be able to talk to my mom about all aspects of my life—my ambivalence about this job opportunity; my reinsertion into Sam's life, or death rather; and this overwhelming sense that I'm living all wrong—but since my diagnosis, I haven't been able to keep her off the topic of removing my body parts like we're trapped in a continuous game of Operation: Hereditary Cancer Edition.

We used to have light conversations about celebrity makeups and breakups. Now when my mom calls, it's always the same. We've been trapped in a cancer loop for years. I worry sometimes that once my ovaries are gone, we'll have forgotten how to discuss anything else.

"These things are important, Alison. You need to take advantage of your chance to mitigate your risk."

"I know," I respond, because I have the gift of living without cancer and don't get to waste it.

"Why don't you see my doctor when you visit for Christmas? She really is the best."

I saw her doctor for the results of my genetic test when this all started six years ago. Before I sat down in front of a neon graffiti *Warrior* painting in that petal-pink office, my breasts were Schrödinger's cat—both the breasts I'd always known and ticking time bags, plotting to destroy me when I least suspected it.

"I have my *own* doctor," I counter, plopping onto my bed.

"Fine. Fine," my mom says, and I can practically hear her hand waving dismissively at me across the line. "Then ask *your* doctor about that fallopian tube study I sent you. Can you at least do that for me?"

"Sure, Mom," I sigh.

"Good." Her relief smacks me in the ears. "Imagine how great you'll feel when you don't need to worry about cancer anymore. You'll be so much happier once this is behind you."

I hear the click of a binder on her end of the line and the flip of the printed medical journal articles. She drones on about studies at Mayo. *Risk, hormones,* and *abnormal cells* reach my ears, but I'm not listening.

Instead, I'm wondering what my mom talks to my sister about. Does she read these articles to Emma and complain about my inaction? Or does she have a relationship with her that has nothing to do with genetic mutations?

For a split second, I picture my other breasts, the ones that were never plotting against me and only wanted to be held close to my chest in a wired balconette bra—a kind of bra that's been verboten since my mastectomy. What would my mom say to those breasts? I'd bet those boobs know nothing of egg extractions and oviducts.

Lucky bastards.

8

Gobble, Baby

I WAKE UP SATURDAY morning to an iCal alert that makes my heart lurch.

Message from the Future: 75 days to Chile!! 🕺 🙂 🏔

"I got you an Americano," I tell Adam when I arrive at Sam's, dropping the drink carrier on the soapstone kitchen island. It's a lame peace offering, but if we're stuck together, I don't want to bicker. We're packing up this apartment and then parting ways forever. We don't need to be friends, but we do need to get through this. "I was going to call it a 'guilt coffee' since I'm dipping out early today, but since I'm going to a children's concert at my friend's elementary school after this, I'm feeling more dread than actual remorse."

Adam accepts the red Starbucks cup with an approving nod. "How did you know I like Americanos?"

I shrug off my coat and drape it on the rack. "You have big Americano energy. I can tell everyone's coffee order. It's my useless superpower."

He smells the coffee cautiously. "You know, Spyhouse is down the street if you're looking for an independent coffee shop," he says, as if I don't live here.

"Spyhouse doesn't have my favorite winter beverage." I take a swig and shimmy my shoulders with my swallow, feeling it tingle in my throat. "Mmm, peppermint mocha."

"Thanks for this. You didn't have to go out of your way." He lifts his red cup, his face contrite.

I have no interest in rehashing how we left things last time—or pinning down my ex's exact level of apathy toward me for the second week in a row—so I shake my head and let him off the hook. "Wasn't out of my way."

He nods, shoulders relaxing, and returns to the corner of the kitchen. Adam unscrews a cabinet door with a tight expression of concentration.

"Did his family ask you to do that?" I ask. Removing cabinet doors doesn't fit within our limited job description.

"They're all beat up, and this stain is peeling. It's easier if I just refinish them." He seems to think this requires no further explanation. He's not telling me something, but I don't care enough to challenge him.

I open Spotify. Music fills the apartment, giving me the energy I need for another day trapped in Adam's company.

"Why are you playing Christmas music?" His voice wobbles between confusion and distress.

My stomach jerks with the vague feeling I might be in trouble. "Starbucks had Christmas cups."

"Because Starbucks is evil."

"Starbucks is a barometer of the people, and the people want Christmas. Wait, do you not celebrate Christmas? I shouldn't have assumed."

He shakes his head, rolling up his sleeves to expose the same irritatingly impressive forearms I spotted last week. Part of me was hoping they'd deflated in our time apart like a leaky tire. He leans against the doorless top cabinet. The pose only emphasizes his height. The apartment shrinks when he stands like that. "I celebrate Christmas *on* Christmas. It's not even Thanksgiving yet. Let Thanksgiving have its moment."

"You're not one of those anti-Christmas psychopaths, are you?"

"Depends. Are you one of those 'War on Christmas' fearmongers?"

I shrug. "I love Christmas. And I don't see why I have to justify it to anyone. If you'd prefer Classic Rock Christmas or Hip-Hop Christmas or Hipster Christmas, Spotify can arrange that."

"What's Hipster Christmas?"

"It's a lot of Zooey Deschanel and that one song by the Pogues over and over again."

He waits a full minute to respond, but at the sound of his resigned breath passing through his nose, I know I've won. "Classic Christmas is good."

For the rest of the morning, I sit on the floor, emptying the contents of Sam's entertainment cabinet, soundtracked by Adam's drill and Classic Christmas. Despite his stoic façade, Adam's head is bobbing along about one minute into "Santa Claus Is Coming to Town." We're all helpless against the power of a Bruce Springsteen Christmas cover.

Adam gives me little more than the occasional grunt as I narrate my every movement before I eventually get lost in the rhythm of the task, sorting video games, ten-year-old Blu-rays, and several generations of gaming consoles into boxes of "Keep," "Sell," or "Trash," but I never relax. After my morning message from beyond, I jump whenever my phone beeps with a push notification. I dismiss each one, attempting to calm my pulse.

"Why are you acting weird?" he asks the back of my head from his seat on the kitchen countertop.

"What do you mean by 'weird'?" I've been having a one-sided conversation with him on and off for over an hour, and earlier I sang the back cover copy of *Olympus Has Fallen* to the tune of "Good King Wenceslas" out of sheer boredom, so when it comes to me and "weird," he'll have to be more specific.

"You were doing your talking thing—"

"My 'talking thing'?" I spin around on the wood floor. "You mean my pointless attempts at conversing with you?"

"Then your phone buzzes, and you stop mid-word and do this shaky-twitchy thing. It's alarming."

"Stop watching me, then."

"What am I supposed to look at?"

I gesture out at the downtown skyline real estate porn outside the wall of windows.

"What's on your phone? It has to be something, or you wouldn't jump five inches in the air every time it makes a noise."

My phone chirps. I try, and fail, to keep still.

"Is someone bothering you?"

"It's nothing," I answer. He's silent again, but his stare has a formidable, claustrophobic effect that would be quite useful in a government interrogation. "Fine. It's . . . uh, did Sam use to leave reminders in your iCal when you left your phone unlocked?"

He freezes at the question. "You mean his 'Messages from the Future'?" Adam asks, his voice all faux nonchalance.

"Yeah, exactly. I got one this morning."

He tilts his head back against the cabinet. "He's been doing it for years." His face transforms as his mouth curves into a small but brilliant smile. "He messed with the settings in my phone, so even when I had it on silent, Doc from *Back to the Future* would yell, 'Great Scott!' It always seemed to go off in the middle of work or class or something." He lets out a light exhalation of air resembling a laugh. "I hated it."

But he doesn't sound like he hates it anymore.

"Yeah." I laugh too, because it's nice to laugh with someone who knows. "Mine are always stuff I should be doing. That's what I didn't like. It pointed out my shortcomings. It still does."

"But he was our friend, not our accountabili-buddy. Sam never understood caution or responsibilities. It was all so simple to him. You want it? Take it. Maybe it was the trust fund."

I shake my head in bewilderment. "Sam had a trust fund?"

"Of course. How do you think he paid for all of those trips?"

"But he didn't care about money."

"Only rich people don't care about money."

"And this condo?"

Adam rubs the back of his neck and shakes his head. "It's technically his parents'. Sorry. I shouldn't talk about him like this."

"Like he was an actual person?" My lips curve into a half smile that's meant to make him feel less twitchy about tattling on Sam to his Current Girlfriend. "Whatever. Trust fund or not, he was right. There are so many things I should be doing that I'm not."

"I was always more cautious than he liked."

Adam looks at me, his hands gripping the sides of the

cabinet like he wants to say more but won't. I pay attention, knowing I'm catching sight of a small, private part of him. I'm not sure how long I've been staring at the tiny changes in his expression when I'm interrupted by my phone's buzz.

"See! That's what it was." He gleefully points out whatever strange jolt shimmied up my vertebrae.

I'm just grateful he thinks it's my phone's fault.

> **1:23 PM**
> **Mara:**
> Sorry. Can't make it. The Guy's thirteen-year-old has been lightly bullying MasterChef Junior contestants on TikTok, and it's becoming a whole thing. Can you find another ride?

"Looks like I need an Uber," I tell Adam, sending a thumbs-up and closing the group chat. "But at least I'm mostly done with the living room."

Adam starts taking apart his drill. "What do you need an Uber for?"

"My friend's holiday concert. Well, her kids' concert. She's their teacher." I pat my pockets before finding my phone still in my hand. "My other friend—my ride—canceled. Why is there surge pricing in the middle of the day?"

"I can drive you." He hops off the counter and grabs his keys from the kitchen island.

"Are you sure? It's thirty minutes away."

"I've got nothing better to do."

I know this to be false, but selfishly, I'm too late and too cheap to question his generosity. "You're sure?"

"I'm happy to do it, Alison," he answers, without a hint of

insincerity. I stand in front of the door, dumbstruck, until he nudges me out of the way of his big leather boots. He puts on his coat—denim-side out—ending any further debate.

———

WHEN ADAM TURNS the ignition, eighties synthwave blasts from the speakers. It sounds like how robots might score a low-budget horror movie.

"I can't with this," I insist, silencing his stereo with the punch of a button.

He starts the noise up again with his forefinger. "At least it's a seasonally appropriate playlist."

"It's terrifying. It's torture. You win. I will sit in complete silence with you if we can turn this off."

He doesn't look at me, but I see his eyes crinkle at the corners. He turns off the stereo, and we ride together wordlessly the rest of the way. Once I settle into the quiet, I don't find myself needing to fill it. I don't need to make Adam feel comfortable, since he seems far more at ease when I'm not doing my patented people-pleaser routine.

He turns into the parking lot, and I half expect to have to tuck and roll treacherously from the slow-moving vehicle. Instead, he pulls into a parking space.

"Thanks for the ride. Very quiet driver. Five stars," I say with a tight nod, but when I climb out of the car, Adam exits too. "Are you coming in?"

"I'm not actually an Uber driver, Alison." He says it all grumbly, like a sleepy bear.

"It's an elementary school holiday concert. It's guaranteed to be terrible." I feel guilty throwing Chelsea's students under the bus, but I have to set appropriate expectations.

"I have nothing better to do." He repeats his argument from the apartment but with a groan for good measure.

"Fine. Hurry up. We're late."

Hand-drawn decorations for every holiday from November to New Year's Day—even Veterans Day—cover the bustling auditorium lobby. A sweet-faced child hands me two programs, and we walk through heavy double doors decked with holly.

"Isn't it a bit early for a holiday concert?" he asks as we shuffle into a pair of aisle seats.

"This is a science and math magnet school. The primary school has a real holiday concert before the break."

He accepts the program I pass to him, opening it with a frown. "So this is the first pancake for the concert season?"

"Yes, but with far more enthusiasm and a greater emphasis on animals and conservation."

Adam surveys the auditorium like he's scanning for threats. Then he grabs my arm, his voice low and subdued. "Why are children in face paint sitting in the audience? Oh god, they're going to start in the audience, aren't they?"

"Probably," I whisper.

"I hate when they start in the audience. It's like being trapped in a flash mob. The only good thing about a flash mob is that I can leave the mall food court. They can't force me to sit in front of Panda Express while Bruno Mars *happens* to me."

I flip through the program. "I don't see any Bruno Mars on the schedule, so I think you're good. But there's a turkey number set to 'Wobble.' Want to guess what it's called?" I turn to Adam, who's performing an ocular pat-down of the crowd.

"Okay, that kid has glitter. Do you have a hood?" Adam leans in to examine my collar, but I swat him away.

"People are looking at us!"

"Suit yourself. You're on the aisle. You'll be finding glitter in your hair for days."

"Let the kids enjoy their holiday show. You're being such a grinch."

"I might have a hat in my truck that you can use for cover."

"Settle down." I place my hand on his bouncing knee until it stills. But then I just hold it there for longer than socially appropriate. When I yank it away, we both become very interested in the particulars of the oil-change coupon on the back of the concert program—$25 off the synthetic blend!—my stomach somersaulting from mortification. I finally look up when a young girl steps into the spotlight.

Jaunty piano music plays, and the house lights slowly fade up as the girl, in a tiger leotard, sings the first verse of Katy Perry's "Roar." The orange-face-painted children in the audience seats gradually join in, and more voices fill the auditorium as the song builds toward the refrain.

All at once, the kids step over audience members in a chaotic attempt to make it to the aisle for a choreographed dance routine. Since they clearly rehearsed the number in an empty auditorium, the children—trapped between audience members—panic when the familiar lyrics start up.

"This one's stuck." Adam nudges me, pointing to the lion next to him. The boy's costume is caught on an armrest, and we watch the poor kid frantically yank at his shirt.

Adam mutters something to the kid, and he nods his head in response. In one swift movement, Adam grabs the boy by his sides, lifts him over the two of us, and gently plops him down in the aisle. "Thank you," the lion yells before running off to his position in the dance. I feel a tug under my ribs. Is that my heart? Did that just literally tug at my heartstrings?

But this spark of joy is short-lived. I spot plastic baggies poking out of the pockets of children dancing into my personal space, and dread sets in.

"You're right," I tell Adam, my voice absorbed by noise. "They're definitely going to throw glitter on us."

"Can we leave?"

"Nope."

He inhales sharply, accepting our shimmery fate. "Their dancing is blocking the exits anyhow."

I paste on a demented grin. "Just smile at the children and prepare to be glittered."

As predicted, the key changes and the children triumphantly douse us in sparkly flecks that will certainly be in my hair for the rest of the week. Coughs erupt throughout the audience, and the kids scurry up front to take their bow.

The concert continues with the classes performing holiday hits, animal skits, and "Gobble" set to the tune of "Wobble."

"Look, they're giving Thanksgiving its moment. Did they know you were coming?" I whisper-tease. Adam looks to the ceiling as if someone might rappel down and rescue him.

I finally feel like I have the upper hand with him until a group of enthusiastic fifth graders ask for audience suggestions for an improvised holiday scene, and Adam's breath grazes the shell of my ear. "What kind of school allows children to perform improv in front of people? Kids shouldn't have this much confidence."

I stifle a laugh and elbow him back into his seat.

Mercifully, Chelsea and her fellow teachers end the meandering skit on North Pole workplace conditions by pushing the rest of the kids onstage for "Jingle Bells," and the adorably puzzling catastrophe comes to an end.

Adam is standing with an arm in his coat before the house lights come up. "The parking lot's going to be a mess. Let's leave now while the parents are looking for their kids."

I grab my coat and point myself in the direction of the stage against the current of parents exiting the theater. "I have to say hi to Chelsea before I go, but I can meet you in the lobby."

"I'm a tall man, Alison. I can't loom over a crowd of children alone."

"What do you think dads are doing if not being tall and looming about?" I scan the stage until I spot a blond ponytail. "There she is. Follow me if you'd rather."

He grouses but trails behind me anyway.

I jump up the stage steps to Chelsea and wrap her in a hug. "Great job, Ms. Olsen."

"You came!" she shouts into my ear, and I flinch instinctually in preservation of my eardrum. Her eyes are saucers at the sight of a man hovering behind me. "And you brought—"

"This is Adam," I say before she can reveal anything damning I've said about him. "He's the one I'm helping with the apartment."

She introduces herself with a demure handshake. "I'm Chelsea, Al's other other half."

"Nice to meet you. The show was great." His flat tone couldn't be more unconvincing.

Chelsea holds up her arms defensively like a perp on a cop show. "I can only take credit for the educational animal skits."

"Oh, I liked those. They were a nice reprieve from the singing."

Chelsea chokes. "You're a real straight shooter, aren't you, Adam?"

Adam's eyes flit to me. "So I've been told."

"The kids did a great job, Chels," I say pointedly.

"Absolutely." Adam fastens his jacket, which he flipped to khaki at some point, and light catches the multicolored flecks falling from his wide shoulders.

"We'll let you get back to work. I'll see you later," I tell Chelsea while pivoting Adam toward the exit. Over my shoulder, I catch Chelsea mouthing, *Text me*. I shake my head as we shuffle out of the auditorium.

At the top of the aisle, we get caught in the musical theater version of a roundabout, children running every which way toward family, classmates, and teachers. Adam grabs my hand to lead me through the chaos.

It's one of those dreadfully lovely gestures that's both deeply intimate and horrifically platonic all at once.

His hand is warm and rough in all the best ways and when he finally lets go halfway through the parking lot, I know I'll be unpacking the significance of the gesture for hours tonight.

"You should know that you're the worst audience member of all time," I tell him while hoisting myself into the passenger side of his truck.

"I saved the show. The lion would still be dangling in the middle of the auditorium if it weren't for me."

Twisting his torso, he places a hand behind my seat to reverse, assaulting me with a close-up of his chin. His beard is shorter than last week, and this close, I can just make out his chin dimple. I've never had a "thing" for chins, but Adam's is forcing me to reconsider this stance.

He pitches his voice lower to account for the closer proximity. "But I'm sorry I interrupted your experience watching ten-year-olds do improv."

With his hand still on my headrest, he fixes his eyes on me for a beat—maybe two. I concentrate on each exhalation as our breaths mix and float toward the windshield in icy clouds. A car honks, and without a word, he brings his hand to the gearshift and pulls the car forward out of the lot.

"My sister was in a kids' improv troupe," I say to cover the moment—or what I think is a moment.

"No. Oh, god. Was it bad?"

"So bad." My wince falls into a smile at the memory of my tenacious sister demanding occupations and vacation destinations from an unwilling audience. "They used to do events in town, like hardware store openings and stuff. My mom always made me go, even though I had horrible secondhand embarrassment. Emma wasn't embarrassed, though. She's nothing like me. She's always been so confident."

"You weren't? Confident, I mean." He glances between me and the other cars.

"Ha. No, I was a dreadfully boring kid and always looking for the manual on how I should be. I still am."

"I don't think you're boring." His sincerity does something to my stomach.

"Well, that's just a blatant lie."

"I don't."

"My whole 'talking thing'?"

"It's certainly not boring." I catch the beginnings of a smile disobediently leaping up his face. The almost-smile raises the temperature in the truck better than the struggling heater.

His hand rubs along the icy steering wheel.

"Are you cold?" I open the glove compartment, hoping he keeps the obvious items in there. Instead, a plastic container of cookies pops out. "Snacks!" I blurt. "Thin Mints?"

The label credits a bakery in Duluth, but they look almost exactly like my favorite treat.

Pink erupts on Adam's cheekbones before he huffs a hot breath into his cupped hands, the frozen wheel balanced by his knee. "I got them yesterday on the way home from work. This place makes dupes of gas station junk food like Ho Hos and Sno Balls, but they do a couple of Girl Scout cookies too. It's dumb. They probably don't even taste like the real thing." He fusses with his rearview mirror, like he's embarrassed to be caught with his own peace offering. My Starbucks gift from this morning looks pitiful by comparison.

I twist toward him in my seat. "This is amazing." I grin at the box, unable to contain my delight. "Really, this is . . . nice."

His mouth relaxes into a smile. "You sound shocked."

"Did you keep them in the glove box so they'd freeze?"

"Happy accident." He turns back toward the road, but his jaw works in thought. He opens his mouth as if to say something but then closes it. "I should probably apologize about last week." He rubs his beard with agitated movements, waiting for my reply.

"Was that the apology or will it come later?" I make him work for it a bit, biting back my grin. I hate a bad apology, and Adam's fun to tease.

"I shouldn't have pretended to know anything about you and Sam." His eyes meet mine when he pulls up to a stop sign, and guilt pinches at my side for giving him a hard time. He knows more about me and Sam than he realizes. "I'm so sorry, Alison. How can I make it right?"

Energy vibrates out of my hand on the bench seat between us, as if interlacing our fingers would be the most natural thing to do. Instead, I press my palm into my lap. "Don't worry about it. It was a stressful day."

He clicks on his blinker. "You don't have to tell me it's fine to make me feel better. I know I was wrong. It's just . . . Sam and I had been growing apart for a while, and his last visit was . . . off. I've somehow been grandfathered into the 'best friend' title, and I put my guilt about that on you."

"You weren't wrong . . . about Sam or how he felt about me," I say, flicking the plastic cookie container with my thumb. "But I want to help his family now, if I can. Sam knows who we all were to him. I think these posthumously awarded titles are more for the people who lost him."

At least that's what I've been telling myself.

He drums the steering wheel nervously. "Can we forget last week? Pretend it never happened?" He glances at me for a long moment and then returns his eyes to the road.

My heart sputters at his boyish earnestness, and I have to bite into a Thin Mint to contain my goofy grin. "I'd love that. But we have to start from right now. I need to wipe my memory clean of what we just watched."

"Do you think Chelsea had to buy the rights to do that to 'Wobble'?" he asks, blinking at me.

I burst into an embarrassing snort-laugh, earning rich, deep-throated laughter from him. My gloved hands mop up my leaky eyes, and I feel something more than awkward acquaintanceship bloom between us. Friendship, maybe? Something approaching friendship, at least.

Because despite all reason, I might like Adam Berg, and that's a truth I'm still reeling from the whole way home.

9

Nips Out, Chilled and Perky

I T'S A MISERABLE, drizzly morning, which means I'll be spending the entire day with Adam fighting my hair. At its best, my hair is light brown with a texture somewhere between *Felicity*-era Keri Russell and *Folklore*-era Taylor Swift, but today's spitting rain only seems to emphasize its wildness.

I smell coffee brewing when I back-step into Sam's apartment clutching two red Starbucks cups. The boxes I filled yesterday are gone, as are the cupboard doors. On the kitchen island are coffee beans, a brown paper bag of bagels, and an extra-large tub of cream cheese. Adam has hit every small business on the block that opens before seven a.m.

"I brought you an Americano for the breakfast buffet." My words bounce around the sparse living room. The furniture's still here, but everything that made the place special is now packed away.

Adam's head pops out of the bathroom door. Scattered around him are several orange Home Depot bags. "Oh, thanks. Leave it there with everything else. I'll need help installing the faucet when you're ready." He bends his head like the matter is settled and disappears behind the toilet.

"Is there a reason *we're* fixing the sink and not, say, a licensed plumber?"

"If you have to hire a plumber to replace a faucet, you're hopeless." His insult echoes off the bathroom tile.

I roll my eyes, kicking off my winter boots and shimmying my coat down my shoulders. Muddy, slushy footprints show my every move like animal tracks. I curse myself under my breath, knowing that every small thing I do to make this apartment messier only adds to our growing to-do list.

Sam's parents couldn't have known the repairs this place needed when they tasked us with getting it ready to sell in only four weeks. Surely they'd forgive us for leaving an imperfect sink, but I don't want to abandon Adam and whatever feelings are compelling him to spend so much of his free time in this apartment.

"I see you beat me to the coffee. Do you want this Americano? I wouldn't want to overcaffeinate you."

"Not possible." He strides out of the bathroom, washing his hands in the kitchen sink before grabbing the cup from my carrier. He lifts it in a gesture of appreciation. "I got a coffeemaker while I was out. This way, you won't have to buy it."

"Oh. Yeah. That's good." I try to conceal my disappointment. I like bringing coffee. It justifies my presence while he's under the sink fitting pipes or whatever light plumbing he's up to.

"And you don't need to worry about missing your mint

mochas." Adam opens the fridge with a flourish, revealing a slim green carton.

"Fudgy Mint Cookie Creamer."

"They can't call it Thin Mint Creamer because of trademarks."

"Sure." I turn the carton slowly, certain it'll detonate in my hands.

"But that's obviously what it is."

If I didn't know better, I'd think Adam sounded the slightest bit excited. It's infectious, even though this creamer sounds utterly repulsive. I settle into a stool opposite him.

"I'll pour some mugs," he says, and I'm about to ask him, *What mugs?* when he produces two ceramic, hand-thrown ones from his backpack on the counter. He places the slate-gray one in front of himself and the forest-green one in front of me.

"These are beautiful." I pick mine up to admire the handsome curved handle, foiling his attempt to pour coffee into it.

"My sister makes them. I stole these from her house this morning. She has all different colors."

"But these are your favorites?"

"The gray one is. But I thought you'd like the green."

Adam pushes the green mug—my mug—to my side of the kitchen island. The liquid inside is a promising dark mocha color. I pull it to my lips for a slow, hesitant sip.

It's revolting.

"Mmm," I say through sheer force of will. My effort is truly heroic.

Adam is practically beaming with pride, meaning one tiny corner of his mouth is tipped upward.

Then the aftertaste hits, and nausea crawls up my throat like the girl from *The Ring*.

"I'm sorry," I say, suppressing a gurgle. "But this tastes like you cut bastardized Thin Mints with antifreeze."

His head jerks backward. "You said you liked it."

"Temporary insanity. A side effect of the antifreeze."

"It can't be that bad." He peers into my mug.

"No, the idea is good, but that's truly heinous. Try it." I push my mug across the counter.

"Why would I drink something bad?"

"I can't be the only person in this apartment made to suffer." I nudge my mug toward him with one finger.

"All right. All right." Adam cautiously places his lips on my mug and takes a slow sip. He swallows, and I wait an eternity for his verdict. "I'm getting the hint of antifreeze you mentioned."

Triumph rises in my body and plays across my face. "See!"

Adam's eyes crease from the smile he's withholding. The tip of his tongue runs between his lips, and an unexpected ribbon of heat twirls through my insides.

"I feel like I can taste the color green. Did you get that?" he asks, oblivious to whatever is happening beneath my surface.

I clear my throat. "Uh, yes. Aren't you glad we both have the shared trauma of tasting a color?"

He chases the sickly-sweet sip with his mug of black coffee. "Enough taste testing. I need you to hold the flashlight while I replace the faucet."

"You couldn't find a loose child in the hallway to help you?"

"I don't lure children into apartments I'm working on," he retorts.

I roll up the sleeves of my white top and hop down from my stool. "All right, Berg. Let's do this."

Adam lies face up with his head in the vanity, his bent leg jiggling restlessly. I crouch next to him, wielding my flashlight like a weapon.

I feel my leg bump his torso and make the devastating error of looking down at the point of contact. His light gray thermal is pulled up, exposing a small strip of skin over the top of his jeans. My pulse sputters, and I avert my eyes back to the pipes. It's too late. Every cell in my body is off-balance.

"So why are we replacing the sink?" I ask, because I need the distraction.

"The faucet—and because it needs to be replaced."

"Isn't this a bit above and beyond the call of duty? I thought they wanted us to pack up Sam's stuff."

"If we only pack everything up, his family will still have so much to do and . . ." His voice trails off, and I wish desperately that I could see his face. He swallows. "If I'd known Sam needed his faucet fixed, I would have fixed it. So I'm doing it now."

I nod, knowing exactly what he means. I've driven Chelsea to the airport at four a.m. and moved Mara into a fifth-floor walk-up, and I'd hide a body for either of them if they asked. Whatever issues they might have had, Sam and Adam were that kind of friends. That doesn't just go away.

"*You're* doing it now? As if I'm not a crucial member of this operation? Is this flashlight floating above you in thin air?" I tease, hoping to lighten the mood. He bumps his knee against mine, and I topple backward onto the white tile floor.

"Just for that, I quit. You can lure a child in here for the rest of the job."

"Alison." His voice frowns.

"Fine, fine." I click the light back on.

Adam loosens and tightens various pipe parts, but I'm too aware of our proximity to pay attention. I'm hovering over him. A light breeze would send me into his lap.

"Do you do this stuff at work?" I ask. More distractions.

"No. In my own house." He adjusts his head under the sink, and I catch a glimpse of his eyes, sharp with concentration.

"Ooh. Homeownership. Brag."

He twists his wrench, biting the tip of his tongue as he works.

I bite my own tongue without thinking. I've captured a small part of him he wouldn't have shown me—the embarrassing concentration face. Something sugary sweet melts in my belly at the thought.

"And at my sister's house in Minneapolis. June's pretty handy, but she's usually busy with my nephew, and her husband, Dev, works a lot."

"You guys must be close. That's nice."

"Yeah, but we're complete opposites. She's bubbly and full of energy. Super chatty. She's like color personified."

"Really? That sounds exactly like you."

A low laugh rumbles from Adam's chest. The sound reverberates through my limbs and disrupts my equilibrium. I grope at the floor.

"What took you to Duluth?" I ask.

"The carpentry master I apprenticed under got me temporary work with a contractor in Duluth until I was ready to start my business in Minneapolis. And that was about seven years ago, so . . ." This laugh is hollow and uncomfortable. "Waiting for the timing to line up."

I want to ask more, but I like talking with him too much. I suspect pressing this particular topic will disrupt our delicate back-and-forth.

"Can you shine the light over here?" His voice strains with the movement of his wrench.

"Sorry." My arm, having drooped under the weight of a whopping half-pound flashlight, is spotlighting the inch of Adam's torso that I'm definitely not thinking about. "So, in Duluth, do you live with roommates or—"

"Alone," he interrupts.

Sam talked about Adam's dating life once. I'd asked him about setting him up with Chelsea. I wanted someone steady and kind for her, and he brought up and dismissed the idea of Adam.

He never dates. No one seems to be worth the effort, he said. It painted a portrait of Adam as an arrogant ass. That image doesn't match up with the man I'm with today. Prickly and stubborn? Yes. But self-important jerk?

"You've stopped talking," he observes, seconds or minutes later.

"Yes, Adam. I'm aware that you think I talk too much."

"*Too much* implies I don't like it." The word *like* wraps around me like a worn flannel shirt. He pushes himself out from under the cabinet and stands.

I side-eye him. "Yeah? Yesterday, did you like when I read off the titles of everything in Sam's entertainment cabinet?"

"Especially the part where you were struggling to sort his Xboxes. Riveting stuff," he deadpans, cleaning the new polished nickel faucet with a dry rag.

"I'm still not over that. It goes 360, One, and then *Series S*? Who names this stuff?" A smile pulls at my lips despite my best efforts to contain it. "I don't mind silence. I actually like it. I don't like when other people feel uneasy with it." Everything they're not saying presses against my chest—it carries a weight—and if I let it go too long, the quiet turns on me. Judges me. It assigns blame.

They wouldn't be writhing in this interminable silence if you were a more interesting, captivating, exciting person, my insecurities whisper.

So rather than face down that voice, I fill the space with my own chatter.

Sam never needed me to crowd out an awkward moment because there never was one. His exuberance was relaxing up until the point where it exhausted me. Granted, some of that exhaustion may have been all of the mountain biking, rock climbing, etc.

But Adam doesn't radiate agitation in silence. He likes it too.

He leans down to put his tools back in his toolbox, and I position myself in front of the vanity. I wince at the frizzy bangs in my reflection and promptly fuss with them.

When I turn the sink handle to wet my hair, I barely register Adam's shout before witnessing the water sputter violently all over the front of my white shirt and numb breasts in the mirror. An unintelligible, startled sound chokes out of my throat, and I stand there, frozen.

"Air bubble," he explains, searching the empty bathroom for a towel. My eyes are fixed on my startling entry to this impromptu wet T-shirt contest. Numb everywhere it matters,

I feel only the damp, cold sensation spreading across my neck and stomach as I twirl away from the traitorous sink.

Wherever my nipples are in the universe, they are no doubt chilled and perky.

Finding no towel in the bathroom—I packed them all the first day—Adam averts his eyes and leaves for the bedroom.

One of the only upsides of not having nipples is going bra-less in a white tee. During my recovery, I met with a tattoo artist specializing in three-dimensional nipple art. She explained that without nipples, my breasts would look *incomplete*—"a face without a nose," she said. She promised tattoos would fill the gaps in my confused brain so I'd no longer do the dreaded double take in a mirror.

By the time I'd healed enough for tattooing, they didn't seem incomplete to me. They didn't look anything like my old breasts, but they looked like *my* breasts, so I decided against the cosmetic substitution. But my first time with a guy after my surgery, I finally understood.

I told him my BRCA story over craft beer and overpriced tater tots. He attempted to sympathize by revealing his precancerous-mole-removal story.

I should have called it then, but I wanted to rip off the intimacy Band-Aid. I took my shirt off and watched his brain short-circuiting at the landscape in front of him—rolling hills rather than twin peaks.

Eyes registering my breasts as *incomplete* looked suspiciously like a man finding them *wrong, gross,* and *repellent.* It's upsetting to watch someone's brain puzzle out your body in real time. I'd never felt so guilty for being in a woman's body with scars and imperfections, for choosing survival over vanity. *I didn't have cancer, yet*, I thought. *I could've risked it. I could've waited until I had someone who loved me with breasts before forcing them to love me without them.*

It was only a moment, and we had fairly routine, uneventful sex after that with no mention of my physical differences. Still, that one moment was enough for me to invest in lacy bralettes for future one-night stands.

I never summoned the courage to have sex with anyone else I actually wanted to see again. The stakes for physical rejection felt too high.

And now I stand here, waiting for Adam to see through my newly translucent shirt and register something lacking. That familiar shame creeps up my spine.

Adam returns holding a sweatshirt with DULUTH TRADING CO written across the front. He presses it to my front without looking, and I clutch it against myself. He starts to rub the sides of my arms but freezes, and I watch the awareness that he's touching me—kind of intimately—amble over his features.

"Sorry, uh, you have goose bumps," he stammers.

Cold bristles over my skin the moment he releases me, and before I realize what I'm doing, I'm leaning forward into him. I know I should back away—I'm making this weird—but he's too warm. I'm always so aware of what my breasts don't have and can't feel, but the pressure of his firm chest against mine just, well, *feels*.

He lets me stand against him a few seconds more before he speaks into the top of my head, his breath tickling my hair. "Where do you keep your clothes here?" he asks.

"I don't," I say into his shirt. The soft cotton is warm on my cheek, and his Adam-y scent fills my nostrils. This close,

I can unravel notes of cedar and oranges, and I wonder if it's fabric softener or soap or just him. His finger brushes a strand of hair away from my forehead. He moves it so gently—so reverently—that his body becomes the only thing keeping me from melting into a puddle on the floor. "I've never stayed over here, you know. We were never . . . I was never ready for that step."

Adam's body goes rigid against me as immediate regret rips through me like a tidal wave. Why am I confiding in a near stranger about my sex history—or lack thereof—with his best friend?

He clears his throat and nudges me toward the bedroom by the hand. "I have a spare shirt. Or you can wear one of Sam's, of course."

Whatever phantom sensations the weight of him shot through my breasts dissipate on my exhale.

I pull open the top dresser drawer and realize I don't know where anything is. I open two more drawers before settling on a plain green T-shirt. Once I'm dressed, I plop onto the bed and hold my boobs protectively.

"I'll throw this in the wash." He points at my soaked shirt, and I toss it into his open hand. "We should take care of this room today." He gestures around the bedroom.

For the rest of the day, we box up Sam's clothes. Any of these sweaters could be sentimental, so we take the coward's way out and every box becomes "Keep." His closet feels imbued with him, like his clothes are an extension of his person—an exoskeleton.

"How are you doing with this?" Adam asks. He tilts his head lazily to look down at me. It's cute. Adam is suddenly extremely cute to me. It's staggering.

I roll my head up in his direction, mimicking him. "How are *you* doing with this?" Because whether he's realized it or not, his relationship with Sam was more significant than mine.

"A bit surreal—like packing him away. But it needs to be done." He looks up at me again from the shirt he's folding. Warmth glows in his eyes. "I can't imagine having to do this for my ex. Not that . . . you know . . ."

I stifle a snort. "If you're only now telling me that your ex-girlfriend died—"

"No." A smile teases his lips. "She's very much alive. And married with a kid and a house on a lake."

"Ooh, the dream," I tease. "How long were you guys together?"

"Most of college." He rubs the back of his neck. "I haven't dated much since. It wouldn't make sense if I'm planning to leave Duluth, and dating itself is such a pain. I get all dirty from work, so I have to change my clothes and figure out what to eat . . ."

I can't help but smile. "You're describing basic human functioning. First-level 'hierarchy of needs' stuff."

We pack until the bedroom looks like a soulless Airbnb— not Sam Lewis's bedroom.

"Do you think we'll be able to make the deadline?" I gesture at the apartment. I feel like we've been at this an eternity, but with our side projects and derailments, it still looks like Sam just walked out for coffee.

"We got a bit done this weekend, but it's the painting and repairs that are the problem. I won't put that on anyone else when I'm more than capable of doing it. You don't have to help if you don't want to. I know you only signed up for packing."

"Oh, you're not getting rid of me now. I've watched too much HGTV to back out as soon as it's getting good." I suppress my grin. Just yesterday morning, the idea of spending a third weekend in Adam's company might have sent me into a stress spiral, but now I'm hoping he wants me to stay. "I'd like to help. If you want me to."

"That . . ." He looks down at the floor, then meets my eyes steadily. "I'd like that," he finally says.

The words zing through my chest. Every bit of it.

10

The Visiting Nephew

I WAKE UP MONDAY morning to a text message.

6:13 AM
Adam:
Your cult of Christmas is far-reaching.

Adam's message sits without context until a picture of a warehouse appears. The wood name placard is cut off, but to the left of SUPERIOR CONST is a giant green wreath with a lopsided red bow.

I hold my boobs in my hands as I consider my reply. It's not sexual—just a thing I do now—like how your tongue absently finds the spot where the Novocain hasn't worn off after getting a filling.

6:16 AM
Alison:
We prefer the Children of the Claus.

6:20 AM
Adam:
Ha.

———————

7:04 AM
Alison:
How do you respond to a text that's one syllable?

7:07 AM
Mara:
What's the syllable?

7:07 AM
Alison:
Ha.

7:09 AM
Chelsea:
Soooo things are definitely heating up with Hot
Adam then? 🔥🔥🔥

7:10 AM
Alison:
Anybody could have sent me a Ha!

7:12 AM
Chelsea:
But you're not crowdsourcing your flirty response to
a Ha from just anybody. 😍

7:14 AM
Mara:
She's right. You're fully obsessed.

7:15 AM
Chelsea:
It's cute!! He's SO your Harrison Ford but from
Morning Glory. He's all crabby and difficult.

7:17 AM
Mara:
Chels, he's fully an old man in that movie.

7:19 AM
Chelsea:
Ford at any age CAN GET IT and so can Adam 🔥

7:21 AM
Alison:
Am I the "it" in that scenario?

7:24 AM
Mara:
Does this guy have plans for New Year's Day? Is he
into sports???

7:25 AM
Chelsea:
Al prefers we call him Hot Adam. Give him the
respect he deserves!!

———

Two DAYS GO by without any new texts to or from Adam, and now that it's Wednesday, I wonder if I killed the conversation. Is it my job to resuscitate it with the next text?

I'm feeling socially out of my depth when Daniella asks me to join a presentation in Duluth. Our company works up there enough that this isn't an unprecedented occurrence, but the timing couldn't be more perfect. What better way to resurrect a text conversation than to casually ask for a restaurant recommendation?

> **10:13 AM**
> **Alison:**
> Where does one eat lunch in Duluth?

I wince at my phrasing, but my stupid thumb already pressed send. I watch my phone for dancing dots until I feel sufficiently pathetic. I groan at myself and place my phone face down on my desk. I have enough time to read and respond to one email on traffic patterns near a proposed railway extension before my phone shakes.

> **10:56 AM**
> **Adam:**
> Who is one?

> **10:57 AM**
> **Adam:**
> Is one me?

11:01 AM
Alison:
One is me, obviously. Boss added me to a
presentation in Duluth. 10 AM tomorrow. I usually
stop at Culver's on the way out of town, but now that
I have an inside source, I want to know where to go!

11:02 AM
Alison:
Unless Culver's is the best your city has to offer . . .

When he doesn't instantly respond, I start to type, then delete. I type again. Delete.

The vibration from my phone physically startles me, and I see Josh register it with a smirk out of the corner of my eye.

11:25 AM
Adam:
Thoughts on sandwiches?

11:26 AM
Alison:
Positive.

11:29 AM
Adam:
I can meet you at Corktown Deli at noon

"Ahh!" I drop my phone like it's on fire.

"What's wrong?" Patty asks. Simultaneously, Josh guesses, "More spiders?"

"No. Sorry. I'm fine. It's one of those banner ads with weird toes."

Patty flashes a sympathetic smile. "I'm sorry, hon. I hate those too."

I lower my eyes to my screen, plunging back into my conversation with Adam.

> **11:36 AM**
> **Alison:**
> You don't need to eat with me if you're busy.

> **11:38 AM**
> **Adam:**
> Well, now I want a Reuben, so . . .

> **11:39 AM**
> **Adam:**
> I can eat when you're at your meeting, so we don't run into each other.

> **11:41 AM**
> **Alison:**
> I'm not letting you eat a sad sandwich alone.

> **11:42 AM**
> **Adam:**
> Reubens are happy sandwiches.

> **11:43 AM**
> **Alison:**
> What's the saddest sandwich then?

11:45 AM
Adam:
Tuna salad. No question.

11:46 AM
Alison:
This checks out.

11:47 AM
Alison:
I'd been planning to use "meeting someone for lunch" as an excuse if the meeting drags on, so this'll actually be perfect. You'll make the story more credible.

11:48 AM
Adam:
Good.

————

THE NEXT DAY, I order a Cozy Pig sandwich from the deli counter while I wait for Adam. Every time the door opens, my eyes dart to it.

Adam eventually walks in and juts his chin in my direction. Relief rushes through me. He points to the front counter, and I mouth, *You go order,* while waving my arms in a series of chaotic gestures. We both find our way back to the table with our sandwiches, and though mine looks good, his pastrami Reuben looks better. I wish I knew Adam well enough to ask if we could split the two halves, but I don't. I eat my sandwich and pretend I'm not jealous of his.

I feel him examine my work attire—an inexpensive over-sized black blazer from H&M over a T-shirt—while we make idle chitchat about the weather and highway construction, finding our conversational groove in this new environment. He's changed into clean clothes, but, having come straight from a construction site, his hair still has a bit of dust in it.

"What brought you up here for the day?" he asks around his last bite.

I point at my full mouth and chew a bit more before answering. "I'm a transit consultant. Bus systems, light rail, the occasional heavy rail. I was updating my recommendations to a team working on the high-speed rail from Duluth to the Cities."

"That'd be convenient. When's it happening?" He takes a sip of his soda, his eyes trained on me.

"Soon, but maybe never. I've been working on it in some capacity since I was an intern. Whenever they want to propose a new budget plan, they bring me back in, but then something happens to the funding. We're always very close to 'getting close.' He's my white whale."

"Are trains a he?" His eyes light up with amusement.

"I've always assumed as much. Thomas is, at least."

He tilts his head, considering. "You're right. Percy, James—are all the trains male? How does that work?"

"I wouldn't think too deeply about the anthropomorphism in the land of Sodor. It gets very dark very quickly."

"I can see that." Adam wakes up his phone to check the time. "Do you have to get back?"

"Nah, I took the afternoon off."

"I could show you around a bit?"

I sip my soda. "I should probably go for a hike. My boots

are in my car. I always intend to but can never seem to get myself to do it."

"Such enthusiasm," he says wryly, brushing the crumbs off his hands and onto the parchment paper.

"I'm trying to embrace the outdoors and adventure in general, but it's a bit of a work in progress. Most of the work seems to be forcing myself to enjoy it, and then I feel guilty for not enjoying it, which only makes it feel more forced." I rummage up something that resembles a smile. "But I *want* to enjoy it, so it's worth it."

It's the first time I've tried to put words to the fight within myself. Like an intense camp friendship, Adam's place in my life is necessarily temporary. He makes me feel like I can peel back the layer behind what I want everyone to see: *My life is big and exciting. I'm worthy, I swear!*

Adam stacks our sandwich baskets and buses our table. "Why does everyone romanticize walking uphill without a destination? Unless you're wild for the woods and have nowhere to go, it's a waste of time."

"So you live in northern Minnesota, which is basically a giant forest, and you've never taken a walk in the woods."

He pops a brow. "I go into the woods when I *need* to be in the woods."

"So only when you *must* craft an emergency farmhouse table do you stride into the cedar trees and chop one down with great purpose? How does a LIVE, LAUGH, LOVE sign rank? Is that a *need* or a *want*?"

"Definitely a need. Could you imagine walking into a home that didn't give you explicit permission to live, laugh, and love all at once?"

Is he making a joke? Adam's eyes hold mine, and the laughter that passes between us is sweet and perfect, like a giant Hubba Bubba bubble. I'd give up talking forever if we could stay just like this. But he pops the moment to say, "You don't need to hike if it doesn't make you happy. That sort of defeats the purpose."

It sounds simple when he says it.

I shake my head, wrapping my green wool scarf around my neck. "It's about embracing a better me." He gives me the blankest expression. "You don't get it. You live out here where it's all at your fingertips. If I lived here, I'd totally be my 'best self.'"

"Yeah? What would your 'best self' look like up here?"

I count off on my fingers. "I'd go hiking every day. I'd finally learn to like camping. I'd travel more. I'd befriend a small-town bookstore owner and fall in love with a Christmas tree farmer."

He raises a snarky eyebrow. "So your best life is a pretty bad Hallmark movie?"

"You have a power ranking for Hallmark movies? Adam, you're holding out on me!"

He buttons up a flannel midlayer before pulling on his coat—khaki-side out. "As someone who has lived both in Minneapolis and on the North Shore, trust me, you'd still be you, but on the North Shore. There would be fewer people and a bigger lake, but all of the things that are keeping you from hiking and liking to camp are coming with you. And you'd be two hours from the airport, so you're not traveling more."

"But I wouldn't mind the drive because Duluth Alison is also very competent at meditating."

"Is the guy selling Christmas trees out of a Walgreens parking lot teaching you to meditate too?"

Coming around to my side of the table, Adam plucks my wool jacket from my chair and holds it open before me, like this is something we do. We dress each other. I school my features and slowly extend my arms into my sleeves, aware of his knuckles brushing my shoulders. When both elbows are draped in fabric, he drops my coat, and I shrug it on the rest of the way.

By the time I spin around, he's already facing the window, his forehead tight and unreadable. I let him lead me out of the deli and pass in front of him as he holds open the door. The cold air hits the skin at my collarbone and I'm reminded again of my estranged nipples as Adam and I walk side by side.

Adam tilts his head down toward me as we walk, a small gesture that closes the gap between us by approximately two crucial inches. "I just think you are who you are." He gestures to a beige truck. "This is me."

I resist the urge to lean two more inches closer. Instead, I adjust my scarf to block the oncoming wind. "I know, Adam. I spent a very traumatic day trapped inside it."

His eyes meet mine as he opens the passenger door, directing me toward him like a homing beacon. My legs carry me over before I can second-guess myself. "So are you going to show me the majestic beauty of your city, or what?"

Something resembling delight tugs at his features. "Hiking's out. What is something you've actually wanted to do here?"

I genuinely consider the question as he crosses over to the driver's side. "I've always wanted to ride the Christmas train at the railroad museum."

"Really?" he asks, incredulous.

"Yes." I lower the visor, trying to conceal my embarrassment. "What else am I supposed to want to do here? I've seen Lake Superior, and it's just a moodier Lake Michigan."

He exhales a laugh and pulls on the gearshift. "All right, Thomas. Whatever you like."

"No. That nickname cannot become a thing."

"Fine. Fine. I don't think we can ride the Christmas train this early in the day, but we can see it at the museum."

"You sure you don't mind spending the afternoon at a train museum? It's not too much of a clichéd 'nephew visiting' afternoon in Duluth?"

He pulls forward out of his parking spot and into the foggy street. "I've never taken my nephew there and it seems like a quintessential tourist experience, which I've never been here."

"All right. We'll be tourists together today." I rub my hands together for warmth. "I want 'Duluth Classic.' I'm talking the equivalent of a 'Spoonbridge, Dylan mural, Mall of America, and cap it off with juicy lucys at Hank's' kind of afternoon."

"Hank's is your idea of a quintessential juicy lucy?" His eyes flick over to me.

The juicy lucy—a cheese-stuffed burger patty—is a necessary element of all Minneapolis burger menus. The location of the perfect juicy lucy is hotly contested by those who care deeply about regional restaurant rankings and "best of" listicles.

I wrinkle my nose. "I don't know. It's a disgusting burger. Do you have a favorite? Is that how College Adam spent his days—eating molten-cheese-filled beef patties, burning the roof of his mouth?"

We debate burgers for the short drive to the museum.

"It's comforting. It's supposed to be warm and gooey,"

Adam argues as we hop out of the truck, defending the sto-
ried Midwest tradition of stuffing food in other foods.

"I don't like scalding-hot surprises when I'm seeking
comfort."

"A little heat never hurt anyone." He opens the door to the
French-château-style building, extending his arm out to say,
After you.

"If it's not a burger from The Nook, what's your comfort
food, then?" His question echoes through the grand hall of
the restored Duluth Union Depot, which now houses the
Lake Superior Railroad Museum and manages the operation
of the scenic railroad along the shoreline.

His face holds a sincere intensity that indicates either a
genuine interest in my banal personal trivia or a fierce deter-
mination to steal my identity. I won't know for sure until he
asks for my mother's maiden name or the street I grew up on.

"Personal pan pizza," I answer. "But I have to earn it
through reading chapter books or no dice."

"See, that's what's wrong with the education system in
this country."

"That's what's *right* with it, because now I associate reading with the taste of pepperoni and peppers. Win-win."

I offer to buy my ticket, and he shakes his head at me, main-
taining he'd never make his nephew pay for a big day out.

We walk past the traditional museum artifacts behind glass
displays and into Depot Square, a re-creation of the turn-of-
the-century downtown hubbub, complete with 1920s jazz
music and façades of old-timey storefronts. In the center is a
collection of train cars: steam, electric, diesel, some dating
back to the 1860s.

The two of us wander the grounds, finding a quiet, easy

rhythm. I set the pace, but every so often, Adam feigns interest in a particular caboose component or a dining car table to sell the lie that he's also getting something out of this.

"You might appreciate this one." I gesture toward a nineteenth-century heavyweight passenger car. My voice tiptoes in the echoey space. "Carpenters and coachmakers used to build ornate wood passenger cars like this."

We step up into the car's salon. I watch Adam take in the floor-to-ceiling golden oak wainscoting. Green panels decorate the ceiling, bordered by gold paint in a floral design. Plush velvet couches sit unused, begging for someone in a bustle to sink into them. The car is textured, moneyed, and teeming with energy, like at any moment we'll be kicked out by men in coats and tails looking for a spot to play cards. It's not a relic, just momentarily out of time.

"These are my favorites." My voice is low, like we might disturb the nonexistent passengers.

"Why did they stop making them like this?" He lightly strokes the curved wood molding as though he's not sure he's allowed to but is unable to help himself.

I laugh. "Money. Also, the wood cars are pretty uncomfortable to ride in. Stainless steel cars are much lighter and make a smoother ride, but they're not nearly as luxurious looking."

I allow myself to admire it a little longer before moving toward the exit. Adam follows and offers his hand as I descend onto the platform. His skin is hot on mine, and I hold on a beat longer than I should, averting my eyes when I finally let go.

11

The Green Plaid Scarf

WHEN WE LEAVE the museum, Adam drives through town pointing out previous apartments and storefronts that used to be something else, like an Adam Berg Personal Memories Tour guide.

"So why trains?" he asks.

"Umm, they were faster than horses and could bear weight—"

"Not 'why do trains exist?'" he interrupts, vexed. "You're clearly enthralled by this place in a way that puts all of the 'visiting nephews' we've passed today to shame. Why do you love trains, Alison?"

I tuck a stray curl behind my ear. "Growing up, we had a model train set under our tree. I was always obsessed with it. My dad and I used to work on it together year-round, scouring garage sales for new cars and components."

I was fourteen or fifteen when I realized it was kind of a lame hobby. My sister was thriving in extracurriculars while I was rewatching a DVD of a PBS special on the transcontinental railroad I'd purchased during a pledge drive with my allowance. Early in my high school career, the train set returned to an exclusively Christmas tradition.

"That's why you got into your line of work?" He looks at me with irrepressible interest—like my dorkiest source of enthusiasm is somehow the most enchanting thing about me.

"I sort of fell into it. I had all these useless train facts rattling around in my brain, so when I wrote a paper in my college freshman seminar that was essentially an ode to the Trans-European Railway network, my professor got me into the right program and connected me with an internship that turned into a job. And here we are today." I swivel toward him with a gesture that says *ta-da*.

His lips quirk. I want to make him laugh—an honest, uninhibited, down-to-his-belly laugh. I think it would be something worth seeing.

"I'm surprised you wound up here." He tilts his head to indicate the Upper Midwest. "And not Europe or somewhere with more trains."

My eyes wander out the window toward the dark, hypnotic swells of Lake Superior. "I like it here, and I like my job, even if it feels a bit Sisyphean at times."

My interest in transportation was never rooted in wanderlust or a desire to escape. Part of what I like about trains is that they're literally tethered to the ground, part of its landscape. Planes make the world feel smaller, but trains remind me that the world has always been big. They connect you to people all over the continent while still granting you permission to pick your favorite corner of it and build a small, simple life there—only to roam exactly when you want or need to.

"But I'm up for a new job. A promotion, actually. It's the next step in a career like mine."

He tilts his head in my direction, eyes dancing between me and the road. "You don't want it."

Self-conscious laughter springs from my chest. "What makes you say that?"

"You're doing your people-pleaser face," he answers, matter-of-fact.

I rear back. "I don't have a people-pleaser face."

"You most definitely have a people-pleaser face. You do it with the Lewises and Russell—"

"And you?"

He shakes his head. "Not so much. You don't seem to care what I think about you."

"That's for sure." I stare out the window at the passing storefronts before I bite, purely out of morbid curiosity. "So what's this people-pleaser face look like anyway?"

His hint of a smile is more cocky than happy. "Your eyes empty out and then your top lip curls up a little in this fake smile—"

I cover my mouth. "Stop looking at my lips."

This earns me another tiny smile. They're getting addictive. "Why can't I look at your lips?"

Because then I'll look at your lips, and I'll wonder what they feel like. I'll wonder if you're picturing the same thing, and this harmless attraction will stop feeling harmless.

"It's useful in moments like this. To identify the people-pleaser face," he says, activating his blinker to change lanes. "I know whatever you say next is something you think you're supposed to say, or what someone wants you to say, or what you—"

"Fine." I let out a swoosh of air, returning to the start of this dangerous thread I shouldn't have pulled. "I'm not sure about the job. I'd spend less time thinking about trains and more time thinking about parking lots."

"It never occurred to me that someone's out there thinking about parking lots in a professional capacity."

"Parking is a very complicated problem." I feel my spine stiffen in defensiveness—even though I too find parking lots fairly soul crushing.

"It doesn't have to be your problem. Not if you like what you're doing now."

"It's the right next move in my career."

"Says who?" he asks, puzzled by my logic. "You shouldn't do anything you don't want to do."

"Is that how you live your life? Doing only what you want?"

"No." He shifts in his seat. "But I don't do anything I *don't* want to do."

We fall into silence until he gestures across me with his arm, his other hand still tapping against the steering wheel. "I live down this street. My workshop is in the garage."

"Oh, yeah? Let's see that."

He turns to me briefly from the driver's side in genuine surprise. "Really?"

"You've pointed out three restaurants that used to be different restaurants you liked better. Of course I'd rather see your workshop. At least it's something from present-day Duluth." He considers me at a stoplight. "Please, Adam. I can't leave Duluth without getting my peepers on some spindles."

"Don't say *peepers*," he says on a weary exhale. Then he turns right.

We park in the driveway of a peeling yellow bungalow. He quickly hops around to the passenger side, grabbing my hand to lower me out of his truck. When my feet hit the craggy pavement, I have to consciously remind myself to drop his hand this time. I'm relieved when all goes as planned.

With a low grunt, he pulls up the garage door and the smell of cut wood hits me like a wall. He sends me a quick, uneasy half smile before tugging the string attached to a lightbulb.

Illuminated in the garage are dozens of unfinished pieces of furniture. I see stools that might become chairs, upturned side tables with four different table legs, and a sideboard that has one door with slats and one door with a wood herring-bone pattern.

Despite the confusing design choices, his skill is evident in each piece. Each component on its own is intricate, delicate, and flawless, highlighting the imperfect beauty of the wood.

"You made all of this?" I ask, unable to hide my astonishment.

"Yeah. It's not that great. Nothing's done. I've been trying out different techniques and styles. I want a collection that showcases what I can do before starting a business in a slightly larger market like Minneapolis. I went down the investor route but . . ." He looks away from me, kneading the nape of his neck. Wood shavings cover everything like a dusting of snow. Next to a belt sander are Sam's cabinets, stripped and sanded down to their original raw wood.

"The plan is to build up a client base eventually—do custom pieces—but I've been tinkering for a while."

"How long's a while?"

"Around six years," he hedges.

"That *is* a while." I walk around the upturned tables. "And all while listening to faux-eighties horror soundtracks." I pull a face of mock terror.

"This morning, I was listening to John Carpenter."

I waggle my eyebrows. "Ooh. The pure, unfiltered stuff. What's with the horror movie music?" I ask, leisurely wandering his garage and admiring his skilled craftsmanship.

The space smells like him—well, part of him. Maybe the inside of his house smells like oranges.

He leans into the frame of the garage door, his eyes following me as I invade his space. "It fades into the background and becomes part of the environment."

"A terrifying environment."

"That's what I like about it. It's immersive. It's impossible to listen to it without having a physical response."

"I could see that." I run my finger along a smooth tabletop. "Can I order a custom piece?"

"Like a table or something?"

"I'd like a wall rack for hanging hiking and climbing gear. Maybe it could have a shelf above it? If I had all of my outdoorsy stuff out in front of me, I'd have no excuse not to use it. Like how the hardest part of working out is getting the clothes on."

"That's not accurate."

I dismiss his comment with a flick of my hand and examine a grouping of furniture. "It's an expression. I like whatever style this is best." I point to one side of an upturned coffee table.

"I like this one best, too." He scrubs his beard with his hand but it doesn't hide his smile.

I love being the source of that smile.

"It's beautiful. It's not too fussy, but it has clean lines and complements the wood grain. It's like high-end IKEA."

"Oh, god!" he chokes. He pushes his hands through his hair, clearly scandalized by my comparison.

"I don't know what I'm saying." I tug his hand down, laughter bubbling out of both of us. "I oversold my spindle expertise earlier."

"You talked a big game."

"I'm sorry." I squeeze his hand, my giggles teetering over into a full-on fit. "I take it back. I take it back!"

Water presses into the corners of my eyes, and our giddy gazes tangle together. The light of the bulb refracts off the warm richness of his brown irises—there's a knotty tone and texture to them I've never noticed before—but then he blinks and steps away from me, toward his truck.

"It's getting late, Alison."

By the time Adam drives me back to the deli, the sun has started to set. He parks in the same spot we started in, and I offer a stiff wave goodbye from the passenger seat. When I hop down, I see him trudging toward me from the other side.

It seems that he's walking me to my car.

So now we're trapped in one of those awkward moments where you say goodbye but then have to walk in the same direction—except he *chose* to do this to us, which only intensifies the discomfort. I keep opening my mouth to make idle chitchat, but nothing comes out. My vision drifts to a municipal employee wrapping twinkle lights around a streetlamp, and I smile. Is there any inconvenient feeling a twinkle light can't fix?

Adam clears his throat. "In a couple of weeks, there's this massive Christmas display on the water." He points to the banner on the light pole advertising the BENTLEYVILLE TOUR OF LIGHTS: 4 MILLION+ LIGHTS! "It's the largest one like it in the country."

"I don't think I'll be coming up for work again for a while."

I don't know why I say it. I know he's not asking me on a date, but this walk back to my car feels suspiciously date-adjacent. My insides are shimmering with sweet, anticipatory end-of-a-great-date feelings. Maybe that's why I think the moment demands clarity.

He looks between my face and the street like somewhere in the space between us he'll find something else to say.

I point at my Subaru. "This is my car," I say, pouncing on the quiet, because old habits die hard. Still, the relief in his eyes is palpable. Giddiness bubbles and fizzes in my stomach at the sight.

"It's a good car for this climate. Do you have snow tires?" He cringes before he finishes speaking, so I know Adam also hears that he sounds like a robot learning passable small talk.

"I do, but I haven't scheduled the appointment yet." What is this conversation? "Okay. I'm going to go now. Thanks for showing me the sights."

Adam doesn't move. The strangeness of this exchange paired with our proximity spikes adrenaline in my blood. How do normal people end interactions with acquaintances they feel a sparking tension with?

I lean in for a hug, and he accepts, his strong arms fully

committing long enough for dopamine to release into my system. It's a lovely, solid hug—warm and firm. I catch a whiff of his familiar scent. Now that I've smelled its source, more notes of his complicated aroma unravel in my nose, like deconstructing a recipe of an indulgent treat.

When he releases me, he doesn't walk away. Instead, his hands go to my arms as he tilts his head sideways. I think our coats are still touching.

His brown eyes travel down my face and land on the green plaid scarf over my jacket, then lift back to mine. This close, I can admire the flecks of gold I discovered under the lights of his workshop. The way he looks at me tickles my ribs.

Too soon, he returns his gaze to the scarf. I'm perfectly positioned to examine the length of his curly eyelashes until slowly—so slowly—his hands move to my scarf. His fingers still and I hold my breath, waiting to see what he'll do. My lips tingle with anticipation and the bitter cold.

Finally, he gently straightens the wool fabric. His right forefinger makes the slightest swipe against the sensitive part of my neck, my pulse thrumming beneath it. He might not have noticed his effect on me if not for my sharp intake of breath.

"That's better," he breathes. His eyes pin me, examining me like a piece of wood, and I can't tell if he sees striking potential or a problem to be solved. They dart to my mouth, only for a second, before he takes a step back.

Every one of my nerve endings—even the damaged ones—lights up like a strand of twinkle lights, but before I'm able to form words again, he's walking away.

12

The Sky's the Limit

THE HEAT'S ON the fritz at work the next morning, so I opt to leave my coat on. When I move to uncoil my scarf, I hesitate, unwrapping it from my neck carefully, like I might find a bit of Adam wrapped inside like a gift. I only find the last flecks of glitter from Chelsea's holiday concert. I shiver off lingering memories of Adam's fingers on my skin.

Since the scarf-touch yesterday, my fingers have been itching for an excuse to text Adam. It's normal to casually text a friend in the middle of a workday for no reason other than wanting to hear how their day is going, right? Friends do that. And Adam is my friend. My attractive friend. My friend who stared into my eyes in a charged goodbye that ended in a feather-light neck graze I'm trying not to think about.

My group chat saves me from compulsively texting Adam an out-of-the-blue "Hey!" like a crushing dweeb.

8:32 AM

Mara:

Why did Patrick send me a formal text breaking up with our trivia team??!!??!!??!!

8:33 AM
Mara:
Chelsea!?

8:35 AM
Chelsea:
It's not my fault! Patrick and Josie are focusing on
their relationship right now without distractions.

8:38 AM
Alison:
She called you a distraction?

8:41 AM
Chelsea:
Just trivia, but I think I was implied.

8:44 AM
Chelsea:
I have to go. The children are here, and they're
forming a mutiny. 🗡️

A text notification from Adam interrupts the group chat,
and I should be mortified by how I beam at it.

8:55 AM
Adam:
Do you like this stain for the cabinets?

A picture of Adam's arm holding a finished cabinet door
in the morning light of his driveway fills my screen. The stain

is light and natural. The warm wood tone juxtaposed with
the cabinet's large, modern shape and chunky, matte black
hardware looks so contemporary-cozy I'm overwhelmed with
the urge to make a potato kale soup.

> **8:56 AM**
> **Adam:**
> Everyone likes white, because it photographs well,
> but I think this will look better in Sam's place.

My chest smarts. We spent yesterday talking about everything other than Sam. It was as if we were becoming more
than forced partners in a funereal task. Or maybe that's what
I wanted to believe.

And then there was the way he looked at me. The way his
finger grazed my neck. The way it seemed like he wanted
to—

Whatever this is, or can't be, doesn't dampen the harmless
delight of talking to Adam.

> **8:57 AM**
> **Alison:**
> I love it! It's perfect.

> **8:57 AM**
> **Adam:**
> Good because I stained them all last night.

> **8:58 AM**
> **Alison:**
> What would you have done if I'd said no?

8:59 AM
Adam:
Nothing.

9:01 AM
Alison:
I see how it is.

Adam doesn't respond for the rest of the morning no matter how frequently I check my phone. When I can't stall any longer for my meeting with Daniella, I walk into her office and immediately relax at the sight of a half-full green juice.

Though she's a mostly even-keeled boss, an eleven thirty a.m. meeting with Daniella can get dicey. A slave to efficiency, she regularly exercises during lunch, relying on juices and powders for sustenance. On cardio days, she fasts until one p.m. to avoid reflux, and at eleven thirty a.m., she's not always at her cheeriest. But today is a strength-training day, so I enter with a little extra confidence.

"Patty mentioned you have reservations about moving into her role with private developer accounts. Now, I don't have much time before Pilates, so forgive me, I'm getting right down to brass tacks." Daniella takes a long slurp of her green juice. Her dark hair doesn't move from its severe, sleek pony. "When you were a young girl in STEM, dreaming of your future, what did you imagine?"

I sink into the modern chair in front of her desk and shrink by approximately a foot. "I think I wanted to build trains."

Her forehead creases. "Hm. I didn't expect that. The rest of this speech works better if you wanted something more enterprising." She sits up in her chair, waving her hand like she's testing the wind direction. "It's fine. I'll pivot. When I wanted to level up in my career, I identified where the money was coming in, and I put myself at the center of it. That's where I want to see you, Alison. At this firm, local government contracts aren't keeping the lights on. Do you want to be the one poring over spreadsheets and modeling transit plans or do you want to be managing the people doing those things?"

I like and admire Daniella, but I'm also vaguely terrified of her, so, under her scrutiny, I grab on to my cushioned seat, feigning a more assertive, powerful posture. Adam's words from yesterday about focusing on what I want—or at least avoiding the things I don't want—buzz in my mind. "I've never seen myself as the corporate-ladder type."

"Then maybe you should reevaluate the way you see yourself. Dream big, Mullally! The sky's the limit."

Behind Daniella's right shoulder is a motivational typography art poster that says exactly that. I wonder if she bought it because she's always been able to say "The sky's the limit!" without irony or if this poster has incepted her over time. The one to her left reads DO THE NEEDFUL, and I thank the god of corporate jargon she didn't incorporate that particular catchphrase in our one-on-one.

"I don't want to pressure you, but I want this tied up by the end of Q-four." She nods, and I'm dismissed.

I check my phone on my way to my desk like a woman possessed, and to both my delight and terror, I've missed a phone call from Adam. Not even my close friends call me unless something's terribly wrong, but something about Adam's no-nonsense persona tells me he might be the kind of guy who uses the phone.

I wanted to hear your voice, I imagine him saying in his low, gruff way and instantly shiver.

I, on the other hand, am not the type of woman who calls, due to modern socialization.

> **11:38 AM**
> **Alison:**
> Sorry I missed your call. I was in a meeting.

> **11:43 AM**
> **Adam:**
> Didn't mean to call. Sorry.

My mouth raspberries as I deflate into my office chair. What was I thinking? Giving in to "happiness" and nursing a crush on a man I met through my ex-boyfriend—an ex whom, despite his death, I'm somehow dating? Again?

My phone illuminates on my desk in my peripheral vision.

> **11:46 AM**
> **Adam:**
> What was the meeting about? How to make your job more appealing to Hallmark writers?

I snort. Warmth floods through me almost like our historic building's heat is working properly.

> **11:47 AM**
> **Alison:**
> No, that's my presentation on Monday.

11:49 AM
Adam:
You have way more presentations in your line of work
than I do.

11:51 AM
Alison:
That's it. I'm quitting to become a carpenter.
Hallmark will write a movie about my move to a small
town to open a bespoke cabinet shop to save the
town Christmas parade, and in doing so, its very soul!
It'll be called *A Cabinet for Christmas.*

11:54 AM
Adam:
I feel like you think I build a single cabinet from
sunup to sundown.

11:55 AM
Alison:
You do in MY Christmas movie.

13

The North Shore Grump Has Left the Chat

ON SATURDAY, ADAM reassembles the kitchen cabi-nets while I pack up the last of Sam's overcrowded closets. We work in companionable silence, except I'm hyperaware of every time our bodies nearly brush against each other.

I don't remember the last time I felt this crazy, like I needed to catalog and dissect every tiny, nearly imperceptible look. After he licks his lips and glances at me before settling his gaze on a cabinet hinge, I spend five minutes deciphering the series of movements. Following an embarrassing amount of deliberation, I decide that if he'd looked at me and *then* licked his lips, it would've meant something. As it stands, he must've had a dry mouth while glancing in my direction.

In the afternoon, he holds the stepladder behind me. I stiffen, studying the feel of his shadow around me for my data analysis. It's pure insanity from sunup to sundown as the pre-occupations of a boy-crazy sixteen-year-old ping-pong around my skull.

In an absolute travesty, we end the day with a noncommittal, one-armed hug. Still, the familiar scent of cedar and oranges unravels me into the door frame.

Sunday morning is a different story. I wake up to a calendar alert—drafted by me, not the ghost of boyfriends past—reminding me of my annual appointment with my breast surgeon at noon. Still, I won't let it dampen my mood, because Sunday is another day I get to see Adam.

I drive into Minneapolis at a snail's speed as icy flakes travel across my windshield in sideways gusts. Color has leached from my knuckles by the time I turn into Sam's parking entrance with a student-driver level of edginess.

"Hello?" I holler once I've trudged through Sam's propped-open door. The sharp scent of paint primer in the air, I cautiously step around boxes clutching the Starbucks drink carrier Adam's come to expect. "If you're a robber, my dad's Liam Neeson," I yell.

"So it's Alison Neeson?" Adam spies me from a ladder in the living room, where he's hard at work spackling over divots in the walls. His pants are slung low on his hips and splotched with different tones of wood stain and paint. His gray long-sleeve has fared a bit better, with only the occasional splatter of white paint. "I've been wondering," he says, biting back a smile.

"Mullally, actually. The Liam Neeson thing was a clever ruse."

Before I can blather on, he pushes up the sleeves of his shirt to reveal the forearms that haunt my dreams. Or maybe this gesture is not for my benefit at all, and he's just warm.

Now I'm warm. I need those hands on me for no other reason than to puncture the tension building between us and free up my brain space for necessary functions. Maybe, if I knew what it felt like to have him touch me—really touch me—I'd stop obsessing over the unknown.

"I can finally change your last name in my phone," he says, interrupting my thoughts.

"What's my last name now?"

I've once or twice saved a man's contact as Peter Good-Hair or Jordan HotFace. My skin tingles in anticipation of the descriptor Adam's used for me.

"SamGF."

The simple statement sucks the air out of the room. Or at least out of me.

He drops the spackling knife and climbs down the ladder. "I saved your contact a while ago. We were on that group chat for the Patagonia trip."

"I remember," I say coolly, removing my coat and juggling the drink carrier.

"You sounded excited about it back then. It didn't seem like you were faking."

I set the drink carrier down on the kitchen island. "I wasn't faking. I was trying. I still am trying. I *should* go on a trip like that. Everyone should." I'm suddenly exhausted and the day's hardly begun.

"*I'm* not going on a trip like that."

"Yes. I believe your response was 'Absolutely not.' Then the North Shore Grump left the chat. A big loss for us all."

"North Shore Grump?"

With the coatrack packed away, I shove my coat over Adam's on the closet doorknob. "You know, because of your geographic location and economy of words."

He crosses the room to the kitchen. "Did I say something wrong?"

Yes! Not only did you point out how I'm failing in my relentless quest toward self-improvement, you also reminded me that, to you, I'm Sam's Current Girlfriend. Possibly forever.

His forehead crinkles in confusion like he's a scolded puppy. I can't help it; I paste on a smile and choose the path of least resistance. "Of course not."

He looks at me in a way I feel in my toes before he lifts one finger and traces the corner of my lip. Then he asks, his voice so low I almost miss it, "Why do you think I want to hear that?"

I inhale, I think. My brain is goo.

"No reason," I tell him once he's dropped his hand. "What do I need to do today?"

He looks around the apartment. Most of it is packed. Aside from the boxes crowding the entry, the place looks cold and bare, like we've puttied over any evidence of the existence of Sam.

"While I prep the walls, can you box up the corner bookcase? I'll drop it off at the Lewises' later today."

Tension grips my shoulders. I've been avoiding the bookcase, and today—Yearly BRCA Appointment Day—it's the very last place I want to be. This bookcase is Sam's life. It's his favorite books, photos, trinkets, and souvenirs. It's proof of a short life well lived. Even looking at it feels intrusive.

I exhale loudly. Theatrically. The baiting way you breathe when you're daring someone to notice how undone you are so you can bite their head off.

"You okay?" Adam asks.

"I'm fine."

"Okay . . ." He walks back to his ladder, clearly confused and hurt.

I walk to my corner and face Sam's bookcase. I have to drag a bar stool from the kitchen to reach the top, but I start there. It's adorned with trinkets that have never made it to his social media feed: faded Polaroids, seashells, a cracked gas station key chain, a stack of handwritten journals, and a receipt for auto-body repair written in Spanish.

I'm struck by how meaningless it all looks to me. I've seen the selfies he's shared of all these places, but these shelves are packed with the bits he wanted to remember—just himself.

Sometime between the breakup and his death, I reduced all of Sam down to a label to be neatly filed away: *that time I was dumped by a travel influencer.* The items on this shelf prove he was so much more than that.

Sam was living his life for himself. Sure, certain poses and pictures monetized a rosy-hued snapshot, but there's no evidence of that on these shelves. Here, he kept the memories of what he truly experienced.

What this shelf reveals is how disingenuous *I* was about him. He was looking for someone to share the real parts of the adventure with. I wanted him to make my life the highlight reel. Guilt buzzes under my skin like a bee trapped behind a curtain.

Sorting these mementos isn't the issue—it's all "Keep"—but I don't know how long these things will sit in a box when I'm done. Will Sam's family immediately take out every item, discussing their memories with each small token? Or will the box sit in a basement for years until someone opens it in search of something in particular, only to slam it shut to hold the painful ghost of grief at bay? I feel like I owe it to Sam to witness it all—one last time—before it gets packed away.

I reach into a small ceramic bowl and pull out a few coins

from other countries and a piece of plastic. My heart clenches when I recognize a chip from Mystic Lake Casino, because I have its mate somewhere in my jewelry box.

He told me a ludicrous story of getting drunk with bikers at a casino in Macau on our third date. *I've never gambled before,* I told him. So on our fourth date, he took me to the local casino.

I bet twenty dollars on a card game I didn't know how to play and lost it all. We played penny slots for the afternoon, and before we left, he handed me one of his last two $1 chips and said, *We'll each hold on to one—for bail money.*

Now I sit on the floor with Sam's chip. He was so sure I could live a life as free and untethered as his if I *wanted* it. When I met Sam, I was certain he was exactly what my small life needed. I thought I wanted my world to get brighter, bigger, and scarier, but I wasn't brave enough to hold on to that light. Or I didn't want it enough. Or maybe I wasn't worthy of it.

I do everything it takes to keep from crying. I don't get to cry over this. Remembering is the absolute least I can do.

My phone beeps, reminding me of my appointment. Two and a half hours have passed in a blink while I've hardly made a dent. I put the chip back in the dish and walk toward the front door.

"I have to go," I say, facing the closet. My coat hugs Adam's over the doorknob. It's denim-side out today, and a grin clambers up my face in spite of my mood.

"Where do you have to go?" he asks from his perch.

I pull on my boring, one-sided black coat. "I have a doctor's appointment."

"On a Sunday?"

"Is that a problem?" My tone slices, but I don't have the energy to dull its hard edge.

"Is this about the name in my phone?"

My cheeks flush. Thank god I'm not looking at him. I don't need my face giving me away, and I don't want to see his either. I don't need the confirmation of how one-sided my feelings are.

But the anxiety building up my spine—that feeling that my brain will peel away from my body if I don't get out—isn't just about him. It's about me. Sam. Everything.

It's like you're pretending to be someone else.

I shake it off. "I don't know what you mean, but I'll be back later."

"Don't worry about it." He sounds more casual than rude, but it still cuts.

I open my mouth to say something—apologize?—but I roll my lips between my teeth and walk out the door.

———

ONE SUNDAY PER month, Dr. Steinberg sees post-mastectomy patients like me for routine checkups. She says it's to allow flexibility for her patients' schedules, but I suspect we're merely an excuse to get out of attending travel hockey tournaments with her husband and two sons. She confirms my theory by waxing poetic on the transcendent silence of an empty house.

Seated on the exam table, I open my gown at the front and watch Dr. Steinberg grope my right breast clinically. Like most breast cancer–adjacent spaces, the room's decor falls on the pink spectrum somewhere between baby and millennial.

I feel the pressure of her touch on my breastbone and the

sharp chill of the clinic air on my exposed arms and stomach. She moves over to my left and repeats the process, her face as vacant as always. I focus on the wall behind her, my attention drifting between an aggressively inoffensive watercolor and a mammogram infographic.

Dr. Steinberg stands as I close my gown. "Everything feels good. Scars look good." Dr. Steinberg doesn't do small talk, but that's never bothered me. I like my clinicians clinical. She rolls across the vinyl floor in her desk chair, and her brows curve inward at the text on her computer screen. "Do you have a plan for the ovarian risk? I can provide a referral."

"I'm seeing someone at Fairview. I'm getting regular ultra-sounds for now until I decide what to do with them."

She rises and offers a nod, like she's checking off a mental bulleted list of bedside manners, as she makes her way to the door. "Good. See you in a year."

I put my clothes back on and walk out of the clinic without looking at anyone. My mom prefers me to call right after my appointments, but I don't feel up for it. Instead, I punch out a dismissive text.

12:45 PM
Alison:
Went great. Phone dying. Call you later.

When I press send—and toss the fully charged lie on the passenger seat—my eyes snag on the sign planted between my car and the navy minivan beside me.

The yearly exam is not what I dread. It's parking in the spaces reserved for patients of the breast cancer clinic, know-ing I *should* have gotten cancer but probably won't because of an unlucky break for my mom. It's knowing my doctor will ask me about my ovaries and I won't have an answer. It's having to call my family and talk BRCA. Again.

I turn my key in the ignition, and the speakers blare "The Christmas Shoes"—the worst and most manipulative holiday song ever written. It's the final insult. I look in my rearview mirror, grab the headrest of the passenger seat, and step on the gas.

Before I have time to react, my car lurches forward, up over the curb and into a snowbank. I slam on the brake and look down at the gearshift to find confirmation that the car's in drive, not reverse.

My Subaru rests on the mound of snow piled directly in front of my former parking spot. I try to reverse, but my car bellows into the snow like a beached whale. I turn off my engine and dramatically rest my head on the steering wheel like a Christmas movie heroine at her lowest point. And yet, a Christmas tree farmer doesn't save me. Chelsea does.

I'm not the only one making snowy road mistakes today, but I suspect mine was the most preventable. Chelsea's uncle Ricky can tow my car to his nearby shop. Since I'm not one of the poor souls blocking traffic or trapped in a ditch, I'm placed at the end of the queue. I definitely won't make it back to Adam today.

I walk back to the doctor's office lobby, pulling my glove off to text him.

1:07 PM
Alison:
Car trouble. Won't make it back.

1:08 PM
Adam:
Are you okay?

1:10 PM
Alison:
Fine. Drove into a snowbank.

Immediately after I press send, Adam calls me.

"Where are you?" his tinny voice asks as soon as I pick up—no greetings.

I fill my voice with all of the faux cheeriness I can muster. I won't let him worry. "I'm fine. I drove into the snowplow pile in the parking lot of my doctor's office."

"I thought you were lying about going to the doctor."

"I wasn't, but now I have to wait for the tow truck." I yank on the locked front door of my doctor's office. "And my doctor left, so I'm in for a long afternoon while I wait outside in the cold or in a car that's mid-takeoff. Perfect."

"Where are you?" Something honks in the background.

"Are you in your car?" I ask past him.

"I dropped some stuff off at the Lewises'. I'm leaving Excelsior now. Where are you?" he repeats more urgently.

"Adam, no. You don't need to do that."

"I'm not leaving you in the cold to wait for a tow truck. I'll wait with you. It'll be fun." He says the word *fun* with the flattest and most unconvincing affect.

I tuck my scarf into the front of my coat and brush against my icy boob. "I'm not super fun right now."

"Perfect, I'm never fun." This makes me laugh, and I swear I can hear him trying not to smile through the phone.

"What if I bring sandwiches? I can't leave you like this. It's too pathetic." Now I'm certain I hear a smirk in his voice, and I smile to no one like an idiot.

"Pathetic?" I repeat. His chuckle pings against my ear, and I relent. "Fine. I want a happy salad."

I know our time together has an expiration date, but I can't help stretching every moment out as much as possible. I want to believe he is too—shouldn't we be done with the condo by now?—but that might be my one-sided crush talking.

"No such thing, but I'll figure it out." A turn signal clicks on his side of the line. "Send me your address."

Crap. "Um. I'll drop a pin."

14

The Flaw in the Design

FIFTEEN MINUTES LATER, Adam pulls into the parking lot of the Susanna Swann Breast Cancer Center and parks next to my skyward SUV. I climb into the passenger side of his truck and close the door behind me. I know what his question is when he faces me, and his warm, dark eyes beg me not to make him ask.

My hands lift defensively. "I'm perfectly healthy. I don't have cancer."

"Does your cancer doctor see a lot of perfectly healthy people on Sundays?" His voice is stiff, and worry etches the lines of his face. His hair is stuck up like he's been nervously pulling at it at every intersection. If I hadn't been staring at that jaw for the past two weekends, I might not have noticed that, right now, it's clenched.

"Yes. Exclusively."

He shuts his eyes. I can't believe I ever saw his face as stiff and unreadable. It's so expressive when you know what you're looking for. Reaching over, I smooth the creases in his forehead with my hand. His breath deepens and slows. His reaction would be proof of something if we were anyone else, anywhere else.

I pull my hand away and sit back in my seat, and he leans away too.

"I have the breast cancer genetic mutation, BRCA1. But I don't have cancer." I blurt the second sentence again for emphasis. I've learned this particular health disclosure requires that frequent reminder.

I take a breath. "You know how Angelina Jolie—" I cut myself off when I realize Adam is likely as familiar with her BRCA journey as he is with the Kardashian offspring.

"Most people have tumor-suppressing genes, but mine don't work. I'm okay now, though. I got a preventative double mastectomy where they removed my breast tissue, and I went from probably getting breast cancer to probably not. So, again, I don't have cancer, despite what the building suggests. I still screen for ovarian cancer until I remove my ovaries, but the risk is only about forty-five percent over my lifetime." I rub at my forehead, clumsily telling Adam in a few sentences what took years to come to terms with and months to recover from.

"That's like a coin flip."

"It doesn't work like that. The risk increases as I get older. I have a little time to decide what to do next, but, yeah, I need to remove my ovaries eventually."

"What would that mean?"

I like that he doesn't ask me when I'm planning to remove them, what my game plan is, or if it's what I want, because the answers are: possibly soonish; I don't know; and of course not, but my genetics don't fit with my personal desires.

He only wants to know what it would *mean* for me, how

it would make me feel to be a single, nippleless woman in her thirties taking hormone replacement medication to stave off the side effects of a self-induced menopause.

"It means . . . I have a lot of decisions to make. But it could be so much worse. Other women with BRCA get breast cancer. My mom did, but now she's healthy, thank god. So it's not like I can be angry or sad about cheating death."

"I'm not sure it works like that. You feel what you feel." Adam moves closer to me, deliberately this time. There's only a wisp of air separating our knees. His eyes have a weight to them that presses me against the passenger window. I swallow.

"Why didn't you tell me what your appointment was for?" He's not accusing me of withholding anything, just curious about the way and why of me, because all of a sudden, we're not some guy and his best friend's current girlfriend. We're something else entirely, and I'm not sure when that happened or if I could stop it if I tried.

When Adam and I were strangers, the detail that Sam had dumped me felt inconsequential. Now it feels important and too late to set him straight. Would it change anything? Would he understand? Would he even care?

"It's not a secret," I answer, smoothing my coat. "But it's something I haven't figured out how to share."

It's true. I never spit it out quick enough, and I watch the emotions pass over the person's face—*But, honey, you're so young,* and when they understand I don't have cancer and feel foolish, *What kind of person allows someone to think they have cancer for even a moment?*

"And then you'd do the thing people do where they indiscreetly stare at my boobs, searching for the flaw in the design."

"Men do that to you?" Adam's eyebrows fly upward.

"Everyone does that to me." I see Adam work to keep his eyes on my face. "You're doing it right now!"

"Only because you brought it up like a challenge. It's like daring me not to think about elephants. It's impossible."

"Likely story, perv."

Shocked, Adam laughs. It's a nice laugh. His whole face brightens, and the low sound rumbles through the truck cab. His happiness vibrates on my skin.

His eyes meet mine, and for a moment, I think he's leaning toward me and closing the space between us. Then he clears his throat, and I lean back—the spell broken.

Adam points himself forward. "I'm guessing Sam knew."

I nod. "Mara and Chelsea think if not for the surgery, Sam and I never would've gotten together."

"How's that?"

"After my recovery, I wanted someone who would push me to live life. I wanted to be more adventurous, outdoorsy, and extroverted. Sam's lazy Sunday was mountain biking in the morning and a raucous barbecue at the lake in the afternoon. He was the human embodiment of exposure therapy." I smile at the memory of my wild and wonderful friend.

"Why do you want to change so much?" he asks, his eyes pinning me in place.

"Near-death experiences *should* change people. Workaholic stockbrokers survive plane crashes and quit to start nonprofits. Cancer survivors become triathletes. I was supposed to have this near-death moment, and I skipped it— mitigated it out of existence—and instead of whatever relief or cosmic insight I would've gotten, there's just . . ." I press my hand to my heart, where the ache prods me. "A life-altering diagnosis *should* alter you. I shouldn't go 'back to normal' after this. I have to make my life mean something."

My left hand fusses with the silicone lining of the cup-holder, but then Adam places his hand over mine, stilling me. His calloused palm burns my skin.

We're both quiet for a moment, like we only have so many words left and the wrong ones in the wrong combination could cost us. Finally, he breaks the silence to say, "You mean something, Alison." My knuckles flex up against his until he gently removes his hand from mine. "Sam pushed me like that too, you know. Mostly in a good way. I was so uncomfortable during my freshman year of college. I was sure I didn't fit in and everyone could see it when I walked into a room. But Sam liked me, and I felt, uh, chosen, I guess. But things changed when we got older. Sam always wanted me to be more like him. He wanted me to risk everything for a half-baked carpentry business, but I had bills and responsibilities. He'd say I was making excuses, but I was never bold enough for him."

"We don't talk much about you and Sam."

Adam clears his throat, but I wait.

"I try not to think about him too much," he finally says. "We'd been drifting apart for a while. He'd always stop by on his way somewhere else, and I'd see him when I was visiting my family, but it wasn't like how we used to be. He was obsessed with my business and when I was moving. We fought about it the last time I saw him."

He closes his eyes. I don't rush to fill the silence. I hold it. Protect it.

"That day, he was so insistent about me starting my company and moving back. He'd tried to get me to rush my plans before, but those conversations had always been like 'Move in with me, man! It'll be epic!'" I can hear Sam's voice in my head when Adam says it. "This was different. He was . . . frustrated. He said I was in a rut, and he wasn't going to watch me stand still anymore. He pointed out everything he wanted me to change. My job, my life, my relationships—or lack thereof. I told him to shove it, and we argued. My last words to him were passive-aggressive directions to a scenic lookout point. But we were supposed to meet up for New Year's, so I just thought we'd figure it out by then. He was planning to set me up at his party with some girl who was 'perfect for me,' and I was already strategizing how to blow it off."

My heart is in my throat. Even though we'd stayed friendly, Sam never invited me to a New Year's party, and I can't stand to hear about some perfect girl for Adam that isn't me—yet another heavy presence between us.

"I remember feeling so relieved he was leaving. I remember thinking, *This is so exhausting. He's so exhausting.* You must think I'm a monster."

"No. Not at all." I clasp his right hand in both of mine. I want to imbue my touch with a small glimpse of how much I think of him. Not enough to give me away, but enough to show I could never see him as a monster.

His eyes tangle with mine, and I'm sure he's going to pull his hand away. Instead, he threads our fingers together.

"I thought he and I would have time to figure it out. Or maybe not. Maybe I was ready to let the friendship go, but now he's gone for real, and I feel so awful." The apple in his throat bobs. "At the funeral, Mrs. Lewis kept calling me Sam's best friend. I kept thinking, *That can't be true.* He deserved someone better than me. That's why I've wanted to take care of everything. I think I thought this condo thing could be some sort of messed-up penance for being a horrible friend."

"Is it working?" I ask.

He doesn't answer. I open my mouth to tell him he's not alone in those feelings of trying to be someone else for Sam's family. We have so much more in common than he knows.

But I forget how to form words when his roughened thumb starts to draw circles on my skin, and goose bumps cascade up the surface of my arm, spreading across my body in waves. I've nearly lost myself in the simple pleasure of holding hands when he asks, "When's the tow truck coming?"

I shake my head and reflexively grab for my phone: a thirty-something's comfort object. I pretend to scroll through text messages before answering. "Soon, I'm sure."

The loss of his touch leaves me cold.

Not for the first time, I wish I knew what I wanted from Adam. There are a million reasons I shouldn't want anything at all. He's a temporary fixture in my life, and he'll disappear back to Duluth as soon as the condo's ready. I know we'll probably never speak again after this.

The heat kicks on and the unmistakable scent of onions wafts upward, killing any mood.

"Is that lunch?"

He blinks. "Yeah, it's from the same place as yesterday. With the salad dressing you like." The plastic bag resting by his feet crinkles as he pulls out a brown, compostable container. "You're lucky you even got a lunch. I figured out this address was a cancer center while I was waiting for my sub and left."

"Without your sandwich?"

He shrugs like it shouldn't have been a question. Like this isn't the most swoon-inducing thing a man has ever done for me.

I stab at a piece of lettuce. "I'm sorry I didn't explain why I was here. I didn't realize it'd, uh, affect you."

He steals a cherry tomato from the top of my salad and takes the container out of my hands to place it on the dashboard. I pivot toward him, because even without saying so, I know what he's about to tell me is important. "You, uh, your health, it . . ." He stumbles over his words, a pink flush erupting on his cheeks. "It matters to me, Alison. You do. Knowing you were here and imagining you might be—" He presses his eyes shut and inhales through his nose before he opens them again. His gaze focuses on me, as if he's reminding himself that I'm still in front of him, healthy and in one piece. "So, yes, it affected me. And I left my sandwich."

These simple words shoot fireworks through my abdomen.

"Admit it." I lower my voice, worried any increase in volume will push him away before I've memorized the intensity in his eyes at this moment. "You didn't want to be my friend, but I wore you down with my delightful personality."

"Don't be ridiculous. Of course we're friends," he says simply. "Personality notwithstanding."

My tension feathers across my skin until it releases into the air, humming around me with a cold, lonesome shiver. "Friends," I repeat. The word echoes in my head until it loses all meaning. Friends. *Friends*. A mixture of giddiness and disappointment curdles in my gut.

His jaw works as he starts and stops before saying his next

sentence. "You're kind of my favorite new person, if that's not too weird a thing to say."

My heart squeezes, and I beam, unable to remain cool and impassive. It's the reaction he wants. His face hardly moves, but his eyes soften into an open, boyish expression. It curls my insides like scissors pulling against a ribbon. "It's a very weird thing to say." The air in the truck has thinned out, leaving nothing but our hot breath. "You're my favorite new person too."

His knee taps mine. I press his knee back, electricity zinging through my nervous system like it's a conductor rail. His deep brown eyes sweep my face before locking on to mine. A blush crawls up my neck as warmth covers my skin like a wool blanket.

"You're also one of the only new people I've met in months," I say to poke him, because I'm not sure what happens next. I sigh out a nervous breath, waiting.

Without removing his eyes from mine, Adam tosses a glove at my face.

"Where did that even come from?" I shriek. His low laugh rumbles, and now I'm laughing too. Our legs tangle together, my free hand drifting up his broad chest with our faces inches apart. Before my brain can register what's happening, he's slipping his hand behind my neck, and I'm clutching his denim jacket to angle my mouth up to his.

It's a soft, sweet breath of a kiss. Until it isn't.

We crash into each other against the cloth upholstery of the bench seat. Adam's mouth catches me, kissing me like we're building something, like we're creating something new and beautiful. His lips glide against mine, and a sigh escapes my throat. Phantom sparks explode over my breasts as my hand fists his hair like it's the edge of a cliff and I'm in free fall. The way his stubble scratches against my face sets me on fire. It's nothing like I imagined. It's *more*. Almost too much. Everything about his touch, his kiss, the press of his body against me, is too much and not enough all at once.

"This is so . . ." His hungry words fall away as his mouth finds my jaw. His tongue burns into my skin. I can't think. I can't see. The buzzing energy of the universe collapses in on his soft lips and sweeping tongue.

He grapples for my hips desperately as rivulets of need flow through me. I can't form any complete thoughts except I need to feel every part of him against me. I scramble up onto my knees as his arms guide me onto his lap, and he gasps into my mouth. His hands tighten on my hips, pulling me impossibly close, eating into space that never existed. My senses are filled with nothing but Adam Berg.

His hands wrestle with the bottom of my coat, and I pry my hands out of his hair to help as we furiously yank at the buttons. He pulls it down my shoulders, my arm knocking my open salad off the dash in the process. Oil-soaked lettuce slides down the console until it all lands on the floor with a wet plop.

"Shit." I shift in his lap, but his hands cup my face and pull me back to him. His eyes drill into me, his pupils so large I hardly recognize him.

"I don't care about my truck right now." He presses our foreheads together as we both catch our breath. "I can't care about anything but this."

His hand strokes my hairline tenderly, tracing down my face over the soft line of my jaw.

"Neither can I," I practically pant before pressing my mouth to his again.

Heat ripples through me as he sinks into me desperately and all trace of tenderness melts away. His mouth is heavy and hot. It's a deep, mind-numbing, stomach-flipping kiss, and I don't know the day, the time, or what postal code we're in when I whimper into his throat at the feel of his fingers toying with the hem of my sweater. His hand travels up my bare back, thumbs grazing my spine, while his other grabs hold of my hair. He grasps at more of me, anchoring me to him as I nearly unravel in his lap.

Whatever is left of my rational brain goes fully offline. I'm all nerve endings and need when the horn from Uncle Ricky's tow truck sends my head into the ceiling of the truck cab.

———

UNCLE RICKY PULLS my car out of the snow with an awful crunch as the metal lurches over the curb and my front bumper falls to the ground with a thud. I sign paperwork and hop back into Adam's truck so he can drive me home, watching my car disappear in the direction of the autobody shop.

Adam squints out at the snow-covered streets. His face is stony. He doesn't say anything right away, and panic swims in my stomach as we sit in heavy silence. I move to turn the radio on for a buffer, but he puts a hand up to stop me.

"I'm sorry about that," he starts, his eyes flitting between mine and the road. "I got, uh—"

"It's my fault," I blurt, falling on the proverbial make-out sword for the both of us. "I shouldn't have. I was—"

His laugh is forced. "We both know it wasn't just you."

He works the back of his neck with his one hand. I rub

circles over my right temple like it will erase the last twenty minutes—a sexual expungement.

"It was a, uh . . ." He's about to say the word *mistake*. I know it in the way he's gripping and releasing the steering wheel. If the word falls from his lips, I'll be sick.

"It wasn't a mistake," I announce. "It was just a thing that happened. A lapse."

"A lapse?" His eyebrows lift with curiosity.

"I read an article about a study on grief . . ." I've read no such article. "It said a, uh, physical connection can be necessary to move into the next stage."

"Which stage?" His eyes dart back to me.

"The fourth one?"

"Depression?"

"No, the one after that."

"Ahh." He knows I'm full of shit. I watch his eyes decide whether he'll play along. "Should we forget it ever happened?"

"I think that's what they recommended. In the article."

"Who produced this study?" he asks, his mouth quirking up to one side. I'll take it.

"Science. All of it." I suppress a laugh.

"I won't deny science." His voice is all faux solemnity as he pulls to a stop behind a van's brake lights. Adam's cheeks are tinted red by the stoplight. "Alison, it's not that I don't want to, it's that I . . . can't."

"It's okay. We're friends," I remind him, but my voice goes up like it's a question.

He turns to face me, looking at me a beat longer than my friends usually do. When his expression turns green, he stiffens and faces forward. "Friends," he agrees, pressing on the gas.

We don't talk for the rest of the ride. The tension between us remains thick. Despite our agreement to forget the kiss ever happened, I imagine his mouth on mine three more times in the warm comfort of his truck. My belly fizzes and pops like soda.

When he pulls in front of my apartment, his arm crosses my body to open my door, brushing my front. My skin ignites at the friction of his coat against mine and the weight of his arm, and I delude myself into thinking he might kiss me again, but he doesn't. I replay his words like they're a broken cassette tape.

You're kind of my favorite new person.

Instead, without leaving his seat, he opens the passenger door to let me out. I turn to him, visibly blushing, and I know he sees it. Hands and lips flash in my mind as he faces forward before I have a chance to register how another charged moment has passed me by.

He waves but doesn't drive away. He lets the car behind him honk to watch me get into my building safely. It's so effortlessly tender, and I wonder if he would've done it for any friend, or if maybe I'm special.

15

Ricky's Towing Isn't Bound by HIPAA

I DON'T REMEMBER WHAT I dreamed last night, but it must have been about Adam, because my cheeks burn at the sight of his name on my phone screen Monday morning.

His message is simply a picture of his familiar hand holding a carrier of two oversized white to-go cups.

7:14 AM
Alison:
Double fisting? Rough start.

7:16 AM
Adam:
Someone shouldn't have driven into a snow pile.
I might've made it home before my bedtime.

I light up alone in my kitchen in front of my Keurig, grateful not to be on FaceTime. The fluttering in my stomach is getting difficult to contain.

I type and delete two messages, one too revealing (*It's good to hear from you*) and one too inconsequential to elicit a further response from him (*Ha ha!*) until I realize Adam is witnessing my overthinking in the form of a dancing ellipsis. Finally, I type out a reply.

7:18 AM
Alison:
Bedtime, Grandpa?

On Tuesday, Adam "Confirmed Friend Nothing More" Berg texts again.

3:34 PM
Adam:
What's your favorite color?

3:36 PM
Alison:
Pass. Only children have favorite colors.

3:38 PM
Adam:
I'm getting paint for the living room.

3:39 PM
Adam:
Not true. My favorite color is brown.

3:41 PM
Alison:
Favorite colors are irrelevant when it comes to painting.

3:42 PM
Alison:
Get a greige with a warm undertone because the
windows are north facing.

I'm at my desk Wednesday morning when my phone vibrates.

8:51 AM
Adam:
I went with light gray. Greige isn't a color, and the
windows are west facing.

8:53 AM
Alison:
I don't know cardinal directions. I'm not a scout leader.

8:55 AM
Adam:
Couldn't rule it out. I've watched you consume a lot
of Girl Scout cookies.

8:58 AM
Alison:
We completely skipped over that your favorite color
is brown!?!

8:59 AM
Alison:
Who hurt you?

"Alison."

Josh is examining me from his desk, fingers still in motion on his keyboard.

I tuck my phone behind a stack of folders. "Are you actually typing something when you do that or is it an intimidation tactic?"

"Both. I ran your vacation days by Daniella. She said it's fine, but we have to switch around onboarding dates for you and the new hire."

"I'm not sure yet if I'm going on the trip. Or taking the job."

Patty pulls off her silencing headphones to interject. "She's panicking about leveling up in her career."

I turn to face her. "You can hear us with those on?"

"They only drown out the typing. I listen until I lose interest."

I rub circles into my temples. "I'm not panicking, I'm trying to figure out what I want." Ever since I told Adam about the job, I can't get his words out of my head. Are all of my attempts to "level up" a waste if I'm not sure it's what I want?

Once they've returned to their work, I pick up my phone. A text from a new number interrupts my conversation with Adam.

9:08 AM
Unknown Number:
Alison—Adam says you're wrapping up early. Will you drop off the keys this weekend with the last of the boxes? I can't thank you enough for all you've done. It means the world to us. ♥ Judy Lewis.

My heart sinks an inch.

So that's it, then. He can't even make it to December 1. Weeks of texts and escalating tension—culminating in a kiss that I'm definitely not obsessing over—are coming to an abrupt end, and I'm finding out from Sam's mom.

What was he planning to do? Give me one last flirty home improvement montage before disappearing from my life forever, doomed to be a name in my contact list that wishes me a happy birthday every couple years? The thought stings like a papercut. My weekends won't be filled with the two of us. Soon, I'll be back to normal. An ache lurks under my ribs.

Why *can't* I go with Sam's friends to Patagonia? It's exactly something Sam would do. What if two weeks of camping and trekking with experienced hikers is exactly the exposure therapy I need to finally embrace adventure? Even if it isn't, it'll be a perfect distraction from whatever isn't happening with Adam. I'll be able to talk about this trip for the rest of my life. I could authentically claim that identity as my own, like people who ran a marathon six years ago and bring it up in every conversation like it's eternally who they are.

"Tell Kyle he's covering me the last two weeks in January," I blurt.

Josh blows his nose and nods, oblivious to the monumental moment he's witnessed. I look down at my phone. For the first time in weeks, I wish I could talk to Sam, to bask in his relentless positivity and enthusiasm. All I have is a text from Adam—another man in my life doomed to be a memory.

9:09 AM
Adam:
Brown like wood, weirdo. From trees.

9:10 AM
Adam:
I like green too. Similar origins.

This is exactly what I wanted from the beginning. Clean the apartment, help Sam's family, and move on to a bigger, more adventurous life. Get in and get out. Those plans never included an impulsive—incredible, mind-blowing—kiss with Sam's friend.

My phone thuds to the bottom of my bag when I throw it in without responding.

———

THURSDAY NIGHT SPORTS trivia is shaping up to be a particularly brutal defeat. Patrick's a no-show, and any questions we manage to answer are through a *Slumdog Millionaire*-esque series of coincidences. Chelsea and Mara know a few of the baseball facts by virtue of being alive in Minnesota, and in the image round, I recognize Kris Humphries from his marriage to Kim Kardashian—not his time as a Minnesota Gopher.

The Wisconsin-themed bar, adorned in green and yellow twinkle lights, subjects us to an entire section on the Green Bay Packers. Chelsea alternates between "Brett Favre" and "Aaron Rodgers" every time we have to guess.

Humphries, Favre, and Rodgers come through for us, and we wind up in a distant, but respectable, third place. It's enough to put Mara in a relatively good mood. We win a complimentary basket of cheese curds that we split three ways, and all check our neglected phones in unison as the jock rock kicks back up.

I have a few unread messages, but only one makes my heart leap pathetically.

9:03 PM
Adam:
This is all your fault.

Below his message is a photo of a single string of twinkle lights draped along his workshop wall. I want to be mad at him, but I can't help but soften in the face of my grump's reluctant Christmas cheer.

Chelsea coos, and I look up from my phone, still smiling like a fool.

"I knew it! Look at your face! When did this happen? In the car? Uncle Ricky said a dude was there when he towed you from the ditch. Did you get busy in the car? Did you swipe your hand on the foggy window like Kate Winslet?" Chelsea's voice climbs higher with each question.

"Oh my god, Chels. It was the middle of the day," I deflect, because who knows whether we would've pulled a Jack and Rose if the tow truck hadn't shown up when it did.

"That's not a denial." Mara's nose is still in her work phone, and she's giving this conversation approximately 40 percent of her focus.

I wrap my arms across myself to intercept the involuntary shiver rolling up my body when I remember how Adam's beard felt against my neck and how desperate I was for more. "Adam happened to be nearby and gave me a ride. And it wasn't a ditch. It was a snow pile on the other side of a curb. If you're going to gossip about me with your uncle, I want you to have every humiliating detail correct."

Mara clicks off her screen and gives me her full attention. "He happened to be near the breast cancer center?"

"Jesus, Chelsea. Hasn't your uncle heard of medical privacy laws?"

"Ricky's Towing isn't bound by HIPAA," Chelsea answers, shaking her head at my attempted diversion. "So how long has this been going on?"

"She's at least made out with him," Mara tells Chelsea. "Her mouth's doing that twitchy thing. That's her tell."

"I don't have a tell!" I slap my hand over my face. "Fine. We did kiss . . . a bit, but we both agreed it didn't happen. Or that it shouldn't have happened. I can't remember the specifics of our not remembering." I'm too busy remembering everything before that *very specifically*.

"But you like him?" Chelsea asks, propping her head in her hands, her eyes soft and wide like a cartoon deer's.

A smile breaks free across my face. "He told me I'm his 'favorite new person.'"

"Cute," she gushes, drawing five syllables out of the word. "Wait, did he say 'new *favorite* person' or 'favorite *new* person'?"

"The second one."

Her pony bobs encouragingly. "Okay. So what does that *mean*?"

"It means he likes her, but she's still his best friend's girlfriend," Mara explains.

Disappointment sags in my stomach. "It's not like that."

"*He* thinks it is." Mara's usually assessing eyes fill with compassion for the mess I've made, which makes me feel all the more hopeless.

My body stiffens the moment a male hand unexpectedly

clasps my shoulder. Scents of the beach and expensive hair products waft into my nostrils.

"Hey, babe!" a familiar voice says.

I inwardly curse, and Chelsea's mouth falls open at the figure behind me.

"Russell!" I turn, greeting him cheerily with an awkward one-armed hug that he turns into a long, full-body embrace.

"Why're you giving me the runaround, girl? I've left you like three messages." He clutches his heart, stepping back like I've shot him, but his wink and big toothy grin in Chelsea's direction confirm my suspicion that he hardly thinks about me when I'm not directly in front of him.

"Sorry. I've had a lot going on." I turn to Mara and Chelsea. "This is Russell. He saved us when Adam and I got a car impounded."

Chelsea flits her eyelashes over her ravenous blue eyes. "Russell, I'm Chelsea."

She extends her hand toward him, but with lightning-fast reflexes, he rejects it and pulls her into a hug. She mouths, *Oh my god!* to Mara and me over his shoulder.

Russell settles into a seat at our table. "Any friend of Sam's girl is a friend of mine."

All three of us recoil physically at the words *Sam's girl,* but Russell doesn't notice. He's waiting for Mara to introduce herself.

She wrinkles her nose, unimpressed. "Mara. We met at the funeral. You hugged me." From her, the word *hugged* sounds more like *sneezed on.*

Russell flashes a Cheshire cat smile, oblivious to Mara's tone. She makes an excuse and heads toward the bathroom.

Chelsea presses Russell's forearm flirtatiously, and suddenly, they're enjoying a lively exchange of Hot People Pleasantries. I pull out my phone and tune them out. Minutes go by while I labor over how to respond to Adam's text. Do I mention Judy's message? How do I casually remind him of our forgotten kiss and find out if our friendship expires this weekend? Should I ask him his preferred flavor of "Goodbye Forever" cake? I feel like it's marble. There's no flavor more ambivalent than marble.

"You're going too, Al?"

Chelsea's wobbly voice pulls me out of my phone trance. "Huh?"

Worry and frustration pinwheel across her face. "Russell says you're going to Chile. The country. To climb a mountain."

Russell and Chelsea stare at me expectantly. "Sam invited me . . . and—"

"Oh, babe, you have to come too," Russell tells Chelsea, throwing his arm around the back of her chair before she subtly shimmies out of his embrace. He's impervious to the nonverbal conversation playing out on our faces.

Mara reclaims her chair, surveying our varying expressions. "Sorry, there was a line. What'd I miss?"

"Alison's going camping in the mountains of South America." Chelsea downs her beer.

Mara straightens. "What?"

My eyes glue themselves to the table, unable to confront my friends' angry faces. Or, not angry—worse—worried. "It'll be good for me."

"For sure," Russell responds, bouncing in his seat. He really can't read a room. "When can I grab that stuff from Sam's place?"

I turn toward Russell, avoiding my friends' stares. "Can you come by this weekend?"

"Perfect. We'll hash out the details for Chile then. Chelsea, it was a pleasure meeting you. Can I DM you?"

She tips her head side to side in disappointed resignation. "Better not," she says. Whatever fun she imagined with Russell, I've shot it in the ass with a tranq dart.

Russell shakes the rejection off. Once he's sauntered away, Mara's eyes tighten at the corners. "I thought Sam's sister gave your ticket away. Why does *Bachelor in Paradise* think you're going mountaineering with him?" she asks.

"I'm capable of buying my own ticket," I snap, frustrated that I'm being forced to articulate actions I may not entirely understand.

Mara throws up her hands. "What're you trying to prove?"

I fidget in my chair.

"When we all had collective heart attacks during *Free Solo*, did you see it as aspirational viewing? You're a woman who loves lazy days on the couch with her friends. *That's* who you are, and you're the best." Mara's voice rises with each sentence, her volume swallowed up by the noisy bar. "But after your surgery, you woke up and decided that you weren't good enough. You signed us up for an *ultra*marathon. I didn't know they made races *longer* than a marathon, and now I'll have to sell my firstborn child to get off that email list."

"What's wrong with wanting to be the best version of myself?"

"Nothing! But this isn't *you*. When you're not off pretending to like the great outdoors, you're playing house with Adam—who still thinks you're Sam's girlfriend, by the way.

So it doesn't matter how much you like him or he likes you, you'll never get what you want if you're pretending to be someone else."

Mara and I never fight, but I can't help but bite back. "You only recognize me when I'm going along with whatever you want. You have to control every part of my life! I knock on doors for your candidates. I study a hundred years of sports trivia so you can win in a one-sided vendetta against a team that doesn't care about us." My words are an erupting volcano, flowing out in a hot rush. "And Chelsea and I don't even like sports. This isn't how either of us want to spend a Thursday night—"

"Please don't involve me in—" Chelsea tries in vain to stop my tirade, gesturing to the waiter for our bill.

"But you steamroll over us." I don't pause. "And now we're sitting under a neon cheese head—yelling at each other— because I'm not doing exactly what you want me to do!"

For a moment, we're all still. I imagine we *could* hear a pin drop if not for the basketball game and jock rock. Chelsea's empty expression settles on the glass in front of her, and Mara doesn't say anything. I feel the tension pressing down on us like dense ash. My lungs fight for oxygen with each breath.

Mara's throat bobs as she places a twenty on the table. "I have some work to finish up. Chels, can you drive Al home?"

"Mar," I say weakly, so much regret woven through that one syllable.

Mara hardens her jaw. "I'm not arguing with you in a fucking Packers bar, Al. That's a friendship low." She slips on her black coat, flinging it around herself like protective armor. "We can talk it out this weekend."

"I'm painting with Adam, and I have to be around for Russell . . ." I trail off.

"Of course." Mara snorts. "Don't worry about it." She shakes her hair out of her collar, and the clack of her heels breaks through the noise as she makes her exit.

"I'm not wrong, am I?" I look to Chelsea for encouragement, but she's avoiding my eyes.

"No, but you're not right either." She turns toward me with her signature teacher face, both tender and resolute. "She loves you. It was hard for me to watch you go through your mom getting sick and your diagnosis and your surgery, but Mara, she's a fixer. She hates to feel helpless. There are a million examples of how gracefully you've handled everything thrown at you, but we can see you're still hurting in small ways."

"Chels, I'm not hurting anymore. I'm healed now, and I'm trying to live my life."

Her jaw ticks in frustration. "Great. Whose life, though? Because backpacking through mountains with strangers isn't yours."

It's the most combative Chelsea is capable of, and I don't know how to respond.

She doesn't make me, asking instead, "Was the kiss good at least?" because I know she's been waiting to ask about kissing Adam since before Russell showed up and knocked us off course.

A laugh falls out of my throat. "Yeah, it was really, really good."

"I knew it," she says, and pops the last cheese curd in her mouth.

When I trudge into my apartment that night, I collapse onto my bed without even removing my coat. Mara's words whir through my brain on spin cycle.

You'll never get what you want if you're pretending to be someone else.

All I wanted was to do my part, move on, and hopefully loosen the knot of guilt braided into my sternum. Why, then, am I so disappointed that this situation is finally coming to an end?

I go still as one thought overtakes all others.

Because when it comes to Adam, I know what I want.

There's no future for Sam's Girlfriend and Sam's Best Friend—sure—but I'm not Sam's girlfriend, and for the first time I want Adam to know that.

I pull out my phone again and look at the photo of his illuminated workshop. My laugh echoes in my empty apartment the second I spot a full mug of coffee lit under the twinkle lights. How does that boy sleep? Next to the coffee mug is a knotty wood board. Is it my shelf?

10:09 PM
Alison:
Are you asleep?

10:12 PM
Adam:
Rarely.

10:13 PM
Alison:
You drink too much coffee. You have a problem.
You need help.

10:14 PM
Adam:
You're 30 percent expired cookies.
YOU need help.

10:14 PM
Alison:
My addiction is helping young women develop
entrepreneurial skills. Yours makes you a jittery
grouch.

10:15 PM
Adam:
I'm not that jittery.

10:16 PM
Alison:
I'm not bringing you an americano on Saturday.
You're detoxing.

10:17 PM
Adam:
Noooooo.

10:17 PM
Alison:
I thought Starbucks was evil.

10:18 PM
Adam:
We've reached an understanding.

10:19 PM
Alison:
Fine. But it'll be half-caff.

He types on and off for a few minutes before his next text appears.

10:23 PM
Adam:
Just so you know, I told Sam's parents we'll be done
this weekend after we paint. They want the keys back
when we're done.

10:25 PM
Alison:
I know. His mom texted me.

10:26 PM
Adam:
Oh.

10:27 PM
Alison:
Can I ask you a personal question?

10:28 PM
Adam:
Do I have a choice?

10:29 PM
Alison:
Before ... the "lapse" ...

10:29 PM
Adam:
Okay ...

10:30 PM
Alison:
You said I was your friend.

Seconds later, Adam's name glows on my screen. Vibrations buzz against my palm, and I anxiously accept the call.

"What are you fishing for over there, Ali?"

My insides turn to goo at the sound of a nickname in Adam's gravelly voice.

"I'm not sure what I'm trying to ask."

Glassware clinks on his end of the line. "So are you keeping me awake to *not* ask me personal questions?"

"It's barely after ten! There's no way you're falling asleep any time soon. You're probably drinking coffee right now."

"Did you just snort-laugh?" He chuckles, low and rumbly.

"Yes."

"It's cute."

Sparks erupt in my belly.

He swallows into the receiver. "I'm drinking water right now. You're a good influence on me. But you didn't send a cryptic text message to talk about that."

"I get it," I say, a giggle bubbling up in my throat. "I

should've texted a more complete summary of my thoughts. I'm guessing you consider phone calls an 'act of aggression.'"

"Not at all. I hate texting. I always come off wrong. So you were saying that we're friends . . . ," he nudges.

"Friends. Of course." Though I'd suppose making out in his truck like teenagers has stretched the bounds of friendship. "I keep thinking about how this all started at the funeral. Mrs. Lewis told you who I was, and maybe I should have said something then, but we weren't friends yet. You didn't even like me. But it's different now. We're—"

His sharp inhale sputters against the phone. "I promise that's not what I felt about you."

The word *promise* in Adam's low voice folds into me like a secret note. Suddenly, the radio frequency between us feels intensely private. I pull myself up over my pillow and prop my head on my hand. "What were you thinking when we first met? I swear you gave me a look like you hated me or something."

Adam pauses. Anticipation trickles through my veins. "That day was kind of a blur," he finally says.

"Of course." I've broken an unspoken agreement by bringing up the funeral. We never talk about it. "It's weird to think Sam's apartment is almost ready. I'd started to think we'd never finish." Or maybe I'd started looking forward to each small mishap that extended our time together. "I'm going to miss you . . . when it's done. I wanted you to know that. This was important to me. You're important to me, in a nonfriend way." I don't know what he'll make of my well-intentioned fib, but I need him to know everything about Sam and his family and my role in trying to make everything a little easier. I need him to know that I'm completely available and have been as long as I've known him. "You should know—"

"Ali." He says it like it hurts. "I think you know how I feel about you. You're . . ." I hear his breath as he searches for the words.

I'm what? I wonder.

". . . you," he says with a breath. I can almost feel it hot on my cheek. "But it's better this ends now. As friends. I don't want it to get any more confusing."

I blush at his allusion to our forgotten kiss and his admission that he might share my desire for more—and suddenly admitting that Sam thought I wasn't good enough for him feels all the more vulnerable.

How can I tell the man I want that his friend found me lacking? I settle on an in-between truth. "Sam and I broke up before he died. I don't know why he didn't tell anyone, but I couldn't bring myself to break it to his family at the funeral, and then Rachel begged me to go along with it for his parents, and then I met you and—"

"Really?" His voice cracks open, sounding almost . . . hopeful, but maybe I'm only hearing what I want to hear. I wish I could see his eyes and puzzle together everything he's not saying. "You broke up with him? Before?"

Relief rushes through my insides, and I can't bring myself to quibble with the details of who dumped who.

"Yeah," I respond, sounding hopeful too. Even if this is too confusing for him, he knows now that it's not confusing for me. That this could be real if only he wanted it.

"It's still weird to think about you and him. And the more I get to know you, the less I can picture it." His voice feels different now—weighed down.

"I was surprised by it at first too, with his whole Instagram-model look. We were always mismatched."

Fabric rustles against the receiver with his groan into his pillow. "Don't do that."

"Do what?"

"Make me tell you how beautiful you are." His voice is a hungry rasp, and the raw sound fills my abdomen with heat.

There's something too intimate about late-night phone calls. I can close my eyes, and Adam is lying on the pillow next to me. I can open them, and we're staring at the same ceiling tiles. I wonder what his ceiling looks like and whether he imagines me looking up at it too.

My body's heavy, like I'm under the weighted comforter Instagram keeps pushing on me. I need to hang up. "You sound tired," I whisper.

"I could talk a little longer."

So we do.

16

Tell the Truth

3:47 PM
Alison:
Minneapolis called an overnight snow emergency.
Did you move Sam's car back?

3:59 PM
Adam:
Shit.

4:02 PM
Alison:
I'll move it. I can tape while I'm there to get a jump
on painting tomorrow.

4:03 PM
Adam:
Okay.

AFTER I MOVE Sam's car Friday night, I invite Russell over to look for his gear. I direct him to the group of three boxes by the living room windows. Aside from this last stack of boxes and a drop cloth held in place by Adam's ladder, the place resembles a staged showroom. Once we paint tomorrow and deliver the last of his things, there'll be nothing left of Sam here. We've packed him away like out-of-season decor.

"This is everything that could be relevant to hiking, mountain climbing, and general outdoorsiness." I nudge a box with my toe.

"No worries. I'm glad we're finally doing this. Want to crack two of those open?" He points to the six-pack of beer he brought. I open up a can for each of us and watch Russell haphazardly empty the boxes I packed so carefully. I reprimand his chaos with my eyes, but he continues un-nesting all of the backpacks I've zipped into one another and tossing them on the ground.

"I'm glad you're still coming." At the sound of his voice—missing its normal blitheness—I look up from the box I'm rummaging through. "I was thinking of calling the whole trip off at first. It's going to be so different without him." He clears his throat. "But I think it will be good for us. It's good to have something to look forward to."

"I get that." I give him a soft smile and watch him blink—too fast, then too slow—until he seems like the Russell I know and . . . tolerate.

"There's a killer new cocktail bar a couple blocks away. We can head over there tonight and talk about the trip. Our crew has a bunch of O Trek virgins, but you'll be in good hands. It's gonna be incredible." Russell's eyes melt, as if he can make out breathtaking views in the distance.

The way he pictures us out in the wilderness is intoxicating. Maybe I could *like* doing something like this—maybe this could shake my life by the shoulders. A genuine thirst for adventure could trickle into all parts of me.

Russell is describing collapsible trekking poles, measuring out about a foot with his hands. "He usually kept it all in a gray bag—" He stops at the sound of the door opening.

"I didn't know we were having a party," Adam says flatly. I react physically at the sound of his voice, body humming. But the look on his face when he walks into the apartment holding a pizza box twists my stomach.

My pulse quickens like I've been caught doing something wrong. *But, Alison, we promised we'd only pack our dead friend's things with each other,* he cries out in the soap opera in my mind.

I swallow and force detachment into my voice. "Hey, Adam. Didn't know you were coming down tonight."

If I'd known, I would've made different decisions tonight, including, but not limited to, not wearing the embroidered train sweatshirt Chelsea gifted me that reads THIS IS HOW I ROLL across the front. I pray the floor will open up and swallow me. "You remember Russell."

"We've met many times." Adam tries for a joke but misses. His tone is all wrong. "What are you doing here?"

"Looking for his gear," I answer for Russell, my voice sounding nervous and guilty.

"For your gear too. Sam wouldn't mind his girlfriend borrowing a pack for our trip." Russell's tone is innocent, but his eyes twinkle with mischief. He knows he's stumbled into something with Adam and me, and I only wish that I knew what.

"Yeah? Are you going on a trip with him, Alison?" Adam's face is expressionless, but his voice is all challenge.

I ignore him. "Russell, you said the bag's gray?"

"What's in there?" Russell nudges his chin at the pizza box in Adam's hand.

Our questions fly past each other, all of us wanting to speak to someone who doesn't want to talk to us.

"Pepperoni and pepper pizza—her favorite."

"Are those cookies?" Russell eyes the bakery Thin Mints propped on top.

Adam doesn't answer, instead crossing the room and taking my can from my hands. "What beer is this?" His look freezes me in place as he presses his lips to the can. He takes a slow, deliberate sip before handing it back to me. "Ooh. Sour. Wouldn't have expected you to like that."

He might as well have peed on me. It would've been more subtle.

"It's different." I accidentally answer with Minnesotan for *I hate it* and internally groan at myself.

Adam swallows his satisfied smirk. He knows he's won this round.

Russell, not to be outdone, combs a hand through his perfectly coiffed hair. "Adam, can you have this stuff cleaned out by Sunday morning? I'm taking the photos, and I don't want to waste the light."

Confusion pinches my forehead. "Wait—you're the real estate photographer?" Will I ever figure out what this man's job is?

"I'm the listing agent. I sold them the condo. Didn't Richard tell you I wanted it on the market by the end of the month? Otherwise, we have to wait until spring. Minnesotans don't move in the dead of winter."

One thousand expressions travel over Adam's face as he registers that the December 1 deadline—and every little upgrade we've made to the condo—has been for the benefit of Sam's family *and* Russell.

I throw my head back. "Are you or are you not a Realtor?"

"I'm not *just* a Realtor. I'm a real estate multihyphenate. I have rental properties, flip houses; I was in talks with Magnolia Network for a home renovation show pilot, but we couldn't make it work. I need full creative control over my brand. This guy gets it." Russell gives Adam an unearned pat on the shoulder. "I like the cabinet upgrade, by the way. The color will look great in the listing photos. Kitchens sell these places. We should talk collabs."

Adam's jaw ticks, and I know it's taking everything in him not to swat Russell's hand with his paw like the disgruntled bear he is.

"Is this it?" I hold up a blue-gray bag like a white flag.

"That's it!" Russell points. Maybe there is a god. "Still want to get that drink, babe? Or are you busy with . . . whatever this is?" He points between Adam and me.

I tilt my head in the direction of the door, too mortified for direct eye contact. "See you around, Russell." I agree to call him about the trip and shut the door behind him.

Adam's humorless laugh reverberates against the walls of the hollow apartment. "Wow. I didn't mean to interrupt."

"Oh, yeah? Was that macho display for his benefit?" I ask, folding my arms in front of my chest.

Adam flips open the pizza box on the counter with practiced nonchalance. "I don't know what you're talking about."

My eyes snag on his fingers, and I shudder at the memory of what those fingers feel like in my hair. On my face. At my waist.

"Were you able to get whatever issue you have with Russell out of your system?" I ask, hating that my voice is higher than usual.

"Are you going to Chile?" He sounds utterly disinterested, his face a portrait of calm.

"Patagonia. And why would you care if I am?"

God, how I desperately want him to care.

"I don't." He removes paper plates from a bag on the counter, unruffled. "You know why you shouldn't go to Patagonia with him?" he asks like he's pondering this for the first time. "Because you shouldn't backpack through the mountains for several weeks, period. Regardless of the company."

"It's only ten days."

"Oh. Well, then, never mind," he says caustically.

I pull my arms in tight like a shield. "You don't think I can do it?"

"I have no idea if you can, but I know you sure as hell don't want to if you can't force yourself to walk along Lake Superior for an hour."

"What are you even doing here?"

"I thought you'd be hungry." He stumbles. "You said you were coming over here tonight, and after what you told me on the phone, I didn't know why I wasn't . . . why *we* weren't . . ." He trails off, pressing his mouth into a hard line. Vulnerability seeps into his expression before it hardens again. "So I got in my car and drove. I wasn't thinking."

He tears at the plastic around the paper plates, turning it over and over, unable to break through.

I step toward him, my body itching to be the smallest bit closer to his. "I'm glad you did."

His hands give up on the plates, and his dark eyes find mine. An unreadable expression clouds his features. "Yeah? Even though I interrupted you and him—planning your romantic trip under the stars?"

"Digging a hole to poop generally doesn't constitute traditional romance."

For a moment, we don't do anything but stare. I'm buzzing with adrenaline.

"Are you jealous?" I ask, accessing every composed molecule in my body to keep my voice even.

His throat bobs as his eyes search mine. The dark quiet of the apartment covers us like a sheet. We've never been here at night. I've never been completely alone with Adam at *night*. He closes the distance, his eyes trained on my lips. He raises his hand, and I stiffen in anticipation of his touch. I'm so aware of every breath, of every inch of my skin.

His eyes scan my face, begging for answers, before they return to my mouth. My breath catches and my heartbeat thrums in my ears. It's all I can hear aside from the rhythm of Adam's steady inhalations. Phantom sensations skitter across my front, and I wonder what my nipples would be doing if they were here. Pinching, I imagine. I can almost feel it.

His breath is hot on my cheek, and suddenly, I can't move. If I move, he might too, and it would be an absolute tragedy to be standing any more than a single inch from Adam Berg.

Friends don't stand this close, I think. *They don't drink my beer or look at me with such unbridled desire.*

I hear his slow swallow.

"I thought you didn't want this to get confusing," I ask.

His other hand tunnels into my hair and my eyelids flutter at the feel of his strong fingers coiling around my curls. My eyes lower to the corner of his mouth that hooks up when my body responds to him. "Are you confused?" he asks, his voice gravel. The gold flecks in his irises glimmer under the kitchen light.

"Adam," I whisper, a secret.

"Alison," he says, a plea. He wraps a strand of hair around his forefinger, anchoring himself to me. It pulls me a millimeter closer still.

Where the truck felt like a spontaneous crash, we both know this moment is different. This is deliberate. This is a choice. A point of no return. I tilt my head up to him, and with agonizing slowness, he presses his lips to mine.

He's soft and tentative at first, as if I might still pull away. The careful caress of his mouth tugs at my bottom lip, and I murmur a sound of pleasure.

"You like that. Interesting . . ." I inhale his words until he presses his lips to mine again, deepening the kiss. Our mouths become desperate, searching for satisfaction. Adam places his hand firmly on the small of my back and pulls me against him.

"Tell the truth," he growls, kissing down my neck. When his mouth meets the spot his finger grazed in Duluth, every cell in my body vibrates. He smiles against my throat. "Did you really like that beer?"

"No." I squeal in surprise, digging my fingernails into his biceps. "I shouldn't pucker at every sip. It's unsettling." He rewards my honesty with a warm laugh against my shoulder that melts into my bones.

"I knew it." He straightens to his full height and smiles down at me, his eyes hooded and wild. "I knew you hated it."

He grabs me by the hips and places me on the kitchen island like I'm lighter than air, his mouth claiming mine again. Heat clenches my center, and Adam separates my thighs to press himself against me. I wrap my legs around his body, aching to be even closer.

In a split second of awareness, I worry about the pizza next to me, but I'm quickly distracted by want. It's an animal, alive in my chest, clawing at my insides. It wants to possess more of Adam's mouth. More of his touch. More. More. More.

I gather the front of his shirt in a tight fist when his hand slips under my regrettably punny sweatshirt, skimming the sensitive part of my hip. His other hand stays firmly at my waist like it's all he has to steady him.

I didn't know a kiss could feel like this, like devouring while ravenous. Like lifesaving breath while drowning.

His firm hand travels to my front, and I feel the pressure of his palm on my breast. Panic instinctually builds up my spine but evaporates into a puff of smoke at the vibration of his hungry groan into my mouth. If he can register the difference in my topography, it's not dampening his enthusiasm. It's the first time a man has grabbed my new breasts with such fiery passion, and I can't help but grip him tighter, needing more contact.

"I've been thinking about this all week," I pant through hungry kisses.

"Try *weeks*."

I run my hand down his hard chest, suddenly aware of the benefits of kissing Adam free of outerwear. "Weeks?"

He nods. "I tried not to, but I couldn't help it."

Dragging my hands to his belt buckle, I think, *I'm going to have sex with Adam on Sam's kitchen counter,* when I hear a key jingling in the lock.

The sound punctures the delicious fantasy.

Wordlessly, we scatter like roaches. Adam's in front of the fridge in an instant, and I brace myself as I jump off the counter. My pinky makes contact with a bit of tomato sauce, and I shudder.

"Hello?" I hear Mrs. Lewis's tentative voice before I see her.

17

Are You Expecting an Edible Arrangement?

AFTER THE BARE minimum amount of polite chitchat with Mrs. Lewis while Adam cooled down behind the fridge door, I fled the apartment and everything that happened on the kitchen counter.

I went to sleep thinking about the kiss. I woke up dreaming about it and imagined his lips the entire train ride and walk to Sam's building.

Even now, I'm still thinking about it when I step into the apartment, currently overwhelmed by the smell of paint fumes and the jaunty notes of Charlie Brown's "Christmas Time Is Here." I look around to find that Adam has nearly finished painting.

"Whoa. Did you paint all night?" I plop the coffee on the counter while respectfully avoiding contact with it. If I return my eyes to the scene of the crime, I'll only replay the kiss in my head to deconstruct it for clues.

"What?" He drops the paint roller in its tray to rub the back of his neck. He's wearing basically what he always wears: a Henley, flannel, and jeans that fit perfectly but have seen better days.

Instead of my true painting clothes—a Pioneer High Robotics Team T-shirt and worn-out leggings with a hole in the crotch—I'm in what all women in rom-coms wear for the falling-in-love-by-way-of-home-improvement montage: a slouchy cropped tee and artfully distressed denim overalls.

He's looking in my direction, but his eyes are darting around too much for me to be sure we've made eye contact. "Oh, because so much is painted. Right. I get it. That's funny."

I shrug my coat off slowly. So as not to spook him. "It's really not."

He stuffs his hands in his pockets and bounces on his heels.

"How much caffeine have you had today?"

He grimaces. "A lot. Too much. I have regrets."

"Did you snort some cocaine too?"

"I had an extra-large coffee, two 5-hour Energy shots, and two Red Bulls. No, three. Two?" He counts on his fingers before he seems to lose interest and gestures in the direction of a wall that is primed, tarped, and taped. "So the paint only needs one coat, which is good. I have you all set up over there. I have my truck loaded with the last of Sam's things. We'll clean up, drop off his stuff, and be done by lunch. Maybe a little after lunch."

"What's the rush? You have big plans this afternoon?"

"Would you rather clean up while I paint?"

"What the hell is going on right now?" I ask, and his eyes double in size at my directness.

"We're painting," he says with infuriating simplicity.

"You kissed me. Twice. In the last week, you've kissed me two times."

"That really was all this week, wasn't it?" A playful glint

touches the corners of his eyes. It brings me the tiniest shred of relief.

"Adam. I'm being serious. Do you regret what happened? Are we forgetting it, again? Are you expecting an Edible Arrangement? I don't understand your energy."

"I'm not a decorative melon guy," he quips, but at my no doubt distressed expression, his aloofness falls away. He crosses the room, extracting his hands from his pockets to pull me into him. His hug unties me like a bow, every knotted-up muscle in my body releasing at once. I bury my face into his shoulder and allow his chin to find its place on my head. It's a relief to know we fit like this, even if he's vibrating with caffeine.

"I definitely don't regret it," he tells my scalp. "I want to talk about it, but it's hard to wrap my head around everything when I'm still in an active text conversation with Sam's mom."

He squeezes my shoulders, pressing me so close that I can feel his racing heart thrum against my temple.

"I realized last night that we needed to close the book on the apartment before we could move forward." He pulls his head back to meet my eyes as he speaks. "And I wanted to move forward as soon as possible. So, yes, I've been painting since four this morning."

I look up at him. "You Billy Crystaled me." His face registers zero comprehension. "It's from a movie. With Meg Ryan. It's a good thing. Don't worry about it."

He presses a kiss to my hair, squeezing me again before stepping out of the hug. "Should we paint?"

"We better. We have a very intense schedule to keep. First, why exactly were you listening to *A Charlie Brown Christmas* all alone?"

"You like Christmas music."

"I wasn't here."

He bounces back to his side of the apartment and picks up his roller, slapping a perfect greige hue on the wall. "You're here now," he replies with a shrug.

In our rom-com-worthy falling-in-love-by-way-of-home-improvement montage, few scenes would make the cut. Sure, he holds me steady on the ladder as I paint near the ceiling, and the shock of his warm hand on my hip nearly topples me into a can of latex paint. And yes, at some point we flick paint across the tarp for no reason other than to prove the other wasn't as good at flicking paint across the tarp. But mostly, we paint while Classic Christmas plays on shuffle.

When Spotify plays two different covers of "Santa Baby" back-to-back and Adam begs for death, I let him switch to an alt-rock playlist while I pour the rest of his Americano down the kitchen drain so his heart doesn't explode.

Painting and cleaning up takes longer than Adam anticipated, so it's nearly six when we climb into the truck for our final funereal duty. He's crashing from the caffeine, so I let him nap while I drive and revel in the headiness of looming over the tiny cars below us in Adam's truck.

He stirs when we exit the highway near Sam's parents', only to burrow his head into my shoulder. "You're so snuggly," he hums, and tiny butterflies flutter in my belly.

I pull into the empty driveway of the large, familiar house.

"You sleep," I tell him, removing the keys from the ignition. "I'll be quick."

I hear the sharp knock at the window but Adam doesn't.

"Kids." Sam's dad appears in the passenger door.

"Shit," I whisper. I shove Adam awake, and he flings his

body across the cab like I'm radioactive. After a slight delay, he recovers enough to roll down his window.

Dr. Lewis leans the elbow patches of his tweed jacket on the door frame. "Is that the last of it?" He points to the truck bed.

We nod.

"Good. Can you help me carry them to the garage?"

We fall all over ourselves piling out of the car. We carry the boxes to the garage, Adam stacking two effortlessly and me attempting the same inelegantly. Dr. Lewis grabs the last box, propping it on his knee while he punches in the garage code. "Judy wants a word," he says ominously. He leads us through the garage door and into the mudroom, while we follow like prisoners to the gallows.

"JuJu, they're here," he calls out to his wife.

Mrs. Lewis putters in looking like a café au lait in head-to-toe cashmere that hangs off her body. She's lost weight since the funeral, and I do everything short of pinching the skin of my wrist to keep my composure. "Alison, I didn't know I'd be seeing you again so soon." She wraps me in a hug and smooths my hair before releasing me.

Dr. Lewis clears his throat. "Judy mentioned running into you two yesterday, but she forgot to invite you to the Cookie Party."

Pain flashes in her eyes before settling back into what is now her default expression: empty.

Adam stiffens at the edge of my eyeline. "You're still having the Cookie Party?"

"Sam was looking forward to it this year, Adam," he tells him. "More than any other year. Rachel's flying in." Mrs. Lewis releases a bemused snort that makes Dr. Lewis flinch. "It would be a betrayal to his memory to cancel." He says it mechanically, like he's repeated this defense verbatim to multiple people, including his wife, if her faraway stare is any indication.

Adam doesn't respond, and silence descends on our quartet, huddled together in the spotless mudroom. I can't take it.

"We'd love to come. I would. I don't know about Adam's schedule, of course," I ramble. "Although I'd hate to impose if it's more of a family thing."

"You're family, honey," she tells me. "Sam would want you here. Both of you."

I feel Adam's rigidity radiating beside me, but I don't look away from the woman in front of me.

"You don't know what it means to me that Sam had you, Alison . . ." She wipes her blue eyes with her hand. "It's such a comfort."

I smile, wanting to be that comfort for her.

"Of course, we'll be there. Both of us," Adam answers, his voice unsteady.

"Yes. Of course," I say, grateful he spoke. "It's so generous of you to invite us."

Mrs. Lewis rubs Adam's arm in a distinctly maternal way, and the smallest bit of tension releases from his shoulders.

Sam's father promises to send the Paperless Post invite, and Mrs. Lewis holds me close as we say our goodbyes. Then Adam and I walk up the long drive toward his truck.

I look over my shoulder at the perfect house on the lake and turn back to the truck window to take inventory of my splotchy face. Adam's hand slips between me and my image and pulls up on the driver door handle.

"I'm awake now," he says.

I don't move right away. Instead, I stare at our watery

reflections. "That's not how Sam thought of me. Ever. We were never like that."

He pulls the door open with a dejected nod. "I know, but knowing doesn't make it easier. Why are you letting them think that you were?"

"I'm not." I wait for him to climb into the cab, trying to meet his avoidant eyes. Emotion crawls up my throat. "It's complicated. She's . . . I want to be what she needs."

He thrums the steering wheel with anxious fingers, squinting into the snow-covered road. "I'm sorry. It's just, I thought today would be the end of it, but it's like . . . you'll always be a little bit Sam's girlfriend, you know?"

His words burn a trail through my insides as he puts the truck in reverse.

18

Otrivia Benson: SVU

WE DON'T TALK the rest of the drive home—which is fine. Shockingly fine, considering how the threat of silence in the Lewis house was so excruciating I would have agreed to anything short of marrying Sam's ghost to fill it. But now I'm happy to stare into the middle distance and stew in my disappointment.

Adam tunes the radio to the Christmas station without my asking, but when I hear the familiar beginning of Darlene Love's "Christmas," I punch the stereo button to silence her. I can't risk ruining my favorite song by association.

At the sight of my apartment building, I leap out of Adam's truck before it's fully stationary.

"Thanks for the ride."

My feet crunch into the fresh layer of snow on the curb. I hear him call out to me, but I can't turn back. The cold air stings my eyes, and water is already pooling in the corners. If he sees me now, he'll think it's about Sam's family or us, but it's all of it. I'll never be the person I'm supposed to be for me or Sam or even Adam.

You'll always be a little bit Sam's girlfriend.

I run inside to safety. My friends will be here any minute to grab me for a night out, and even though Mara and I haven't talked since our fight, Chelsea—ever the good-natured meddler—found a bar hosting trivia two blocks away.

It's a perfectly diabolical setup: Mara can't resist an opportunity to train for her showdown with Risky Quizness, and I can't avoid them if they're within shouting distance of my window.

I peel off my painting clothes and survey my sweater drawer for options, settling on a white turtleneck sweater that I pair with black chunky-heeled boots to cancel out the Maine lobsterman effect.

At the buzz of my intercom, I release the security door with the press of a button.

"It's open!" I answer the knock from inside my closet. "Are we walking? Because that will affect my coat choice."

"Walking where?" The voice is low and familiar and, most crucially, not Mara's or Chelsea's.

I spin around, thanking all of the available gods that I'm fully clothed. "Adam! What are you doing here?"

"You left your phone in the car when you were sprinting away from me." He holds out my mint-green case.

I grab it from him, avoiding skin-to-skin contact. "Thanks."

"You have a nice place." He can see all of my belongings in a single eyeful.

"It gets the job done. I hope you didn't have to fight someone for a parking spot."

"I did have to parallel park." For a brief moment, he flashes his familiar smirk, but it breaks into a serious expression. "I think I gave you the wrong impression. I didn't expect to see Sam's parents today. They've never come out any other time I've dropped stuff off. And seeing them with you—"

"I know. It was uncomfortable, considering . . ." I trail off, anxiety swimming in my gut. Adam's face is drawn with dread and disappointment. Everything in his expression says this is goodbye. The condo's packed, and we're over: Sam's friend and the eternal almost-girlfriend.

I'm overwhelmed by one true and undeniable fact: this can't be over. Last night's kiss changed everything for me, and no matter what we call last week's—a mistake, a lapse— I'll never stop replaying it in my mind. I'll be old and gray describing the hungry look in his eyes to fellow retirees on the shuffleboard courts.

I take his hand, lacing our fingers together. "We can't leave it like this," I plead, my words floating off on a puff of air.

His face reacts, but I can't read it. I hold his gaze, memorizing his bottomless mahogany eyes just in case. Outside, the snow continues to fall, but my focus is entirely on Adam.

"Ali." His low voice is soft and tinged with awe, like I'm something rare.

"No one else calls me Ali."

"Does it bother you?"

My heart sputters beneath my ribs. "No, I like it."

Light dances across his eyes as he decides what happens next. Anticipation teases at every nerve ending. "Ali." His thumb swipes across my palm. I press my eyes shut and feel it everywhere.

A distant shout from out the window drops between us like a bucket of cold water.

Adam's forehead creases in confusion. "Is someone yelling for you?"

"What?"

"Al! Al! Al!"

Adam drops my hands, and disappointment shoots through my abdomen.

I force the crank on the living room window and see Chelsea hanging out of Mara's Jeep, yelling up to my apartment. Her blond blowout is perfect, and her burgundy sweatshirt is oversized in that way that makes petite people look even more petite. "There you are. I thought I had the wrong apartment. I've never Romeo'd you before."

I cup my hands around my mouth. "I think you Romeo'd everyone in Lowertown."

Chelsea's eyes gape. "Do you have *a man* up there?"

I glance at Adam, feeling my face redden, before calling out to my friends, "I'll be right down, okay?" I close my window and face him.

He clears his throat. "You're busy. I'll go."

I can feel him slipping out of my grasp like sand.

Please, don't go, I want to shout. *I have so much to say to you, and I need more time than the two minutes before Mara starts honking.*

"Adam."

We're frozen at the window when Chelsea busts into my apartment with a reluctant Mara in tow.

"Is everyone decent?" Chelsea's cheery voice might as well be a door slamming shut.

"Thanks for that, Chels." I shuffle Adam in the direction of my friends and follow behind. "Chelsea, Mara, you remember Adam."

Chelsea greets him with a hug, and now we're all stuffed in my tiny entry.

"Adam." Mara widens her eyes at me. It's not as discreet as she thinks it is. "Glad you could join us tonight. We're a teammate short and need the numbers if we want to dominate. Do you know facts about any sports other than football?"

Adam blinks in the face of Mara's competitive ferocity. "Hockey and a little basketball."

Mara clasps his hand in hers, closing the deal. "Perfect."

I shake my head at them. "He said he's leaving."

"I can stay if you need me." Adam looks at me as if waiting for my approval. It makes my pathetic heart leap in my chest.

Mara pulls her beeping phone out of her pocket. "Our main rival's there, so we need the win."

I reach into my closet behind her for my jacket. "How do you know Risky Quizness's schedule?"

Mara absently shoots off a text. "I do my research. I follow the team members on my catfish Instagram. That's how I knew this guy's a Vikings fan." She tilts her head at Adam without looking up from her phone.

I narrow my eyes. "You stalked him?"

Mara shoos away my concern. "Lightly. The most basic of recon."

"What did this invasion of his privacy produce?"

Mara's unruffled. "Mostly public information. I did one sketchy thing, but he was clean, so no harm."

"Mostly?!" I squeak just as Adam responds, "So I passed the background check?" He's fighting an indulgent smile that puts me immediately at ease.

Chelsea pops an eyebrow. "You reshare too many pictures of chairs in your Instagram stories."

"Yeah. Cool it on the chairs, bro. Mix up your content strategy," Mara piles on.

I raise my hand in Adam's defense. "He likes chairs, guys. Let him live. Now, are we doing trivia, or what?"

Adam bounces on his toes, nearly concealing his amusement and possible aftershocks of his earlier caffeine overdose.

Mara finally stuffs her phone in her pocket and accepts his enthusiasm as a formal request to join our team. "Know that if you choke on any Vikings questions, I'll forgive, but I'll never forget."

"So which member of Risky Quizness are you catfishing?" Chelsea furtively examines the group across the room as we settle into our usual table. It's one of those anonymous modern bars that pops up in any vaguely historic building in Saint Paul: infinite craft beers on draft, warm wood accented with brick, and high industrial ceilings bedecked with Edison lightbulb fixtures. It's the kind of place that is always enjoyable and never memorable. "'Glasses,' 'Beanie Boy,' 'Handlebar Mustache,' 'Too Tall,' or *Amélie* Haircut'?"

Adam, like every oblivious man ever, openly gapes at the subject of our gossip. "That table over there? None of them have facial hair."

I gulp my complimentary water, already overheated by the proximity of Adam in the crowded bar. "The guy in the Hawaiian shirt shaved the 'stache last summer, but it's all we'll ever see."

"Poor Handlebar," Chelsea says, pouting. "We should give

him a new signifier. Unless Mar caught feelings in her cat-fishing scheme. Then we should really learn his given name."

"I don't actively reel anyone in, but I use Ashleigh with a *gh* to keep tabs on my nemeses," Mar explains, perusing the menu lazily, despite never having once deviated from her deceptively nonalcoholic drink of choice: soda water with lime.

"A person probably shouldn't have more than one neme-sis," I say into the void. Mara spares me a glance.

Chelsea and Mara discuss fake Ashleigh and her interests in knitting, *Grey's Anatomy,* and Target designer collabora-tions, until Mara pulls the profile up on her phone. "Only Beanie and Too Tall followed me back."

"I think Ashleigh and Too Tall would make a cute couple. She could knit him an extra-long scarf!" Chelsea claps her hands together gleefully.

"Too Tall doesn't know how to turn off geotagging, so he's the most useful for my purposes." Mara winks conspira-torially.

"What constitutes 'too tall'?" Adam squints at the Risky Quizness table, searching for clues.

"If you have to duck when going into the bathroom at the Pizza Lucé on Selby." I tap his forehead lightly, and he nudges me with his shoulder. Just like that. Like we're two people who touch each other affectionately.

"Too Tall hit his head on the ceiling there and bled all over the place. We're talking *The Staircase*–level blood splatter. Total gusher." We collectively wince at Chelsea's visceral de-scription.

Adam turns to face me, deep brown eyes catching the light of the Edison bulb over our table. "And now it's all you see."

A smile sneaks across my lips before I can contain it.

Mara points to Adam, disrupting our flirtatious exchange of glances and half grins. "I wouldn't worry, Bob Vila. I'm the one who prefers men not to loom over me. Alison likes 'em tall."

Hot embarrassment creeps up my neck.

A teasing smile pinches the corners of Adam's eyes. "Too Tall. Handlebar Mustache. Am I 'Bob Vila' when you talk about me?"

Mara nods. "Yep."

"Sometimes 'Hot Adam,'" Chelsea says over her.

"We don't talk about you!" I choke out, but not quick enough to beat the others or prevent Adam's self-satisfied lean against the table. I chug the rest of my water to cool my red-hot cheeks and hope for a well-timed natural disaster to divert everyone's attention.

"Focus up." Mara's eyes sharpen as she enters competition mode. "Since you're playing with us tonight, Adam, you're eligible to play in the tournament on New Year's Day if—and only if—you prove useful to me."

"Don't listen to her. There's no pressure." I cover Adam's hand with mine but then lose my nerve and remove it to tuck my hair behind my ear, like this series of movements was utterly intentional. Luckily, Chelsea gives Adam a friendly shoulder pat that I hope cancels out my too-familiar touches. *Look, Adam, we touch each other here. All friends do.*

Chelsea eyes the bar. "Don't be dumb, and you'll do fine. I'm putting in an order for tater tots. Anyone thirsty?" Adam and I both want IPAs, Mara asks for her standard soda water, and Chelsea trots off to fetch them along with her typical order—whatever beer is light and cheap.

"We're a pretty tolerant team. You can be dumb and quiet, but you cannot be dumb and *persuasive*. No convincing Al to back your wrong answers. Team rules," Mara decrees.

Chelsea finally returns with a tray of beers and the quiz sheet, which Mara immediately snatches to study the image sections on the back. "Who's the host?"

Chelsea sighs in relief. "Darren. We can use either name."

"Mara got our first team banned by insulting the host," I murmur to Adam.

"I wasn't insulting Stu. I was describing him. He's the one who didn't like what he heard."

I lean closer, and smell oranges and wood shavings. "It was a whole ordeal. We changed our name, and Mara dyed her hair brown for a couple of months."

Chelsea leans across the table. "Her reverse Sydney Bristow. Oh! We should keep Sydney Quiztow in our back pocket for when your thing with Risky Quizness escalates to criminal levels."

Mara looks to the ceiling. "It wasn't a disguise. It was an unrelated hair mistake. Are we Otrivia Benson: SVU or Marquizka Hargitay tonight?"

Under the table, Adam's hand swipes against my knee, and it sends a jolt up my spine.

"Let's be bold," he says, and I try not to notice what the words do to me. "Go with the original."

Playing as Otrivia Benson: SVU, we coast through the first few categories. Adam answers a few but primarily watches our practiced game of mental table tennis with awe. The general trivia round is reliably straightforward. Round two perplexes the neighboring teams with a series of pop culture questions in the form of palindromes, but Chelsea inexplicably knows every answer. By the end of the second half, we've only been stumped by two questions.

The music turns back up to the typical Saturday night bar volume—too loud—and Mara leaves to submit our sheet for scoring. On his way to the bathroom, a stranger thanks Chelsea for inspiring him to reconcile with his mom, a life-altering conversation I'm assuming Chelsea squeezed in while picking up our tater tots.

I take a swig of my beer and freeze, feeling the heat of Adam's mouth on my ear.

"You guys are incredible." His breath makes me squirm in my seat.

I turn my head toward his, only slightly. It's so loud that he doesn't move away. His nose—his lips—barely graze my cheek.

"It's Mara, mostly. She's always been a trivia and cross-word addict, and if you play enough, you catch on to the structure—hear variations of the same questions." I manage to make words come out of my mouth, but he's watching me with an intensity that sucks the air from my lungs.

He places a hand on the back of my chair, turning his body to face me dead-on. I scooch forward, and our knees puzzle-piece together until my leg can't feel anything but his, like he's water and I'm weightless in a pool of him.

How could I be this consumed by him and belong to any-one else?

"This is fun." He tilts his head back slightly and I get an even better angle of his boyish grin. I'm desperate to get a peek inside his brain. What could possibly be making him smile like that?

"And that surprises you?" I push myself closer until our bodies are entwined.

He presses his lips closed and inhales. The music lowers so Darren can make an announcement, and Adam's knees knock mine as he turns back toward the table, like our physical closeness was merely a matter of bar acoustics. Just when I'm getting used to the loss of his accidental touch and the subsequent drop in temperature, he shakes his head and takes a slow sip of his beer. I track the movement like a creep.

That mouth kissed me, I think. *Twice.*

He catches me staring, and I don't even have the good sense to be embarrassed. My eyes must look wild, because his expression is thrown by them.

"You can't look at me like that, Ali." His pleading tone is confirmation he's feeling this same torturous pull.

"Like what?" I tease, my voice low, leaning so close I have to crane my neck back to look at him.

I consider a retreat until his hand grabs my thigh.

19

Lewis Hamilton at the Sink, with a Hand Towel

THWAP!

Mara slams our score sheet on the table. The sound breaks the spell we're under, and our bodies snap forward. Her finger pounds into the tabletop. "Risky Fuckness has a perfect score!"

"Oh look, Mar. We only missed two questions. That's not so bad," I say, my voice drenched with the disappointment of Adam releasing my leg.

Mara fusses with her necklace. "You think Evil Incarnate cares we only missed two?"

Adam's hand drifts to the back of my chair like the sharp November breeze. "Wow. You really hate those guys."

"She's pretty competitive," I respond, still catching my breath.

"I'm in love!" Chelsea announces, bouncing into her seat. "There's a guy at the sink who looks *exactly* like Lewis Hamilton. It's uncanny. He's my future husband."

Adam grabs his drink. "Do you follow Formula 1?"

Chelsea shakes her head. "The Netflix show."

Mara plops into her chair "It's a docuseries that follows the sport, but it's a year behind. If you know what's happening in real time, don't spoil it for her."

Chelsea cranes her head toward the bathroom in search of her racing lookalike. "I'm very invested in the future of Mercedes racing—except last year. Do you think that guy's British?"

"He didn't speak?" I ask.

"He offered me a paper towel, but I wasn't listening until I *looked* at him."

"I'm getting a beer. Do you want anything, Ali?" Adam touches my back when he asks.

"I'm fine, thanks." I look at Mara and Chelsea, exposed by my creeping blush.

Chelsea mouths *Ali* as Adam walks away.

Mara raises an accusatory brow. "Al, what's going on with that?"

"I'm sorry, I think you mean *Ali*." Chelsea's in a full-on giggle fit.

I sip my beer for cover. "You're the one who invited him."

Mara rolls her eyes. "I'll invite anyone with a pulse if it gives us a shot at winning."

I shove a tater tot in my mouth. "We were supposed to be having a girls' night—not falling in love at the communal sink."

Chelsea flutters her lashes. "I can only watch you making love with your eyes for so long before I have to get back in the game."

I gag on a tot. "Don't say 'making love.'"

"Are you gonna hook up with this guy? Because he's *very*

interested." Chelsea's face is plotting our pathway to the bathroom stall for our unsanitary quickie, but Mara eyes me over her glass.

"It's complicated. We may have kissed again. Then it got weird. Now it's not, and I'm not sure why." I sip my beer, noticing it sounds fairly uncomplicated when I put it like that.

"They're announcing the top three now," Adam says from behind me, casually placing a hand on my shoulder and sitting down. The warmth of it skitters across my skin.

Darren announces Otrivia Benson: SVU's second-place victory, but I barely register it. My body is buzzing with anticipation. We walk out of the bar into the late November air, and the cold wind hits my face like a slap. I gasp, and Adam rubs the sides of my arms with his thick leather gloves. I shiver under the weight of his hands.

"This coat isn't warm enough for a night like this. Don't you have a parka?"

"This is it. I just have to flip it inside out," I say wryly.

He gives me an admonishing head shake but can't hide his amusement.

We walk to my apartment two by two, knuckles grazing. Chelsea gives me a big, dramatic hug before hopping into Mara's Jeep, and Mara studies Adam and me with an inscrutable look before pulling away, Chelsea in the passenger seat.

I turn to Adam. He's leaning against his truck with his hands in his pockets. He's phenomenal at leaning. As the silence stretches, Adam looks at me.

He just *looks*.

The chill is biting, but I don't make a move. It feels too heavenly to be looked at like this. By *him*. If I collapse on this sidewalk of hypothermia, I'll accept it. I'll have died how I lived: happy, aroused, and with poor circulation in my little toe.

"I liked seeing you tonight . . . with all your friends. I'm glad you invited me." There's a sweet vulnerability in his voice.

"Technically, Chelsea and Mara invited you." I nudge his arm teasingly, and lit by nothing but the glow of the twinkle lights, it feels like an accelerant.

"I like Chelsea. Mara too, but I'm not sure she likes me."

"Any weirdness was more about me. We argued the other day . . ." I should let the conversation drift off—let him drive home—but I can't let go. "And she doesn't know what to make of us."

"I don't know either," he says thickly.

I go completely still. "We're friends," I tell him. *Who kissed yesterday,* I finish within the privacy of my mind. Replaying the kiss while staring into his eyes feels too filthy, so I do it quickly at three times the speed.

"I don't know. I don't think about my friends the way I think about you."

"How do you think about me?" I lick my lips, knowing I'm playing with fire.

I don't need him to answer. Everything I need to know is written all over his face. He reaches out and lightly grabs my mitten-covered hand in his. My body heats despite the freezing air. The juxtaposition of the hot and cold is too much to bear. I stare back at him, preparing to combust.

He pauses, closing his eyes to consider my question. "I imagine your every detail. Constantly. God, imagine the things I could accomplish if I could think about anything other than you: my favorite person." He tilts his head down to mine, and his gaze buries itself into my lungs. Basic breathing becomes difficult.

"I'm only your favorite *new* person."

"No, you're not," he answers, refusing to let me back away from this.

A shiver chases up my spine. If he steps back now, I might fall over the precipice of whatever comes next all by myself.

"Just tell me I'm crazy," he whispers, pressing his forehead to mine. "Tell me you don't think about me the way I think about you. Tell me you don't want me, and I'll drive home, and you'll never see me again."

My eyes flutter shut. I could end this. I could stop everything right here. I'd never have to watch him realize I'm not enough, like Sam did. I open my eyes before my mind's made up. It's a mistake—or a miracle—because his expression is so bare and vulnerable, like what I say next is as vital as water or air. When his eyes flash down to my lips, his mouth quirks, pleased by whatever he sees in my expression.

"Adam . . ." Our hot breaths mingle, and I feel his every shallow inhalation like it's my own.

"Do you want this?" His voice is hushed.

I do. Every molecule in my body has been pulling me toward him since we met. It doesn't matter if I was with Sam or when I was with Sam, how it ended or when, because this—right here, this moment—feels inevitable.

Seconds pass, but he doesn't move. My chest rises and falls, and I feel my last bits of self-control leave me with each exhale. "Yes. I want this. You. So badly."

When we pass the threshold of my studio, the place has never looked more like a room with a bed—the overhead light a spotlight for the single feature in the space below.

But then he hooks his hand into my coat pocket, expertly spinning me around and pressing me against my front door with his body. It isn't even fully closed before he's kissing me against it, but I hear it click under our weight.

With the door against my back, we remove our boots, scarves, coats, and other winter bits, trying our best not to fully break contact. His lips move down my jaw, onto the hollow of my throat. I smile into his hair at the feel of him against me.

His fingers tug at my sweater, and I gasp when he brushes my bare skin. He pulls it over my head so I'm in my entryway with nothing but a lavender lace bralette. When he starts to toss my top on the floor next to our boots, I risk breaking the moment to grab it.

"I like this sweater, and it's kind of wet over—"

"Yeah, yeah." He speaks into my mouth. "I wasn't thinking. I can't think."

"We should make it to the bedroom at least."

"Isn't this all the bedroom?" he teases, and I rebuke him with a bite to his lip, pulling him toward the bed.

Adam grabs me by the hips, and I pull myself on top of him. Everything about this kiss is different. His mouth is slow, languid, sensual. There's no desperation. No fear. Just us. Bodies alone in the dark.

My world has shrunken down to the space between us. Need flows into my fingertips. I need to feel the roughness of his beard beneath them, comb my hands through his hair and grab the back of his neck.

His calloused hand greedily scrapes up my stomach before he pauses. "Will this feel good?"

I look down to see his thumb is grazing the bottom of my

breast. "I can't . . . I don't feel that," I answer, referring to the featherlight touch of his thumb.

A knee-jerk apology plays at the back of my throat, but in the face of his worshipful expression and the tender way his hand moves to cradle my head, nothing comes out. I'm just me—literal scars and all—and he's looking at me like I'm enough. Like I'm everything.

"I can sometimes feel the pressure of, uh—"

I consider how to say it—how to explain it—as he waits patiently while kissing my neck, like he can't bear the momentary loss of contact. I laugh into the pillow beneath him, and he smiles into my clavicle.

I feel my fear and apprehension fall away with the thin top sheet. "I want you to touch me the way you want to touch me. It feels sexy to be wanted by you, even if I can't feel every part of it. Is that okay?"

"Yes. Very." He yanks off the last bits of fabric between us, and there's not a moment of hesitation in his eyes, his hands, his mouth. There's nothing between us. No one between us. Just Adam and me. Nothing has ever felt so much like mine.

20

The Morning After

I WAKE UP FACING the wrong side of my room. I blink open my eyes as the sun assaults me through the gauzy cream-colored curtains. Adam's arm is draped over my stomach. He stirs and pulls me into him, cocooning me under his larger frame. When he nuzzles himself into my hair, I can't help but let out a giggle, luxuriating in the feeling of being safe and warm and held against him like this.

"Morning." It's the same voice, but in my hair—in my bed—it's low, gruff, and tinged with affection.

"Morning." I try to flip over, so we're eye to eye, but he playfully keeps me nestled against him.

"No. Too comfy. Don't ruin it," Adam faux whines with an audible smile in his voice.

"I want to look at you. I need to see your bedhead for blackmail material."

"Then I'll see your bedhead for counter-blackmail material."

"On second thought . . ." I move to make a break toward the bathroom, but he pulls me back and flips me around.

"Just know that I have curly hair and can't wake up with it looking cute. It's impossible." I take in his sleepy face. It's sweet and guileless with the tiniest bit of awe, like he wasn't sure I was real until now.

"I love your hair. And your eyes. What color are they? Sometimes they're green, sometimes they're brown." He gently wraps a strand around his finger and tucks it behind my ear. The lightness of the touch makes me shiver.

I furrow my brow in a show of mock seriousness. "They're this rare, coveted shade called 'hazel.'"

He tugs at a sex-flattened curl. I pinch my lips together to conceal how stupidly happy I am.

Brushing my hand through his soft hair, I settle my fingers on the back of his neck. "I love your hair too. And your chest. I've always wondered what it felt like. That sounded a little creepy. I don't want to make a sweater out of you or something."

He smiles. "I've wondered what you feel like too."

I shrug. "Now you know everything."

"I don't know. I think I have more questions." He pulls me into him, kissing my neck, and I let out a high laugh.

When he comes up for air, he just stares at me. "So I'm the only one who's ever called you Ali?"

"Yep."

"That's crazy to me. You're such an Ali."

"It's my last name."

The moment he hears it, he rolls his head away from me dramatically. "Ali Mullally! You let me call you that?" His face is the portrait of mortification, and he holds me even closer.

I wriggle in his arms. "No, it's nice. Mara and Chelsea are

the only people who have given me a nickname before. Never from a . . .”

I’ve fallen headfirst into the issue at hand. Is this a one-time-to-get-it-out-of-our-systems-and-say-goodbye-for-forever thing? Is this a to-be-repeated-many-more-times thing? Is this the beginning of a relationship?

Now that it’s morning, the rest of the world threatens to burst our happy bubble. With a rush, fear is creeping up my body like vines, threatening to strangle me.

Could this possibly work? He’s Sam’s best friend, I’m Sam’s ex, and we live hours apart.

“Hey. Where’d you go?” He places a thumb on my chin and pulls my face toward his. He analyzes my eyes, slowly leaning in for a kiss. It’s not like the passionate, starving kisses of last night. It’s soft and unwavering. It’s a hug—a caress—but it’s also vitalizing. If I woke up to Adam every morning, I might be able to give up coffee. Though Adam is clearly a caffeine addict, so I can’t imagine there would be a shortage of coffee in a life with him.

The realization that a future like that is unlikely makes me stop the kiss.

“We need coffee,” I say.

Adam stares at me for a beat, deciding whether to let whatever is brewing in my brain be. He nods but doesn’t release me. “I can make it. You stay in bed.” He kisses my nose and hops off the mattress, throwing on his boxer briefs. I take the opportunity to admire his broad, shirtless body in the daylight.

I watch him hunt through my cabinets before putting him out of his misery. “The K-Cups are on the tree next to the Keurig.”

"Keurig? No, Mullally! Unacceptable."

"Your coffee snobbery is unacceptable."

He pops in a K-Cup and presses the button on the machine. "There are so few good things about the morning. The smell of fresh ground beans is the only thing that makes waking up bearable."

"The only thing?" I prop myself up in a casual pinup-girl pose, and I very nearly pull it off.

"I guess there are a *few* other things." He lets a true smile escape before turning back to the coffee mugs.

I take advantage of his time in my kitchen to sneak into the bathroom, still naked. My hair's worse than I feared, so I pull it into a loose topknot. When Adam approaches from behind, mug in hand, I realize he has a full-frontal view of my mastectomy scars in the mirror.

They've faded over the last year, but the horizontal lines remain a visible pink. As the first man who's seen them since that ill-fated Bumble hookup, I brace myself for the moment they catch his eye.

I see the quick eye flit of a double take, but nothing resembling disgust. His expression hesitates, like you might pause over a tattoo or a beauty mark or some other feature that, though unexpected, is not unwelcome.

His lips meet my neck while his eyes capture mine in the mirror. "Do you have any idea how many times I've wanted to do that when you put your hair up in front of me?" he asks with a sexy grin. "I put your coffee on the table next to your book stack."

With a quick peck on my jaw, he exits the bathroom. I grab my robe from the hook and sneak on a swipe of mascara and berry-colored lip balm.

I find coffee and a single freezer Thin Mint on top of my bedside book tower. I scooch myself under my bedspread beside him and sip from my mug cautiously, swiping any residual crumbs off of Glennon Doyle.

"You need a bookshelf for those." Adam gestures from beside me.

"If only I knew a hot carpenter."

"Are they going on the shelf I'm building?"

"No. That'll go by the door for all my hiking, climbing, and backpacking stuff. My bookcase is over there—mocking me." I point at the tall Wayfair box propped in the corner.

"We'll put that together today." Adam looks pleased to have a building task on the agenda. "You seem to enjoy the self-help section." He points to the pile of books next to me.

"My BRCA books." He looks puzzled. "They're the books I bought after I got my mastectomy."

His eyes scan the spines: *Braving the Wilderness*; *Wild*; *Eat, Pray, Love*; *The Year of Yes*; *Walden*; *The Wilderness of Grief*; *Untamed*; and *If Your Dream Doesn't Scare You, It Isn't Big Enough*.

He eyes Glennon. "I'm sensing a theme, and it's not boobs."

"There aren't a lot of BRCA-specific books—though I do have a couple of those too—so after my mastectomy, I bought a bunch of general female-empowerment memoirs and grief books."

"Why is the wilderness such a large part of female empowerment? Do you know how many first-time hikers die each year?"

"*More* people die in cars."

"More people are *in* cars," he retorts.

"Are you seriously taking a stance against the natural world?"

"I reject the idea that a person is automatically self-actualized by hiking the Pacific Crest Trail."

"I've read at least three memoirs that would refute that." We're rattling the rock of messy BRCA-related feelings growing moss inside my chest, and since I'd rather wrestle a coked-up grizzly than uncover what lies beneath my buried neuroses, I drink from my mug and stare down at my bedspread for conversational inspiration. "I don't know what we're supposed to do today. Usually, on a Sunday, I'd be getting ready to see you."

He lifts his brow. "We can meet downtown in an empty apartment."

"Kinky."

"You're hopeless." He gets up and pulls on his jeans, jumping a little to fasten himself into them. "I need some breakfast before I can do your talking thing with you."

"I'm supposed to feed you? It's been so long since I've had an overnight sex guest."

Adam's face trips a bit. I reach out and grab his hand, forcing him to meet my eyes. "Since the mastectomy—"

"You don't have to—"

"I want to." I squeeze his palm and the small gesture loosens the tight rope of muscles in his shoulders. "You're the first person I've trusted to see me. All of me."

My words, however clumsy, have the intended effect and his thumb swipes over my knuckles. "You're so beautiful, Alison. Every part of you is beautiful."

My heart explodes in my chest. I do the only reasonable thing and pull him toward me for a kiss, spilling a drop of coffee on my bedspread in the process, but I can't bring myself to care.

We get dressed and walk the few blocks to my favorite breakfast spot. One part bakery, one part restaurant, and all parts country cottage aesthetic, the Coffee Cake caters to the weekday lunch crowd and Sunday brunchers. We sit at the counter facing a large window peering into the kitchen, and I order cinnamon French toast while teasing Adam mercilessly for ordering oatmeal.

So much is just like always, but everything's changed. For one thing, we never stop touching.

My knee presses against his.

His thumb draws circles in my palm.

I nudge his shoulder with mine, and he presses a quick kiss to my lips.

I feel drunk with hormones and giddiness. Anxious to get back to my apartment, I curse myself for choosing a breakfast order with such a long cooking time. I see Adam's knee jiggling and wonder if he's thinking the same thing.

When his phone rings on the counter, the name flashing on the screen is a pinprick to our happy little bubble.

Dr. Lewis's name glows up at me like a stoplight. "You should take that."

His jaw ticks. "Yeah. I'll just . . ." He trails off, pointing to the sidewalk outside the restaurant.

I watch him answer through the window, his face tight. I feel like a snoop staring at him like this. I feel like the other woman, tucked inside while he sorts out his business just out of earshot. The stool squeaks as I force my legs to swivel away from my view of the sidewalk and peek into the kitchen.

The chef is preparing a mini pot pie. It isn't until he calls for a coworker that I recognize him as Glasses from Risky Quizness. I pull my phone from my coat pocket to message Mara, so she can add another red string to the serial killer board she undoubtedly keeps on their team—but I stop myself.

She wanted to talk things through after our argument, but I haven't made the time. I've been consumed with Adam and the shift in our relationship. Would Mara welcome a casual text from me right now?

Adam's tap on my arm releases me from my thoughts. "What are you staring at?" He rubs my shoulder, and I cover his hand with mine to keep it in place.

"Glasses from the enemy trivia team works here." I tilt my head discreetly in the chef's direction.

"Better alert Mara." His breath kisses my ear.

"What was Sam's dad calling about? Is there something more he needs us to do?" My voice is remarkably nonchalant.

"Reminding me of their party." He sniffs, and I know better than to press. "But mostly, he was telling me about his friend who wanted to hire me for a carpentry project. They're envisioning a shed that doubles as a playhouse or something."

"That's great!" I cheer with too much enthusiasm. I'm making it weird. "Do you need to go measure a baseboard or a stud or . . . how long are you going to let me say words I don't know before you rescue me from myself?" I ask in the face of his rapidly growing smirk.

"No, please go on. I'm loving this." He spears a piece of my French toast. "I'm not taking the job, so it's fine."

"You don't have to give up work on my account. I could help. I recently went through a home improvement crash course. I got very high marks, but full disclosure, I am sleeping with my instructor." He ends my bit by planting a kiss below my ear.

"I can't take a job like that anyway," he says, pulling himself away and leaning against the counter at an angle that emphasizes that fairly devastating jawline. "I'd have to take too much time off work. It's not possible."

"Why? You're moving down here to start your carpentry business anyway. Isn't this exactly the type of job you'd want?"

He rolls his shoulders. "Yeah. Eventually. But not now. And I've dealt with Paul before. When I'm halfway through the shed, he'll decide it's too impractical and want me to repurpose the material for a basement bar or some shit. I'm not committing to something with someone who doesn't know what they want. Plus, I don't want to tangle myself up with the Lewises if we're—"

He's saved by our server, who asks a flurry of questions (More coffee? Do you need butter for that? What about sugar for the oatmeal? Jam? It's lingonberry!). It veers us off course from the conversational landmine we were sprinting toward.

We bicker about oatmeal—perfection or gruel?—and settle back into our routine of quick pecks and addictive touches, as if the phone call—and the unanswerable questions it prompted—never happened at all.

———

THE FIRST THING Adam does is search my apartment for additional home improvement projects. Once he's zeroed in on something that needs fixing, he grabs his tools from his truck, and, to avoid more tow trucks, I text my landlady Adam's license plate number. When he sent me the photo of his front bumper, it felt like the first real indication that this might happen again.

Adam strolls through the door, wielding a drill like a handyman fantasy. "Put me to work."

"I want to do it myself. Make more coffee. You're already off pace for the day."

"Really?" His expression's dubious.

"I hate to tell you this since it's your chosen vocation and all, but using a drill is not that hard."

He yanks off his backpack and removes a pouch holding different drill bits. "Putting together prefab furniture is not my job. Is riding the light rail your job?"

"I've ridden the Green Line while on the clock, so I can't say it's *not* part of my job." I position the tool in both hands like it's a Super Soaker. "Enjoy your coffee and pick out a Christmas movie for us."

I walk to the corner, where that bookcase box has been splayed for the better part of autumn. With the appropriate tool, I make quick work of building it while Adam searches Netflix from my bed. I pick up the narrow bookcase unsteadily for the final reveal.

"Can I . . ." When he speaks into my hair, his voice is so close to me, I startle. "Oh, don't drop the . . ." The bookcase tilts forward, but Adam acts quickly, catching the top above my reach. He helps me right it, and I hold it steady while he silently picks up the drill from the end table and anchors the piece to the wall. "Being tall helps with this part."

"Sorry. That was a bit dramatic."

"It all worked out. And now you have a bookcase."

"It's a miracle," I say flatly, blowing an escaped curl out of my eyes.

"Look at it. You built this!" He congratulates me, rubbing my shoulders.

"I *assembled* it."

"Don't do that. This is my favorite part of making something, seeing what was just pieces of wood become beautiful and useful. You have a space in your home for books and photos and memories, and you made it."

He's the most animated I've ever seen him as he talks about building something "beautiful." It must have been hard for him to do the opposite each day in Sam's apartment— hollowing out that space.

He pushes my hair back and kisses my nose, oblivious to my melancholy thoughts. "I think I've found the perfect Christmas movie."

"That's the spirit. Remember how hostile you once were to Christmas in November?" I grapple with the bedside book stack while Adam queues up a movie on my TV.

"I've only known you four weeks, and you've completely corrupted me."

"I reverse grinched you." I grunt, turning my tower of books sideways and pressing them into the shelf like a broken accordion. "There."

I plop myself on the tiny couch, and Adam pulls my legs over his lap, grasping my thigh like we do this every Sunday morning. I'm looking at this Polly Pocket apartment in a whole new light today. "What do you think?" he asks.

I don't answer at first. I sink into his deep brown eyes and admire the way the light from the TV dances on the hard lines of his face. Finally, I look at what he chose. "Dear Lord! What's this?"

"*Krampus*. It's the only Christmas horror film on Netflix. The ultimate compromise."

"A great man once said, 'A good compromise is when both parties are dissatisfied.'"

He tightens his grip on my thigh and curves his brow upward. "Henry Clay?"

"Larry David."

"Fine. You pick." He tosses the remote in my lap.

"What was your favorite Christmas movie as a kid?" I ask.

He considers the question for a moment before answering, "*Babes in Toyland*."

"Which one?" I ask cautiously.

"Keanu Reeves, Drew Barrymore, trolls . . ."

I gasp dramatically. "Oh, that's very dark, Adam. I'm so worried about your childhood now."

"It's about toys," he says, like it makes that waking nightmare of a movie reasonable.

"We're watching *Elf*. End of discussion."

And we do, but Adam is up and wandering around my bed before Will Ferrell has taught anyone to embrace Christmas cheer.

"Buddy is about to ruin spaghetti *and* maple syrup for you, and you're missing it!" I holler over my shoulder from the couch.

"I need my other sock. My left foot is cold." His voice is muffled under my bed.

"Is it at the bottom of the sheets?"

"I already checked."

"Then it's lost forever. Maybe your right foot will share with the left every so often."

"What's this?" he asks mischievously.

I jump off the couch to intercept whatever humiliation he's set in motion. When I spot my plastic bin of model train cars, I'm equal parts relieved and mortified. "Oh. Those."

His long fingers remove the clear lid almost reverently. "Is this your famous model train? Your locomotive superhero origin story?" He carefully pulls a forest-green steam locomotive out of its bubble wrap. "Why are they in a box under your bed?"

"One, they're incredibly dorky, and, two, have you seen the size of my apartment? If we hold hands in the center, we can each touch a wall."

"You built these with your dad?"

"We just fixed them up. We used to find cars with missing wheels and broken engines at rummage sales and discount bins and paint them in festive Christmas colors. My dad used to give them to me as Christmas presents until he realized how embarrassed I was by them."

I remember bouncing into the garage, shoving a reference photo of a new tunnel system or car we needed to be on the lookout for under my dad's nose. New railcars could go for over $200. Luckily for my family's finances, my dad and I agreed that the joy was in the hunt—finding the discarded treasure and breathing new life into it.

Adam holds a train car in his hand like it's a precious artifact. "These should be prominently displayed."

"No." I laugh self-consciously, rewrapping the car. I snap the clear lid back on the bin and tuck it away again. "Your home is the vision board you live in. The hobby I share exclusively with elderly men and nine-year-old boys is not the version of myself I'm building toward."

"So the self-improvement books get prime real estate and this special thing you love gets shoved under the bed?" The edge of frustration in his voice catches me off guard.

"Those books are aspirational and empowering."

"What about the hiking junk? Forget that shelf you wanted. I could build a display case for your trains instead. It'd be perfect."

"It'd be mortifying. I want to see the things I should be prioritizing every day, not my embarrassing secrets."

Adam shakes his head. "I don't understand why you'd prioritize something you have to remind yourself to tolerate over something you actually love."

I cross my arms. "I love hiking."

"Now say that with a straight face."

"I respect hiking," I clarify. "And I'm challenging myself to love it. That's what healthy people do. I'm healthy."

Adam growls out a soft sigh. "Fine. Yeah. I'm sorry I said anything."

I want to pull us out of the weird energy field we've fallen into. Whatever we are feels too vulnerable to withstand even the smallest of conflicts. I shove him playfully, hoping to jolt us out of the negative charge. He catches my wrists to keep me close, feeling it too. Giddy warmth radiates from our point of contact.

"Okay," Adam says with a forehead kiss. "I hear you."

I pull myself into his chest. "Good. The shelf for my hiking gear makes more sense anyway. You'd probably have to take off work to build a big display case here."

"There are other things in your apartment that I might be

interested in skipping work for." He kisses the top of my head before pulling me onto the bed. We cuddle in positions that prevent attentive viewing of Will Ferrell and Zooey Deschanel. When Adam rises to drive home, he kisses me so casually, like there will be a thousand more kisses just like it. I tamp down the longing that rises in my belly and close the door behind him.

Two hours later, my phone beeps.

5:03 PM
Adam:
I already miss you.

My heart swells and swoops at the message from my new favorite person, and I'm starting to wonder if Adam and I were ever only *friends*.

21

The Only Explanation, Aside from a Lobotomy

IT'S IMPOSSIBLE TO concentrate at work now that I know Adam biblically.

This weekend has upended my life, and yet, I'm still expected to return emails and follow up on ongoing projects. Monday, I catch Daniella on her way to lunch cardio and volunteer to go to Duluth more often if necessary. She doesn't bite, instead asking whether I've decided to accept the new position. I respond with a noncommittal combination of a nod and head shake, until I'm saved by the arrival of the elevator that she marches into. Tuesday, I hum along to lobby music like a lovesick lunatic.

By Wednesday, I'm fantasy shopping for RVs after reading an article about the life-changing experience a cancer survivor had while traveling America. Once I find her blog post about a fecal plumbing mishap, though, I quit browsing Winnebagos and stare at my silent phone in anticipation.

"Why's your face like that? Are you sick?" Patty asks me from her neighboring desk. I've spent the last three days staring down at my hidden cell phone screen, alternating between grinning at my messages and grimacing at the lack of his instantaneous response, deciding Adam must hate me because I've used the wrong *Schitt's Creek* GIF. To her credit, my face must read a bit like food poisoning.

"It's her boyfriend," Josh says for me.

"No, Joshua. Her boyfriend's . . ." The hard line of her lips might as well be a strip of duct tape with the word *dead* scrawled in Sharpie.

"No. The new one," Josh says past me—like my desk isn't the middle piece in our U-shaped configuration. "She's checking her phone obsessively. She gave Kyle the last sparkling water at the team meeting. She even changed her email sign-off to 'Cheers' with an exclamation point. There's only one explanation—aside from a lobotomy."

"Oh! That's wonderful. How long?" Patty asks Josh. I may as well not be here.

"Sometime this weekend. Definitely before the Monday stand-up meeting. But it's been ramping up for a while."

"I'm not seeing anyone," I say in protest, because Adam and I never defined anything.

Patty, using gossip as an excuse for a break, pops open a bag of vending-machine mixed nuts. "Is that why you haven't decided about the job? You're worried how it would affect your new relationship?"

"What? That's not—" Poorly timed, my phone buzzes violently.

Patty beams. "Oh, it's him!"

Josh flashes a self-satisfied smirk.

"It's my mom," I say truthfully, flashing her "Happy Thanksgiving" message out to the room.

"It's Wednesday. Thanksgiving's tomorrow." Josh's tone is soaked in suspicion, as though even calendars support his hypothesis.

I shoot her back a smiley face, and then spot a missed text from Adam.

Josh ceases typing to point at my pink-cheeked grin. "See. That's the look."

"I've earned a free cookie from Panera, Josh. That's all."

Josh grimaces. "Whenever you get excited about your Panera rewards, I feel so sad for you."

Patty tsks. "Let her have her cookie, Joshua."

> **3:47 PM**
> **Adam:**
> Where are you right now?
>
> **3:52 PM**
> **Alison:**
> Work.
>
> **3:54 PM**
> **Adam:**
> In front of your place.
>
> **3:55 PM**
> **Adam:**
> Cut out early.
>
> **3:56 PM**
> **Adam:**
> I need to see you. Can't wait.

After making my transparent excuses to Josh and Patty, I sprint home through the skyway and find Adam's truck next to my fixed-up Subaru in my apartment's parking lot.

"Can you get the door?" He steps out of his truck holding two paper grocery bags. "When did Uncle Ricky finish your car?"

"He dropped it off Monday," I answer, dismissing a notification on my phone that would plummet me to the truck floor if I weren't mostly numb to them by now. I swallow the lump in my throat.

He smirks. "Is that work? Are you in trouble?"

"Patagonia reminder. From Sam. One of his 'Messages from the Future.' I really should delete those," I explain, as casually as I can, but Adam's face is frozen in place.

I shake the moment off my body and pull open the security door, peering into Adam's shopping bags. "You know, your caveman texting style is much less frustrating when this is the result." I spot a baguette, a bottle of wine, a bundle of green parsley, and a clear bakery box of Thin Mints before my eyes are drawn to a clay pot of delicate pink flowers. "Is this an orchid? Did you bring groceries and flowers?" My eyes take in Adam's appearance behind the paper bags. His signature reversible jacket—khaki-side out—is covering a charcoal crewneck sweater and navy slacks. "Are you wearing fancy pants?" I paw at his clothes to get a better look.

He groans, seemingly embarrassed by my attention. "I changed out of my work clothes. It's not a big deal. Can you let me up so I don't drop these?"

I gingerly remove the orchid and lead Adam up the stairs.

"What are the groceries for?" I ask as we walk into my apartment, immediately turning into the kitchenette.

He unloads the contents of his grocery bags into the fridge. "Pies are for Thanksgiving. The rest is for dinner. I noticed you didn't have any food that wasn't cookies."

"How long can you stay?" I ask, sidestepping the accusation.

"As long as you'll have me. Or work on Monday. Whichever comes first."

"Don't you have Thanksgiving plans?"

"Yeah, but you're coming with me," he says into my lower cabinet.

"To your family's Thanksgiving?"

He places my largest pot under the faucet. "When I asked you if you were busy and you sent me a GIF of a girl eating on a toilet in a bathroom stall, I didn't realize that was like a *firm* plan."

I consider explaining the scene from the cinematic classic *Mean Girls* but opt to stay on message. "Are you inviting me to the Berg Family Thanksgiving?"

"It's just my sister's family. My parents are on a cruise."

I struggle to picture any human sharing DNA with Adam on a cruise, but I push past it. "Do they know who I am?" The moment the question falls out of my mouth, I want to suck the words back in like a rogue spaghetti noodle. My shoulders tense, anticipating Adam's retreat at the suggestion of Sam, the Lewis family, and this scheme I'm trapped in.

Instead, he pulls me into him, and his chest shakes with a suppressed laugh. My body relaxes. "You're Alison." He tips my face up to his, splintering me with his mahogany eyes. His voice is sweet and reassuring. "I really want you to meet them."

"Then I can't wait." I press my lips to his chin. "What're you cooking for me?"

He moves the full pot to the largest of the three burners on my undersized range. "Carbonara. It's not fancy."

It looks fancy. He didn't skimp on anything. The guanciale is from the butcher counter, and he bought two kinds of expensive Italian cheese. I recognize the pinot grigio as one that sits two whole shelves above what I deem a reasonable wine splurge.

When he bends into the fridge, I notice neatly trimmed hairs on the back of his neck. His beard is just as impeccably groomed when he turns to face me.

I narrow my eyes, and his cheeks turn the loveliest shade of pink. "What?"

My face splits in two. I can't contain my amusement. "Did you get a haircut today?"

He rubs the back of his neck, but the gesture doesn't erase the evidence.

I pull his arm back down and slide my hand into his. "No, wait. I don't mean to tease you. It's just . . . this is *very* romantic."

"Why do you sound so shocked? I can be romantic." He threads his fingers through mine.

"I'm not shocked you're romantic. I'm shocked that I'm someone who inspires romance."

"That's ridiculous."

"I'm serious! I don't know what to do with myself." I swing our clasped hands to demonstrate this.

"You inspire me." Adam squeezes my hand and pulls me toward him, his back against the kitchen counter.

I've never felt such reciprocated attraction with another person, but it's so much more than lust. When I overhear someone complaining about Christmas creep or make it on the train just in time or have some minor work success, I want to tell Adam. I want to earn one of his rumbly laughs. He makes me feel desired and wanted for every odd and boring part of me.

"What do the subjects of your romance normally do?" My voice is lighter than air.

He leans his head down, placing a firm hand possessively on the small of my back. "You could start by kissing me."

"Why didn't I think of that?"

I tip my mouth up to his, and he responds with a slow, deliberate kiss. Quickly, the fire between us builds. It was four weekends of forced proximity before the heat was too much. Now we can only kiss for a minute before we're flicking off burners and backing out of the kitchen to frantically pull each other's clothes off.

It's too good, my brain worries.

But with Adam, nothing feels *too* anything. It feels exactly right.

22

A Pikachu Balloon

JUNE? WHERE DO you want the pies?" Adam hollers through the doorway. The rosemary wreath bounces against the door knocker, sending the scent of herbs into the late November chill.

We step into the sunny yellow entry of his sister's 1920s bungalow. He removes his boots on the hallway runner while balancing a pair of pie boxes overhead, and I follow suit.

"You brought the pies?" A honeyed female voice greets us.

His sister's house is irrepressibly joyful. We walk through the minty-green living room—packed with pops of oranges, corals, and blues—into the cheery peach kitchen.

A tall brunette in a pink knit sweater smiles from behind her dishwasher.

"I told you I was bringing them, didn't I?" He greets her with a kiss on the cheek and sets the boxes in the only open spot on the counter, which is otherwise occupied by three bowls of chips, a cutting board of vegetables, and six Crock-Pots of varying sizes, putting the Minneapolis power grid to the test.

"But there was that one year—"

"Am I ever going to live down that power outage? It was the ice storm's fault. It took down all of Two Harbors."

"It's a shoddy carpenter who blames his tools."

He removes the pies from their boxes and breaks them down to recycle. "Just for that, you're not getting any of the caramel apple pecan. Did you hear that, Dev?" she shouts across the house. "More for us."

"No! Fine, fine. You're perfect and nothing is ever your fault."

"That's what I thought. Happy Thanksgiving, by the way." Adam snatches a carrot from the wood board and crunches. "Where's Otis? I want to introduce him to Alison."

I smile at his mention of me but continue to stand in the kitchen doorway like a vampire waiting to be invited in.

"Jesus, Adam. Were you raised in a barn? Use a plate." His sister empties enough clean plates for five before shutting the dishwasher. Adam bumps her hip so he can unload the rest of the clean dishes for her, like they've done this millions of times before.

She wipes her hands on a lemon-patterned towel and crosses the checkered floor to wrap me in a hug. I take a step forward to meet her, feeling a bit of my anxiety release. "The famous Alison. I've heard so much about you. I'm June, Adam's sister."

"Nice to meet you." I punctuate her affectionate hug with an awkward back pat. I want June to like me more than I care to admit, so obviously, I'm at my most socially inept.

"I don't like turkey anymore," a tiny voice shouts. A waist-height human barrels into the kitchen like a tornado. Arms full of ceramic plates, the Berg siblings dance around him without missing a beat.

"You eat turkey all the time," his mom coaxes.

"Not anymore. It's yucky."

"Not this turkey. This is the good stuff. You like it." Adam gives the seven-year-old no room to disagree.

"Who's she?" Otis asks, pointing straight at my nose in that shameless way in which all elementary-school-aged children move through the world.

June lowers her son's finger and shuffles him in the direction of the sink. "Is that how we meet new friends? Wash your hands for snack."

"Hi, I'm Otis," he says, stepping up to the stool in front of the faucet. He has the same round, nut-brown eyes as June and Adam, with darker brown hair and tan skin. His expression is so sweet and open like his mom's.

"IIi, Otis. I'm Alison."

He looks between his uncle and me. "Are you Uncle Adam's girlfriend?"

I think my eyes pop out of my skull.

"What do you know about girlfriends?" Adam asks his nephew with a surprised cough. He's putting glasses away in the cabinet behind me. I resist the urge to flip him around with each thud of heavy ceramic and analyze his expression.

"I know what girlfriends are. I have two girlfriends," Otis says proudly.

"Otis, can you tell Dad that Adam and Alison are here?" June steers the subject away from girlfriends, real or imagined, and Otis hops off the stool and skips out of the kitchen.

June looks at me. "So are you two . . ."

His hand finds the small of my back. I lean into him, like an innate call and response.

"Of course we are." His voice is so sure and uncomplicated.

The sound of it lights me up from the inside. "But I didn't want to reward his precociousness with a straight answer."

June reaches over her head for a pair of hand-thrown ceramic mugs. She ladles something warm and spicy into the peacock-blue one and hands it to me. "He's not half as bad as some of the kids in his class. Arabella caught me vaping in front of a Sky Zone and told me my insides were going to turn to Jiffy Pop."

Adam takes the yellow mug from June with his right hand. His left hand is otherwise engaged drawing small, achingly slow circles on my lower back.

I blow into my steaming cup, and the appley scent wafts into my nose. "What did you do?" I ask, a smile in my voice. I like June. I like how loose and comfortable Adam is here.

I like Adam. Full stop.

June spoons a bit of the liquid into her mouth straight from the Crock-Pot. "I said, 'Thank you for that fearless feedback. I'm trying to quit.' And that her mommy puts wine in her Starbucks cup during playdates, so Arabella should place her eagle-eyed focus on what's happening on the home front."

I choke on my hot toddy.

June shakes a bit of cinnamon in the mixture before stopping to look at me. "I'm joking, I promise. I would never say that to a child. And Hallie doesn't drink *that* much. I swear."

Adam rolls his eyes, and I catch a glimpse of him as a little brother. "She knows you're joking. And she's not going to narc on you to Hallie."

"Sorry. Adam hasn't brought anyone home before. I'm all in my head."

Adam groans. "June—"

"Hallie sounds like a blast," I interrupt. "And now I know to keep an eye out for the moms carrying opaque venti Starbucks cups if I'm looking for a good time."

June's mouth turns up in the corners, and she sends Adam a secret sibling look I can't decode.

"But the Sky Zone Jiffy Pop part was true, though. Arabella is *super* judgmental for a six-year-old."

"You have to stop vaping, June," Adam scolds. It's as though they have this back-and-forth every time he comes by. Just another sister-brother dance they do. It makes me a little homesick.

She tosses her head. "I know, Dad." She turns toward me, a potential sympathizer. "It's a holdover from art school. Smoking behind the ceramic studio became vaping on the back porch. I managed to quit for a while, but then—"

"Pikachu!" Otis screams.

"Inside voice!" June, Adam, and a man's voice I can't place yet parry in unison.

"It's a Pikachu balloon!" he cries out again, undeterred.

"Looks like the parade started." June's eyes go wide. "I need to wrangle my animal. Alison, make yourself at home. Adam, can you set the table?" She marches out of the kitchen, sipping from her mug.

I head for the cupboard, but Adam grabs me by the belt loop and tugs my back into his chest. The thrill of his semi-public manhandling zips up my spine.

His mouth tangles in my hair. "I heard my sister order you to make yourself at home."

"At home, I set the table."

He twists me to face him. "Not in the Berg house. You're a guest. Pretend you're relaxing at your apartment right now."

I tilt my head to get a better look at that chin dimple. I can't get enough of it. "There's entirely too much space here for me to pretend I'm at home."

"What about *home* home? What are the Mullallys doing on Thanksgiving?" he asks, lacing our fingers together.

"Emma's probably with her wife's family. My mom gave us all food poisoning from an undercooked turkey twenty years ago, so she usually makes a Stouffer's lasagna while my dad holes up in the den and murmurs at the Lions in distress."

"Can't help with the lasagna, but I'm pretty sure Dev is watching football on his phone in the other room. Might even catch a frustrated murmur or two."

I play with his fingers, relishing the feeling of being the first woman Adam Berg has brought home to his family.

"Don't send me away." I push out my bottom lip. "I'd rather see what trouble you get up to in here."

The look in his eyes is searing.

We're interrupted by a South Asian man with brown hair, clear plastic glasses, and a strong resemblance to Adam's nephew. He strides into the kitchen with a giggling Otis over his shoulder. "Don't mind us. Just checking on my bird." He plops his son on the floor next to him and squats in front of the lit oven window. "Should only be another hour. Maybe two. I'm Dev, by the way. You must be Alison."

Adam tilts his head toward his brother-in-law. "Dev's in charge of the turkey, and you should probably add three hours to his meal ETA."

He squints at the glistening bird resting primly in the roast pan. "Not this year. I've been watching *Barefoot Contessa* all week. I've got this down to an exact science."

"I'm starved," Otis whines.

Adam grabs a carrot off the platter behind him. "Here."

He winces. "I'm not starved for that."

"Then you're not starving, are you?"

Otis pokes his uncle when a new thought occurs to him. "I added blankets this morning. Can you go look at it?"

Adam tilts his head toward the dining room. "Your mom put me to work, but you can show Alison your improvements. I'll find you guys when I'm done."

"We're making Uncle Adam an apartment in my room."

I smile at Otis. "Sounds cozy."

"It's a bunk bed fort, but I connected it to the rocking chair with a quilt, so there's more space for reading."

His dad peers over his glasses at him. "Make sure I still have a path around the room."

"I'm really, really good at forts," Otis declares. "But Uncle Adam's still better than me."

"Not for long, bud." Adam touches the top of his nephew's head affectionately.

I melt just a little.

Otis reaches for my hand and tugs me up the stairs to his room. "It's not as tall as the last one, but Mom won't let me use the couch cushions anymore."

"That's good. Rules spark creativity."

Otis throws me a look that says he's not convinced by my design philosophy. Like his mom, he's a mini maximalist in the making.

I peek into Otis's room through the open doorway. He hasn't followed his dad's instructions, and there's no space to move about the room. Still, there's an architectural method to the madness of stacked pillows and blankets tied to the metal posts of the twin bunk beds. The blankets create a lean-to tent off the bed frame with the ends secured under a bookcase and a wooden rocking chair.

Unable to stop myself, I get closer to admire it. "Did your uncle make that?"

"Uh-huh. He made it before I was born. I want him to make a bed loft now, like my friend Phoenix has in his room, but my mom says he doesn't make stuff anymore."

I run my hand along the chair's smooth arm. The piece is so functional, but it's more than that—it's art. Organic curves and clean lines emphasize the warm golden wood. It looks both sturdy and airy—masculine yet delicate. There's a sky-blue crescent pillow tied to the spindles where Otis's back can rest while reading a story. There's so much life in this chair. I can't picture something so confidently itself coming from the messy and confused workspace Adam showed me in Duluth.

"Did you add another side already?" Adam appears in the doorway, his shoulder pressed against the emerald-green accent wall behind Otis's bunks.

Otis's eyes sparkle at the sight of his uncle. "I wanted to make two sides around your bunk, but Dad said we won't be able to see if we do."

"We can take away the blue blanket to make a skylight and hold the other ones together with zip ties. They're in the glove box of my truck."

Otis's eyes go wide. "You brought them? Mom! Uncle

Adam brought the zip ties!" he yells to his mom on the way down the stairs toward the driveway.

Adam chuckles at his nephew, high-stepping over blankets to cross toward me. "Otis is easy to impress."

"This chair is amazing. Seriously, Adam."

"I'm happy with the quality. The teak's held up well to abuse." He snorts, likely imagining an Otis-designed stress test.

"It's beautiful."

Adam's cheeks pink. "Do you mind if I help Otis with this?" He points to the mass of blankets and pillows behind us. "June's emptying pop into the cooler on the back porch."

"Perfect. I have so many questions for her."

Adam's head shake produces a barely detectable breeze. "I regret bringing you already."

I plant a kiss on his cheek. "Too late."

While Adam is helping Otis install a fort skylight with zip ties and a rainbow knitted throw, and Dev is moaning "Come on" at something the Detroit Lions did or failed to do, I'm sitting on my heels in a crouch on the back porch with June. She passes me a twelve-pack of Coke while she pours a bag of ice over bottles of Spotted Cow, a cult favorite beer sold only in Wisconsin she snagged from a border gas station for this occasion.

"He's been different these last couple weeks. He must really like you." June's tone is as cheery as ever, but her eyes size me up.

"It's been nice having this time to get to know each other—despite the circumstances."

"So you're Sam's, were Sam's . . . ," she stumbles.

The bitter-cold air finds every hole in my orange sweater.

I bob on the balls of my feet to generate heat. "We dated for a little while. Before."

June's big brown eyes are brimming with sympathy. "I'm sorry. Sam was a good guy, and I know Adam's been taking it hard."

My eyes fall onto the Coke box I'm breaking down.

I'm ashamed to admit that for the past week, we've existed in a mostly grief-free bubble. Since we delivered Sam's keys, I've been too preoccupied with my growing feelings for Adam to notice much else.

Not sure what to say, I change topics. "I can't get over how Adam's been sleeping in that tiny bunk bed this whole time."

June cracks open a Coke and laughs into the can. "That ridiculous bunk bed!" she says before taking a sip. "I want to buy something nicer, but every time I bring it up, Adam swears he's going to build whatever Otis wants. At this point, I'd take anything that doesn't sway when I sit on it."

I smile at the image of Adam swinging into the bunk each night.

June leans her back against her house. I do the same, so we're shoulder to shoulder drinking pop and looking out over her small, snow-covered lawn. The chicken coop stands in the back corner like a dollhouse on stilts, surrounded by an out-of-season soccer net, orange Adirondack chairs, and abandoned tiki torches. The whole scene looks vaguely post-apocalyptic in the way it all peeks out from under the white blanket as nature reclaims the city.

"I bet it's a challenge to get a big piece down from Duluth. When he starts his shop down here, it'll be easier to build something for Otis."

Her laugh is sharp and thin. "Yeah. I'll be counting down

the days." June's face falls when she registers the confusion on mine. "I didn't mean . . . Adam's always *supposed* to move back here, but it's not something we're counting on anymore."

I guess seven years of stasis will do that.

"Might be different now. Like I said, he's different with you." She takes a gulp of her Coke, and the silence drifts from comfortable to stilted to tense, hitting every possible step on the way down.

Adam appears in the open sliding door. "Did she give up all of the blackmail material?"

I shoot upright like he's busted us in the middle of a drug deal, even though we were only quietly drinking pop.

"I didn't tell her about your childhood obsession with *The New Yankee Workshop,* if that's what you're asking."

His sister hands him a beer, and he does that fratty thing where you pop off a bottle cap by slapping it on the ledge of a patio railing. I know I must be far gone because I find every bit of the maneuver—the easy confidence with which he does it, the tiny flex in his arm muscles it produces, the way he catches the cap in midair—unbelievably sexy.

"But the girl deserves to know that you used to cry out for Norm Abram when our parents turned off the TV."

I delightedly mouth, *Norm?* at Adam. Color creeps up his neck.

June shuffles us back inside with a cheeky big-sister smile. "His first words were *drop leaf table.*"

I squeal in delight, but Adam's face reddens by the second. "That's an exaggeration."

"Is he telling you about the radial arm saw he asked for every Christmas, even after the mall Santa lectured him on age-appropriate gifts and blade safety?" Dev hollers from the living room.

"I was like six years old!"

His protesting only makes me laugh harder. "That doesn't make you sound more normal!"

Otis appears out of thin air. "Cleo's sister said that mall Santas aren't Santa and he won't make any of the gifts you ask for."

Dev and June trade telepathic parent looks.

"I wouldn't listen to her, bud." Adam swings his nephew onto his back. "Cleo's sister doesn't understand the complicated bureaucracy of the North Pole. Now, let's show Alison the new skylight before dinner in . . . ?"

Dev stands and studies his smartwatch. "Two hours. Definitely no more than three."

"See, Adam? You make fun of Crock-Pot Thanksgiving, but these are the conditions I'm working under," June argues before instructing us to not fill up on chips like last year.

With that, she shoos us kids upstairs until dinner is served.

Three and a half hours later, there's a turkey carcass on the counter, a platter of meat, and six simmering slow cookers filled with every classic Midwestern Thanksgiving side. Since I followed instructions and did not fill up on chips, I load up my plate with mashed potatoes, gravy, green bean casserole, stuffing, sweet potatoes topped with marshmallows, and, finally, a bit of turkey.

Despite Dev's variable cooking time, the turkey is perfection, and I see the wisdom in Crock-Pot Thanksgiving when every bite hits my tongue at the optimal temperature.

"This food is absolutely delicious. I can't thank you enough for letting me crash your Thanksgiving."

"It's not crashing if you're invited." Adam nudges me with his shoulder.

I try my best to stop the goofy smile curving up my lips. "All the same, I'm grateful to be here. It's been a while since I had a family Thanksgiving like this."

A warm, maternal smile spreads across June's face. "You're always welcome, Alison." She sucks in air through her nostrils like she's harnessing the extra oxygen to suppress whatever emotion is bubbling up under her lungs. "It looks like we've moved into the gratitude portion of the evening."

Otis sits up straighter, apparently too young to be embarrassed by expressions of familial love. "I wanna go first."

"Try again," Dev corrects him rotely.

"Can I go first, please?" Otis asks, and we all nod back at him. "I'm thankful for my fort. For Mommy, Daddy, Nana, Dada"—he counts off each name on his fingers—"Grandma Nance and Grandpa Tom, Uncle Adam, Al . . ." He looks at me, now apparently just listing people he sees.

"Alison," Adam finishes for him.

"And Pikachu balloon . . ." His voice trails off like he might continue counting gratitudes indefinitely, but when he starts in on his green beans again, we collectively realize he's satisfied with his list.

"Okay then," June picks up. "I'm grateful to have my happy healthy family here today. I know it wasn't under the best circumstances and this hasn't been the easiest few weeks, but I've loved seeing a little more of my brother lately." She wipes her eye with her pink sleeve. "And that you won't look like Bigfoot in the pictures I send Mom from today. Which means I'm most grateful for Alison, since that was clearly for your benefit."

"Oh, yeah. You look good, man." Dev combs his fingers through his own beard. "Refreshed. And did you get a haircut?"

"He's trying to impress Alison," June says by way of explanation. "So now we're all treated to his cute widdle face."

"It's just a beard trim, guys." Adam's cheeks are crimson.

"Well, I'm thankful for the family and our health and . . ." Dev trails off, mentally rifling. "You took all the good ones, hon."

June gives him a satisfied nod.

"I guess I'll go next," Adam starts. "I'm grateful that we could all be together today. Family, health . . ." He waves his hand like *yada yada*. "I'm grateful for friendship, even when it . . ." His eyes cloud with emotion, and he tries to clear it away with a cough. "But I'm grateful I got to spend this time with you, Alison. When I first saw you last month, a part of me knew we'd be here right now."

I make a sound I've never heard come out of my mouth before. I think I guffaw.

"What?" he asks, tripping over the laugh in his throat.

"That is some serious revisionist history."

He shakes his head and reveals a new smile to me, his nervous but excited smile. "No, it's not. I knew. I knew from the moment I saw you."

"How did you know?" My voice is incredulous but my face is all dumb, happy grin.

"Because I was asleep—in this walking, talking, waking coma. And now I'm awake. You woke me up."

Something warm and wonderful curls beneath my ribs, and I want to kiss him, hold him, and cry into his neck all at once. But we're still sitting at the Thanksgiving table with his family, so I settle for rubbing his shoulder blade as the happy tears build behind my eyes.

Once we've finished eating and cleared the table, Dev gets swallowed up by the floral-printed pillows on the couch, watching whatever football content is still playing. Adam reads a story to Otis while June has me blind taste-testing wines from the Wine of the Month Club Arabella's mom gifted her. I learn I have no idea what expensive tastes like, but I'm slightly buzzed by the end of it, which is a perk of the game.

After Otis is tucked in bed, June sends us home with more food than will fit in my fridge and pretends not to hear Adam when he objects to the second container of turkey. They wave us off, and Adam guides me by the hand down the front steps.

The glow from the multicolored twinkle lights dances across his features, and I'm overwhelmed with a sense of rightness. *This is what it will be like,* I think, *this is what being in love with him will be like.*

23

Denise Richards
Was a Scientist

I N THE TWO weeks after Thanksgiving, Adam only manages one overnight visit. I offered to drive up to Duluth,
but between his catching up on hours before the winter
slowdown and my covering Patty's duties until Daniella hires
a replacement (or maybe *my* replacement since I still haven't
given her an answer on the position), nothing seems to line
up until the annual Lewis family Cookie Party.

We arrive separately, keeping our relationship under wraps
today out of respect, or possibly cowardice. I'm choosing not
to examine my motivations.

I don't know what I expected from the words *Cookie
Party,* but it was not this. There are no children frosting cookies on coffee tables or parents passing around Tupperware
containers of maimed gingerbread people. This is an elegant,
catered affair with charcuterie, two different fig preparations,
and holiday whiskey punch with a punny name spelled out
on a letterboard. The titular cookies were ordered in from a
local high-end bakery and are so stunning, I feel uncomfortable eating them.

Unlike Adam's cozy Thanksgiving celebration, the dress

code at the Lewises' appears to be Minnesota Cocktail Casual, which translates to women in their finest wool sweaters and men in their golfiest golf shirts. Not much of a linksman, Adam is in a cream fisherman's sweater, awakening within me a new—and decidedly sexual—*Deadliest Catch* fantasy. My cranberry sweater dress is doing something similar to him if the conspicuous charge in the space between us is any indication. I'm shocked the hair of passing guests doesn't stand on end.

The Lewises' decor consists of Pottery Barn's best approximation of "Farmhouse Americana." The whole house is painted like different-flavored lattes. The vanilla foyer transitions into a hazelnut formal living area. There's an unlit Christmas tree in every room. I can't discern whether this is an aesthetic choice or if they weren't in the decorating spirit this year. The whole house *approaches* "festive" without quite crossing the finish line.

The vibe is more of a free-flowing cocktail party than a sit-down affair, and to my relief, very few people ask who I am to the family. Sam exists in stories, but direct mention of him is avoided at all costs.

The less relevant a guest is to an immediate family member, the greater the burden they seem to bear in keeping the conversation light and snappy. In some spaces, that person is Adam or me, but in the sunroom overlooking Lake Minnetonka, a neighbor is carrying the conversation on her back. Against a chai latte wall of floor-to-ceiling windows, she asks everyone their favorite James Bond film and refuses to let anyone off the hook until they've provided a bulleted list of reasons why they prefer it.

"I've only seen one of the Pierce Brosnan ones," I answer,

gripping my appetizer plate like a security blanket. "I can't remember which one." For our trivia team, Patrick is the expert on the Suited Men Saving the World genre (both tuxedo and latex).

This answer doesn't seem to satisfy her. She pushes her icy blond hair behind her ears, agitated. "What country was he in? Who was the villain? Which Bond girl was it?"

"I want to say Denise Richards was a scientist?"

It's not what she wants to hear, and I'm finally dismissed.

"You couldn't have just said *Casino Royale*?" Adam grins against the shell of my ear. I look around on instinct, finding only a pregnant cousin, Lucy, napping with her eyes open while her oblivious husband, Greg, holds court in the corner with a nineties-style stand-up routine on mini quiches.

"You couldn't have jumped in and saved me?" I ask, biting into my bottom lip.

"And miss the trivia expert struggling to name the movie where Denise Richards played a nuclear physicist? You're still trying to remember it, aren't you?"

"*The World Is Not Enough,*" I blurt with a snap of my fingers. "I should go find her."

He pulls me back by the arm. "Let her find someone who appreciates British spy films the way she does." His thumb swipes the sensitive part of my wrist, igniting my insides.

"Adam, my man!" a voice booms from behind me. "It's been too long."

A corn chip flees my plate, and Adam takes a small step away from me, his left eye twitching at the tall, forty-something man in a fleece vest. "Paul. How's the house?" Adam asks stiffly.

"Don't get me started on that money pit." Paul's smirk tells us he'd love nothing more than to detail every small construction setback. "It was such a shame we couldn't get that partnership off the ground. Are you still doing carpentry? I have a million projects I could use you on. The deck railings are a mess, and come summer we'll want one of those fancy She Sheds for the girls."

"My work up north keeps me pretty busy." Adam must register my confusion because he glances my way before looking back at Paul. "Sorry I couldn't be more helpful. If you'll excuse me . . ." Adam starts to walk away.

Paul initiates a Sorkin-style walk-and-talk, detailing the hail damage to his deck. Adam increases his pace, refusing to relent, and I trail behind like a lost puppy. Once we're in the matcha mudroom, Paul must realize that Adam *will* walk out the door in his socks to escape this conversation, and he retreats to the kitchen with his tail between his legs.

"Why wouldn't you take that job?" I ask Adam once Paul's out of earshot.

"I can't rebuild a deck by myself in a weekend. Or make a She Shed playhouse for his daughters. Why call it a She Shed? Sheds are for everyone."

"I think it's a Pinterest thing." I tug at a stray piece of hair that's fallen out of my half-up half-down thing. "If you lived here it wouldn't be a problem. Plus, you'd have more time to focus on your furniture. He wants your work."

"He doesn't know what he wants."

"What partnership was he talking about?" Adam doesn't respond, instead digging through his pockets with the frenzied intensity of a truffle pig. "What are you looking for?"

"Sam's condo keys. I forgot to return the other set."

He frees the key ring from his pocket. The touristy key

chains clink together like discordant wind chimes. He places it on the rack like an eerie parting gift from beyond. It dangles between his parents' keys like a denial, as though Sam might stroll through the side door and pluck them off the hook.

It's the most unsatisfying ending imaginable.

"I'm sorry. I think I'm a little off today, Sam's birthday and all."

"It's Sam's birthday?" I ask too loudly. My head swivels around to see who might have overheard. "Today?" I ask, in a whisper this time.

"The party's always *near* his birthday, but this year it fell on the actual day. Sam was making a big deal about it. That's why his dad wouldn't cancel. How do you not know his birthday?"

"I knew he was a Sagittarius." Chelsea unearthed this information in one of her two-minute soul-baring conversations.

I'm reminded again that Adam and I are grieving two different losses. Though mine is not insignificant, I missed out on a future with Sam as the friend who could push me out of my comfort zone. Adam lost history.

He looks back at me quizzically, waiting for translated subtitles to pop up on my forehead. "We didn't date that long, remember?"

His eyes drift over my head at the guests milling in the other room, and for the first time since I told him the truth about me and Sam, he looks weary. Defeated.

Anxiety swirls in my stomach. "You *are* moving to Minneapolis, right?" The words burst from my mouth inelegantly. I sound panicked and needy and all I can do to stop myself from spewing more emotional vomit is stuff a carrot in my mouth from the hors d'oeuvre plate I managed to hold on to in the Great Paul Getaway.

"Of course," he answers simply. "When I'm ready."

My tension mutates into dread and picks up speed like a tornado. "It's okay if you're not—Duluth isn't so far—I just want to know what to expect."

His agitated hand tugs at the back of his hair. "I'll move when I want to move, Alison."

It's the wrong thing to say. I want him to want to take it back—say his words didn't come out right—but he doesn't move. My eyes fall to my plate. I dip a carrot in the baked brie like it's an important task requiring all of my focus and follow Adam back into the crowded sunroom, where we can't discuss anything real. My only hope is that Bond Lover will return with follow-up questions, but instead, something far worse happens.

"My two faves are here!" Russell shouts from where he's holding court across the room.

Adam's face tightens. I half murmur, "Shit." I let myself forget I'm only here to play a part for ten minutes, and Adam and I are sent the one person who could blow this all up.

I stuff a loaded cracker in my mouth, sputtering, "Russell. What a surprise."

"Well, I am their Realtor." He says *Realtor* as if the role is on par with a godparent or religious leader.

A cracker shard stabs my throat, forcing a choking cough, but it doesn't do the kindness of suffocating me. Adam takes my plate and pats my back. I force out hard hacks until

I finally will it loose, ending a small part of this waking nightmare.

Russell, wearing his most smug smile, asks, "Are you guys officially a thing yet?"

His question rings out like a warning shot. Is it me or did the whole party just go still? I stroke my throat like I'm still recovering from my brush with death and let Adam answer for the both of us. "We're here for Sam's family, Russ."

Russell squints. "Two things can be true." He turns to me, and his smile is more earnest. "Excited for Chile?"

I nod quickly, rolling my lips under my teeth. Adam white-knuckles my plate of assorted dips.

"Sam said it might not be her thing," Russell continues. "But everyone should endure the rain on a trail in the Andes at least once. Right, Alison? It's a rite of passage."

"Oh, good. The weather will be bad. It was starting to sound like *too* much fun," Adam says, his voice drier than sandpaper. He doesn't sound like my Adam. He sounds like the North Shore Grump.

"Right?" Russell laughs, seemingly oblivious to Adam's tone.

"Sam said it wasn't my thing?" My brain is snagged on Russell's evocation of Sam. It's like picking at a barely healed scab and revealing the all-too-fresh wound beneath.

"He just meant that you're sort of set in your ways. Like Adam."

Before Adam can say something needlessly petty, I bring the focus back to my self-improvement. "That's weird, because I can't wait for Chile." I snatch my plate back from Adam, mostly for effect. "I love hiking in the rain and sleeping outside where bugs live and carrying heavy things. It's going to be great. Now, if you'll both excuse me, I saw someone walk by with a bacon-wrapped date that I'd very much like to eat." I snap a piece of jicama between my teeth and follow the scent of meaty appetizers at top speed until I'm in front of a table of food next to my old friend Bond Lover.

I learn her name is Elin and that we've both seen enough Marvel movies to reach agreement on the superhero movie genre: we tend to enjoy them but couldn't explain the plot of any of them if there were a loaded gun to our heads. I grab on to small talk with Elin like a lifeline as the energy of the surrounding party becomes increasingly fraught.

First, no one's seen Mrs. Lewis. Dr. Lewis is buzzing between conversational clumps to ease our minds, but it's clear from his stammering that he hasn't settled on her excuse. From what I overhear, it's a bit of food poisoning but more like a cold—but certainly not the contagious kind, lest she come out of her room at some point. When he makes his way to us, it's a headache.

Dr. Lewis doesn't speak to Elin and me so much as *at* us. He gets his lines out and surveys the room above our heads in search of his next exit.

I feel Adam come to stand behind me at a respectful distance, but I don't turn to talk to him. I'm sick of today. I'm sick of fear and guilt and puff pastry with spinach surprises that get stuck in my teeth.

The string-quartet-Christmas-cover soundtrack can't quite compete with the concerned whispers of the party guests. *Has anyone seen her? Someone should check on her. Did you know today was Sam's birthday?*

I feel Adam hovering but don't stop talking to my James Bond superfan—mostly afraid that if I do, Adam won't have anything to say to me anyway.

"What about Netflix? Name every show you've ever seen on Netflix. We must have some overlap." Elin and I are getting desperate.

Dr. Lewis puts out cookies. He thinks the green tray is vegan but when Elin presses, he can't be sure. "Judy usually handles this," he tells us. I wander from room to room looking for where they stashed the coats to make a run for it. Adam finds me in a small room of floor-to-ceiling mocha.

"Patagonia with Russell is happening?" He asks the question like he doesn't care about the answer.

"It never wasn't happening. I'm excited."

"You're excited."

"I'm excited about the prospect of a life-altering experience." I feel his brain working. "What is it?"

He rocks on his heels. "Just wondering if you'll let me drive you to the airport or if you'll fly off on your adventure without telling me."

"Since you don't know if or when you'll want to move here," I argue, keeping my voice flat, "it probably wouldn't be convenient for you to drive me."

To anyone who would overhear, this conversation sounds like emotionless small talk, but it feels like plates smashing against the wall of my chest.

"I knew you were still thinking about that," he huffs. I say nothing, moving the pattern of the Persian rug with my toe when I hear the slap of slippers approaching us.

Mrs. Lewis walks in in shearling slippers and a robe with the emblem of a European river cruise line embroidered on the collar. She looks impossibly disheveled and bone tired. If I didn't know the true source of her appearance, I'd assume she was wandering the house after being roused from a surgical procedure.

When she sees us, she smiles for one beautiful second before her face empties out. We watch her remember all over again. The broken look in her eyes burns a trail through my heart.

"Mom." A woman's voice carries from the hallway.

"Rachel, we're in the office," Mrs. Lewis answers, awareness flickering back to her face.

"We? Mom, you should go back to bed." Sam's sister, Rachel, appears in the doorway, and my eyes lock on my original coconspirator. "Alison?" My name has never sounded so much like a curse word.

"Rachel!" My voice is too jovial to be genuine. "Good to see you again, I was just leaving," I say. My fingers buzz, itching to turn the knob of the front door. I can't stay in this house for another second.

Mrs. Lewis places her hand on my arm. My chest constricts at this wrinkle in my escape plan. "I have a gift for you. Richard, can you grab the box from the sideboard?" she calls out to her husband, who advances toward her voice.

"Judy, are you down here in your robe?" Dr. Lewis's question holds no judgment or embarrassment, only concern. "I'm sending everyone home. I thought this would be good. I thought—"

"You thought we could eat charcuterie and drink wine on my brother's birthday and pretend he didn't die?"

The room collectively winces at Rachel's direct shot.

Mrs. Lewis pinches the bridge of her nose. "Please, Rachel. Not now."

"Why are you turning on me? I flew all the way out for a party I knew was a bad idea."

"Richard, get the box from the sideboard in the hall so I can give them Sam's presents and go back to sleep."

"Presents? Mom, you don't have to—"

Mrs. Lewis cuts her daughter off with a wave of her hand. Her whole body shakes. Adam swallows hard, and I know he sees how frail she looks.

Her husband fulfills her request, returning to the room holding an envelope and a tiny box. The small room is packed with bodies that suddenly feel like an audience. Dr. Lewis hands his wife a box, but everyone's eyes fix on me.

The room feels elastic, like it's stretching around me and snapping against my skin. I paste on a smile, my face hot.

Mrs. Lewis tightens her terry cloth belt. "I'm sorry you have to see me like this. It's a, uh, hard day." The word *hard* seems insufficient.

Dr. Lewis cleans his glasses with his sweater. "Russell tells us you really went above and beyond with the condo. I know you must be anxious to have his more valuable personal effects distributed," he says.

"No," Adam assures him. "Please don't worry about that."

"It's a bit more complicated than I anticipated. These things take time."

"But these are things we can give you both now. They're from Sam." Mrs. Lewis's clasped hands shake as she speaks. I think I'm shaking too.

Rachel looks confused. It twists my stomach even more.

Mrs. Lewis hands Adam an envelope. "That's your Christmas gift from Sam. His phone had a calendar alert this morning. He wanted Rachel to make arrangements while she was here for the party."

"A calendar alert?" I ask, just as Adam says, "What arrangements?"

He opens it carefully, reverently, aware it's a message from beyond, something every other person in the room is desperate for. He unfolds a piece of printed paper. "A plane ticket?"

"To Chile," Rachel explains to him. "A week before he— we switched your name on the ticket for . . ." We trade glances. "Someone who could no longer go. He was going to invite you. He said he wanted to 'shake things up' for you."

Mrs. Lewis claps her hands together and smiles through tears, the thought of her son, his gift, and a trip he'll never go on eliciting warring emotions. Adam hasn't taken his eyes off the ticket.

"Alison." Mrs. Lewis faces me. "I don't know what Sam had planned for you for Christmas, but I have something I can give on his behalf. It's technically mine. It's a family heirloom—"

Rachel grabs her mother's arm. "Mom, you shouldn't . . ."

"You don't have to . . . ," I say. Neither of us has any idea how to stop this speeding train.

Mrs. Lewis shakes her arm free. "Rachel! Please. This was for Sam to give to the woman he loved when he settled down and got serious about his life."

"He *was* serious about his life. He was serious about living it." Rachel's voice cracks.

Sensing the impending crash, Adam takes my hand. I think I take his too, but I'm not sure. I'm frozen in place. My limbs are too heavy to move.

I feel the blood coursing through my body even before she

reveals a silver pendant I remember her wearing at the funeral.

"It was my grandmother's," Mrs. Lewis continues. "I always knew he would give it to the woman he chose. I wish he could have given this to you himself . . ."

Mrs. Lewis is trying to smile through her tears as she removes the necklace from the box. I can see her holding it up to my neck, but my vision is pulsing.

Dr. Lewis is confused.

The light is flickering out behind Adam's eyes.

Rachel is trying to pull the necklace away from her mother.

I observe every movement as both immediate and delayed as their arguments fade beneath the sound of my thunderous heartbeat.

My limbs are stiff. My hands are shaking. My chest feels like it's being pulled tightly together and zipped up. The rock of guilt presses against my lungs as my breaths become too thick. Too heavy.

"It wasn't supposed to go on this long. You were supposed to forget about her," Rachel shouts, shoving a hand through her perfectly tousled blond waves.

"They didn't," I hear my voice say.

Adam squeezes my hand. "Take a breath, Ali. Please."

"I was just trying to help you. And him. I wanted you to be proud of him. He deserved that," Rachel cries.

Now I'm crying.

"What is she talking about?" Dr. Lewis presses.

Everyone's looking at me. My throat tightens like hot fingers gripping my neck. "I'm sorry. I can't accept this." But I can't make myself move my trembling hands. I feel a familiar touch guide me to the floor.

"Breathe," Adam says, but I barely register it. He's underwater.

My heaving sobs come faster. I gasp for air, but it's no use.

Mrs. Lewis grabs her husband's sleeve. "Richard, you're a doctor. Do something!"

"I'm a podiatrist!"

It's the last thing I hear before I fall underwater too.

24

A Minnesota Goodbye

Dr. Lewis diagnoses me with a "fairly generic" panic attack. I could live without the color commentary, but I'm in no position to take offense. Despite the foot focus of his medical expertise, he remembers enough from his emergency rotation to talk me down until the panic subsides.

In the privacy of the Lewises' office, it comes out all at once.

"Sam meant so much to me," I start, because despite all of the lies, this feels like the most important truth. "But we were never very serious. I didn't know he hadn't told you about the breakup until I was at the funeral."

The Lewis family speaks on top of each other. All at once, I hear:

"You're not his girlfriend?"

"I thought Sam wanted it this way."

"What kind of person does something like that?"

With the simple raise of his hand, Adam stops the cacophony. "She broke up with Sam a while ago, but at the funeral, Rachel asked her to go along with the whole girlfriend thing."

"He broke up with me, actually," I say, correcting him. "Right before Labor Day."

I turn to Adam to watch the moment he realizes I wasn't enough for Sam, but he's staring at the door with a faraway look.

"You knew?" Mrs. Lewis asks Adam. He nods, never looking away from the door.

It's then she notices that he's still holding my hand. He grabbed it when I started panicking and hasn't let it go since. She clutches the silver pendant in her palm. "You two are together." Her voice isn't angry or betrayed, just tired. Of me. Of this. Of today, maybe. Of missing her son who's not coming back, no matter how many necklaces she gives away.

Adam drops my hand.

Rachel cops to her part of the ruse. How she never imagined I'd become this entangled in everyone's lives. How she was only trying to help the family heal from this terrible loss.

I want to tell them that Sam and I were just becoming friends again and how I still feel stunned by the permanent loss of him. I want to apologize and beg their forgiveness. Instead, all I say is, "I only wanted to help."

The Lewises look back at me, faces depleted.

Adam walks out. I mumble more useless *sorrys* at the family and chase him to the front door. His legs are longer, but my boots don't have laces, and I manage to catch him before he makes it off the porch.

"Adam. Adam. Where are you going?" I start to grab his hand, but I stop myself.

"I need some air." Adam already sounds miles away from me.

"What's going on?"

"This isn't the right time for this, Alison. You just—" He cuts himself off and faces me. "Are you okay?" he asks, concern carving ruts in his face. Hope billows through me. "Does that happen a lot? The panic attacks?" he asks.

"No, but it's happened before." When my mom was diagnosed with cancer and I was diagnosed with BRCA and suddenly our insides were lying in wait to attack. I've been seeing a therapist on and off ever since.

Adam doesn't speak again. Silence fills the space between us on the snow-covered porch, choking out any conversation before it starts, like suffocating fumes. I feel the pressure of what he's not saying pressing against my lungs. Every so often, he twitches as if about to speak but no sound comes out. His mouth doesn't move.

Apprehension is flooding my heart, and I want to be more like Adam right now—capable of sitting in silence until it forces the other person to reveal themself—but I've never been like that. I'm always yapping my every thought, giving the Adams of the world emotional ammunition.

"What's going on? Please talk to me. Is this because he broke up with me?" My voice is quiet, as if it's the volume and not the content that's bothering him. "Is it making you second-guess—"

"What? No. I don't care that he broke up with you. I care that your relationship with him is clearly unresolved."

"What are you talking about? It's resolved."

"That's not what it looks like." He forces his words out like sawdust in his throat. "I spent hours lying to everyone, acting like I hardly knew you, and then I watched his parents give you a fucking family heirloom like their daughter-in-law. And I just stood there."

"Are you mad at me about that?"

"I'm mad at myself for pretending this was even possible."

My throat dries up. "This? You mean us? Of course this is possible."

"No, it's not. You and Sam? We'll never be past it. Relationships shouldn't be this complicated."

"Everyone knows the truth now. We won't need to pretend anymore."

A breeze slices between us, and at his shiver, I tug the collar of his jacket closed to keep him warm like he's done countless times for me.

His eyelids droop closed. "Why did you agree to go along with Rachel in the first place?"

I let my hands drift down to his chest. "I wanted to make things easier for them. What was I supposed to do?"

"What about Patagonia?" he asks, shaking my hands off and patting the envelope from Rachel in his pocket. "Why did you ever agree to that trip? Why are you still entertaining it now, even though Sam uninvited you? Why didn't you tell me any of this?"

I stuff my hands in my coat pockets. "Why would I tell you that Sam dumped me and switched my ticket because I wasn't enough for him?"

"Because *I* thought you were enough. I thought you were more than enough." His voice shakes, and my heart clambers up my throat at how we've already become past tense. "And for some reason you don't. But I've wanted you since the moment I saw you at his fucking funeral. That's what I was thinking when I first saw you, Alison. I'd been so awful to him, assuming I'd have a chance to make it right. But he was gone, and I wasn't sure I'd feel anything else again until I was at the front of the church. Until I saw you."

He rubs his hand on his face and keeps going, barely pausing to breathe. "I'd never felt that way before. Then, a second later, I recognized you, and thought, *That's Sam's girlfriend. I'm such an asshole.* That's what I was thinking. My best friend *died,* and the first thing I did was go after his girlfriend. What kind of person does that? What *best friend* does that? God, did you see the look on his mom's face?" Guilt and heartache carve his face into tormented lines. "And now I can't even think about him without feeling like trash over how I couldn't stop thinking about you."

His words are a blow to my gut. I want to fix this, but a toxic combination of defeat and frustration drowns my system. Because despite his words on this porch, we didn't fall apart today. He never gave us a real chance.

Guests spill out the door, and we turn away from each other like strangers. I sniff, pretending my heart isn't breaking until the family backs out of the driveway.

I finally let out my breath. "You've been looking for a reason to bolt all day—since the moment you met me, really. If it hadn't been this, you would've found some other excuse to give up. It's what you've done this whole time. One step forward, two steps back."

"How am I the problem here?" he says, dumbfounded.

"Are you ever going to leave construction? Move to Minneapolis? Start your own business? Choose one table leg? Finish my stupid shelf?" Tears stream down my face. When our eyes finally meet, his are red rimmed too.

"You want me to finish your shelf so you can stare at your climbing gear and your trekking poles and whatever other crap you never want to use? You spend all your time doing things you hate and hiding what you actually like under your bed. And you think *I* was looking for a reason to give up? How am I going to be with you if you're so busy trying to be someone else?"

I wipe at my wet face, smudging my makeup. "I'm just trying to be a better person."

His laugh doesn't have a shred of humor in it. "Better how? What does that even mean? I don't care what's in those books. Going trail running won't make you better or more deserving. You know what might? Being honest with yourself."

My stomach bottoms out at his words. He rakes a hand through his hair. I want to touch it. I barely got a chance to touch it.

"I'm sorry. I don't want to argue with you," he pleads. "It's just that . . . do you know that I hardly let myself think about Sam? I felt so guilty over what I'd felt for you since his funeral that I've never let myself feel sad or angry about him."

For the first time, possibly ever, I have no words. I don't know what to say or how to fix this.

Minutes pass before Adam steps off the porch. On the last step, he turns back and reaches for me.

"It's icy. Are you wearing good boots?"

My heart clenches. I accept his hand, my wellie-covered feet stepping down. Our faces meet inches apart, and for a moment, I wonder if we'll kiss, but of course we don't. Instead, Adam lets go of my hand and points at my hip.

"Someone's calling," he says to my buzzing pocket. I didn't notice it. I'm basically a zombie.

"It's my mom. Give me one . . . don't go anywhere. Please."
He nods, and I take two steps away from him to answer.

"Alison, honey!" my mom yells cheerily through the receiver. "Did you book your flight for Christmas? I've been
thinking about your oophorectomy." My mom starts in with
the ever-present BRCA talk, picking it right back up from the
last conversation.

Bitterness builds in the back of my throat. "Mom, I can't
discuss my ovaries right now, this isn't a good time."

She tuts. "It'll only take a second, Alison. It'll be tight, but
my doctor said she can squeeze you in for the first week in
January—"

"Mom!" I explode like an overinflated balloon. I shouldn't
have to make major fertility decisions on my ex's front lawn
with the source of my cracking heart just feet away from me.
I should be able to have one conversation with her about anything else besides my genetic inability to suppress tumors. "I
don't care if Dr. Logan's making time for me. You didn't even
ask or consider what I wanted. I can make a plan with *my*
doctor, and it won't involve an oophorectomy in January,
because I'll be in Patagonia—"

"Alison!"

"Love you. Bye." I punch the end call button, nostalgic for
the cathartic release of my high school flip phone.

I lean back against the porch railing. Adam's staring down
at the ground next to me.

"So you're really going to go to Chile," he says, his voice
wrung out. I hate how my body responds with frayed sparks
of electricity. "This isn't you."

"But I want it to be." My tone is just as defeated.

"I like you, Alison. Sometimes I think I—" He stops himself. "I can't do whatever this is with you." Adam sighs. I turn to meet his gaze, and I'm struck by how beaten down he looks.

"So this is it? You don't even want to try?" I grab for his hand, then think better of it.

He looks so wounded. I can't imagine what he's seeing looking back at him. He rubs his beard, his eyes focusing on a slush-covered garden gnome. "It shouldn't be so complicated."

"I want this. Us." I wipe away the building tears with my glove. "There. I uncomplicated it for you."

"I can't be with you when you're so determined to be someone else."

This simple statement guts me.

"I'm always me when I'm with you." It's the closest I get to breaking through to him, but I watch his walls go up at the last second.

"I need some time to think."

"How much time to think?" I ask, my voice pitiful.

"I honestly don't know. But I'll tell you as soon as I figure that out."

25

Going Full *Into the Wild*

I PROBABLY NEED A tent, right? A waterproof one?" I muse aloud.

I stayed at Chelsea's after the party. I couldn't bear to go back to my apartment and see Adam everywhere. Then I spilled the tragic story of the Lewis Cookie Party and promptly fell asleep.

Now I've lured Chelsea to the Mall of America.

One part theme park, one part capitalist nightmare, the Mall of America may be the worst place to find yourself on a Sunday in the middle of December. My foot slides on a Yeti bumper sticker as I yank Chelsea by the arm past the picked-over cooler display at the entrance of L.L.Bean.

My eyes dart around the store until they find a pop-up tent display in the distance. I charge toward the orange vinyl, chewing my bottom lip while I compare features of the tents. I have no idea what I'm looking for, so I grab the one in the smallest box. Compact is best, right?

"Do you need to shop for camping supplies *right now*?" Chelsea asks, worry laced in her voice. I barely register her concern.

I can't be with you when you're so determined to be someone else.

Adam's words play on repeat when I give myself a moment to think. So I don't let myself think. I just do. I woke up this morning with energy that needed to be expended and a bone-deep desperation to be the woman I'm supposed to be. Adam's wrong. I'm not *being* someone else. That better, more worthy someone *is* me.

"I'll need it for next weekend," I explain, wrenching my cart with a herky-jerky 180-degree pivot. Chelsea trails behind me, her mouth agape.

"Are you going somewhere?"

"The Boundary Waters. Ely, maybe? I'm just gonna play it by ear." I mention the wilderness within the Superior National Forest near the Canadian border casually, like it's a bagel shop I want to stop at on the way home.

"It's like five degrees there if it's a warm day." Chelsea follows me through the racks of clothes, removing a hammock from my cart and placing it back on a shelf. Before her hands have left the box, a man with an ash-blond bun snatches it for himself. Never underestimate the brutality of a Midwesterner near discounted outdoor equipment.

"If I don't get some practice camping, I'll never hack Patagonia in January."

"Why do you *need* to go to Patagonia in January?" she asks in her best patient-teacher voice. When I disappear into the depths of the thermal underwear rack, she tries a different tactic. "Patagonia is in the Southern Hemisphere, right? Is it even that cold there in January? Northern-Minnesota-woods cold?"

"It's in the mountains." I haven't looked into the weather conditions yet. "Should I dehydrate my own food, or can I buy the store-bought stuff?" I barrel away from her with three sets of wool long johns.

"I think there's some unnecessary risk in dehydrating your own." Chelsea's mollifying words don't match the distress in her voice. Her eyes flit toward the entrance repeatedly as I compare the temperature recommendations on windproof pants.

I see Chelsea's shoulders slump in relief out of the corner of my eye. "Mara! Thank god you're here. She's gone full *Into the Wild*. Have you watched that one, Alison? I think it's on Netflix."

"With Reese Witherspoon? Of course." My thoughts are miles away, contemplating whether I need new hiking boots or if I can double up on socks.

Mara wrenches the pants from my grasp. "Nope. *Into the Wild* with Emile Hirsch. It's a true story in which someone traveling alone in the wilderness starves to death in a bus. A *bus,* Alison!"

I roll my eyes. "I'm not going to die in a bus. But if I did, at least I'd know I really lived."

My mantra sounds dramatic and disturbed even to my own ears.

"You know how else you can live? By living. Come on, we're going to eat waffles. You're not maxing out your credit card on whatever's happening right now. I can't believe you dragged me to the Mall of America during Christmas shopping season. A hugely pregnant woman shoved me in front of a Pandora store, and this was after I'd already witnessed her other child vomiting on the log flume." Mara grabs me firmly by the shoulder. "I love you, but there's only so much trauma I can withstand before noon on a Sunday."

"But my cart," I whine in despair. It's then my eyes catch

on the thing that rips me in half. Collapsing onto the floor next to a circular sale rack of performance vests, I clutch the source of my devastation on my way down: a fucking denim-khaki reversible jacket.

"Come on, sweetie. We can come back later after we do some googling." Chelsea pats my head cajolingly.

"Yes, I'm sure Wirecutter has an article on the beginner's guide to frostbite," Mara says.

I'm crying on the floor of an outdoor retailer over a men's jacket. I'm a manipulative teaser on the five o'clock news: *Holiday inflation devastates shoppers (more at eleven!).* And my friends are hardly fazed. I'm utterly pathetic.

I drop the jacket, and Mara and Chelsea lead me by the arm past the canoe display and out of the store.

I've eaten four bites of waffle when it begins.

"First . . ." Chelsea folds her hands sweetly on the lacquered-penny tabletop of our booth in the assertively trendy restaurant. "We want you to know we love you. It's just—"

"This is an intervention," Mara erupts.

"Subtle," Chelsea murmurs, letting her head fall back on the black vinyl. "What's going on, Al? Is this really only about Adam?"

"No." My voice cracks. "Yes. Probably not."

"Does it have to do with the mastectomy?" Chelsea asks gently.

I consider her question, brushing my hair out of my tear-stained eyes, the wet pieces sticking to my face. The fresh wound to my heart smarts, but something older and thornier twists at my sternum just above it. "I was supposed to get cancer," I say in a stuttering breath.

"It wasn't like one hundred percent happening," Chelsea says softly.

She hands me her napkin as tears stream down my face. I blow my nose into it pitifully. "My mom did, and I was supposed to *probably, someday* get cancer. And now I probably won't. I can't shake this feeling that I cheated."

Chelsea shakes her head, her eyes filling with water. "You didn't cheat, Al."

"Maybe. But my mom beat cancer, and she's still consumed by it because of me. It's all we talk about. How much she doesn't want to see me go through chemo. How I can mitigate my risk until I never have to worry about it. But I want to be someone who deserves it, like Sam. Sam deserved his life."

Mara reaches across the table to take my hand firmly in hers. "What happened to Sam was a horrible accident—and it has nothing to do with you—but, I'm sorry, 'mitigating your risk'? Is that what we're calling having a fucking mastectomy, Al? You had a scary diagnosis and made the decision to take control of your life at a pretty big cost. You want to talk about earning things? You did something hard and brave, and you have more than earned the life you have."

I've never liked when people call me brave for making a cautious medical decision. But from my forthright friend, it doesn't sound like a sympathy card from the hereditary-cancer section of Hallmark—it sounds like a badge of honor.

"You have to call your therapist. Today. We're not taking no for an answer," Chelsea says.

I lean my head on Chelsea's shoulder. Mara leaves her side of the booth and scooches in next to me. I close my eyes, feeling safe and still for the first time today.

"Do you ever feel like you're doing life completely wrong?" I ask shakily.

Chelsea's shoulders jostle my head when she lets out a puff of air that's equal parts laughter and tears. "Yes. Constantly."

"I have a lot of opinions on how other people are living their lives, but my own?" Mara shakes her head with a smile. "I'm sorry if I made it worse by trying to control everything. I know how I can be—it's very helpful in most areas of my life, but I didn't see that I was doing that to you. I'm sorry for that, but you need to tell me when I'm going too far. You have to stop doing things because you think it's what you *should* do and silently keeping a scorecard."

I lob my head from Chelsea's shoulder to Mara's. "I think I can handle that."

We eat too many waffles, and I'm consumed by that fizzy, silly feeling I only have around my best friends—that intoxicating invincibility of being known, understood, and loved as the most beautiful, brilliant idiot the world has ever seen. No one else, not even Adam, could make me feel so lovably ridiculous as these two weirdos.

26

How to *Eat, Pray, Love* Your Way Through Minnesota

"WHAT DO YOU want to talk about today?"

It's how my therapist, Denise, starts every session, though we rarely stay with the benign topic I present for long. This Thursday lunchtime session, just two weeks after my friend-tervention, is no exception. In the last two weeks, we've met five times, discussing BRCA, Sam, and everything leading up to my full *Into the Wild* at the Mall of America. The two of us have dissected my relationship with my mom, now that I'm headed home for Christmas in a few days.

We've also discussed Adam, but the hurt feels too close up to look at it with any clarity. If therapy is a pair of binoculars, my breakup with Adam is a tree trunk two inches in front of my nose.

But today, I don't want to talk about him, so I broach a more palatable subject. "I'm supposed to go on vacation next month, hiking through the Patagonian Andes."

"Supposed to . . . ," she repeats with a smile from her Scalamandré zebra-print chair. Denise's office aesthetic is Mental

Health Whimsy, as if Wes Anderson and Esther Perel collaborated on a collection for Anthropologie. "What makes you say 'supposed to'?"

"It's supposed to be an incredible experience. Anyone would want to go on an adventure like this." My lips curve up in one of those unconvincing smiles that Adam can spot a mile away.

"Do *you* want to go on an adventure like that?"

"I should want to. I know I shouldn't do things just because I *should* want to, but I'm worried that if I pass up on this trip, I'll always regret it."

Denise is ramping up to something, but her poker face offers no clues. "Why is that?"

To stall for time, I take a sip of water. "I get that this trip isn't *me,* but I still *want* to like stuff like this more. I don't want to feel guilty for squandering an opportunity just because I won't enjoy the trip itself."

The word *guilty* rings in my brain like a bell, and I know we'll be pivoting to my many other issues now.

Denise hears it too, but her face remains placid. "And what are you feeling guilty for in this instance?" she asks.

My eyes find the pilling fabric on my sweater sleeve. "Same as always, I guess. For being me. For being a homebody when I should want excitement and spontaneity."

"And there's a greater value to excitement and spontaneity than contentment?"

"Isn't there?" I ask.

Her brow furrows curiously. "I generally don't rank feelings."

"There are no empowering memoirs about women finding *contentment* after tragedy."

"I would argue *most* are about that."

The brown leather armchair groans as I shift my weight. "No. It's like, something awful happens and—rather than sitting in the debilitating sadness and fear—you fly around the world or hike the Pacific Crest Trail or sail around the Caribbean. Through the journey, you become self-actualized and a person worthy of happiness and success."

"And contentment?"

"No. It's . . ." I trail off.

"What happens to the sadness and fear? Do they dissolve into the ocean?" She smiles kindly. "Before your mastectomy, we talked a lot about sadness and fear. You were fearful of the surgery. You were scared they would find cancerous tissue. You were sad about the loss of your breasts. Where did those feelings go?"

"They didn't find cancer, and the surgery went well, so the whole thing was moot. My mom was still getting regular scans, and suddenly, I never had to think about it. I shouldn't have wasted time worrying about myself."

"So you felt guilty you no longer had to have that fear anymore?"

I shrug. "Maybe. And I was still sad too, about losing my breasts, but I was so lucky. Being sad felt ungrateful."

"And you didn't want to 'sit in the debilitating sadness,' as you put it?"

"No. I didn't want to feel that. I wanted to *do* something. It felt . . . easier." I squirm, picking at my sweater. "But this trip isn't about guilt. Maybe I haven't clicked with the outdoors because of how solitary it is. Being surrounded by a group of avid adventurers could make all the difference."

"Could you test that out?" she says, challenging me, because Denise is the kind of therapist who gives homework. "Go on a hike with friends who love the outdoors and see if that feels joyful to you? It might be worth a shot, before flying to South America."

———

"BUT IT WASN'T opening the relationship that broke us. It was the lies," Russell laments, twigs snapping underfoot on this uncharacteristically warm December day, two days before I'm set to fly home for Christmas. Out on the trail that Russell chose for our Patagonia trial run, we've hardly escaped the parking lot and he's already baring his soul to Chelsea.

"Nonmonogamy requires the deepest levels of trust," Chelsea assures him. "But, Russell, a boundary you don't reinforce isn't a boundary at all." Russell blinks like this conversation has unlocked a new level of personal growth.

The dawn light spills over the Mississippi River like flickering embers, and we climb the steep bluffs in search of the breathtaking views I was promised when I drove two hours south before daybreak. The devil on my shoulder argues we had the perfect view when we parked the car and everything we've seen since then has been more of the same, except now my right knee hurts, my cheeks are lightly windburned, and I can't feel my pinky toe. Still, I am determined to see the positive.

"Oh! A goldfinch." Chelsea points enthusiastically at a bird that looks like every other bird we've seen today. Since part of Denise's requirement for this trial run was eager participants, I immediately ruled out Mara, but Chelsea and Russell have proven to be happy hiking partners.

"This is where I filmed my audition tape for *Survivor*. And *Naked and Afraid*. And *Dating Naked*. No, wait, *Dating Naked* I filmed over . . . there." Russell pivots to point out a nondescript cluster of rocks. "Speaking of hot dates, how are you and my guy Adam doing? I added him to the Patagonia group chain, but he *immediately* left the chat. New record for him."

The pot of coffee I chugged this morning sloshes in my stomach. "I wouldn't know. We haven't really talked for a couple weeks."

"No! You guys? It would've been epic."

"Russell, tell me about your current dietary restrictions," Chelsea buffers, because we've never met a bulky, chiseled man who could resist fetishizing what he was depriving his body of to stay so bulky and chiseled. Between the small talk and bird spotting, she's been running interference at every turn.

After exhaustively detailing his specific brand of keto—a rotation of boiled chicken, coconut oil, and starvation that would violate the Geneva Conventions—Russell disappears behind a curtain of trees.

"Can you believe this exists here?" Chelsea leans against amber-colored rock. "This was left behind by glacial melt from the last ice age. It's been here for thousands of years and will be here for thousands more. This scenery is literally stepping back in time and into the future. It's incredible." Chelsea's excitement echoes off the surrounding bluffs. Jealousy that she's able to so easily enjoy herself out here twinges in my belly.

I uncap the water bottle clipped to my pack and offer it to her before taking a swig for myself. "Why don't you want me to do this?" I ask, feeling the cold water travel down my throat. "You seem to love it out here."

"I do. You don't, and it's not fun to watch you torture yourself. The worst part is, if you weren't determined to make adventure your personality, I think you'd like it in small doses—a way to drift out of your comfort zone. Instead, you're so angry that you're uncomfortable. This could be a nice day with one of your best friends and the hottest man I've ever seen—like, he's currently holding a branch, defecating, behind us, and I still haven't ruled him out as a sexual option—and you're not even enjoying it. You're glued to everything you don't like and criticizing yourself for noticing those things. Stop trying to have a life-altering epiphany in the woods and just have a pretty okay time with me." She nudges me with her shoulder.

I smile, imagining what it could be like to feel things without judging my every thought. Then her earlier comment catches up to me. "Wait, he's pooping?"

Russell jogs up from behind us, adjusting his outer layer. He accepts Chelsea's proffered hand sanitizer with a wink before we're back on the trail. We walk for an hour or so up steep paths of snow-covered rocks. Our ice cleats crunch with every step. The farther we walk, the more patches of limestone peek out from blankets of snow like a mouth packed with too many teeth. As we begin to descend, a droplet plops onto my nose. It's slow at first, but soon the skies open up, and icy December rain is biting my cheeks.

"Should we wait it out?" I ask. The above-freezing temps felt like a godsend this morning, but I'd kill for snow right now.

Russell shakes his head. "We're not far from the car. We should keep moving." We keep walking, but the slippery, sloped terrain slows our pace. My foot slips in a flooded crevice and water seeps into my socks.

Coffee rebels in my intestines. "Can we take a shortcut straight down?" I ask with more urgency than I intend.

"No way, Mullally," Russell shouts over the rain. "Not safe."

"Can we pick up the pace then?"

Chelsea blinks off the water collecting on her lashes. "Al, we're moving as fast as we can."

"I have to . . ." I shift unsteadily. "Use the restroom."

We stop, rain beating down on our shoulders. Russell tips his head in the direction of a naked, emaciated tree.

My jaw falls open. "You can't be serious."

"I did it," he argues.

"And it was weird!"

"There won't be toilets on our trip, and it's going to rain. Like all the time."

I point my head toward the ground, my soaked knit hat weighing heavy on my head. I wipe my brow, but the rain keeps falling to replace it. Dampness seeps through my water-resistant layers, rattling my frigid bones. "Why do people think this is fun? Am I crazy or are they?"

Chelsea leans in to pat my shoulder, but her foot slips out from under her. I lunge for her jacket, and she grabs at my arms, hood, belt bag, anything she can to steady herself, but we topple into the icy mud. My hip crashes against stone and my cheek scrapes against a frozen branch that might as well be an ice pick.

In the flurry of arms, my bag rips open, spilling its contents over the rain-soaked terrain. Emotion catches in my throat when I spot a small white disc. It's my casino chip—the mate of the Mystic Lake chip from Sam's bookcase.

An unexpected snort spits rainwater out of my nose, because that great memory couldn't be more different from where I am right now. For one thing, we were dry. Stale cigarette smoke filling our noses, we overindulged at the buffet, shared drinks at the bar with a bickering octogenarian couple, and snuck into the amphitheater for Boy George and Culture Club's sound check.

That day was nothing new and special to Sam. It was so . . . simple. I didn't have to hide the nausea creeping up my throat at the top of a mountain bike trail or feign confidence rappelling down a rock wall. I was *me* the whole day—boring me—with someone I cared about. That's what made it perfect.

Grief and joy grip my insides, because Sam didn't keep that chip because it was an Instagrammable thrill that fit his "nomad aesthetic." He kept it because it was real. He kept it to remember a great day with a good friend. He was a collector of great days, and I could be too, if I could admit that my happiest days haven't been any of the adrenaline-fueled ones.

A happy day was that perfect first warm day in May when Mara, Chelsea, and I wandered the tiny beaches around Lake Harriet. Mara and I flipped a pedal boat, and we all ended up at Chelsea's, watching romantic comedies late into the night.

It was starting the day doing something awful like packing up a bookcase or going to a dreaded doctor's appointment and ending it in Adam's arms. A perfect day was spending it with Adam as myself and absolutely no threat of nausea-inducing thrill.

Why am I forcing these grand adventures like I googled

"how to *Eat, Pray, Love* your way through Minnesota" when my best days are filled with contentment?

Well, shit, Denise.

The familiar rock in my chest doesn't pulse at the prospect of bailing on Patagonia. It's not even a rock anymore—when did that happen? It's more like a tangled ball of Christmas lights. You groan when you find it buried at the bottom of a box, because you know it *can* be untangled. You can't justify paying $19.99 for a new strand when you know it's possible to sort this strand out if you only try.

I have to start looking at what really makes me feel lighter, and if I'm honest, I've known for a while that forcing myself to be someone else isn't it.

Icy ground squishes under my gloved hand, and I wipe my hair from my eyes, dragging the mess across my face. "I'd rather die than poop outside," I burst out, because I can't stand pretending a second longer.

"What?" Russell asks, his voice louder than before. The rain is slowing down to a merciful sprinkle. His eyes monitor me like I'm a rabid animal.

"And I hate parking lots. I won't spend every day being paid to consider where people park so I can poop in the mountains on vacation." My pulse is skyrocketing with adrenaline. I keep wanting to make myself fit this mold of a person I think looks right from the outside: the survivor. But I can only be me. "I can't keep forcing it. It won't make me better or worthy. It'll just make me full of shit."

"And you don't want to shit outside," Chelsea repeats. A smile dances across her mud-splattered face, her blond braid now a wet, dingy rope.

I grin up to the sky, leaning back against the frozen wall of sandstone. "Exactly."

We make it down the rest of the hill, and even though mud squelches in my boot, my bruised hip throbs, and I'm pretty sure my lip is bleeding, I manage to enjoy the downward climb. Without my self-imposed pressure to make this hike the key to my enlightenment, the surrounding bluffs become what they always were: a beautiful, cold place to spend a day with one of my best friends. And Russell.

We find our cars in front of the mostly empty strip mall where we left them, and my heart smiles at the fact that I won't be planning traffic flow in retail parking lots any time soon. With the drop in temperature, the rain's caked onto our cars in a thin sheet of ice. Russell scrapes at our windshields while Chelsea and I relieve ourselves at the only open business: a zombie-themed escape room.

"The guy at reception didn't even bat an eye," Chelsea chuckles.

I pull a stick from my hair. "He must think we're part of the cast." We look a bit undead.

Back outside, I thank Russell for his part in my emotional epiphany. He presses me into a firm hug. "It won't be the same without you, babe," he says, I think sincerely.

We wave to him, and high on my own power, I shoot off a text.

11:11 AM
Alison:
I'm not going to Patagonia. Or taking that job.
You were right about everything.

It's not enough, but the things I need to say can't be communicated over text. It's an olive branch. Dancing dots appear. Disappear and then reappear. My heart is a pattery mess as I wait eagerly for his response. We can fix everything—I know we can—if he just responds.

> **11:14 AM**
> **Adam:**
> No.

> **11:14 AM**
> **Adam:**
> I wasn't.

I wait for more, but more doesn't come. My heart flickers like a candle burning out.

I step into my apartment hallway picking at the dirt caked on my jacket and find a familiar face sitting on my doormat.

"Rachel?"

"Sorry to show up like this. I have a sixteen-hour layover, and I wanted to talk in person. I was worried you wouldn't answer if I called. Not that I'd blame you."

"How do you know where I live?"

"I got your address from Adam."

My body clenches. "You talked to Adam?"

"Not really," she answers. "He wasn't very chatty over text."

My heart sinks as I shove my key in the lock. "I wouldn't take it personally. Do you want to come in?"

She nods and follows me. Her eyes examine my limited

seating options before she settles into a bistro chair in my kitchenette. I shrug off my stiff jacket and sit opposite her.

She eyes the dried blood on my cheek. "Are you okay?" I'm not sure if the question is asking after my current physical appearance or my general well-being, but it doesn't matter because she keeps talking. "I shouldn't have asked you to lie. I didn't consider what that would be like for you." Her jaw shakes and eyes swim with each word. "This has been the worst time in my life—in my parents' lives too—but before Thanksgiving, I felt so . . . alone in it all."

I clutch her hand across the table to steady her. "Would you like coffee? This feels like a conversation that requires coffee."

Her face pinches in confusion until I reach my other hand out to my counter and pop a K-Cup in the Keurig without missing a beat. The joys of tiny living.

Her laugh is a warm breeze. "Yes, actually. I've been up since yesterday. Coffee sounds really good."

I hand Rachel the full mug and replace it under the coffeemaker with another while she tells me about growing up with Sam. How they were each other's closest confidants. How their parents were always anxious about their children's insatiable wanderlust. She tells the kind of stories you'd share at the funeral of someone very old, where guests are capable of celebrating a loved one's long, full life, rather than dwelling on the unfairness of a shortened existence in a numb stupor. It's as lovely for me as it is cathartic for her.

"They loved us, but they didn't get us. I knew I was never going to please them, so I figured why not drop out of college and become a flight attendant—travel the world as much as I could. Sam couldn't disappoint them like that. He didn't move out with me, even though we talked about it all the time. He lived in their condo and tried to be both people, but he just felt so guilty that he didn't crave the settled life they wanted for him. That's why I wanted you to go along with it, so he'd get to be both people. I didn't realize it would feel like I was the only one mourning the real Sam. They were so fixated on the guy he wanted them to see and not the amazing person he actually was."

"That must've been really lonely. I'm sorry I bolted as soon as it all came out."

"No, that part was actually really great. Everyone left, and we were finally able to have a real conversation. It was . . . nice—healing, even. We've been seeing a family counselor over Zoom and working through it all together. I'm not sure we would've gotten there without all of this nonsense."

A sad laugh tumbles from my throat. "I'm glad my mess accomplished something."

"They know I asked you to do it. They don't blame you."

I press my forehead into my hand and feel my energy drain into the floor. "I'm not sure it was all so selfless. Sam dumped me because he realized I wasn't the person I wanted him to think I was. Through all of this, a part of me got to pretend a little longer. Now I'm just me again. And that might not be so bad, but 'me' is . . . sad, I think."

She lifts her mug, a small smile teasing the edges of her lips. "Welcome to the Sad and Lonely Club. Thrilled to have you."

I take a restorative sip and—against all odds—feel a little happy to be just me. "Thrilled to be here."

27

A Midwest-Tuscan Christmas Aesthetic

WHEN I LAND in Michigan on Christmas Eve, my first meal is at Buddy's Pizza. Usually, it's Zingerman's Deli—an Ann Arbor staple—but today, I want crispy corners and stringy cheese. It's a quintessential winter day in southeast Michigan, meaning the skies are a dreary gray and the snow surrounding the strip mall parking lot is more of a dirty beige slush than a winter wonderland.

"They must have pizza in Minnesota." My mom turns out of the parking lot, the smell from the pizza boxes on my lap filling the aging Chevy Malibu.

"Nah. They're still figuring it out over there."

"Well, that settles it. You're moving back. Or at least moving to Florida." She punctuates her flat delivery with a flick of her turn signal, oncoming headlights lighting up her curly brown bob.

"Yes, Florida—the state known for its pizza," I respond dryly.

"Your father and I went to Clearwater last spring, and they had great food."

"Were you meeting with L. Ron Hubbard for a slice?"

"Elron who? I never have any idea what you and your sister are talking about."

"Nothing. A Scientology joke. They're headquartered in Clearwater, Florida."

"Oh, them? I left Scientology ages ago, back when they were mostly a bunch of boats." She shrugs as she turns into our neighborhood, as if escaping Scientology is tragically mundane and not fodder for a ten-episode HBO series. Bored, she changes the subject. "Emma's pregnant, by the way."

I know my sister Emma has always wanted kids, but I had no idea she was trying to get pregnant. "She must be so excited. Can we stop at the bookstore for a baby gift?"

"She won't be telling you. She's not telling anyone yet, but she's visibly pregnant, so I thought you should know not to bring it up. And don't offer her wine or anything."

"Why would I offer a pregnant woman wine?"

"Because you don't know she's pregnant."

I point between the two of us. "I'm not participating in this, so I'll just follow her lead. Anything else I should know?"

She shakes her head. "I printed some articles for you to look at on increased risk of skin cancer with BRCA," she says. "We can look at them after dinner."

Slumping deeper into my pizzas, I lean my forehead against the window with such helpless melancholy, I put my inner high schooler—the one who wrote sad, strange poetry in pastel gel pen—to shame. Every time I get on a plane to Michigan, I tell myself this will be the visit when I don't regress back to my seventeen-year-old self. This year, I couldn't make it past the ride from the airport.

. . .

My dad doesn't leave the den for dinner until my mom and I have finished eating and are settled on the couch searching for a Christmas movie. "Working or studying?" I ask him when he emerges.

He startles mid-yawn, as if the sight of me on the couch doesn't compute, and adjusts his black Coke-bottle glasses. "Well, hi there, Alison. Studying. Classes start next week."

I point to the kitchen. "Pizza's in the oven." For as long as I can remember, my parents have stored pizza, in its cardboard box, in the oven, at two hundred degrees. I never considered it a hazard until I got my own apartment and made the conscious decision never to do this, lest I burn the place to the ground. Still, whenever I visit, I instinctually stick the pizza box in the oven without a thought, as if basic fire safety doesn't apply to childhood homes.

He makes himself a plate and shuts himself back in the den. When my mom got her cancer diagnosis, he went down to part-time at his job as a machinist. Worried her cancer might return, he stayed part-time. After years of clean scans and too many free hours, he decided to fill them with a master's degree in medieval literature. For fun. It's a decision I still find baffling, but I suspect he finds the women in his household a bit baffling himself.

My extremely introverted and cerebral father has always existed in sharp contrast to my extroverted, gregarious mother. I remember road trips to the Sleeping Bear Dunes where my mom spoke for hours on end as my dad received her words without response. Once, I followed him into the gas station and found him standing in front of a wall of Gatorades with his eyes closed. When I asked if he was sick, he responded,

"No, sweetie, it's just . . . your mom's a verbal processor. That's all."

I've never viewed my parents' marriage as a bad one, just one that has never made sense to me. I always assumed he was retreating to his study to escape his chatty wife and two loud daughters, but now that he's an empty nester, I can see it's who he is. My dad has always felt more comfortable in the quiet refuge of a book, where my mom only reads enough to get invited back to her many book clubs.

"How did the ultrasound go?" she asks.

"Fine," I answer.

"Did the cyst go away?"

I throw my head back against the overstuffed chocolate-brown couch cushion. My parents last invested in home decor in 2005, so the aesthetic of the seventies split-level is Midwest Tuscan, all oversized brown furniture and red accents. My eyes rest on the faded, color-washed walls my parents painted themselves with yellow-gold paint, a wet rag, and a rerun of *Extreme Makeover: Home Edition*.

"I rue the day I told you about the cyst."

"Well, did it?"

"Yes. My ovaries look perfectly ordinary," I answer, irritation burning a hole in my throat.

"Why is my love and concern for you so annoying?"

I clench the brick-red pillow on my lap. "Because BRCA's the only thing we talk about."

She rolls her eyes. "It's not that bad. I don't think you realize how much I worry about you. I passed this mutation on to you. I just want to make sure nothing bad happens because of it."

I watch her braid the tassels on the throw blanket over our

legs. I've spent so much time imagining how testing negative for the BRCA mutation would have released *me* of guilt that I've never considered the guilt my diagnosis pressed into my mother's chest. She's as desperate to alleviate misplaced feelings as I am, but instead of forced hikes and ill-conceived camping trips, she's ensuring I'm attending appointments and scheduling procedures. My mom, Adam, Rachel, Sam, we're all powerless against guilt.

"At my last visit, I asked her about the article you sent— the fallopian tube removal. She agreed it's a good option for me, but I have to take these steps on my timeline. No one else's. I can promise I'll take care of myself, but I need to be able to talk to you like my mom. Not my genetic counselor."

As she nods, her face stiffens like she's working to hide an emotion from me. "I didn't realize we were talking about it that much. I only want to know what you're thinking. It's like pulling teeth with you sometimes."

"Yeah, I'm realizing I don't like discussing how to avoid cancer with you, of all people."

"Why me 'of all people'?"

"Because you had to actually survive cancer so I could skip it."

"You think you *skipped* cancer? Like you overslept and . . ." She flicks her hand like she's brushing something out of her way. "Missed it?"

"Not like that."

"Explain it to me then."

I turn toward her on the couch, perched on my crossed legs. "I have this mutation, and because of it, I was supposed to get cancer. In an alternate timeline, we don't know I have the gene yet, and—"

"Alternate timeline? Is this like a Marvel thing? You know I can't pay attention to those movies."

"No, but, absent medical intervention, our bodies were supposed to get cancer. Yours did, and you fought for your second chance. You had to suffer through chemo. I didn't do anything. I didn't lose anything. Why do I get to cheat cancer when you couldn't?"

"You didn't lose anything? Honey, you lost your breasts. You will lose your ovaries. In an alternate timeline, we've figured out a way to keep you healthy that doesn't involve removing body parts." She reaches for my hand across the couch, her familiar gold rings cold against my knuckles.

"I'm working through it with Denise, but I've been overwhelmed by this feeling that I'm not deserving. Like my life isn't big enough to justify what I've been given. I can't quite explain it yet."

She fusses with one of my rogue curls, unable to help herself. "No, I think I know what you mean. You know the breast cancer support group I went to? I swear to you, I had the best prognosis of the bunch. I felt like such a jerk every time I talked about my fears or the treatments when the Stage Four women had no idea what was happening next. One of them was even a little younger than you. She'd just had a baby when she was diagnosed. I remember thinking that she was really fighting for her life, while I was just . . . I don't even remember what I thought I was doing. I only remember feeling so guilty that I was going to live when some of those women weren't."

She shifts on the couch, settling in. "You know how your dad went back to school? I was the one who first wanted to go back to school. I was going to get an MFA and write the next Great American Novel like I'd always said I would back when I was getting my teaching certificate."

"I didn't know you wanted to write."

"Ugh. I don't. I barely like reading—it's all too solitary—but in the back of my brain there was this thought spinning round and round. *What if the cancer comes back? What if this is your only chance? What if it comes back* because *you didn't do this?* But you know what was so much more terrifying than owing a debt to the universe? Realizing it's all random. And that's the truth, there's nothing to pay or prove. We're all just living."

I feel a bit of my guilt lift from my chest. Those feelings I clung to—that living life to the fullest was objective and identifiable—don't fit so neatly beneath my ribs anymore. My mom turns on the couch cushion and faces me straight on when she tells me, with the steadiness and certainty reserved only for moms, "You don't need to prove you deserve your life to me or anyone. You deserve it, because everyone does. When they die or get sick or have to get a mastectomy, it's not because they deserve it. It's not fair, and it's random. There's nothing we can do other than live how we want to live."

I don't realize I'm crying until I rub my eyes with my hand, and they come away wet. "I hate hiking," I blurt. "I want to like it, but there are so many bugs." My voice is so pathetically weepy, my mom can't help but laugh at me.

"I know, honey." She pushes the top of my hair back and kisses my head like she did when I was little, and I feel protected in the same way I did back then. "I want to watch *Meet Me in St. Louis,*" she says, grabbing the remote.

"I love that one."

"I know you do."

I snuggle against my mom as the black-and-white image of the familiar St. Louis house transforms into that dreamy 1940s Technicolor, and we watch Judy Garland—in all her glory—croon about the boy next door.

———

EMMA WADDLES ACROSS the travertine tile floor in her red velvet maternity dress, conspicuously holding her belly. Her wife, Theresa, trails behind, balancing a Pyrex of her mother's cuccidati cookies, greeting the house with a cheery "Merry Christmas."

Emma grunts.

I grab the Italian fig cookies from my sister-in-law's hands and set them on the counter, freeing Theresa to help her wife flop into a chair at the kitchen table.

"How's life, Em?" My hands move from the table to my neck to my arm with transparent awkwardness.

Her nostrils flare. "Mom told you I'm pregnant."

I suck in a breath. "She told me you wouldn't be telling me you're pregnant. So, yes? No? It's unclear."

Emma snatches a carrot from the veggie platter. It cracks in half between her teeth. "That woman could never keep a secret."

"I think your belly is the tip-off," I say, pointing to Emma's bump. Theresa's laugh sprays cracker into her hand.

Emma lifts her sandy blond waves off her neck to reveal droplets of perspiration. "Alison, you don't tell a pregnant person they look pregnant. Don't you know anything?"

"You're my first pregnant peer. I don't know the rules."

"You're supposed to say you'd never know I was pregnant if I hadn't told you and that I'm glowing even though it's clearly sweat."

I refill the bowl of green and red M&M's I ate for breakfast and tuck the bulk bag back in the cabinet. "So . . . lie?"

"Don't listen to her, babe," Theresa says, flipping her long, dark hair. "You look like a pregnant celebrity who's so tiny she can still shoot her movie. So long as she's carrying an oversized bag or a houseplant at all times."

Emma leans across the table to flick my shoulder. "You're both the worst."

I wince and swat her hand away. "Why single me out?"

"Because you're the worst person in this house. And the closest. And a bad influence on Tree," she tacks on.

"I'm not even the worst Mullally daughter in this house."

I love Emma for her boldness, but no one's mistaking her for the sweet one. The running joke in the family is that 30 percent of her sentences start with "You know what I don't like about . . ."

"I'll leave you two to duke it out." Theresa kisses her wife's temple before escaping to watch TV with my dad.

"So how's the pregnancy going?" I ask.

"Good. I had morning sickness for like eighteen weeks—second trimester is easy, my ass—but now that I'm at twenty-one weeks, the Linda Blair memories are starting to fade."

I pluck a stalk of celery from the tray. "Why didn't you want me to know?"

She scoops a handful of M&M's into her mouth. "It's not just you. I haven't told Tree's family."

"Do you hide behind large pieces of furniture at Sunday

dinner?" Theresa has a giant Italian family that gets together for mandatory weekly dinners at her aunt's house. Neither illness, weather, nor a light coma will excuse your absence.

Emma glares at the suggestion. "I've only gotten bigger recently."

"Sure, you don't look *that* pregnant for a pregnant person, but you look *quite* pregnant for a nonpregnant person. I think they'll start to suspect."

"IVF was this whole thing"—she waves her hand in an attempt to simplify something that's too emotionally fraught to describe over a Kroger veggie platter—"and I didn't want to bother you with my fertility stuff with everything you've been going through."

I stare at her, snapping open the Christmas Coke can in front of me and waiting for her to fill in the dots.

"You're going to get your ovaries removed. You don't really want to hear me cry about my egg retrieval." She picks a loose strand of hair from my sweater sleeve and frowns at it. I know my sister well enough to spot this bit of misdirection when I see it—her attempt to distract from how Emma Mullally just admitted to tears.

Is this how I sound with my mom when I compare our burdens? "I love you and Theresa, Em. You don't have to hide stuff from me just because you tested negative. I want to be there for you through all this stuff. This baby too."

She folds her lips shut, holding back whatever's bubbling underneath. Emma's always felt more comfortable roasting than emoting. I watch her wrestle with the urge to pinch me rather than continue on the path of sisterly vulnerability.

"How did it all happen?" I ask, taking a sip.

"So when a woman and a woman love each other very much, then Dr. Kirby—"

"Not that, you idiot. How did you know this was the moment to take that step? How did you know it was what you wanted right now?"

"I didn't."

"What?"

"How am I supposed to know if any time is a good time for anything? Does anyone? You just have to make the choices that feel true to the life you want and hope like hell it will all work out."

"The life I want has been a bit of a moving target lately."

"Yeah, your social media's been all over the place. Were you in a hot-air balloon at some point?"

"I was. Yes." The hot-air balloon pilot took the photos for me while I held my knees to my chest on the floor of the basket and did breathing exercises.

"This is just like when we were kids and you tried out for track even though you're a garbage runner, because you liked the *idea* of it better than the geeky stuff you did with Dad. You only let yourself be all obsessive with that train thing during Christmas. Theresa thinks it's why you're such an unbearable Christmas monster."

"I thought it was my fun quirk."

"Alison," Emma huffs. "It's literally the most unbearable thing about you. You watch *The Holiday* year-round. It's deranged." The future mother and person in this house most likely to put me in a headlock kicks me in the kneecap for emphasis.

"Stop with the violence," I demand, resisting the impulse

to tack on *or I'm telling Mom*. "Nancy Meyers transcends the holiday season, and Cameron Diaz is criminally underrated as a comedic actress."

Emma furrows her brow. "You know what I don't like about Cameron Diaz?"

I throw a red M&M at her face, but when she catches it in her mouth, we're both too impressed to remember what we were arguing about in the first place.

Dinner goes by in a blur of mashed potatoes, green bean casserole, and honey baked ham, and I can't help but wonder what slow-cooker creations June's made for the Berg family today.

For dessert, my mom passes the cookie tin around the table as she weaves her culty tales.

"What's even weirder"—she bites into a jelly thumbprint shortbread—"is I was supposed to go to the Rajneesh compound with that roommate, but Emma and Alison's father got the flu. The girl said it was a yoga retreat, but yeah, she was in the documentary."

"Ms. Mullally, you seriously need to write a tell-all book," Theresa implores.

My dad rubs small circles between my mom's shoulder blades. "I'm always saying she has a story to tell," he agrees. My mom eyes me knowingly.

Emma stands, making a meal of every minute articulation of her bones. "I love you all. This was wonderful, but I'm too pregnant to be up this late."

My mom gasps theatrically, clutching her chest. "You're pregnant?!"

28

Survivor's Guilt Is an Ongoing Theme

WHEN THE MOVIE—ONE of the many Hallmark Christmas movies that poses the unanswerable question *What if Santa's son could get it?*—ends, my mom yawns strategically, signaling the official end of the holiday season. When I turn in for the night, I spy light glowing from under the office door—the room formerly known as EMMA'S ROOM—KEEP OUT UNDER THREAT OF DEATH. I knock lightly, and my dad beckons me in.

"I thought you were asleep," I whisper, closing the door behind me.

My dad chuckles gently from his roller chair. "I don't sleep anymore. But I'm glad you knocked." He opens the bottom drawer of his heavy wood desk. "I found this for the Christmas train. I'm sorry I was so busy this year with schoolwork."

I sit cross-legged on the floor at the foot of his desk, shaking my head with a smile. "It's fine, Dad. There's always next year. I wasn't here long anyway."

He reveals a miniature tunnel portal. It reads CASCADE TUNNEL in chipped painted print. "I found it at that flea market in Ohio your mom likes. It's the tunnel from our road trip to Washington, remember?"

I take the small piece of plastic in hand. "Of course. I made Emma read my book on its construction in the car, and she threw up right as we entered it."

He chuckles, his eyes lost in the memory. "I didn't think that tunnel would ever end."

I reach up, placing the piece back on his desk. "It's the longest railroad tunnel in the United States. Maybe we could paint it when you're done with classes this summer."

"That would be great, sweetie."

"I couldn't help but notice I didn't get a train car this year." I poke the armrest of his swivel chair.

"Yes. It was a big year for Target gift cards." He cleans the lenses of his glasses with his shirt. "I didn't think you liked getting those old cars anymore."

I chew on the corner of my mouth. "I've decided to embrace my rail enthusiasm. Year-round. Wear it on my sleeve from now on."

Adam was right. I'm sick of hiding the things that make me happy under my bed.

I shut the door after we wish each other good night and make my way down the wallpapered hallway to my old room. The space has functioned as a guest room ever since my mom swapped my twin bed for a double, but the walls remain a light periwinkle adorned with the same sheer black butterfly curtains that fluttered over the heating vent in a way that delighted my teenage self.

My homework desk is missing, but a flimsy Robert Pattinson poster still marks its old home. What can I say? Teenage Alison Mullally had a thing for the strong, quiet type.

I'm nearly tucked into the guest bed when a name lights up my screen.

Adam's calling me.

For the first time in weeks, Adam wants to talk to me. What could this mean? It has to at least be a courteous, *Good evening, Alison. In the New Year, expect me to be blocking your number. Have a lovely holiday.*

In danger of the call going to voicemail and missing this moment altogether, I frantically swipe at my screen. The phone jumps out of my hand, and I fumble with it twice before it lands on the bed with a thud.

"Hello?" I shout at my phone on the comforter. "Hello?" I answer again when the phone is on my ear.

I hear nothing but silence.

I sit on my bed, one hand on my phone and the other pressed into the stress crease forming on my forehead. "If this is a misdial, I'll kill you."

"Suddenly, I'm wondering why I was so nervous to call you." His familiar voice swims against my ear. It's warm and gravelly and as lovely as I remember. I resist melting at the sound of it.

"No need to be nervous." I try to pitch my voice sweet with a hint of sultry, but I don't think I nail it.

There's the briefest awkward silence before Adam speaks again. "Merry Christmas, Ali."

The nickname hits me in my chest. I reach for my headphones and place my pillow on my lap, worried lying down might jinx this. "Merry Christmas, Adam." I wait for what he might say next but hear only muffled voices in the background. "Where are you?"

"I'm at June's. I've been here a few days."

"How was Otis's Christmas?"

"Perfect. He's at that age where he still wants to believe in Santa but is questioning the logic. We had to work a bit harder to sell it. After he fell asleep last night, I walked on the garage roof so we could show him Santa's boot prints in the morning."

"Adam! That's stupid dangerous."

"No way. It was smart." His voice sparkles with the beginning of a laugh.

"You thought it was smart to reenact the dad's death in *Gremlins*?"

"I'm impressed you've seen *Gremlins*. That's nearly a scary movie."

"First, how dare you? Second, *Gremlins* is terrifying. I can't watch *Snow White* without picturing those little goblin thingies singing along."

"They're gremlins, Mullally. It's in the name." His voice widens the way it always does when he's pretending he's not amused by me. "How was your Christmas?"

"Good. Really good, actually. The best one in a while."

"I'm glad."

The silence grows until I can't help but squash it. "Did you call just to say Merry Christmas?"

"No. I wanted to talk. I just needed to get some privacy."

I hear a car door shut on his side of the line. I imagine him in his truck in his sister's driveway and the way he looked at me from the bench seat the last time I was there with him—like he was drinking me in.

"Okay." I reshuffle the pillows to lie down. I've talked to a few boys while staring up at this popcorn ceiling, but I've never felt as on edge as I do right now talking to Adam.

"Where are you?" he asks.

"My childhood bedroom. It's weird being back here. The whole house is a 2000s time warp. This morning, I stepped on a butterfly clip that's been caught in my rug since elementary school."

"I hate butterflies," he says easily, like he hates Mondays or anchovies and not a majestic creature of the natural world.

Pleasure creeps into my voice. "How can you hate butterflies?"

"Okay, I don't *hate* butterflies. But I don't understand why people treat them differently than other bugs because they're colorful."

I snort.

"What?"

"Nothing, I just love that. It's such a *you* opinion."

"Delightfully misanthropic?"

"Grumpy," I answer. "And something I might agree with but would never say out loud." I can hear him thinking, smiling maybe.

"I'm seeing a therapist." The confession bursts out of him. "Maybe I should start there." He laughs nervously. It's deep and rumbly, just like I remember.

"Me too. I've seen her on and off for years, but I'm *on* again."

"I'm newer to it than you are. Things kind of fell apart for me after Sam's birthday. June begged me to see someone."

"I'm so sorry, Adam." I count his breaths as the silence stretches. "I got your text." The word *No* flashes above my head.

"That's why I called." He exhales. "I didn't know how to say it over text. When you reached out, you said I was right, but I wasn't right about anything. I volunteered to help with the condo because it was something to do. A way to put off processing everything I was feeling after Sam's death. We weren't growing apart. I pushed him away.

"Sam was the one who I made all these life goals with—go up north for the apprenticeship, make it back to the Cities, and strike out on my own. He made it sound simple. It *was* simple at first. When I finished the apprenticeship, he talked me up to his parents' friends, looking for investors. Paul, that guy at Thanksgiving with the She Shed, he went back and forth with me for almost a year on investing. He had me re-design the same dining set countless times, wanting something more 'marketable.' By the end of it, I had a garage full of furniture I hated, and he had a vegan juice company that was a better fit for his *Shark Tank* fantasies." He chuckles bitterly.

"I never got over that, what felt like the dismissal of everything I worked for. I lost who I was to create something someone else might deem worthy of their investment. For years, I've been sort of . . . hiding, I guess? So stuck in my life and so afraid to try again and fail. Sam was always pushing me to take another chance, and I pushed him away rather than risk taking a single step forward."

He swallows audibly, and in my mind, I can see the way his throat moves. "When he died," he continues, "instead of allowing myself to feel sad he was gone, I felt so guilty for pushing him away by choice. I was still sad, but I wasn't letting myself feel it. I didn't think I deserved to feel the loss, like there was only so much of Sam's memory to go around and I hadn't earned my piece."

I finish his thought for him. "And I only made everything worse."

"No, that's the thing. I blamed you for that guilt, but it was there before Mrs. Lewis introduced us. Don't get me wrong, thinking I was falling for his girlfriend didn't *help*, but what I was feeling wasn't your fault."

For a moment, I let his words—*I was falling*—float deliciously around my insides before I force myself to hear the past tense of it.

"But you also made me feel like things could be better, like it wouldn't always feel so lonely," he says, his voice cracking with emotion. It makes me wish I could hold his hand. "I'm sorry I put all of those feelings of anger and shame on you. It wasn't fair."

"I'm still sorry I complicated those feelings further. I'm no stranger to guilt. It's my favorite feeling."

"How's that?"

Finally getting comfortable, I snuggle deeper into my pillow. "Not my favorite as in 'most enjoyed,' but I seem to prefer it over feeling anything else. I don't know. Maybe I enjoy it a little. So many emotions want you to just sit and feel them until they go away. Guilt demands action. You have to atone for it. It tells you exactly what it wants from you. Sadness doesn't do that. At least it doesn't for me."

"You sound like my therapist." He chuckles lightly, and the sound makes my insides fizzy.

"I sound like *my* therapist. Survivor's guilt is an ongoing theme for me. After my mastectomy, I was kind of . . . depressed. Mara and Chelsea were amazing, but the recovery was more than I anticipated. And I wouldn't let myself be sad because what kind of asshole feels sad after escaping cancer? Deserving people feel grateful. Deserving people survive and go climb mountains and live life to the fullest. I grabbed on to that last one and ran with it."

I clear my throat. "Rather than figuring out how my new body fit into who I was before the surgery, I created a new personality: someone worthy of a second chance. Because an introverted couch potato couldn't possibly deserve it. When I met Sam, I thought he was living exactly the right life. He was colorful and alive. I thought being the person he chose proved I was too, and being the person he dumped proved I wasn't. Now I've come around to the idea that I might not be cut out for sucking the marrow out of life, and it might be okay to just be myself."

"There's no one else like you," he responds, his voice a secretive hush. "I don't want to torment myself anymore. And I don't want to feel sad, but I am. Whether I like it or not."

I want to ask if he feels my shadow in his life, the way I feel his—but I'm not brave enough to hear the answer. "Are you in the bunk bed tonight or driving home?"

"Air mattress, actually. For Christmas, I built Otis this lofted bed thing he wanted. I've been down here a lot the last couple weeks. Figuring some things out."

"Wow. No more bunk beds. It's the end of an era." I hear his laugh, which transforms into a yawn. "Should I let you go?"

"Probably. I should go inside and head to bed."

"It was nice to hear from you," I say, forcing a formal distance into my tone. "Good luck, Adam."

"Good luck?" I almost feel his light chuckle on my cheek. "Is that better or worse than wishing me well?"

"Better, I think."

"Okay. Good luck to you too. Night, Ali." He starts to say something else but stops himself. "Night."

"Night," I say, and hang up the phone, already impatient for our next late-night call.

29

Ruth Bader Winsburg, Night Cheese, and Risky Quizness

I DON'T HEAR FROM Adam again after our late-night Christmas call. I considered reaching out at midnight on New Year's Eve, hoping this would be our new thing—emotional late-night phone calls on bank holidays, and by Memorial Day we'd be making declarations of love—but I fell asleep at nine p.m.

On New Year's Day, I have no missed calls on my call log, and it's time to move forward. This morning, I purged my closet of my fake life. Now I'm at Chelsea's apartment before our trivia tournament, and I can't resist showing off my personal growth to her and Mara.

Chelsea's apartment is a third-floor unit in a 1920s colonial in the Como Park neighborhood of Saint Paul. The architecture mixes perfectly with her floral-forward, English-country-home styling.

I plop a laundry basket on top of her fluffy blue bedspread. The bland-colored bits of my performance fabrics—grays, olives, and khakis—drape over the top and fall onto the cheerful floral print.

"The remnants of your Cheryl Strayed period," Chelsea says reverently. She holds my dark green North Face shell jacket to her chest.

"Taking to the woods is always a cry for help," Mara says from the hallway.

I lean against the tufted headboard. "But in movies it's always a positive thing."

"No, in movies it's the wake-up call to get therapy. They never choose to stay in the woods for eternity. There's nothing for anyone there. You always have to come back out to civilization." Mara walks around the bed and settles onto the upholstered bench at its foot, balancing a teacup on her knee.

"Your movie was never the 'take to the woods' movie. It was a 'buy a house in a quaint Christmas town and learn to love yourself with the help of quirky strangers' movie," Chelsea explains.

I furrow my brow. "What are *your* movies?"

"Mine is 'Christmas Man teaches me about love,' and Mara's is the classic 'girl moves to the city and gets the big promotion,'" she says, like the answer is obvious.

I pass Mara my hydration backpack. "I wanted you guys to have first dibs before I donate it all to mark the end of this phase. And the beginning of something new."

"Make sure you keep some of this—base layers aren't just for camping—but I don't see a lot of uses for a pair of UV-protective cargo shorts." Chelsea flicks the khaki shorts away from her like they're radioactive.

"They seemed necessary at the time."

"Did they, Al? Did they really, though?" Chelsea asks.

I shrug.

"Were you able to get Patrick to change his mind for the tournament today? He can join late between rounds if he has a conflict," Mara asks with a sip.

Chelsea shakes her head. "He's on a New Year's getaway at a fancy couples' resort in Wisconsin with Josie. There's no way he's coming. Sorry, Mar. Is there anyone else eligible to play with the team we haven't tried?"

Mara raises her eyebrows indiscreetly. "Just, uh . . ."

I groan, ignoring the emptiness beneath my ribs. "We can say his name." I swallow to clear the knot of emotion lodged in my throat. "It's fine. Adam and I . . . it was never going to work out with us."

I clap my hands on my knees and stand, ready to leave the trappings of adventure and talk of Adam behind. "Come on, we have a trivia tournament to get to."

Mara cheers. "Yes! Let's obliterate some poor, delicate nerds."

Every New Year's Day at two p.m., a different venue in the Minneapolis–Saint Paul area hosts the Twin Cities Trivia Tournament. This year, we're at Union Depot, a historic railroad station in Saint Paul that continues to serve as the city's transit hub, community center, and—thanks to the stunning neoclassical architecture—event venue.

Obviously, I love it here. It's one of the rare places in the city where a bride in Vera Wang can mingle with a hungover college sophomore waiting for a Megabus to Milwaukee beside a local senior downward dogging on a rec center yoga mat.

Today, the ornate room is cordoned off for the tournament. Skylights in the vaulted ceiling bathe the dozens of round six-top tables covering the marble floors in warm natural light. Each table is bare, with the exception of a few pencils, scrap paper, and a basket for phones and smartwatches. Bars and food carts are set up on either side of the room to maintain the pub quiz aesthetic, along with a small stage, lights, and a speaker system. The gravitas and solemnity of the building are both out of place and completely fitting for the boozy trivia showdown about to commence.

The moment we walk in, Mara grabs Chelsea and me by the elbow to relay reconnaissance. "Based on my intel, the teams to beat are Ruth Bader Winsburg, Night Cheese, and Risky Quizness."

"Quizly Bears is here again," I warn her. Despite the cutesy name, the team knocked us out of last year's semifinals in a vicious tiebreaker.

Mara shakes her head, her shark eyes fixed on her nemesis two tables away. "Not a threat. Man Bun carries that team, and he's on family leave with Pixie Haircut."

Chelsea coos. "Aww. Good for them. I didn't know they were together."

"They weren't at the time. She was cheating on her long-term partner Faux-Hawk with Man Bun," Mara explains like a spy providing crucial wartime intelligence. "When Faux-Hawk found out, he defected to Ruth Bader Winsburg. Now Ruth is stronger than ever, and Quizly Bears is a pathetic shell of what it once was."

Chelsea titters. "Can we trade tables near them? I want to hear about that."

Mara twists her necklace. "We're not here to make friends, Chels. We're here to crush dreams."

"Whatever. I'm putting in our order for beer and fries before it gets crowded." Chelsea hops off in the direction of the bar.

"No alcohol, Olsen. I'm serious!" Mara hollers after her through cupped hands.

I pick a seat at the table displaying MARQUIZKA HARGITAY. "Chill, Mar. This is for charity."

Mara's eyes circle around her like she's a defensive animal before she finally sits. "Don't let that affect your killer instinct. The animal shelter gets our money no matter who wins."

"Mara, I promise you, we'll do everything in our power to decimate the competition."

"Thank you, Al. I needed to hear that from you. I was beginning to question your commitment."

The tournament is made up of eight rounds with an elimination of the lowest-scoring teams each round until the final five face off. By round three, all of the casual players are out, leaving only the teams with at least one Mara-caliber competitive maniac. When our team name is announced as a semifinalist, Mara barely contains her squeal.

My pen is poised for the next question, but Darren interrupts the round to announce, "We have a latecomer for Marquizka Hargitay."

Mara cups her hands around her mouth. "Send him in."

I'm at the top of a roller coaster about to plunge down the first steep descent as the sound of men's boots echoes offstage. My hands start to tingle with anticipation while I wait for the tall figure in a khaki-colored jacket to come into view under the harsh stage lights. He steps out of the shadows, and my heart sinks through the floor. I thought it'd be Adam walking out there.

"Patrick?" Chelsea's voice echoes off the curved ceiling. We watch his red hair glowing in the spotlight, his pristine leather boots and nonreversible tan puffer coat. "I thought you were with Josie this weekend."

"We broke up," he says onstage, in front of the house of quiz nerds. The mic picks up his deep voice and carries it to every corner of the room. "The vacation was a plot to guilt me into getting rid of my cat."

Multiple strangers join Chelsea in a horrified gasp. She peels her hands off her mouth to speak. "Not Colonel Corduroy!"

He nods solemnly. "She said it was her or the cat, and it was finally too much. She hates my family. She hates my friends. Now she hates my cat too? I couldn't take it anymore."

Strangers slow-clap him in either sarcasm or solidarity. Their motivations are unclear.

Mara's eyebrow arches up. "So you were fine with her hating your friends and family? Cats are where you draw the line?"

Dozens of onlookers share Chelsea's appalled expression. "Those are just *people*, Mara. Colonel Corduroy is blind in one eye."

Darren, the tournament host, cuts through the crowd's murmurs. "You can join your team, but per the bylaws, I need your excuse to log into the spreadsheet."

"I would have gotten here earlier but we broke up *during* the couples massage, and then we had to drive home together—"

Darren moves the mic to the side. "Just say traffic, man."

"Of course. Traffic. Sorry." Patrick jumps down the steps two at a time to join Chelsea on her side of the table.

We wait for the questions to pour in, but the visibly perturbed cohost, Stu, is conferring with Darren, who steps back to the mic. "I promise we'll start the semifinals in a minute, but we have a problem in the lobby. There's a guy out front demanding to speak with someone on an unregistered team . . ." He looks down at the sticky note Stu passes him. "Otrivia Benson: SVU. Anyone know what he's talking about?"

My heart stops.

Stu crosses his arms dramatically in front of the mic stand. "He's refusing to leave. And we all know Otrivia Benson is banned from this event, so he isn't here for any team participating *legally*."

"Shit, Stu. It's pub trivia. Let the guy talk to one of the Marquizka Hargitays."

I look to my right at our defender—none other than Glasses from Risky Quizness.

Mara stands, fueled by righteous indignation. "Seriously, Risky? You're resorting to getting us thrown out of the tournament?"

Glasses rears his head back in exasperation. "Everyone knows you're Otrivia Benson! It was the *least* subtle name change of all time."

Other teams start to express their own opinions until Darren gestures for the crowd to calm down. "We can't actually 'ban' anyone from participating as a new team if they qualify. Stu, let him in and see what he wants. Then we can get on with it."

I spot the jacket first, but I stop breathing the moment I see his face.

"Adam, wh—what are you doing here?" I stammer around the longing in my throat. He's in that ridiculous jacket—denim-side out—with a red flannel underneath. My body registers pain at the sight of him, like how a perfectly warm bath stings when you're freezing. My heart wants him so badly it hurts.

Stu ushers him to the mic stand. "You weren't answering your phone," Adam says, adjusting his volume to account for the microphone.

I point to the phone basket before asking the first of the one thousand questions buzzing in my brain. "How did you know I was here?"

Adam holds up his cell phone. "Sam invited me."

I twist my face in confusion, and someone from Agatha Quiztie yells, "Who's Sam?"

"How's that possible?" Chelsea asks.

Adam shrinks a bit, noticing all eyes are on him. "Uh, can I speak to Alison privately?" he asks. My mouth opens, but no sound comes out.

Blunt Bob from the Quizly Bears shakes her head defiantly. "He can't tamper with the team, so unless he's staying, whatever he has to say he says in front of all of us."

"Tampering? Seriously?" Mara throws up her hands. "Fine. Adam, say what you came to say so we can finish the tournament."

"Mara!" Chelsea reprimands her.

"What do you mean Sam invited you?" I ask.

Adam grabs the mic stand. "Should I just . . . in front of everyone?"

"Is he talking about the Sam who's . . ." Patrick mouths the word *dead* to Chelsea.

Host Darren is now bouncing on his leg. "You can join their team. We just need to log your excuse, per the bylaws."

I stand up so I can see Adam over the crowd. "What do you mean Sam—"

"The calendar alerts." He points to the phone in his palm. "'December twenty-ninth—Get a haircut. You'll be so glad you did after your date with destiny and your hair always looks weird for a couple days after a cut. December thirtieth—DON'T bail on Sam's NYE party like you always do.'" Adam's voice cracks, and my heart clenches. "'This is the beginning of EVERYTHING!' And there's like ten exclamation points after that last one. 'January first, two p.m.—Trivia tournament with your perfect woman.'"

The memory of playing trivia with Sam after our breakup flashes in my mind. **We should do it again. I'll bring a ringer.**

How many times have I reread that text since he died, never once wondering what he meant—or who?

Adam keeps reading from his screen. "There's also a note about not wearing flannel, but I didn't see it until after I left."

"Sam invited you," I repeat with renewed understanding. I issue either a wobbly laugh or a sigh of relief or a shocked gasp. Maybe all three, because my body is coming to grips with the notion that somehow Sam did all of this. Something that feels a bit like magic whirs between Adam and me.

Darren steps up to Adam's mic. "You can just tell me you were caught in traffic, bro. I just need to—"

Adam grabs the stand back with more conviction. His eyes drill into mine, and, for a moment, I forget we're making a spectacle of ourselves. It's *him*—and he's *here*—and I might be about to get everything I ever wanted.

"It was you he was talking about that night. I was supposed to go to his party this weekend so he could bring me here. Today. It was always you!" Adam wets his lips, waiting for me to respond.

Sam was always right about me. I was so determined to see

it as a negative thing, but he saw how right I was for someone he loved.

I want to say something, anything. Our problems aren't in the rearview. I'm finally grappling with my diagnosis and my mastectomy. We're both facing our grief over the loss of our friend. I've only recently started accepting myself for who I am—a nippleless homebody who's as deserving of life as anyone else. And Adam's still stuck in his rut, by all accounts.

"And I bought a house. Here. Well, not *here* in this train station, but nearby. I'm done making excuses for why I can't have the things I want, because I know what I want." Adam looks around the open space surrounding us and the crowd in rapt attention. He makes a face that says, *The hell with it,* and it's unspeakably sexy. "I love you. I love that you love trains and hate my music. I love that you listen to Christmas songs way too early. I love that you snort when you find something truly funny."

I snort a little at that, and the sound emboldens him.

"I love that you love that I hate butterflies and that you're afraid of gremlins. I love that you can't help but tell me when you think I'm being ridiculous or too rigid. That you want me to move forward with my life, but you want me to want it for myself. I love everything about you, Alison. I only want to be with you. Exactly as you are."

My heart stutters to a stop. Adam stares back at me like I'm the only one who heard his declaration. Everyone holds our silence, waiting for us to say something, but neither of us can speak. I don't know any words.

Stu shoves his way in front of Adam's mic, meeting the resistance of his rigid body. "I hate to interrupt, but this feels pretty personal . . . so if you're not here to participate in this event, you'll have to wait in the lobby until the end of the tournament."

"Wait!" I cry out. Chelsea squeals directly into my eardrum before shoving me in the direction of the stage. I bound up the steps two at a time, unable to waste another second, because I know I love him too. The feeling doesn't hit me like an oncoming train. It slipped inside my heart long ago when I wasn't looking. When I didn't think I deserved it.

A teary laugh bursts from my open mouth. I'm finally on the stage and the hot lights hit my eyes sideways, temporarily blinding me. Without the benefit of sight, I reach out for his waist to draw him closer. He loops his arm around me, and I hit his chest with a delicious thud.

He presses his forehead to mine, and I breathe him in, only vaguely aware that we have an audience. He smells so familiar. Like a warm drink on a cold day and a bonfire on a summer beach and a workshop garage in Duluth. Like Adam, everywhere I want to be, every time of year.

He lifts my face to meet his eyes, reintroducing me to every gold fleck within his chocolate-brown irises. "That was a good speech," I whisper.

"I watched the Billy Crystal movie. I watched three, actually, before I figured out which one was the right one. But I wanted to Billy Crystal you again. More intentionally this time."

"I love you." The words escape my mouth on an exhale. They couldn't wait for air.

He moves his hand, tipping my chin toward him so he can kiss me. My whole body relaxes at the feel of him against my lips, and he drinks me in with sweet, warm sips. I never want it to stop, but a rapidly shrinking part of me knows we're standing in front of a crowd of impatient trivia junkies. A disgruntled throat clears, and Adam and I slowly break apart. His heated gaze never breaks mine.

"I've loved you this whole time," I whisper. "Even when I was Sam's girlfriend. The second time, I mean, after his funeral." The mic picks this last part up, and we start to lose the audience's goodwill.

"It's less weird in context, guys. Come on," Mara says, defending me to the rapidly turning crowd. "Darren, put 'traffic' on the spreadsheet for him too. He's with us."

Adam and Patrick join us for the rest of the competition. In the semifinals, the Chelsea-Patrick mind meld comes through for the team in the form of prehistoric literary puns.

"Anne Brontosaurus." Patrick points to the answer sheet.

"Not Charlotte or Emily?" I bite down on my thumbnail, the anxiety of getting so close to victory finally hitting me.

Patrick shakes his head. "No, it's Anne. Stu said it was an epistolary novel."

Adam bounces his knee with a bit more agitation than normal, competitive tension thick in the air. "I thought the brontosaurus wasn't a real dinosaur species."

Chelsea writes furiously. "It is now. It's like Pluto. We're always changing our mind about it."

Adam and I are merely an impediment to the lizard-lit dream team, so I seize on the opportunity to lean in close and ask, "So you bought a house?"

"Yes, but it was a long time coming. I've wanted to be closer to my family for a while. I was going to tell you about it when I called, but I didn't want to put any pressure on you. I wanted to invite you over for something very romantic that I still haven't planned, if I'm honest. I wanted to show you I was serious about moving forward for myself. But then . . ."

"You got the calendar alert."

"And I couldn't spend another second counting down the days until everything else was ready. I was ready, and it was so like Sam to push me off the cliff. Our favorite 'real estate multihyphenate' showed me some places and a couple were ridiculous—like one had a pool? Why waste your entire yard with a pool in this climate?"

I gesture for him to get to the point.

"But one was perfect. Two bedrooms. A workshop. Nice neighborhood. Yard for a dog. But we don't need a dog if—"

Mara snaps her fingers in front of her face. "Hey, guys. I'm thrilled for you and your many future rescue dogs, but can we focus on the task at hand?"

In the final round, Adam proves his worth early on by naming every Kurt Russell/John Carpenter collaboration for the "Famous Kurts" section (other Kurts being Browning, Vonnegut, Gödel, and Cobain).

"Snake Plissken was such a great action hero name that it was reused—"

Mara holds her left hand up to stop Adam's chatter while scribbling *Escape from New York* with her right. "Demonstrate your value to Al another time."

"Sorry, I was excited I knew the answer." Adam squeezes my thigh under the table, sending a blush up my whole body.

"We're going to have to figure out what happens next."

He frowns. "I think Stu just handed Mara the image-round questions."

"No, with us," I explain while examining the pictures of men Mara shoves in my face. "So you live here?"

"In three weeks."

"And we're dating . . ."

"Obviously we're dating, Alison."

"Exclusively?"

"I am."

"Is it serious?" I ask playfully.

"I think so," he answers mockingly.

"I'm going to kill you, dismember you, and sell you both for parts," Mara says simply. It successfully puts an end to our nausea-inducing love fest.

For the first time ever, Marquizka Hargitay breaks into the top three teams. For a tiebreaker, we send our fearless leader to the stage for a sudden death against Glasses from Risky Quizness and a man from Night Cheese. Chelsea, Patrick, and I groan when Darren names the category. "What's wrong with animal land speed records?" Adam whispers.

Patrick exhales in defeat. "Chels would have killed this category."

Chelsea—our resident science teacher and animal lover—covers her eyes, unable to watch the massacre. Mara's face pales when Stu reads the question. I rub my arm anxiously, uncomfortable watching Mara lose at something. It's like seeing a costumed grizzly performing in a circus act, heartbreaking and unnatural.

Mara's guess is completely off, and we end the tournament in third place behind Night Cheese and Risky Quizness.

"Third's good, right?" Adam asks.

Mara pats his cheek. "Oh, Adam, you sweet, gorgeous dummy. There's only winning and losing." She drains her pint from our free round of loser beers. "Next year, we're taking this seriously."

Chelsea whines, "This year wasn't taking it seriously?"

Adam brings my hand to his lips, and we can't get out of there fast enough. The cool air whooshes in my ears as we spin out of the revolving door into the bitter January air.

Immediately, he pushes me up against a column and captures my mouth in a wild, starving kiss. This kiss isn't sweet. It's heavy and hot. He pushes his hand into my hair and grabs hold, grasping at more of me, anchoring himself.

"God, I love you so much," he says when he breaks the kiss to search my eyes. "Please tell me if this is too much, too soon."

"This is the exact right amount of 'much.'" I punctuate each word with a kiss on his nose, cheek, chin, and wherever else I can get a bit of him.

"Oh, wait." He stops short. Worry flashes across his face, and my mind rushes to fill in the gaps. "I forgot your shelving in my workshop."

"You built the shelf? I just gave away my camping stuff."

"Not the one you asked for. I built you a display case for your trains."

"I love you so much it hurts," I blurt before I can overthink it. Even when I wanted to be someone else, he only ever saw me. And he loved me for it. "It's the most thoughtful, incredible gift I've ever received. I can't wait to see it."

"Should I drive back and get it?"

I lean my head on his arm. "Let's just go home, Adam."

He rewraps my scarf around my neck to block out the chill with the same precision as before. Then he takes my hand and leads me down the stone steps in the direction of the river.

"I'm dying to know what other Billy Crystal movies you watched while preparing to sweep me off my feet."

"I started with *The Princess Bride*."

I nod. "Wise choice."

"Veered off course with *City Slickers*—but that was mostly for me." He gives my hand a squeeze. "Then I found my way to the right one."

"So if I'd said no after all that, were you still going to move into a house fifteen minutes from me?"

We break apart on the sidewalk so Adam can hold open an apartment-building door for a mom juggling a grocery bag and an infant car seat. "I was going to very respectfully woo you. Slowly. Over time," he tells me, letting the door swing shut behind them.

I hold back my snort. "Now I'm sorry I didn't go that route."

He sighs like I'm the most infuriating woman he can't live without—it's the loveliest sound. "I'm not."

He pulls me into him again as we walk past the store owners packing away their twinkle lights and presses a kiss into my hair.

We walk hand in hand like that all the way home, and I can't imagine anyone else I'd rather be.

Epilogue

Three Months Later

G ET YOUR HEAD in the game, Mullally!" Mara yells, my cell phone pinned to her forehead.

Sprawled out on Adam's leather sofa with my legs on his lap, I'm hardly in a game-ready stance, but while I'm recovering from surgery, Heads Up at Adam's house is our group's temporary pub trivia stand-in.

Yesterday, I had my fallopian tubes removed laparoscopically to decrease my risk of ovarian cancer until I decide when to have an oophorectomy and hysterectomy. I made the choice not for my mom, but for me. If Adam and I decide to have kids someday, it'll happen in a doctor's office, but I don't want fear to force our hand.

Back in November, I would've found the prospect of fertility planning with Adam Berg ludicrous. Now I don't know how it could have gone any other way. He's my favorite person and—as he's constantly telling me—I'm his.

"*Cheers!*" I shout.

"*Cheers* was an ensemble show!" The buzzer cuts her off. Her lips narrow to a tight line when she reads the celebrity name on the screen. "Danny DeVito wasn't even in *Taxi Driver,*" Mara bites out.

"You were thinking of *Taxi.*" Adam rubs circles into my knee, swallowing his smile.

I wince. "Oh, yeah. Sorry, Mar. I think I'm still foggy."

"What's taking Chelsea so long with the food?" Patrick asks. "Adam, do you have any snacks?"

"Thin Mints in the freezer," Adam says. Despite his rants on the Girl Scout business model—*What kind of company requires adults to engage in financial transactions in Target parking lots with children, Alison?*—he keeps a stash ready for me at all times.

"Sorry about that." Chelsea breezes in through the front door, arms loaded with carryout bags of Thai food. "Riley's neighbor filed a complaint over his backyard chickens, and it's really shaking his sense of community."

"Who's Riley?" Patrick asks from the freezer.

"The DoorDash delivery driver," Chelsea answers, plopping the bags on the coffee table in front of me. A starving Patrick rushes to pick at the appetizers. "I hope you don't mind, Adam, but I gave him one of your cards from the workshop. He wants to hire you to design a more suitable coop for Thelma and Louise."

Adam's hand freezes on my thigh. "You went into the garage?"

Chelsea bobs her head, oblivious to the tension building in Adam's posture. "Yeah, that rocking chair looks amazing. Who's it for?"

"Someone ordered a rocking chair? I want to see it." I start to stand, but Adam holds my legs down on his lap.

"Sit down. You're horrible at surgical recovery," he complains.

I scrunch my nose. "I'm phenomenal at recovery. You're a grouchy caretaker. And that was *barely* a surgery. They didn't even give me the good drugs."

"Yes," he groans. "You complained about that to *multiple* nurses. I think they put you on a list."

Flatware clanks together in the kitchen as Chelsea and Patrick bicker over dinner, but Mara and I have our eyes trained on Adam.

"It's for you," he admits. "It's a rocking chair like I made for Otis. I thought we could put it next to your bookshelf."

Patrick delivers me a bowl of green curry. "I hope it's more stool than chair. Have you seen Al's apartment?"

"It's for here. I built the bookcase in the spare room for you. I thought it could be your office. I was going to give it to you as a gift and ask you to move in when your lease is up in May, but now you know, and the surprise is ruined." His boyish pout is too adorable for words, and a face-splitting grin blooms between my cheeks. Even my heart smiles.

"Are you serious right now?" I ask him. Chelsea squeals somewhere behind me, but it's like the world has faded out around the edges. I only hear him.

He grabs my hand. "Of course. I love you, and I want you here all the time. I can't wait to take that next step with you."

An unwelcome thought douses me in cold water. "I signed a new lease."

He freezes. "You said your lease is up in May. Like the end of May."

"Everyone knows that means the new lease starts on May first. And even if it meant the end of May, you were planning to ask me *in* May. Have you never read a lease agreement?"

Mara marches past the couch with my phone to her ear. "I'm already calling your landlady. What's her weak spot?"

"Her family doesn't really *see* her," Chelsea provides around a mouthful of pad Thai. "I ran into her by the garbage cans once."

"So is that a yes to moving in?" Adam asks me through the flurry of activity, like I'm the only person in the world.

"Of course it's a yes." Giggles bubble in my voice. "I'm obsessed with you, and this house is adorable. I'm obviously moving in. I've even got my team on logistics." I tilt my head in the direction of our friends conferring by the large window, dappled in the fading evening sun.

He pulls me closer and presses his forehead against mine. Longing shudders through me, and I wish we were alone and not in the middle of Game Night chaos. "We're going to live together," he says, his words traveling down my spine on a low growl. "I'm going to wake up next to you every morning."

I tug him by his shirt a millimeter closer. "You're going to see my bedhead every day, not only on the weekends. Can you handle it?"

He kisses my cheek and drags his mouth to my ear. "Of course. I want way more of you than weekends."

Sparks crackle in my heart. "Now that you've made a

romantic proclamation in the form of a rocking chair, you're officially a sexy carpenter cliché—"

He interrupts me with his lips, and any intruding thoughts dissolve away.

He releases my mouth, pulling his head back to meet my eyes. His fingers snag a loose curl behind my ear, and joy shows freely on his face. "Alison, I've never felt so ready for everything to change."

ACKNOWLEDGMENTS

I've always loved the acknowledgments section in the back of books. Even before it occurred to me that I could write a book, I'd read the list of thank-yous in the author's own voice and marvel at the sheer number of people it took to make a book appear on my shelf. The community of individuals who rallied around the author and made this fairly solitary work a little less solitary. No matter a book's content, the acknowledgments are always earnest and warmhearted, which is exactly what I love about them. Through writing this book, I discovered that it truly takes a village of incredibly generous and brilliant people to bring a book into the world. I never dreamed that I would be writing an acknowledgments section, but here we are, so get ready for things to get a little earnest and warmhearted. And pretty sappy.

Endless thanks to my phenomenal literary agent and advocate, Laura Bradford, who literally made all of my dreams come true, and to my foreign rights agent, Taryn Fagerness, whose expertise has taken my words across the globe.

To my editor, Kate Dresser, you've understood this story and these characters from day one, and your incredible insight and expertise have made this book more than I ever thought possible. Working with you creatively has been a gift, and I can't wait to do it again.

Thank you to Tarini Sipahimalani, who has all of the answers to my questions, and the entire G. P. Putnam's Sons team, especially Sally Kim, Ashley McClay, Alexis Welby, Aja Pollock, Janice Barral, Tiffany Estreicher, Emily Mileham, Maija Baldauf, Christopher Lin, Meg Drislane, Chandra Wohleber, Molly Pieper, Nicole Biton, and everyone else who helped get this book into the hands of readers.

To my mentor, Meredith Schorr, thank you for plucking Alison and Adam from the Author Mentor Match submissions pile and sending my life into a wild and wonderful new direction. Your unwavering belief in me gave me permission to believe in myself.

To all of the writers I admire who took the time to read my book and publicly write kind things about it, I cannot thank you enough for your generosity. The writing community continues to astound me. You are truly the best people.

Millions of thank-yous to the friends and creative partners I've made along the way, especially Naina Kumar, Ava Watson, Scarlette Tame, Amanda Wilson, Elizabeth Armstrong, Kjersten Piper Gresk, Karsyn Zetah, Jenny Lane, Sarah T. Dubb, Kate Robb, Jessica Joyce, Livy Hart, Cara Stout, Vienna Veltman, Bella Lucas, Amy Buchanan, Ingrid Pierce, C. B. London, Danica Nava, Myah Ariel, Laura Piper Lee, Jill Tew, Maggie North, and Alexandra Vasti, who read early drafts, critiqued scenes with love and positivity, or helped me polish up a punch line or two. Also thanks to the SF 2.0 community, the 2024 Debut Slack, the AMM R9 Slack, the Kitchen Party group chat, the Bad Bitch Writers Club, and the bookish community who have offered me laughs, support, and true friendship. You have been the most wonderful surprise on this journey.

To my Lifers, Natalie, Devon, BethAnn, Katie (KTB), Katie (KSG), Kelly, and Lilia: You all are as funny and kind as you are gorgeous (and you're all absolute smokeshows). Thank you for being the reason I love writing about friendship.

I'm so grateful for my in-laws Al and Susan, who not only raised my wonderful husband but have been so supportive of this crazy new venture from the beginning. Thank you for every trip to the zoo and day at Papa and CiCi's that kept my son happily distracted while I brought this book over the finish line.

To my mom, who took on both cancer and raising teenage me with grace and humor (never tell me which was worse), thank you for encouraging me to dream and for teaching me to face the scary, hard things. Thank you to my sister, Meg, who was subjected to my earliest stories on family car trips and so magnanimously gave me the confidence to keep telling them.

John, I hope you aren't reading this book, but I hope my writing it has made you proud (since, not to brag, Dr. Seuss and I share a publishing house). You make me brave, and I hope I make you brave too.

Chris, I wish I could put words to the way you've encouraged me and made me believe in myself. Thank you for reading every version of this book and begging me to keep going. Thank you for being the most generous partner, the most patient and attentive parent, and the greatest person I'll ever know. I love everything about you. You're better than anyone I could ever write.

And to you, dear reader, time is a precious resource. Thank you for spending a little of it with me.

FOUR WEEKENDS AND A FUNERAL
DISCUSSION GUIDE

1. At Sam's funeral, Alison goes along with others' assumption that she's still dating Sam. Would you have made the same choice? Discuss the identity changes that come with being Sam's *most recent* girlfriend, and the role Sam's family assumes of her.

2. Alison and Adam are quite the grumpy-sunshine combo. Why do you think Alison is drawn to Adam?

3. In cleaning out Sam's apartment, Alison and Adam are forced to confront the impact Sam had on their lives. To what extent do objects hold memories of a person? How do you think this task brought them together, or pulled them apart?

4. Preemptive survivor's guilt plays a big role in how Alison approaches her life as a BRCA1 carrier, and to an extent, how Adam copes with Sam's passing. How do these feelings push them forward, or guide their decisions?

5. Alison tries to convince herself that climbing mountains (and otherwise being "outdoorsy") means she's living her

best life. What does "living life to the fullest" mean to you? Discuss the day-to-day moments in which you honor your vision and when you fall short.

6. This novel's title pays homage to the classic romantic comedy *Four Weddings and a Funeral*, and the author was inspired by another classic rom-com: *While You Were Sleeping*. Have you seen these movies? If not, plan a screening for your group and discuss how inspiration shows up in the novel.

7. Alison and Adam's relationship is built on a secret. In what ways was this secret necessary for the story to have panned out the way it did? Are secrets ever a good thing in a romantic relationship?

8. Both Alison and Adam have friendships that mean a great deal to them. Discuss how their friends played a role in their individual journeys. Which friend was your favorite?

9. Alison and her friends enjoy competing in bar trivia against other punnily named teams. If you were competing in a trivia tournament, which knowledge category would be your area of expertise? Brainstorm your own team name to go up against Otrivia Benson: SVU.

10. Ellie Palmer pays tribute to Sandra Bullock's Chicago transportation-worker character in the movie *While You Were Sleeping* with Alison's career in public transportation. How did Alison's perspective on her lifelong passion for trains shift over the course of the novel? Are there any

childhood interests or traditions that you've revisited later in life?

11. In turns hilarious and heartfelt, *Four Weekends and a Funeral* offers many poignant observations about life. Which of the story's messages spoke to you most? To what extent do you think humor is essential in telling this story, and why?

12. At the end of the novel, we discover a truth about Alison and Adam's relationship. Discuss to what extent fate and choice coexist, and if Alison and Adam were fated to meet. If so, brainstorm Alison and Adam's alternate not-so-meet-cute.

13. Where do you think Alison and Adam are today?

14. In *Four Weekends and a Funeral*, author Ellie Palmer offers a unique take on the fake-dating trope. If you could tweak one well-known romance trope, discuss which trope you would choose, and how you would turn it on its head.

ABOUT THE AUTHOR

© Morgan Lust

Ellie Palmer is a lifelong lover of love stories, a carrier of the BRCA1 mutation, and a prototypical Midwesterner who routinely apologizes to inanimate objects when she bumps into them. When she's not writing romantic comedies featuring delightfully messy characters, Ellie's at home in Minnesota, eating breakfast food, watching too much reality television, and triple texting her husband about their son.

elliepalmerwrites.com
ⓘ ElliePalmerWrites